PRAISE FOR THE NOVELS O[...]
BESTSELLING AUTHOR J[...]

"Castle is well known for her playful lo[...]
of romantic suspense runs delightfully true to form . . . [...] [...]
effervescent romance mildly spiced with paranormal fun, this novel
won't disappoint." —*Publishers Weekly*

"A fun read, as are all Castle/Krentz's books." —*The Pilot*

"Writing under Jayne Castle, Jayne Ann Krentz takes her trademark
combination of witty, upbeat action, lively sensuality, and appealing
characters to [a] unique, synergistic world." —*Library Journal*

"Jayne Castle, one of the pioneers of the futuristic subgenre, continues to
set the standard against which all other such books are judged."
—*Affaire de Coeur*

"As always, the characterizations and plot blend perfectly for a thrilling,
funny, and fully satisfying read." —*RT Book Reviews* (4½ stars)

. . . AND JAYNE ANN KRENTZ

"Good fun." —*Cosmopolitan*

"Entertaining." —*People*

"Fast-moving . . . Entertaining . . . Highly successful."
—*The Seattle Times*

"Fast-paced . . . Interesting characters . . . A good time is had by the
reader." —*Chicago Tribune*

"Quick and witty and the romance sizzles . . . Reads fast and will make
you smile, wince, and sigh. What else could you want?"
—*The Columbia (SC) State*

"Along with Nora Roberts, Krentz is one of the most reliably satisfying
romance writers publishing." —*Sunday Times (CA)*

"Jayne Ann Krentz is one of the hottest writers around."
—*Albuquerque Journal*

Other titles by Jayne Ann Krentz

COPPER BEACH

IN TOO DEEP

FIRED UP

RUNNING HOT

SIZZLE AND BURN

WHITE LIES

ALL NIGHT LONG

FALLING AWAKE

TRUTH OR DARE

LIGHT IN SHADOW

SUMMER IN ECLIPSE BAY

TOGETHER IN ECLIPSE BAY

SMOKE IN MIRRORS

LOST & FOUND

DAWN IN ECLIPSE BAY

SOFT FOCUS

ECLIPSE BAY

EYE OF THE BEHOLDER

FLASH

SHARP EDGES

DEEP WATERS

ABSOLUTELY, POSITIVELY

TRUST ME

GRAND PASSION

HIDDEN TALENTS

WILDEST HEARTS

FAMILY MAN

PERFECT PARTNERS

SWEET FORTUNE

SILVER LININGS

THE GOLDEN CHANCE

Specials

THE SCARGILL COVE CASE FILES

Anthologies

CHARMED

(with Julie Beard, Lori Foster, and Eileen Wilks)

Titles written by Jayne Ann Krentz and Jayne Castle

NO GOING BACK

SINISTER
AND
FATAL

THE GUINEVERE JONES COLLECTION, VOLUME 2

JAYNE CASTLE

BERKLEY BOOKS, NEW YORK

THE BERKLEY PUBLISHING GROUP
Published by the Penguin Group
Penguin Group (USA) LLC
375 Hudson Street, New York, New York 10014

USA • Canada • UK • Ireland • Australia • New Zealand • India • South Africa • China

penguin.com

A Penguin Random House Company

Library of Congress Cataloging-in-Publication Data

Castle, Jayne.
[Novels. Selections]
Sinister and fatal / Jayne Castle.
pages cm.— (The Guinevere Jones collection ; volume 2)
ISBN 978-0-425-27184-1 (alk. paper)
1. Businesswomen—Fiction.   2. Women private investigators—Fiction.   I. Title.
PS3561.R44S535 2014
813'.54—dc23
2013042209

PUBLISHING HISTORY
The Sinister Touch Dell Books edition / October 1986
The Sinister Touch InterMix eBook edition / August 2012
The Fatal Fortune Dell Books edition / December 1986
The Fatal Fortune InterMix eBook edition / August 2012
Berkley trade paperback omnibus edition / February 2014

PRINTED IN THE UNITED STATES OF AMERICA

10   9   8   7   6   5   4   3   2   1

Cover background photo © Shutterstock.
Interior text design by Tiffany Estreicher.

CONTENTS

Dear Reader:

If you've been keeping track of my titles, you probably know that a while back I did a four-book series featuring an amateur sleuth named Guinevere Jones. (No relation to the Arcane Joneses – at least I don't think so). The books are all straight-up romantic-suspense and they were written under my Jayne Castle name. They have been out of print for some time but now I am delighted to tell you that my publisher is making them available again. The second two titles, The Sinister Touch *and* The Fatal Fortune, *are contained in this book, Volume 2 of the Guinevere Jones Collection.*

I hope you enjoy the ride with Guinevere Jones as she solves crimes and falls in love with the sexy, mysterious Zac Justis.

Sincerely,
Jayne Ann Krentz
(AKA: Jayne Castle)

SINISTER
AND
FATAL

THE
SINISTER
TOUCH

CHAPTER 1

The night had been a long one. No, that wasn't strictly accurate. It had been *lonely*.

Guinevere Jones glared at the stylish new coffee machine as it dripped with agonizing slowness. She could have bought a cheaper coffeemaker when she went shopping for one yesterday if she'd been willing to settle for a plain white or beige model. But this little sucker was an exotic import, and with its dashing red-and-black trim it had totally outclassed all the bland models on the shelf next to it at the Bon. Even the glass pot was elegantly different from the ordinary coffeepot. Definitely high-tech style. She hadn't been able to resist it. It lent such a perfect, snappy note to her vivid yellow kitchen. Unfortunately it was proving to have more style than efficiency. Zac would undoubtedly have a few pithy comments to make when he tried it out.

If he ever got around to trying it out, Guinevere reminded herself resentfully as she stood in front of the coffee machine with a yellow mug dangling uselessly from one finger. Zac had been very busy with a new client lately, a client who seemed to find that the most convenient time to consult with the head of Free Enterprise Security, Inc., was in the evening. The fact that the client was Elizabeth Gallinger wasn't doing much to mitigate Guinevere's prickly mood. Guinevere's own firm, Camelot Services, which specialized in providing temporary office help, had had a short secretarial assignment a few months ago at Gallinger Industries. Guinevere had only seen Queen Elizabeth from afar, and then just briefly, but the memory of that regal blond head, classic profile, and aristocratic posture had returned in all its glory last week when Zac had mentioned the name of his new client.

Elizabeth Gallinger was thirty-two, a couple years older than Guinevere, and already she was running one of the most prestigious corporations in Seattle. Queen Elizabeth, as she was rather affectionately known by her employees, had inherited the position of president when her father had died unexpectedly last summer. Everyone had anticipated that Elizabeth would be only a figurehead, but everyone had underestimated her. Elizabeth Gallinger had very firmly assumed the reins of her family business. Four generations of old Seattle money apparently had not led to serious mental deficiency due to inbreeding.

Guinevere was beginning to wonder if Zac was the one with the mental deficiency. If so, it couldn't be blamed on inbreeding. Zachariah Justis had a pedigree as ordinary and plebian as Guinevere's own.

Guinevere frowned at the slowly dripping coffeemaker. It occurred to her that an ambitious entrepreneur with no claim to illustrious predecessors or illustrious family money might find Elizabeth Gallinger a very intriguing proposition. Zac had never been overly impressed by money, but there was always a first time.

Damn it, what was the matter with her? If she didn't know better, Guinevere decided ruefully, she might think she was actually jealous. Ridiculous. The fact that Zac hadn't spent a night with her for almost a week was hardly cause for turning green-eyed. She and Zac didn't live together. The affair they had both finally acknowledged was still at its very early, very fragile stage. Neither wanted to push the other too far, too fast. They were both carefully maintaining their own identities and their own apartments.

Fed up with the slowness of the coffeemaker, Guinevere yanked the half-full glass pot out from under the dripping mechanism and quickly poured the contents into her yellow mug. In the meantime coffee continued to drip with relentless slowness, splashing on the burner. Deciding she'd clean up the mess later, Guinevere hastily put the pot back onto the burner and turned away to sip her coffee.

Through her kitchen window she could see the high, arched window of the second-floor artist's loft across the street. This morning, as usual, the window was uncovered. Guinevere had never known the artist who lived and worked in the spacious, airy apartment to pull the shades. Artists were very big on light, as she had once explained to Zac when he'd had occasion to notice the tenant across the street. She smiled slightly as she recalled Zac's annoyance over the small morning ritual she went through with the anonymous man who lived in the loft.

Guinevere had never met the lean, young artist. But she waved good morning to him frequently. He always waved back. When Zac happened to be in the kitchen beside Guinevere, the unknown artist tended to put a little more enthusiasm into the wave. Zac's invariable response was a low, disgusted growl. Then, just as inevitably, he'd close the mini blinds on Guinevere's window.

But Zac wasn't here to express his disapproval of the anonymous friendship this morning. He hadn't been here to express it for the past several mornings. So Guinevere sipped her coffee and waited for the appearance of her neighbor. Idly she studied the canvas that stood facing her on an easel tilted to catch the northern light. The young man with the slightly overlong hair had been working on that canvas for several days now. Even from here Guinevere could recognize the brilliant colors and dramatic shapes.

But there was something different about the painting this morning. Guinevere's brows came together in a new kind of frown as she tipped her head and narrowed her eyes. There was a large black mark on the canvas. From her vantage point it appeared to be an uneven square with a jagged slash inside. It didn't fit at all with the wonderful brilliance and lightness of the painting.

Guinevere went forward, leaning her elbows on the window ledge, the mug cradled between her hands. There was more than just an ugly black mark on the painting. She could see that something was wrong with the canvas itself. It was torn or slashed. Terribly slashed.

Slowly Guinevere began to realize that the huge canvas had been horribly defaced. Her mouth opened in stunned shock just as her unknown neighbor sauntered, yawning, into the brightly lit loft.

He was wearing his usual morning attire, a loosely hitched towel around a lean waist and a substantial amount of chest hair. Guinevere had decided that he always wandered into the loft just before he took his morning shower. Perhaps he had an artist's need to see how his work looked in the first light of day. He glanced at her window before he looked at his painting.

Across the narrow street his eyes met hers. Even from here she could see the questioning tilt of one brow as he made a small production out of looking for Zac. When she just stared back, her expression appalled, he finally began to realize that something was wrong. The amusement faded as his glance turned to curious.

Guinevere lifted one hand and pointed behind him. The stranger turned and glanced over his shoulder. His gaze fell at last on his ravaged canvas.

His reaction answered Guinevere's silent question of whether he had done the damage himself. The artist stood staring at the ruined

canvas, his back rigid with shock. When at last he turned to meet
Guinevere's eyes again, all traces of amusement had vanished. He
just stared at her. Unable to do anything else, consumed with sympathy for him, Guinevere simply stared back.

How long she stood like that, Guinevere wasn't sure. It was the
artist who broke the still, silent watch. Swinging around with an
abruptness that underlined his tension, he picked up a huge sketch
pad and a piece of chalk. Hastily he scrawled a brief message in fat,
charcoal-colored letters.

"Coffee downstairs. Ten Minutes. Please."

Guinevere nodded at once, then turned away to finish her coffee
and find her shoes. She was already dressed for work in a narrow-
skirted, gray pin-striped suit and yellow silk blouse. Her coffee-
brown hair was in its usual neat, braided coil at the nape of her neck.
She slid her stockinged feet into a pair of mid-height gray pumps
and slung a leather purse over her shoulder.

Quickly Guinevere made her way through the red, black, and
yellow living room with its red-bordered gray rugs and high, vault-
ing windows. The old brick buildings here in the Pioneer Square
section of Seattle had wonderfully high ceilings and beautiful windows. When they had been gutted and refurbished, they made great
apartments for the new, upwardly mobile urbanites. The busy harbor
of Elliott Bay was only a couple of blocks away, and although Guinevere didn't actually have a view of the water, just knowing it was
close gave her a certain satisfaction. Many mornings she walked
along the waterfront on her way to her First Avenue office.

Closing and locking her door behind her, Guinevere hurried
down the two short flights of stairs to the security-door entrance of
her apartment building and stepped out into the crispness of a pleasantly sunny late-spring morning. On mornings such as this, one
knew for certain that summer really was just around the corner.

Another sure sign was the fact that several restaurants and taverns in the area had started moving tables and chairs out onto the sidewalks. The rain was due late this afternoon and would probably last for a while, but this morning the air was full of promise.

The missions, which were one of Pioneer Square's more picturesque features as far as Guinevere was concerned, had already released the crowd of transients, derelicts, and assorted street people that had been sheltered overnight. Without much enthusiasm the ragtag assortment of scruffy mission clients were slowly drifting out onto the sidewalks, blinking awkwardly in the sunlight as they prepared for the day's work.

Soon, either under their own power or aboard one of the free city buses that plied the short route, they would make their way toward the Pike Place Market where the tourists would be swarming by midmorning. One particularly ambitious soul decided to practice on Guinevere. She smiled vaguely and shook her head, ignoring his outstretched palm and the request for cash as she hurried toward the restaurant.

As soon as she opened the high doors, the smell of freshly baked cinnamon rolls assailed her, reminding her that she hadn't had a chance to eat breakfast. A fire burning on the huge hearth on one side of the enormous, old brick room took the chill off the morning.

Guinevere glanced around and, when she didn't see her neighbor, decided to throw caution to the wind and order some cinnamon rolls. They arrived with butter dripping over the sides. Of course, you couldn't eat a cinnamon roll without a cup of coffee. Something was required to dilute the butter. She was paying the check when the artist slid into line behind her.

"Hi." His voice was pleasantly deep, edged with a trace of the East Coast and laced with a certain grimness. "What a way to meet. Thanks for coming. I'm Mason Adair, by the way. I feel as if I already know you."

Guinevere smiled at him, liking his aquiline features and the large, dark eyes. It struck her that he looked exactly like a struggling young artist should look. He was taller than she had thought, towering over her as she stood in line beside him. His height coupled with his leanness made him appear aesthetically gaunt. He was also younger than she had imagined. Probably about thirty. His paint-stained jeans, plaid shirt, and heavy leather sandals fit the image, too.

"I'm Guinevere Jones. Want a roll?"

"What? Oh, sure. Sounds good. I haven't had a chance to eat yet."

"Neither have I." Guinevere picked up the tray.

"Here, I'll take that." Mason Adair scooped the tray out of her hands and started toward a seat in front of the fire. A few drops of the coffee in Guinevere's cup slopped over the side as he set the tray down on the wooden table. "Sorry. I'm a little clumsy by nature. Finding that canvas slashed this morning isn't improving my coordination. Shit."

Guinevere smiled serenely and unobtrusively used a napkin to wipe the cup as she sat down on one of the short wooden benches. The fire felt good even though it was produced by fake logs. Mason Adair dropped down onto the opposite bench and reached for a roll.

"I was shocked when I glanced out my window and saw that huge black square on your beautiful painting. At first I thought maybe you'd gotten disgusted with your work and had deliberately marked it up." Guinevere stirred her coffee.

"I've got a certain amount of artistic temperament, but I'd never do anything like that to one of my own paintings. Hell, I liked that one. Really liked it. I think it might have been inspired by your kitchen, by the way."

"My kitchen?"

"Yeah, you know. All that yellow. Every morning I look in your window, and it's like looking into a little box of sunlight."

Guinevere smiled with pleasure at the unexpected compliment. "I'm flattered."

"Yeah, well, somebody wasn't." Morosely Mason chewed a huge bite of his roll. His appetite was apparently unaffected by his depression. "It isn't just the vandalism that got me. It was the fact that someone was actually inside my apartment, messing with my stuff. I know now why people who've been burgled say they feel as if they've been personally violated. It's a strange sensation. It gets to you."

Guinevere sighed in sympathy. "I'm terribly sorry, Mason. I know it's a terrible feeling. Have you any idea who would do a thing like that?"

Adair hesitated. "No, not really. I asked you to meet me here because I wondered if you'd seen anything or anyone. I never pull the shade, and you usually have your kitchen window blinds open. I thought that maybe you'd noticed something out of the ordinary last night. It must have happened last night. I was out all evening, and I didn't look at the painting before I went to bed."

"Mason, I'm really very sorry, but I didn't see a thing. I worked on some papers in my living room. I do remember going into my kitchen around nine o'clock for a snack, but your window was dark."

"No lights on?"

She shook her head. "Not then."

"Whoever did that would have needed some light, don't you think?" he asked broodingly.

"It would depend on what time during the evening he did it. It's not getting really dark until after eight o'clock now. I suppose someone could have gone into your studio and defaced your painting sometime before then and not needed any light."

Mason took another huge bite of his roll, dark eyes focusing blankly on her concerned face. Guinevere had the impression that he was trying very hard to sort out some very private thoughts. She let him chew in solitude for a moment, and then she asked, "That square that the vandal drew in black. It looked a little odd. Of course, I couldn't see it very well from my window, but there was something about the shape of it that looked awkward. Was it a child's work, do you think? Youngsters into mischief?"

"This isn't exactly suburbia. We haven't got a lot of children running around Pioneer Square. Just an assortment of street people, artists, and upwardly mobile types. All adults. At least physically. Mentally, who knows?" Mason chewed for another moment. "And it wasn't a square. It was a pentagram."

"A what?"

"A five-sided star."

Guinevere blinked. "I know what a pentagram is. What was the mark in the middle?"

"Just a zigzag slash." Mason looked down at his plate, still half absorbed in his own thoughts. "Whoever slashed the canvas must have brought along his own knife. None of my tools appeared to have been touched."

Guinevere frowned, leaning forward. "Mason, don't you find it rather odd that whoever did that to your painting chose to draw a pentagram?"

"Odd? The whole damn thing is odd. Spooky, too, if you want to know the truth."

"Yes, but a pentagram? With a bolt of lightning in the center?"

He raised dark eyes to meet her intent gaze. "I said it was a zigzag shape, not a bolt of lightning."

Guinevere hesitated. "I always think of pentagrams as being symbols of magic."

Mason didn't say anything for a long moment. "Yes," he finally admitted. "I believe they are."

There was another lengthy pause. Finally Guinevere asked, "Was anything taken?"

Mason shook his head. "No. Nothing. Didn't touch the stereo or the paints or the cash I keep in the drawer of my workbench." He sighed. "Look, this isn't your problem, Guinevere. I shouldn't have bothered you with it."

"I don't mind. We're neighbors. Going to call the cops?"

"I'll report it, but I don't think it's going to do much good. What's a little malicious mischief these days when the cops have their hands full with real live murders?"

"Real live murders," Guinevere repeated with a trace of a smile. "I think that may be a contradiction in terms."

Mason stared at her for a second, and then he laughed. "I think you may be right."

"Has anything like this ever happened before, Mason?"

His brief humor faded. "No."

"What about the possibility of jealousy? Are any of your friends resentful of your success?"

"What success? I've got my first major showing tonight, down the street at the Midnight Light gallery. I'll be lucky if someone offers me more than a hundred bucks for one of my pictures. That doesn't qualify as sudden success."

"Your first showing?"

Mason nodded. "Yeah. I just hope I live through it. I've been kind of jumpy lately, waiting for it. Whoever did that hatchet job on my painting last night couldn't have picked a worse time to rattle me. It's all I needed."

Guinevere drummed her fingers on the table, thinking. "You know, if there's anything more to this than a fluke case of malicious mischief, maybe you should do something besides just reporting it to the cops."

"What more can I do?"

"Hire a private investigator to look into the matter?" Guinevere suggested.

Mason stared at her. "Are you kidding? When I can barely pay my rent? I don't have that kind of money. Forget it. There isn't much an investigator could discover anyway. How's he going to locate a vandal?"

"How about the little matter of how the vandal got into your studio? Was the door forced?"

Mason's brows came together in a solid line. "Not in any major way, or I would have noticed. I didn't see any pry marks, and none of the locks were broken. But my apartment isn't exactly Fort Knox. It wouldn't have taken a lot of expertise to get inside. You sound like you've been watching a lot of TV lately."

"Not exactly. But I have been keeping some questionable company," Guinevere said blandly.

Mason's brows shot upward as he put two and two together. "Let me guess. That solid-looking guy with the dark hair and the super-conservative business suits?"

"Zac is trying to dress for success. He's learning the fine points of making a forceful statement in the business world while upholding the image of his firm."

"I see." Mason's dark eyes lightened with amusement. "Unlike me. How's he doing?"

"At maintaining his image? Rather well, as a matter of fact. He's just landed a very nice contract with a local firm."

Mason nodded. "So he's doing okay maintaining the image. How about in the category of making a forceful statement?"

"Oh, Zac has always had a knack for making a forceful statement when he wants to do so," Guinevere said cheerfully. Memories of Zac hunting human game on a cold and windy island in the San Juans several weeks previously flickered briefly in her head. She had to suppress a small shiver. Zac was very, very good at making force-ful statements on occasion.

"I'm not surprised," Mason murmured. "I think he's made one or two forceful statements in my direction recently. The last time he closed your kitchen blinds I got the distinct impression that he would have preferred to have his hands around my throat rather than the mini blind rod. So he's the questionable company you keep? What does he do in the business world that necessitates all this forceful-personality and image-building stuff?"

"He runs a company called Free Enterprise Security, Inc. He does security consultations for business firms."

"How big is Free Enterprise Security?"

Guinevere swallowed a scrap of her cinnamon roll. "To date there is only one employee."

"Zac?"

"Uh-huh." She grinned. "But he manages to get things done. You know, this isn't exactly his line of work, but I might mention your situation to him and see if he's got any advice. He's terribly discreet. He has to be. Businesses don't like their security problems publicized. That's why they consult outfits such as Free Enterprise Security."

Mason looked at her askance. "I have a funny feeling he's not going to be overly sympathetic."

"He has no reason to be jealous and he knows it. I've already told him that you and I have never met."

Mason chuckled. "You won't be able to tell him that anymore, will you? I can't wait to hear his reaction when you tell him you've taken to meeting me for breakfast."

Zac's reaction was forthright and to the point. He looked up in aston-ishment from the plastic bucket of steamed clams from which he was eating and stared at Guinevere as if she had just announced that she had made a brief trip to Mars. "The hell you did." He went back to his bucket of clams.

Guinevere pushed her own lunch aside, leaning forward to get his attention. The lunchtime crowd was heavy down here on the waterfront. She and Zac were sitting in the corner of a small sidewalk café that enjoyed an excellent view of the harbor and the tourists who were strolling the broad sidewalk that linked the boutique-lined piers.

"Zac, you're not listening to me."

"I heard every word you said." He scooped another clam out of its shell. "You claimed you had breakfast with that artist you've been ogling for the past few months. There are laws against that sort of thing, you know."

"Having breakfast with an artist?" She was getting annoyed. Deep down inside, Guinevere wondered if she'd hoped to see at least a spark of romantic jealousy inflame Zac's smoke-gray eyes. All she was detecting was irritation.

"No, ogling artists." Zac forked up another clam. "Stop trying to bait me, Gwen. I've had a hard morning. You're just mad because I had to cancel our date last night."

Guinevere set her back teeth very firmly together. "Contrary to what you seem to believe, I am not indulging in a fit of pique. I really did have breakfast with Mason."

"Mason?"

The name brought his head up again. This time there was something besides irritation in the steady gray gaze, and Guinevere wasn't sure she liked the too-quiet way Zac said the other man's name. She shifted uncomfortably on the chair.

"Mason Adair is his name. He's very nice, Zac, and he's got a problem."

Zac stopped eating clams. "Is that a fact?"

"Zac, I'm serious. This morning, when I looked out my window, I could see that the painting he's been working on had been terribly defaced overnight. Someone had drawn a huge black pentagram on it and then taken a knife to the canvas. Mason was shocked. He saw me looking just as shocked and held up a sign suggesting we meet for coffee. You know, that place with the cinnamon rolls just around the corner from my building?"

"I know it," Zac said grimly.

"Well, he was rather shaken up, as you can imagine. Has absolutely no idea who could have done such a thing. He asked me to meet him on the outside chance that I might have seen something from my kitchen window. He hoped I might have spotted someone moving around in his studio last night." Zac's gaze could have frozen nitrogen. "Did you?"

"No." Guinevere sighed in exasperation.

"Good." Zac went back to eating clams. "That's the end of it, then. No more breakfast meetings with naked artists. Hell, Gwen, I credited you with more common sense than that. You've lived in the city long enough to know better than to agree to meet absolute strangers. What got into you? Were you really that upset because I had to cancel our date?"

"I hate to break this to you, Zac, but I did not rush out to buy cinnamon rolls for a starving artist this morning just because you broke our date last night."

"He made you pay for the rolls?"

"Speaking of broken dates," Guinevere continued stoutly, "how was your little business meeting last night?"

"All business. Elizabeth is a very impressive executive. She focuses completely on the problem at hand and deals with it. Great business mind."

"Does she know how much you admire her, uh, mind?"

Zac looked at her steadily. "Are you by any chance jealous, Gwen?"

She lifted her chin with royal disdain. "Do I have cause?"

"No."

Guinevere went back to the fish and chips she had been nibbling earlier. "Then I'm not jealous." The thing about Zac was that he had a way of dishing out the truth that made it impossible to doubt him. She couldn't ignore that tingle of relief she was feeling, though. It annoyed her. "Now that we've disposed of the personal side of this discussion, perhaps we could get back to business."

"What business?"

"Well, I told Mason I'd mention his little problem to you."

"Guinevere." He rarely used her full name. When he did, especially in that soft, gravelly voice, it usually meant trouble. "What exactly did you tell Mason Adair?"

She concentrated on sprinkling vinegar on the French fries. "I just said I'd mention to you the incident in his studio last night. He's going to report it to the police, of course. But, as he said, they won't be able to do much. Just another small case of vandalism as far as they're concerned. They might even write it off as a case of professional jealousy. Mason's going to have his first show tonight. It could be that not everyone wishes him well. At any rate, Mason's fairly sure it isn't something one of his acquaintances would do. And there was something odd about that particular kind of vandalism, Zac. I mean, that business with the pentagram and the bolt of lightning in the center. It wasn't just malicious or nasty. It was weird. Pentagrams are associated with the occult."

"You're rambling, Gwen. Get to the point. What exactly did you tell Mason Adair?"

"I told you," she said with exaggerated patience. "I said I'd mention the matter to you."

"And?" Zac prompted ominously.

"And maybe see if you had any advice for him," she concluded in a mumbled rush as she munched a French fry.

"Advice?" Zac ate the last of his clams and pushed the plastic bucket out of the way. He leaned forward, his elbows folded on the table, his hard, blunt face set in a ruthless, unrelenting expression that seemed to slip all too easily into place. His dark, rough voice was softer than ever. "No, Gwen, I don't have any free advice for your starving artist. But I do have some for you."

"Now, Zac—"

"You will stay clear of him, Guinevere. You will not get involved with pentagrams, slashed canvases, or artists who run around wearing only a towel while they wave good morning to their female neighbors. Understood?"

Guinevere drew a deep breath. "Zac, I was asking for advice, not a lecture. If you're not willing to help—"

"But I am willing to help, Gwen. I'm helping you stay out of trouble. Or have you already forgotten what happened the last time you tried to involve me in a case I wasn't interested in handling?"

"Now, Zac, you collected a nice fee for that business in the San Juans. You can hardly complain about my involving you."

"Hah. I can complain and I will complain. Furthermore . . ."

Zac was warming to his topic now. The lecture might have continued unabated for the remainder of the lunch hour if a small toddler dressed in a designer-emblazoned polo shirt and shorts hadn't come screeching down the aisle between tables and made a lunge for Zac's empty plastic clam container. The child, giggling dementedly, scrambled up onto Zac's lap, grabbed for the container, and spilled the contents across Zac's trouser leg. Empty clam shells and the accompanying juice ran every which way, splattering the restrained tie and the white shirt Zac was wearing with the trousers. There was a shriek of delight from the toddler, and then the child was racing off to wreak more havoc and destruction.

Zac sat looking after the small boy, a stunned expression replacing the hard one with which he had been favoring Guinevere. In the distance two distinctly yuppie parents ran after their errant offspring. They had the same designer emblems on their polo shirts that their son had on his. A coordinated family.

"Have you noticed," Zac asked in an odd voice, "how many small children there are around these days? Whatever happened to all those women who said they were going to have careers instead of babies?"

Guinevere tried to stifle a small grin. "I'm still keeping the faith."

Zac pulled his stunned gaze back to hers. "It's the biological clock syndrome, you know."

"Biological clock?"

"It's running out for women your age," he explained in that same odd voice.

Guinevere's grin disappeared. "Zac, what on earth are you talking about?"

"Babies," he said grimly. "My God, even Elizabeth Gallinger is talking about babies."

"Elizabeth Gallinger! Zac, what in the world were you doing talking to Elizabeth Gallinger about babies?"

But Zac was staring sadly at the clam shells strewn across his trousers. "I have the feeling this suit will never be the same."

CHAPTER 2

As usual disaster had struck when he'd tried to exert a little masculine authority over Gwen. Zac glanced down at the clean shirt and slacks he'd changed into at home before returning to his small office downtown. It was going to cost a fortune to have the other suit cleaned. If he hadn't known better, he would have easily believed that Gwen had summoned up the small demon child at the appropriate moment just to cut off his lecture on that damned artist.

There was more trouble involved here than just a clam-stained suit, Zac thought morosely as he opened a file labeled GALLINGER. Gwen had a knack for taking other people's problems too seriously. People liked her, and they tended to confide in her. Hardly anyone willingly confided in him, Zac realized. Not unless he had the potential confidant by the throat or pinned against a wall or standing in front of a gun. Must be something in his personality that people failed to find sympathetic.

Now here was Gwen discussing pentagrams, slashed canvases, and naked artists over lunch. Zac just knew that combination spelled trouble. He had been right to instruct Gwen to steer clear of it. But, as usual, she had dug in her heels and resisted. He hadn't accomplished much at lunch, and Zac was well aware of the fact. Hell, he hadn't even arranged to see Gwen this evening. After the disaster with the clams she'd excused herself to hurry back to her First Avenue office. Zac had been left to deal with clam-juice-stained trousers on his own.

Clam juice he could handle. He hadn't wanted to spend another evening alone, however. It had been a long week, and he'd seen very little of the woman with whom he was supposedly having an affair. Zac frowned at the notes he'd made on Gallinger Industries' security situation and wondered why labeling his relationship with Gwen as an affair hadn't made as much difference as he'd expected. Somehow, being the methodical, detail-oriented man he was, he'd assumed that putting a label on the situation would define it and cut out all the uncertainties and ambiguities. It hadn't.

What exactly had he expected? Zac wondered. That she'd move in with him? He hadn't actually brought up the subject of living together because he'd had no encouragement. Gwen had shown absolutely no interest in giving up her apartment, and she certainly hadn't invited him to move into hers. It was true he managed to spend more nights in her bed lately than he had before they'd officially agreed they were involved in an affair, but Zac still had a strong sense of uncertainty about Gwen's feelings toward him. She had never told him she loved him. He was afraid to make the assumption. Some assumptions could destroy a man.

A few weeks ago when they had returned from the island jaunt that had nearly gotten them both killed, Zac had gotten Gwen to admit that their relationship definitely had evolved into something more than a dating arrangement. At the time he had assumed the admission would settle everything between them. Instead it had only opened up more questions.

For a while there at lunch he had gotten the impression that Gwen might be a bit jealous, and in a way it had given him hope. It wasn't that he wanted her to feel insecure or hurt, but it would have been nice to know she cared enough to get jealous.

That was juvenile, Zac told himself irritably. That sort of thing was for kids, not for adults.

Adults. Gwen was thirty years old, and he was thirty-six. They were both very definitely adults. For women that meant a ticking biological clock, just as Elizabeth had mentioned the other day.

Zac gazed thoughtfully across his desk. There was a glass wall opposite him, but the view was somewhat limited. It revealed only the corridor between his office and the glass-walled office on the other side of the hall. The rest of the tiny office consisted of bare walls and a small storage cabinet. Piled on top of the cabinet were the new genuine simulated-leather binders he'd ordered from the office stationery supply house down the street. Each binder was engraved with FREE ENTERPRISE SECURITY, INC. Zac thought they looked quite impressive. He would use them for presenting final reports to clients. Other than the new binders there wasn't much else to look at except the top of his desk. But he didn't notice the scenic limitations as he considered the matter of biological clocks.

Perhaps Gwen wasn't able to commit herself completely to him because she was starting to fret about the matter of babies. All around the nation women who had postponed babies for careers were reportedly starting to panic. There had been an article on that subject in the *Wall Street Journal* just the other day. Maybe, deep down, even unconsciously, Gwen, too, was getting ready to hit the panic button and decide that she wanted a baby, after all. If that happened, would she see him as good father material?

Probably not. He didn't even look like good father material to himself. It didn't take much imagination to see how a would-be mother might view him. If Gwen was getting restless because she had decided she wanted a baby, she might easily have written him off as a long-term commitment in favor of some guy who wanted sons and heirs.

On the other hand, if he was wrong and he brought up the subject of having a child, Gwen might panic for the opposite reason. She might decide that he was about to make an unreasonable demand on her. It was a decidedly tricky situation.

Zac tapped a pencil on his desktop and wondered how a simple, straightforward affair could get so complicated. The phone rang before he could come to any conclusions. With a sense of gratitude for the interruption he lifted the receiver.

"Free Enterprise Security, this is Zac Justis."

"Mr. Justis, this is Sarah, Miss Gallinger's secretary."

Zac straightened in his chair. The Gallinger account was the biggest one he'd gotten so far. He paid great attention when someone from the company called. "Yes, Sarah, what can I do for you?" He should have a secretary of his own, Zac thought worriedly. It probably didn't make a good impression on a high-level secretary from another company when she called and got right through to the head of the firm. Image. As Gwen kept telling him, you had to have a good image.

"I have a message from Miss Gallinger. She would be pleased if you would attend the cocktail party she's giving tomorrow evening. She apologizes for the short notice but assures you that she'd love to have you come. Will it be convenient?"

"Uh, yeah, sure." Zac floundered. He hated cocktail parties, but business was business. "May I bring a guest?" Gwen could handle things like this.

"Certainly. I'll tell Miss Gallinger to expect a party of two. That's eight o'clock tomorrow evening. You have the address?"

"I've got it."

"Thank you, Mr. Justis. I see you have an appointment with Miss Gallinger this afternooon at five?"

Zac winced. Another evening shot to hell. "It's on my calendar."

"Fine," Sarah said smoothly. "Good-bye, Mr. Justis."

Zac hung up the phone and went back to thinking dark thoughts about babies and biological clocks.

"Babies!" Guinevere glowered at her sister, who was sitting at a small desk in the corner. "He's been discussing babies with Queen Elizabeth. The nerve of the man. He's supposed to be having an affair with me, and he's talking babies and biological clocks with Elizabeth Gallinger."

Carla flipped a handful of precision-cut blond hair back behind her ear and smiled serenely. Her beautiful gray-green eyes scanned her sister's grim expression. "You can't deny that the clock is ticking, Gwen. Elizabeth Gallinger's only a couple years older than you. It's ticking for her, too. Lots of women are starting to worry, you know. They're hitting thirty or thirty-five, and panic is setting in."

"The thought of a panicked Elizabeth Gallinger boggles the mind," Guinevere said dryly. "She's beautiful, rich, and powerful. What on earth does she have to panic about? If she wants a baby, I'm sure there are plenty of well-bred studs around who will be glad to marry into the Gallinger millions."

"Perhaps she's not looking for a husband," Carla said thoughtfully. "Maybe she's only interested in having the baby. A lot of successful women are considering single parenting these days."

Gwen was stricken by a horrifying thought. "You don't think she's decided Zac is good genetic material, do you?"

"How would I know?" Carla wrinkled her freckled nose. It was the freckles that softened the exquisite beauty of her features and turned her into an approachable female. "I don't travel in Elizabeth Gallinger's circles."

"Neither do I. But Zac has been traveling in those circles a lot for the past couple of weeks." Guinevere's mouth tightened just as the front door opened. She instantly composed her face into a polite, businesslike smile. Then she saw who the caller was, and pleased surprise lightened her smile. "Mason. What on earth are you doing here? Carla, this is Mason Adair, the artist who lives across the street from me. Mason, my sister, Carla."

"I've heard all about your, er, towel," Carla murmured, gray-green eyes full of sudden humor.

"I'm sorry I can't say the same about yours."

Mason and Carla exchanged in-depth glances, and Guinevere blinked, sensing something new in the atmosphere. She ignored the feeling and motioned Mason to a chair. Men frequently reacted this way around Carla.

"What can I do for you? Have the police turned up anything concerning your slashed canvas?"

Mason yanked his eyes away from Carla and dropped into the nearest seat. "Nah, not a thing. I doubt that they will, either. That's not why I'm here. I came to invite you and"—he glanced at Carla again—"your sister to my showing tonight. It's occurred to me that there's a very good chance virtually no one will come, and with you there I'd at least have someone to talk to while the gallery owner chews her fingernails."

Guinevere smiled. "Are you really concerned that no one will attend?"

"It's happened before to artists. The other possibility is that people will show up, but they'll hate my work."

Carla tilted her head. "Those are the two chief possibilities?"

Mason groaned. "Who knows? I just thought I'd try to make sure a couple of friendly faces are there tonight. Don't worry, you won't be obligated to buy a painting."

Guinevere glanced at her sister. "What about it, Carla? Want to come with me?"

"Sure. Sounds like fun. We can all stand around and sip champagne and make snide remarks about Mason's paintings."

Mason glared at her. "You've never seen my stuff. How do you know you're going to want to make snide remarks?"

"Intuition. What time are we supposed to arrive?"

He shrugged. "Sometime around eight."

Guinevere looked at him keenly. "You're really concerned about this showing, aren't you?"

"It's important to me. If it goes well, it could be a very nice break. A good start for my career."

"And if it goes badly?" Carla inquired.

"Then I go back to snitching free crackers at salad bars so I'll have enough money to buy paints and pay for the studio." Mason grinned at her. "Either that or I find myself a wealthy lady patron of the arts."

Carla assumed an expression of horrified shock. "Sell your body for money to buy paints?"

"Anything for the sake of my art," Mason intoned. His eyes narrowed as he studied her face. "Have you ever modeled?"

"Nope. And from the sounds of things you don't have enough to pay me what I'd charge if I did decide to take up the career."

"One must be prepared to make certain sacrifices for the arts, Miss Jones."

Guinevere watched the byplay closely. There was nothing surprising about Mason's immediate interest in Carla. Most men who met Carla for the first time were immediately interested. But there was something about the way her sister was responding that was a little different from usual. The sparkle in Carla's eyes was genuine, and the expression in Mason's gaze was very honest and very male. The evening ahead should prove interesting.

Mason's worst fears concerning his first gallery showing were not realized. Guinevere and Carla arrived at the Midnight Light art gallery to find that a healthy crowd had already descended on the small, discreet establishment.

"It's the free champagne and canapés," Mason explained as he met them at the door and ushered them inside. "Theresa, the owner, really went all out for me in that regard. Food really brings in the locals. Unfortunately, most of them are fellow artists, who are, by nature, freeloaders, not potential buyers. Still, it makes for a crowd."

Carla, dressed in a sweep of crinkled peach-colored cotton belted at the waist with a black sash, glanced around the room with a critical eye. "Anyone from the press here yet?"

Mason looked startled. "The press? Well, I don't know. I'm not sure who Theresa invited. The press doesn't usually pay much attention to this sort of thing, not unless the artist is really important."

"The press will turn out for free food, too," Carla informed him. "But you have to get the word to them. Remind me to talk to the gallery owner later and see just who she contacted."

Guinevere grinned at Mason. "My sister has a talent for organizing."

"Oh." Mason nodded vaguely, taking Carla's arm. "Well, come on over and get some of the freebies before they're all gone." He looked around a little nervously. "I never thought this many people would show up."

Guinevere followed her sister and Mason to the champagne table, scanning the collection of paintings hung on the stark white walls. It was the first time she'd had a really good look at his work. Her previous viewings had been across the distance that separated her apartment from his studio. She had always liked the colors in his pictures, though. Through her kitchen window she'd seen canvases done in warm, vivid hues that appealed to her. But up close she realized that his work was subtly complex, the kind of painting that rewarded detailed study.

There was an abstract quality to Mason's work, but the pictures were powerful and surprisingly comprehensible. Some, such as the painting of one of the Pioneer Square missions on a cold wintry day, contained a definite social commentary. The line of men waiting for free shelter and a free meal was strangely affecting, even though Guinevere saw such lines every evening as she walked home from the office.

But other canvases were devoted to the integral play of light and color, drawing the eye with disarming ease. Guinevere liked them and found herself stepping closer to one that was predominantly yellow in an effort to read the tiny price tag.

"A thousand dollars!" She gasped. "Mason, if you sell a few of these, you won't have to eat free crackers for a couple of months."

Mason turned his head to glance at the canvas behind her. "I know," he said, not without a certain hopeful satisfaction.

"I'm glad to see the gallery owner had the sense to put decent prices on the paintings," Carla murmured as she accepted her glass of champagne. "It's important to keep the values high right from the start."

Guinevere looked at her. "I had no idea you were such an authority on the sale of art."

"I'm not. It's just common sense. Show me some of the other

paintings, Mason." Carla smiled brilliantly, and Mason took her arm with a kind of stunned enthusiasm.

Guinevere found herself standing alone by the champagne table. She picked up a cracker that had a piece of smoked salmon stuck into a dab of cream cheese and wondered what Zac was doing. He'd told her earlier that he had another of his late-afternoon meetings scheduled with Elizabeth Gallinger. Perhaps they were even now discussing babies.

For the first time Guinevere wondered just how much appeal the subject would have for Zac. He'd never expressed any interest in a family life, but maybe the prospect looked more appealing to him than she'd realized. After all, he was thirty-six years old, and he'd spent a lot of time knocking around the world. Maybe he'd suddenly realized he'd missed having a family. His past had been violent at times and strangely rootless. She knew his coworkers in the international security firm for which he'd once worked had called him the Glacier because of the slow but painstakingly thorough way he went about doing a job. The nickname Glacier, she had decided, could also have referred to the coldly lethal capacity he had for dealing with certain kinds of situations. Guinevere had twice seen Zac when he was on the hunt. It was a chilling vision.

But babies? Diapers? Day care? Strollers? Guinevere couldn't imagine Zac suddenly becoming fascinated with fatherhood. Unless, of course, the potential mother was the main draw. Guinevere chewed her lower lip and thought about Elizabeth Gallinger.

When she was sick of the thought of Queen Elizabeth, she picked up her champagne glass and went to study a painting of Elliott Bay at sunset. Telling herself she would not let her imagination run wild on the subject of Zac and babies, Guinevere concentrated on wishing she'd had the sense to wear something artsy such as Carla had worn.

As it was, Guinevere was very aware of the fact that she was the only one in the room wearing a skirted suit and proper pumps.

"Not bad if you like sunsets," announced a masculine voice from just behind Guinevere's left shoulder. "A little trite in some respects, but this is one of his earlier works. Mason has changed a lot during the past couple of years, and it shows in his painting, don't you think?"

Guinevere turned to face the short, wiry young man who was eyeing the painting behind her. Something about his features reminded her of a ferret. "I've just met him recently. I don't know much about his earlier work."

The man smiled with an air of superiority. "I see. You're new on the scene around here?"

"If you mean new on the art scene, the answer is yes. I'm Guinevere Jones."

"Henry Thorpe." He waited impatiently for some sign of recognition, and when it didn't come, he frowned. "I've had a couple of showings here myself, but I guess if you're new in the art world, you wouldn't have known about them."

"I see." One of Mason's freeloading fellow artists, Guinevere decided. There was a certain nervous energy about Henry Thorpe that she found curious, almost unnatural. It was as if he were operating at a higher internal speed than most of the others in the room. Perhaps Henry Thorpe indulged in other substances besides free champagne. Anything for the sake of art.

"You don't look like you're here for the free food," Thorpe announced, scanning her neat suit. "So I assume you're a potential buyer?"

"I'm very interested in Mason's work," Guinevere said politely.

"Yeah, so are a few of the others," Thorpe said slightly grudgingly. "I guess it's the superficial accessibility of the stuff. People who don't know much about art like it because they think they can understand it."

Detecting more than a small measure of professional jealousy, Guinevere deliberately turned back to study the painting of the bay. But Henry Thorpe edged closer.

"You'd never guess it from that sweet little painting of sunset on the water, but ol' Mason wasn't exactly a sweet character when he did that picture. He was running pretty wild a couple of years ago. Hung out with a weird crowd."

Guinevere frowned. "Mr. Thorpe, I'm really not interested in hearing this."

"If you want to buy a painting from a guy who used to run around with witches, that's your business. But personally I—"

"Witches!" Astonished, Guinevere swung around to confront Henry Thorpe. Memories of a black pentagram flashed into her head. "Witches? What on earth are you talking about, Mr. Thorpe?"

Sensing that he may have blundered socially, Thorpe tried to back off. "Oh, well, it was no big deal. You know how it is. People sometimes get mixed up in strange things, and Adair was pretty strung out a couple of years ago. Had a bad time with his family back East, and I think he tried to forget his problems by getting involved in something really off-the-wall. But that's all over now. I mean, it's not like he would have painted hidden symbols of the occult into these canvases or anything. You don't have to worry about that."

"What doesn't she have to worry about, Thorpe?" drawled Mason Adair as he came up behind the smaller man. Carla was still firmly tucked into his grasp.

"Nothing, Mason," Thorpe assured him hastily. "Just talking about some of your paintings. Not a bad crowd tonight. Any buyers?"

"Most people seem to be here for the same reason you are," Mason said, assuring him smoothly. "The free champagne."

Thorpe risked a cynical smile. "You can't hold that against us, friend. You've been known to hit a few showings for the free food yourself. Excuse me." With a nod for both women Henry Thorpe slipped back into the crowd.

Mason watched him go with a wry expression. "He's right, you know. I have made a few meals off a showing like this. Can't blame the others for turning up tonight. I just hope they don't elbow all the potential buyers aside in their lunge for the food."

"I don't think you have to worry about that," Carla said with a certain satisfaction as she watched the gallery owner hang a SOLD sign on a painting across the room.

Mason followed her gaze and whistled silently. "Jesus. Theresa put a price of fifteen hundred on that sucker."

Guinevere grinned. "Congratulations. You're going to have something to celebrate when this is all over." And then, remembering the comment Thorpe had made about Mason's past, she couldn't resist adding, "Your family will be excited." The reaction was immediate and grim. Mason's expression of dazed pleasure vanished beneath cold, hard lines.

"My family," he said far too calmly, "can go to hell. That's where they sent me." Then he saw the concern on Carla's face and made an obvious effort to shake his suddenly savage mood. "Hey, forget it. It's no big deal. My family and I don't exactly communicate these days. My old man wrote me off the day I made it clear I was going to make a career in art instead of law. That's old history. Let's get some more champagne."

Several more SOLD signs went up before the evening ended. A certain subdued excitement had infected the crowd. Theresa, the gallery owner, was bubbling over with heady enthusiasm as she darted about, answering questions. By the time he and Guinevere had put Carla into a cab to send her back to her Capitol Hill apartment, Mason's mood was euphoric. He stood on the sidewalk until the cab was out of sight and then started walking Guinevere back to her apartment building. It was nearly midnight and the streets were empty.

"Hey, it went okay, didn't it?" Mason said for what must have been the fiftieth time. "It really went okay."

"It went better than okay," Guinevere said, assuring him. "You heard Theresa. She's ecstatic. You're all set, Mason."

"Are you kidding? This is just the beginning. There's no such thing as being all set in this business. Every new painting gets judged against all the others you've done. But at least I've proven I can sell. Dad never thought I would get this far, you know."

"Didn't he?"

"Hell, no, he—" Mason broke off abruptly. "Forget it. I don't want to talk about him. Not tonight."

"How about witches, Mason?" Guinevere asked gently. "Want to talk about them?"

He stopped short and stared at her under a street lamp. "Witches! You mean that stupid pentagram business?"

"Mason, that man, Henry Thorpe, said something about your once having been involved in some kind of occult group. And that damage to your painting last night looked pretty vicious. If there's any possibility of a connection, don't you think you ought to tell the police?"

Mason muttered something that sounded quite disgusted. "Thorpe. God knows what he was running on tonight. He hasn't been able to paint decently for almost a year, and it's eating him alive. What did he tell you about witches?"

"Nothing much. Just that for a while a couple of years ago you'd been mixed up with some sort of odd group."

Mason shoved his hands into the pockets of his leather jacket.

"Yeah, it was odd, all right. But it wasn't dangerous. Bunch of folks sitting around playing games with stuff they learned out of old books. For a while it was just a friendly group that met to get a little high on some homegrown agricultural products and have a few laughs. An excuse to party. A couple of the members started taking things too seriously, though, and I got out. So did almost everyone else. The partying was getting in the way of my painting."

Guinevere frowned, considering. "You don't think there's any possibility of a connection between what happened last night and that group?"

Mason shook his head impatiently and resumed walking. "Not likely. Most of the people I knew who were part of the crowd have long since dropped out. Like I said, it was just an excuse to party. I haven't seen any of the original group for months."

"Where did you do all this, er, partying?"

"One of the members, a guy named Sandwick, had inherited an old house. Mostly we used it. Had a spooky old basement that was soundproof. Neighbors couldn't hear us if we got too loud, not that the neighbors would have cared. It wasn't exactly a high-class area."

"Where was it located?"

"Near Capitol Hill." Mason sounded totally uninterested. "Let's talk about something more to the point."

"Such as?"

"Such as your sister, Carla."

Guinevere smiled. "As I told you, she's an organizer. She used to be an executive secretary, but lately she's been working for me."

"Is she free?"

"No, actually, she can be quite expensive," Guinevere remarked, remembering certain incidents from her sister's recent past.

"Come on, Gwen, you know that's not what I meant."

"All right. She's not involved with anyone special at the moment. Does that answer your question?"

"It does."

"There's just one other thing, Mason," Guinevere went on slowly. "Please excuse the big-sister spiel, but I'm afraid it comes with the territory. I *am* her big sister and I don't want her hurt. She went through a bad experience a few months back. She's over it now, but I wouldn't want anyone undoing all the progress she's made." Carla's "progress" had cost a bundle in therapy, Valium prescriptions, and patience. It had also led directly to Guinevere's first meeting with Zachariah Justis. That first encounter had been very unnerving. It had taught her right from the start that Zac could be quite ruthless.

Mason grinned. "You do sound like a big sister. But don't worry. I'll take good care of Carla. If she'll let me."

"Be prepared to be organized."

"I can't wait." Mason stopped in front of Guinevere's security door. "Here we are. I'll walk you up the stairs like a good Boy Scout. I really appreciate you and Carla coming to the gallery tonight. I was not exactly cool and calm ahead of time, and it was good to know there were going to be some friends there."

"It was a very successful evening, Mason. You should be proud of yourself." Guinevere dug her key out of her shoulder bag as she climbed the second flight of stairs.

"*Relieved* is the word, I think." He waited, lounging against the wall, while she slipped the key into her lock. "Well, good night, Gwen, and thanks again for showing up tonight." Mason straightened and turned to start down the stairs.

"There seems to be something wrong with the door." Guinevere pushed tentatively against it. "I was sure I left it locked. I always lock it."

Mason paused, glancing curiously back over his shoulder. "Anything wrong?"

Guinevere shoved open the door and stood looking into the living room. "Nothing you can do anything about, Mason. Good night." She closed the door very gently in his face and turned to confront Zac.

Zac put down the glass of tequila he had been holding and leaned his head back in the chair where he had been sitting for the past two long hours. The expression in his ghost-gray eyes made Guinevere think again of glaciers.

"I think," Zac said in a voice that showed all the rough edges, "that we have a communication gap here." He got up out of the chair and came forward with grim deliberation. "You and I are supposed to be having an affair. That, for your information, implies exclusivity. What the hell do you mean by coming in at midnight with that goddamned artist?"

CHAPTER 3

"I'm not an errant wife coming home late after a night on the town," Guinevere managed to say in a surprisingly even voice. She wasn't feeling at all even inside. She'd never seen Zac in quite this mood. There had been times when he'd been annoyed with her, and she'd seen him concerned and had been around him when his temper grew a little short. But she'd never seen such blatant anger and outrage.

"No, you're not an errant wife, are you? You're a bored mistress coming in after a night on the town."

Guinevere's head came up with a snap. Furiously she tossed her shoulder bag down onto a black leather chair. "Don't you dare call me your *mistress*, Zac. A mistress, for your information, is a kept woman. And you don't keep me, Zac Justis. Lately you haven't even kept me company!"

"So you decided to go out and find someone else to keep you company?"

"It's none of your business what I did tonight." She was moving farther and farther out on the thinnest possible ice, but her own anger was in full sail. "You have no right to yell at me like this."

"No right? You come home at midnight with that naked artist in tow, and you tell me I don't have any right to yell?"

"He wasn't naked."

"How long would it have taken him to get naked after you invited him into your apartment?"

"I didn't invite him in, not that it would have made any difference. Mason walked me home after his gallery showing tonight. He invited Carla and me to attend. Since I didn't have anything else to do tonight and since he's a very nice person, I decided to accept the invitation. I had a couple of glasses of free champagne and half-a-dozen salmon canapés. I resisted the impulse to buy one of his paintings. Primarily because I couldn't afford one. That, Zac, is the sum total of my wild night on the town. Mason and I left the gallery about fifteen minutes ago, and I can produce witnesses if necessary. Is there anything else you'd like to know?" Summoning up a courage she wasn't sure she actually felt, Guinevere walked right past Zac, flung herself down onto the black sofa, and glared across the room at the egg-yolk-yellow floor-to-ceiling bookcase. She refused to glance at Zac, who was watching her the way a predator watches its prey.

"Yes, goddammit, there are a few other things I'd like to know. Were you planning on inviting him in for a nightcap? What's his view of the evening's entertainment? Is it as charmingly innocent as yours?"

Guinevere swung her gaze from the bookcase to Zac's glittering gray eyes. "Mason is falling rapidly for my sister. A typical male reaction around Carla. She's about all he talked about on the way back here this evening. Now, if we're going to discuss innocent evenings, why don't we dissect yours? How long did the after-work session with Elizabeth Gallinger go? Did you find it necessary to conclude your business over dinner and a few drinks? Did you go to her place or yours after that?"

Zac ran a hand through his dark hair, his expression turning frustrated. "My meeting with Elizabeth was all business."

"Really? No more chitchat about babies and biological clocks?" His eyes narrowed quickly, and Guinevere knew she'd struck gold. "Oh, I see. The subject did arise, then? Before or after you gave her your analysis of Gallinger's security needs?"

"You don't know what the hell you're talking about. I left Elizabeth several hours ago, went home, and started trying to call you. I thought you might be in the mood for a late dinner. When you failed to answer your phone for over two hours, I finally decided to come over here and make sure everything was all right."

Guinevere couldn't stand the way he was starting to pace back and forth in front of her. The movement reminded her too much of a stalking cat waiting to pounce. Uneasily she kicked off her pumps and got to her feet. She walked past him, ignoring his glare, went into the kitchen, and turned on the light. The mini blinds were raised, and she could see that Mason hadn't yet let himself into his apartment. The studio window was still dark. Guinevere reached for the teakettle. She didn't feel like waiting for the new coffeepot to crank through its elegant ritual. Zac appeared in the kitchen doorway as she switched on the burner.

For a long moment they looked at each other without saying a word. With a woman's instinct Guinevere knew that some of Zac's initial fury had cooled.

"Everything was just fine, Zac. There was absolutely no need for you to be concerned. We don't have to account to each other for every moment, do we? We're having an affair. We're not married. The simple truth is that Carla and I spent a pleasant evening at the gallery. Mason walked me home afterward. That's all there was to it." She kept her tone quiet and remote.

He was silent for a moment. "I discussed business with Elizabeth and then went home and started calling you. That's all there was to my wild evening, too."

"I don't like being called your mistress."

"I'm sorry. Lately I've been feeling"—he paused—"possessive." His gaze was steady. "What should I call you?"

"The name is Gwen. You don't have to use any other labels." She turned away to reach for a couple of mugs and saw the light come on across the street in Mason's apartment. There was no sense adding new fuel to a fire that was starting to die out, Guinevere decided. Catching sight of Mason through the kitchen window would probably not set well with Zac. Out of sight, out of mind. She put the mugs down on the counter and went to lower the blinds. Her hand was on the cord when an abrupt movement in the studio caught her eye.

"Zac!"

He was at her side instantly. "What is it?"

"Zac, there's someone in Mason's studio. Oh, my God, look!"

Mason had sauntered into the high-ceilinged room, automatically turning on the lights. A dark, hooded figure, who had apparently been inside the apartment when Mason opened his door, dashed across the floor, hand upraised. From their vantage point Guinevere and Zac could make out Mason's startled reaction, and then the hooded figure was upon him.

"Call 911." Zac was already on his way out of the kitchen, heading for the front door.

Guinevere reached for the phone, punching in the short emergency code. With her eyes riveted to the drama taking place across the street, she quickly gave the address and situation to the person on the other end of the line. "Just hurry, will you?" she snapped when the dispatcher patiently asked for her name and address as well as that of the victim's.

Guinevere slammed down the receiver and leaned forward, staring out the window. She could see Mason's crumpled body on the floor. The hooded figure was straightening slowly. Some instinct must have warned him that he was being watched. Turning, the man glanced out of the studio window. For a taut moment his gaze locked with Guinevere's.

She couldn't see much, Guinevere realized as she frantically tried to take mental notes. The hood fell forward around his face, hiding almost all of the details one was supposed to recall in this sort of situation. Besides, she was too far away to make out such things as the color of his eyes. But she could see the heavy line of the jaw, and there was a certain sense of bulkiness under the old shirt and pants he wore. A heavy man. She was almost positive she wouldn't be able to identify the man if she ever saw him again, though. Frantically she tried to find some unique feature. The hood, itself, was the oddest part about him. It was shaped like a cut-off monk's cowl. It shadowed his face and fell into a short cape around his shoulders.

As they stood facing each other through the windows, it occurred to Guinevere that the cowled man had as good a view of her as she had of him. Belatedly she reached out and turned off her kitchen light.

But the man in Mason's apartment was already swinging around in alarm. He must have heard Zac's footsteps on the stairs. Or perhaps seeing Guinevere had jerked him into action. Whatever the trigger, it sent him running out of the apartment.

Helplessly Guinevere watched as Mason's attacker fled. With any luck he might run into Zac on the stairs, she thought. But a few seconds later Zac burst through the door and went straight to Mason's prone figure. There was no sign that Zac and the cowled man had tangled.

Guinevere raced across the kitchen and out her front door. At the last minute she remembered she wasn't wearing any shoes. As she grabbed a pair of sandals out of the closet, she heard the first police sirens in the distance. She shoved her feet into the sandals and hitched up the narrow skirt of her suit. Then she was running down the two flights of stairs to the street. Out on the sidewalk she dashed toward the entrance to Mason's building. The security door was propped open with a copy of the Seattle Yellow Pages that belonged on the shelf beneath the pay phone in the small lobby. Zac's work, Guinevere assumed. Perhaps to make access quicker for the cops. She wondered how he'd gotten inside the security entrance so quickly. But Zac had a way of doing things like that.

She flew up the stairs to the second floor and glanced down the old, linoleum-lined hall. Mason's building hadn't been as expensively renovated as hers. In fact, it looked to be in what was probably a sadly original condition. The dim halls and shaky banister on the staircase made the place look a little like a cheap hotel. At the opposite end of the hallway there was a faded exit sign, indicating a fire escape. If Zac hadn't met the escaping attacker on the staircase, it was probably because the man had used the other exit.

The door standing open at the end of the hall had to be the one to Mason's apartment. Guinevere rounded the corner just as the sirens whined into silence outside the building.

"Zac! Is he all right?"

Zac was crouching beside Mason. He didn't look up. "He'll live. Whoever it was got him on the side of the head, but the blow must have been deflected. He's groggy but not unconscious. Did you see any sign of whoever it was who did this, Gwen? I didn't pass him on the stairs."

"I think he must have used the fire escape. I got a brief glimpse of him through my window while I was dialing 911."

Zac did glance up at that, pinning her with grim eyes. "Did he see you?"

"I . . . I think so, but he must have heard you about that time and dashed out of the room. He was wearing a weird hood, Zac. It was very strange." Guinevere broke off as footsteps echoed on the old stairs.

"I'll handle this," Zac said, getting to his feet.

Guinevere nodded obediently. Zac was good at this sort of thing, too.

On the floor Mason groaned and opened his eyes. "Hell of a way to celebrate my first show."

It was a long time later before Guinevere found herself alone with Zac back in her apartment. She was tense and troubled. Zac sprawled on the sofa, eyeing her as she stalked back and forth in front of him.

"I don't understand it, Zac. Why didn't Mason tell the police about that incident with his painting last night? Damn it, he told me he'd filed a complaint. Or at least he implied he was going to file one. But tonight he didn't mention it. Instead he acted as if he'd just been unlucky enough to walk in on a routine burglary this evening. He didn't try to relate the two incidents."

"I didn't hear you rushing to fill in the missing pieces," Zac observed quietly. "You didn't say a word about that pentagram or the canvas slashing, either."

Guinevere threw up her hands in frustration. "Because I could see Mason looking at me, practically begging me to keep my mouth shut." She turned to glance at Zac accusingly. "And you went right along with Mason's limited version of the story, too. Why?"

Zac shrugged. "The same reason you did, I suppose. It was pretty damn obvious Adair didn't want to link last night's incident with tonight's, and even more obvious that he'd never mentioned the slashed canvas to the authorities. I could see him watching me as I talked to the cops, and I knew he wanted me to say as little as possible."

"So you did."

"I told them what I'd seen through your window tonight, which wasn't much. Hell, I didn't even get a look at the guy. He was long gone by the time I reached Adair's apartment."

"But you knew about the pentagram and the slashing," Guinevere reminded him.

"All right, so I decided to respect Adair's wishes and keep quiet about it. I'm used to dealing with clients who prefer not to involve the cops. I guess it's getting to be second nature to abide by the client's wishes."

That much was the truth, Guinevere thought. Many of Zac's business clients had no desire to see their company's name dragged through the newspapers or to have any association at all with criminal activity, even though they were the victims. That's why they hired discreet security firms such as Free Enterprise Security, Inc. Precisely so that such unpleasant matters would be handled *discreetly*.

"Are you saying Mason is now a client?" Guinevere asked brightly.

Zac glared at her. "No, I am not saying that. I merely made the point that I'm used to working for people who don't want the police involved. Out of habit I respected Adair's wishes tonight. That's all there is to it."

Guinevere sighed and sank down onto the opposite end of the sofa. "I wonder what this is all about, Zac."

"Beats the hell out of me." One arm draped along the back of the cushion, he continued to watch her closely. "But whatever it is, I don't want you involved. I've told you that before, Gwen. I mean it."

"Zac, Mason's a friend."

"I thought he was just a ship passing in the night."

"Well, it's more a case of a permanently anchored ship. With a porthole that looks straight into my porthole."

"I've been aware of that for some time," Zac drawled. There was a short silence. "I heard him tell the cops that he'd been to the show at the Midnight Light gallery tonight with you and Carla."

"So?"

Zac exhaled heavily. "I shouldn't have chewed on you earlier this evening."

"Is that an apology?"

"Yeah."

Guinevere risked a small smile. "I shall treasure it always."

"You do that. I don't apologize very often."

"I know."

There was another short pause before Zac said promptingly, "Well? Don't I get one, too?"

"An apology?"

"You owe me something for all those not-so-subtle accusations about the meeting with Elizabeth."

"I guess I do. I know she's an important client for you, Zac. And I'm a businessperson. I understand about client demands."

"So when do I get the apology?" he pressed.

"I thought I'd already given it!"

"No," he said, leaning forward to haul her onto his lap, "you haven't. But you will."

Her mouth curved tremulously as she automatically braced herself with one arm around his broad shoulders. "Going to exact your pound of flesh?"

"And then some." Zac brushed his mouth against hers, sampling her lips with easy, possessive familiarity. His large palm spread warmly across her thigh. "You have such nice flesh."

Guinevere relaxed against him, luxuriating in the welcoming heat and strength of his hold. Her fingertips lost themselves in his thick, dark hair. He murmured something sexy and outrageous into her ear.

"What was that?" she demanded, pulling slightly away.

"I said I adore the pink perfection of your rose-colored lips, the column of your throat reminds me of a Grecian statue, and I could kiss the ground upon which your dainty feet tread."

"Funny, that's not what I thought you said." She tugged at the first button of his shirt.

"Okay, so it lost something in the translation. Let's not quibble."

"Wouldn't think of it." She slipped her fingers inside the white shirt and found the dark, curling hair on his chest.

His hand tightened on her thigh, and he began unfastening her silk blouse. When the delicate garment fell unheeded to the gray rug, Zac groaned softly and kissed her shoulder. "I've missed you lately, sweetheart."

"Not as much as I've missed you." She snuggled more closely as he undid the front catch of her bra and pushed it off her shoulders. When his palm rubbed gently across her nipple, she closed her eyes and let her fingertips sink into his chest.

"Do you know what you do to me when you respond like this?" Zac lowered his head and put his mouth on the crest of her breast.

"Ummm." She could feel the rising need in him. Under her thigh he was growing heavy with desire. His immediate response was every bit as exhilarating for her as he claimed hers was for him. Their physical attraction for each other had been intense and immediate right from the start. But as their relationship deepened into a full-fledged affair, it seemed to Guinevere that the physical side of things was changing, growing more complex and variable. Vaguely she wondered why it should be that way. It was as if there were more questions now than when they had first started making love, questions they hesitated to ask each other.

"We both have too many clothes on," Zac muttered as he slid his hand down her side to her bare waist and found the opening of her skirt.

"Do we?"

"Definitely." He surged to his feet, lifting Guinevere in his arms, and strode toward the bedroom. "But I think we can handle the problem."

He finished undressing her in the shadowed bedroom, his hands gliding over her with a hunger that was building rapidly in its intensity. Guinevere struggled briefly with his slacks, but he grew impatient and unsnapped them himself. As the last of their clothing fell away, Zac eased her down onto the bed, pushing apart her legs so that he could lie comfortably between her thighs.

"You're in a hurry tonight," she teased, her eyes gleaming.

"It's been too long." He ducked his head to kiss the hollow of her throat. Deliberately he let her feel him poised at the damp, silky opening of her body. "I'm a creature of habit, Gwen. And lately I've gotten into the habit of going to bed with you as frequently as possible. You can't just cut a man off from his habit without a few serious consequences. I've been suffering withdrawal symptoms for the past week."

"It's your own fault you've been suffering," she couldn't resist pointing out.

"Don't remind me. I finally get an evening that's at least partially free, come rushing over here, and what do I find?"

"No more lectures, Zac."

He sucked in his breath as he felt her lift her lower body against his with tantalizing emphasis. "No," he agreed fervently. "No more lectures." He caught her shoulders and eased forward, just barely entering her. He waited eagerly for the small intake of breath that told him she was reacting as passionately as she always did to his possession. Zac ached with need, but he had grown addicted to that first little gasp with which she always greeted him, and he always held himself in check until he heard it. When he felt her nails dig lightly into his shoulders, he surged forward, burying himself in the tight, clinging warmth.

"Ah, Zac. *Zac.*"

Her passion made him forget all that had happened that evening. It wiped out the memory of the long nights he'd been spending alone lately, and it obliterated the jealousy that had gripped him earlier. At this moment she was completely his once more, and he thrived on the knowledge. Thrived, hell. It made him feel complete and alive and filled him with a satisfaction that nothing else could equal. Zac reveled in the mental sensation just as thoroughly as he gloried in the physical. There had never been any other woman who could do this to him.

His body drove into hers, setting up an inevitable cadence that could only lead to one conclusion. Guinevere's eyes were closed as the passion crystallized within her. He could feel the strong, feminine muscles in her thighs as she wrapped her legs around his waist and held him close. She wanted him as completely as he wanted her, and Zac knew he would cheerfully kill to keep her in his arms.

When he sensed the delicate tightening that signaled the beginning of her climax, Zac fought the familiar battle to restrain himself until she was so far along the path that it would be impossible for her to turn back. Then, when the little shivers gripped her, he surrendered to his own pounding desire, a stifled shout of triumph and satisfaction mingling with her small cries.

Zac waited a long time before rolling reluctantly to one side. He felt pleasantly exhausted. Guinevere lay cradled inside the curve of his arm, and he idly toyed with the nest of damp, dark hair below her flat stomach. Her lashes lifted with lazy, lingering sensuality as she looked up at him.

"Apology accepted?" she asked throatily.

"Hell, yes. I'm not an unreasonable man."

"Hah." She grinned and tickled him.

"Watch it," he advised, not bothering to move.

"Why?"

He groaned. "Why is it you always have so much energy after we do this, while I'm always in a state of total exhaustion?"

"Don't whine about it. Just a basic constitutional difference between male and female. It's not your fault men have this fundamental weakness."

"If we're weakened so much afterward, it's only because we have to do all the hard work."

"Excuses, excuses." She leaned across him, folding her arms on his chest and resting her chin on them.

"Speaking of excuses . . ." he began slowly as he remembered something.

"What about them?"

"I wasn't able to think of any to get myself out of a cocktail party tomorrow night. A business thing. Will you come with me so I don't have to stand in a corner by myself?"

"Luckily you've caught me in a generous mood. Who's giving the party?"

There was a slight pause before Zac said quietly, "Elizabeth Gallinger."

Guinevere deliberately allowed herself to pause before responding. She thought she could feel Zac tightening a little beneath her. "Received a royal summons?"

"Something like that. She's a good client, Gwen. I don't want to offend her. At least not until she's paid for the analysis I've been preparing."

"That much I can understand. And since I definitely don't want you standing alone in a corner all evening, I'll be gracious and go with you."

"You're too good to me."

"I know." She drummed her fingers lightly on his chest and grinned wickedly. "Much too good to you."

"Fortunately for me," Zac murmured, ruffling her hair, "I don't let humbleness cripple me."

"I can see that." One of his legs moved between hers, and Guinevere was suddenly aware of a resurgence of the throbbing heat that had consumed him earlier. Her fingertips slipped down his rock-hard belly to the stirring shaft of his manhood. "I thought you were exhausted."

"I am. This time you'll have to do all the work." He reached down and gripped her waist, lifting her lightly and settling her on top of him. "Show me how much energy you've really got."

Guinevere sank down along the length of him, a secret, sensual smile curving her mouth. "More than enough for both of us," she promised him softly.

Guinevere woke the next morning to a muttered expletive that reached her all the way from the kitchen. She blinked slowly and peered at the clock. Almost seven. Usually she was up and moving by six. Last night Zac had been determined to make up for several lost evenings. As she stretched, she felt the results in the muscles of her thighs.

"Where in hell did you get this stupid excuse for a coffee machine, Gwen?"

She groaned and pushed back the covers as Zac's shouted question reached around the corner into the bedroom. "Don't yell, you'll wake the neighbors."

He appeared in the bedroom doorway, two mugs dangling from his left hand. He was already dressed, his hair still damp from the shower. "You chose that sucker for its color, didn't you?" he accused. "It was the red-and-black trim that seduced you. You can't resist anything bright when it comes to decorating this place, can you? Do you realize that at its present rate of production that coffeemaker is going to take an hour to produce two cups of coffee?"

"Possibly, but it will be really terrific coffee, Zac. Trust me."

"I'll bet you didn't even bother to research coffee machines before you went shopping for one. I should have gone with you. At least I could have kept you from buying some off-brand piece of junk."

"You're wrong. It's not off-brand; it's imported." She got up and reached hastily for her robe. There had been several mornings now when Zac had seen her rising naked from a tangled bed, but she still wasn't accustomed to the way he watched her when she was running around nude. "And I did research coffee machines. But when I got to the display at the Bon, this one just stood out from all the rest. It was as if it had 'Buy Me, Guinevere Jones' written all over it. I couldn't resist it. It's beautiful."

"It's a disaster."

"Details, details." She finished tying the sash of the robe and smiled brilliantly. "Relax. It'll have the coffee ready in a moment. I'm going to take a shower."

"Maybe we'll have one mug of coffee out of that idiotic device by the time you're dressed, but I wouldn't count on it." The phone rang in the kitchen, and Zac turned away to answer it.

Guinevere traipsed after him. It was, after all, her phone, her apartment, and her kitchen. Zac had a way of assuming a lot of rights around the place on the mornings after he'd spent the preceding nights. She'd seen this syndrome previously. When she reached the kitchen, he was already speaking into the phone.

"Okay, Gertie, I'll take care of it right away. Thanks for the message." He replaced the receiver and glanced at Gwen. "That was my new answering service."

Guinevere smiled contentedly. "I'm glad you took my advice and hired one. Answering machines don't leave the best impression on clients. Much better to have a human answer your phone when you're out. How did Gertie, or whatever her name is, know to call here?"

"I left this number with her last night." Zac busied himself with the toast that had just popped out of the toaster.

"I see." Guinevere considered the implications. Zac had obviously intended to spend the night when he'd arrived the previous evening. Well, she could hardly hold his rather arrogant assumption against him. After all, they were involved in an affair.

"Want a bite of toast?"

Guinevere nodded. "So who was the message from?"

"Elizabeth Gallinger. She wants to see me first thing this morning." Zac was taking great pains with the buttering process. "Breakfast meeting."

Guinevere gritted her teeth and forced herself to smile sweetly. "Oh, good. You won't have to worry about getting coffee out of my new machine. *Liz* can buy you a cup."

With a certain air of defiance she glanced toward her kitchen window, but there was no view into Mason Adair's apartment this morning. Zac had lowered the blinds.

CHAPTER 4

Carla glanced up disapprovingly as Guinevere walked into the office that morning. "You're late." Then she added with great interest, "Did Zac spend the night?"

"It occurs to me, sister dear, that your extensive interest in my social life is due to the fact that you're bored. I don't think you've got enough to do around here now that you've got all of Camelot's files in order. Your skills as an executive secretary are being wasted." Guinevere hung up her umbrella. It was a myth that Seattle residents never carried umbrellas, a myth perpetuated by the locals, who liked to pretend that they were indifferent to the misty rain that was a major factor in their environment. Hers hadn't been the only umbrella out there on the street this morning, and there was no way those others could have belonged to tourists. It was only eight o'clock. Most self-respecting tourists were still in their motel rooms at this hour.

Carla gave her sister a strange glance. "I thought you appreciated me getting your office organized."

Instantly Guinevere was sorry she'd made the comment. From the force of long-established habit she backed off, not wanting to hurt Carla's feelings. But damn it, she told herself, it was time Carla was out on her own again. Besides, Guinevere wanted her office back, even if she might not run it quite as efficiently as Carla did. "You know I've been extremely grateful for all the work you've done. It's just that now you have everything down to such an efficient routine that I'm beginning to feel like an unnecessary accessory around my own office. It's time you took on a new challenge, Carla." She waved a hand around the room, indicating the sum total of Camelot Services' headquarters. "This place is just too small for you. You're trained for bigger and more exciting things. You're too skilled, too much of a professional, to continue working here as a clerk."

Carla's mouth trembled a little. "I'm not sure, Gwen. I just don't know."

"What I need is part-time clerical assistance," Guinevere said gently. "Hiring a skilled executive secretary such as you to work here is like hiring a Thoroughbred race horse to pull a wagon. I've got a dozen people in my files who can handle the clerical work required by Camelot Services. You should be out earning big money and managing an executive office. Carla, you mustn't let that incident at StarrTech keep you from going back to the kind of work you were trained to do."

Carla's beautiful eyes were wary and wistful. "I know, Gwen. It's just that I've felt, well, safe here."

"I realize that. But you're also getting bored here. You were born to organize someone or something."

"You don't get bored here," Carla pointed out.

"I own the place. It may be humble, but it's mine." Guinevere smiled. "It makes a difference, you know."

Carla sighed. "All right, I can take a hint. I'll start keeping an eye out for another position."

Instantly Guinevere was stricken with guilt. "There's no rush, you know. We can watch for something interesting that might come through Camelot Services. Lots of times people ask for short-term, temporary secretaries whom they then wind up hiring as permanent staff."

Carla's insipient depression disintegrated beneath a wave of humor. "I know. And you chew nails every time it happens."

Guinevere was pleased to see how quickly her sister had thrown off her bad mood. A few months ago such a mood might have settled on Carla for a full day or more. Her sister really was back to normal, and it was time she went back to the kind of work she liked. "Well, it is a little irritating to have some of my best temps stolen, but I guess it goes with the territory. Besides, it's good advertising in a way. The people who get full-time jobs tell others how they landed them through Camelot Services, and the new employers are impressed with the quality of the people we send them. You have to look on the positive side."

"I'm glad you're feeling so positive and philosophical this morning, because Bonny Hatcher's husband just phoned to say Bonny went into labor last night and had her baby at three this morning."

Guinevere stared at her. "But she wasn't due for another couple of weeks!"

"These things happen, Gwen. Healthy baby girl. Seven pounds, two ounces."

"Good grief. Zac was right?"

"About the sudden onslaught of baby making?"

Guinevere nodded dolefully. "It's scary, isn't it? Everyone is either talking about babies or having them. And you read all the time about how well all those new fertility clinics are doing. It's the latest fad among educated, successful women. Biological clocks. Probably just a craze, but when it's all over, there are going to be a lot of kids running around."

"Oh, my God," Carla breathed. "You are really starting to worry about this, aren't you?"

"My imagination has been running riot a lot lately." Guinevere pulled a stack of folders toward her as she sat down at her desk. "But business comes first."

"Wait a second," Carla said bluntly, "What about Zac? How does he feel about the new fad of having babies?"

Guinevere opened a folder and stared unseeingly at the contents. "I don't know," she said quietly. "I just don't know."

Carla grimaced. "Haven't the two of you talked about the subject?"

"Not directly."

"But, Gwen—"

"Look, Carla, I don't have the answers to your questions, so let's get down to work. As long as you're sitting at that desk, you might as well do something useful. Get on the phone and see who you can find to replace Bonny Hatcher at Fogel's today. She was due to work there for another five days to replace his secretary who's on vacation. We can't let Fogel down. He's been a small but very loyal client." She glanced at the clock. "His insurance office doesn't open until ten. That gives us less than two hours."

"I'll find someone. I can always go out myself if necessary." Carla reached for the phone and the folder full of temps who were qualified for Fogel's kind of office.

"Oh, and Carla, when you're finished, you'd better send flowers to Bonny's hospital room. And maybe one of those little designer baby suits."

Carla chuckled. "A designer baby suit?"

"Don't laugh. It's what the new brand of baby is wearing these days."

"Okay." She started to dial.

"And when you're finished," Guinevere added deliberately, "I've got something important to tell you about Mason Adair."

Half an hour later, as Guinevere finished her story of the events in Adair's studio, she was glad she hadn't brought up the subject until after Carla had located a replacement for Bonny. Carla nearly went into shock.

"Good Lord! Is everyone all right? What about Mason?"

"He's okay. He got a few bruises in the struggle, but he wasn't badly hurt. He refused to go to an emergency room."

"And you and Zac?"

"We're fine," Guinevere assured her. "It was probably the sound of Zac racing up the stairs that drove off the intruder."

"I've got to call Mason." Carla was already dialing.

"I don't see why," Guinevere began calmly, only to be interrupted by Carla as she spoke urgently into the phone.

"Mason, what's this I hear about an intruder in your apartment last night? I can't believe it. Are you all right?" Pause. "Are you absolutely certain? There can be delayed effects from this sort of thing, you know." Another pause as she listened to Mason. "Yes, yes, I realize that, but all the same—" Long pause while Carla listened impatiently. "I know, but I still think you should take it easy today. What do you mean, you can't? Just don't try painting until tomorrow. There's no sense pushing things. Besides, you deserve a break after your brilliant show last night." Carla frowned. "Oh, I see. I didn't realize. Your cousin? Well, I'm not sure. After all, this is your family and all, and I know there are problems. I wouldn't want to make things awkward." One more pause. Carla suddenly seemed to change her mind. "I understand completely. Of course we'll be there. One o'clock. Yes, I know the restaurant. See you then, Mason."

Guinevere leaned back in her swivel chair and eyed her sister.

"What on earth was that all about? Where, exactly, are we going to be at one o'clock?"

Carla appeared to remember something. "You're not already scheduled for lunch with Zac, are you?"

"Zac didn't schedule me in for anything today," Guinevere said dryly. "He left my apartment in a big hurry. Had a hot breakfast meeting with Liz. My next appointment with Zachariah Justis is tonight. I'm due to escort him to the queen's party. Zac was afraid that if he went alone, he'd be a wallflower. Fat chance. I'm sure Ms. Gallinger would have found some way of entertaining him."

"Gwen, I hate to tell you this, but you're losing your objectivity. Are you jealous?"

"Of course not. Forget that and tell me what's happening at one."

"Mason's cousin is in town. Just showed up without any notice. Called Mason's apartment this morning. He's been sent here on family business, apparently. He's taking Mason to lunch, and Mason doesn't wish to be alone with his cousin. Feels it will be a stressful situation, to say the least. I volunteered you and me to run interference. The lunch is free, Gwen. Cousin's going to pick up the tab."

Guinevere eyed her sister appraisingly. "Carla, haven't you learned yet that there is no such thing as a free lunch?"

"What could go wrong?" Carla asked with perfect confidence.

"We could become embroiled in an embarrassing family conflict."

"Nonsense. By going we'll be helping Mason to avoid a conflict."

Guinevere gave up the argument and went to work.

Dane Fitzpatrick turned out to be something of a surprise. He was, according to Mason, the son of his father's sister, an only child, just as Mason was. Apparently the family had always expected Dane and

Mason to be close friends, but the truth was, they had very little in common. When they were very young, Mason said, there had been a distinct hostility between himself and his cousin, probably promoted by the fact that the other family members tried to force them to be buddies. But there were also some very basic differences between the two men. Dane had been content to fulfill family expectations as far as career and lifestyle were concerned. Mason had been of a more independent and rebellious temperament.

Given Mason's surly comments on his cousin, Guinevere wasn't expecting the gallant, charming, thirty-five-year-old man who looked as if he had just stepped out of a fine East Coast law office. Impeccably dressed in a gray suit and old-school tie, his slightly thinning hair meticulously trimmed, Fitzpatrick exuded quiet confidence and the sense of authority that came naturally to those who are descended from a long line of successful upper-class lawyers and a good family. He was a handsome man, with the kind of physique that spelled tennis courts, golf, and sailing on a regular basis. He had what must have been the family's dark eyes, judging from the fact that Mason had them, too. He also had excellent manners. Guinevere was surprised by the gracious way he covered up his astonishment at seeing Mason walk into the restaurant with two strange women in tow.

"Please sit down," Dane said with quiet gallantry as he accepted the introductions. "Mason, you should have mentioned you were bringing guests. But no matter. This table will seat four."

Guinevere glanced around at the interior of the expensively paneled restaurant. The place was noted for its fish, of course, just as most of Seattle's good restaurants were known for seafood. But this particular restaurant was also known for its prices. It looked as if it had been established for fifty years, but Guinevere knew for a fact that it had been built only recently. Nevertheless, the mahogany walls, old-fashioned chandeliers, and heavy green carpeting gave the impression of a much older heritage. She had been looking for an excuse to dine here, and she wondered now whether Mason or his cousin had chosen the place. A waiter materialized near Dane Fitzpatrick.

"Would anyone care for a drink?" Fitzpatrick asked.

"Sure," Mason said. "I'll have a beer."

Mason hadn't bothered to dress for the occasion. He was wearing his usual paint-stained jeans, a scruffy-looking pullover, and an even scruffier pair of Nikes. There was a certain air of defiance about him that touched Guinevere. She had the feeling that Mason had been battling his family a long time. Carla was watching him with a protective expression, as if ready to jump between Mason and Dane, should violence erupt. But violence wasn't about to erupt, Guinevere knew. Dane Fitzpatrick would never stoop to such blue-collar behavior. Above all, he was a gentleman.

"Well, Mason, I had planned to discuss business with you, as you well know, but since we have guests . . ." Fitzpatrick let the sentence trail off. His meaning was clear. This was family business and not meant for the ears of outsiders.

"Don't worry about Carla and Gwen. I've already told them why you've flown three thousand miles just to take me to lunch. You can talk in front of them."

"Perhaps they would prefer that we didn't," Fitzpatrick suggested with grave politeness. It was obvious he was seeking a socially acceptable path out of an uncomfortable situation.

It was Carla who took charge of the conversation at that point. She buttered a chunk of French bread and said blithely, "Did you hear about Mason's show last night? Very successful launch. Several important paintings were sold, and next time there will be press coverage. He's on his way in the art world."

Fitzpatrick looked directly at Mason, who was nursing his beer. "I'll be sure to tell your father."

"Why bother? Dad could care less. But he must have been the one who sent you out here on this wild-goose chase. You wouldn't have come on your own. Why, Dane? What's happening back home to make him suddenly start wondering how things are going with the black sheep of the family? And how did you get my address? I haven't communicated with anyone back East for nearly two years."

"Your father asked me to try to find you, Mason. It's taken quite a while. When I told him that I had a Seattle address for you at last, he asked me to come and see you. You know him. He's much too proud to contact you himself. As it so happened, I had business out here on the coast. After I finished meeting with my clients in L.A., I flew directly here. I think you should consider it an overture, Mason. Your father is a stubborn man. He'll never be able to bring himself to contact you first. Not after what happened between the two of you. But this is his way of trying to tell you the door is open."

"But I'm the one who's supposed to take the big step and apologize? What good would that do, Dane?" Mason asked wearily. "An apology isn't going to solve the problem. As far as my father is concerned, nothing will solve the problem except for me to give up trying to make a career out of my painting. You know as well as I do what kind of lifestyle he thinks I'm living out here. As far as he's concerned, I'm beyond the pale. Decadent, addicted to God knows what, and totally immoral."

"Mason, perhaps you should give the old man a chance," Fitzpatrick said earnestly. He appeared to have forgotten Guinevere and Carla now, as the conversation came down to brass tacks.

"What chance did he give me or my painting? He drummed me out of the family the moment he found out that I was absolutely serious about art. Forget it, Dane. Go back home and tell my father that I haven't changed my mind."

"Your father's will—" Fitzpatrick broke off with an uneasy glance at the two women. Obviously this was too important to discuss in front of strangers, regardless of Mason's lack of concern.

"I don't give a damn about my father's will. I know I'm out of it. But I just don't give a damn. You're welcome to enjoy every penny, Dane."

"Mason, it doesn't have to be this way."

"Yes, it does," Mason said stonily. "The only thing that will ever change it is if the old man admits I have a right to live my life the way I want to live it. What do you think the odds are that he'll do that, Dane?"

Fitzpatrick sighed heavily. "Not good. He's a stubborn, willful old man who has ruled the family for too many years to back down now. He'll never accept your art. You're right about that. If you come back, he'll still want you to give it up."

"Sending you out here to see me was just one more maneuver to try to coax me back into the fold, wasn't it?"

"You're his son," Fitzpatrick said. "It's natural he would try to bring you home."

"On his terms."

"As I said, he's a very stubborn man."

Mason put down his beer mug and glared at the older man. "Tell my father that unless he's prepared to accept me for what I am, I'm never coming home. Not after the things he said to me two years ago. He's the one who threw me out, Dane. There's no way I can come back until he takes the first step. Having you stop by and take me to lunch doesn't constitute a first step as far as I'm concerned."

Dane Fitzpatrick seemed to accept the fact that he had done his duty and that it wasn't going to have any major impact on Mason. He nodded sadly and summoned a deliberately charming smile for Guinevere and Carla. "I fear we are ruining lunch for your friends, Mason. Let's change the topic."

"Good idea." Grimly Mason signaled for another beer.

Guinevere sensed Carla's silent sympathy for the brooding young artist and sent her sister a commiserating glance. All things considered, it was an awkward situation. She hoped her other social engagement of the day would fare better, but she had her doubts.

At ten o'clock that evening Zac found himself exactly where he had feared: standing in a corner alone, drinking tequila. Guinevere was here, all right, but not at his side. She had been easily snagged by a small knot of women her own age, and from what he could overhear of the conversation, they were all discussing babies. He couldn't tell if Gwen was participating enthusiastically or just keeping up her end of the conversation in order to be polite. He wished he knew. If Baby Fever was striking her, he wanted to know about it and be prepared for it.

From the shelter of his corner Zac watched Guinevere as she chatted with the others. He always took a certain possessive satisfaction in watching her. Tonight she had her dark hair in its customary twist at the nape of her neck. The style looked businesslike when she wore a suit and absolutely elegant when she wore the kind of thing she had on tonight. He liked the fact that she wore her hair up during the day and on social occasions. It lent a certain intimacy to the act of taking it down for bed. Zac was aware of a fierce possessiveness as he thought about taking the pins from Guinevere's hair later on tonight.

The red silk dress was scooped at the neckline, gracefully full in the sleeves and bodice, and pulled in snugly at the hips. Zac had liked the feel of the material under his palm earlier that evening when he'd guided her into Elizabeth Gallinger's beautiful Mercer Island home. It had made him think of how good Gwen's skin felt when he was making love to her.

Zac took another swallow of the tequila and decided he probably shouldn't get started thinking along those lines. This was a business party. The last thing he wanted to do was embarrass himself in front of Elizabeth Gallinger's wealthy guests. If he wasn't careful, he'd have to go hide behind a potted palm. It still amazed him that Guinevere could so easily affect him. Tonight, after the party, he would take her home and then to bed. He could wait. She was his for the evening. His for as long as he could hold on to her.

Zac just wished he knew how long that was likely to be. There was still a strange element of uncertainty in his relationship with Guinevere Jones. It worried him primarily because he didn't know how to go about fixing the problem. Zac was accustomed to solving problems. He might be a little slow at it, but he was thorough. It annoyed him that this one wasn't getting resolved. How the hell did she really feel about him? How committed was she to the affair? And just how interested was she getting in babies? He looked around the room, and all he could see were two-dozen biological clocks dressed in evening gowns. It was a daunting image. Maybe he'd had a little too much tequila.

Across the room, prominently displayed over a white couch, was a Mason Adair painting. Guinevere had spotted it the minute she'd walked into the room. It was a canvas full of life and interest, a study of an old woman reading a book. For some reason, although there was a wealth of aging character in the face, the feeling projected by the painting was of youthful discovery. Even Zac, who admitted to himself that he knew next to nothing about art, could feel the effect of the painting.

"I've heard that Queen Elizabeth prides herself on being a patron of the arts. She enjoys 'discovering' the best and the brightest of the new talent. I saw a lot of good stuff on display in the lobby of Gallinger Industries when I worked there for a while a few months ago. It's a real coup for Mason Adair that she obviously thinks enough of his work to have a picture hanging here in her home. I wonder if he knows she bought one?" Guinevere had commented in low tones when they had walked into the glass-walled living room. She had then given him a brief résumé of her experiences at lunch with Mason and his cousin, Dane Fitzpatrick, describing how alienated Mason was from his father. Before Zac could tell her he didn't approve of her having lunch with Mason Adair, Elizabeth Gallinger had come gliding across the room to greet them.

Now, as Zac stood contemplating the picture in greater detail, a soft, throaty voice made him glance to the side.

"Ah, Zac, there you are. I've been looking for you." Elizabeth Gallinger swept through a cluster of her guests who parted for her automatically. Elizabeth had that effect on people. She was a very beautiful woman who projected the kind of self-confidence that came from old money and old family. Zac couldn't imagine her giving a party that was anything less than an unqualified success. Everyone she invited would come. What had Guinevere called such an invitation? A royal summons. But then, Guinevere had been acting strangely whenever Elizabeth's name came up lately.

"Hello, Elizabeth. Looks like a great party." Zac winced inwardly at the inanity. He wasn't sure what else to say. It was easy enough to discuss security matters with Elizabeth Gallinger, but on any other topic he simply couldn't think of much to say. What did you talk about to a woman who moved in Elizabeth's circles if you weren't talking business?

"You don't appear to be enjoying yourself," Elizabeth complained, her crimson fingertips settling lightly on his jacket sleeve. "What happened to that nice Guinevere Jones?"

"She's talking to some of the other guests." Zac glanced across the room. Guinevere still appeared to be trapped in the baby discussion. Either that or she was staying in it of her own free will. He wished to hell he knew which.

"Oh, yes, I see." Elizabeth smiled with great charm. "It's getting a little stuffy in here, don't you think? What do you say we go out onto the patio for a few minutes?"

Zac looked at her in mild surprise and then nodded. "If that's what you'd like. Sure."

"Once this kind of party is up and running, no one really needs the hostess," Elizabeth confided lightly as she led the way out of the white-and-pastel living room. The royal-blue bodice of her gown was sequined and cut to reveal a surprising amount of cleavage. For some reason the look was elegant on Elizabeth. Not at all tacky, Zac decided. Just the same, he wouldn't want Guinevere wearing anything like that out in public. Elizabeth's blond hair moved around her face as if it had been privately trained by her hairdresser. Until now Zac had only seen Elizabeth Gallinger in French designer suits. It didn't surprise him that she looked just as at home in what was probably a French designer gown.

They stepped through a pair of open French doors and out into the cool evening. The rain had disappeared shortly after noon today, and the temperature had immediately climbed into the low seventies. Some of the pleasant warmth still lingered although it was fading rapidly. Elizabeth walked over to a teak railing and leaned against it to gaze out over a discreetly lit garden. Acres of sloping lawn stretched down to the waters of Lake Washington. Across the expanse of dark water the lights of Seattle and Bellevue glittered.

"A lovely evening, isn't it, Zac?"

He nodded again and then realized she might not be able to see the affirmative motion because of the shadows. "Very nice." God, he was a stunning conversationalist. It wasn't like this with Guinevere. He had no trouble at all talking to her. And she had no trouble talking to others. It was one of the reasons he'd wanted her with him tonight. She could keep a conversation going. Unfortunately she was wasting her talent in a discussion of babies this evening.

"I've been extremely pleased by your analysis of Gallinger's security needs, Zac. Now that the project is almost concluded, I want you to know that I'll be recommending you to other people in my position."

"I appreciate that, Elizabeth."

"We've spent a lot of time together over the past few weeks. I feel as though I've gotten to know you quite well," Elizabeth continued in a thoughtful tone.

Zac, who didn't feel he knew this woman at all well, except as a client, tried to find something neutral to say. "It's been an interesting project."

She was silent for a moment. He could see her perfectly chiseled profile as she continued to gaze out into the garden. "On occasion during the past few weeks I've found myself talking to you about a subject I haven't discussed with anyone else, Zac. Something about you made me think you would understand."

Zac froze. Babies. She was going to bring up biological clocks agin. He knew it. Where was Gwen when he needed her? "Uh, well, Elizabeth, I'm sure a lot of women are discussing the same thing these days."

She swung around, a smile curving her perfect mouth. "You see? I knew you sensed what I was getting at. I've made the decision, Zac. I'm going to have a baby. I'm going to become a single parent."

He cleared his throat. "That's terrific, Elizabeth. I'm sure you'll make an excellent mother."

"Oh, I will," she assured him serenely. "I'm in a position to give a child everything. And I will. But the most important thing I can give my baby, Zac, is good genes. My own are impeccable. But I must make certain the father's are equally sound."

Zac felt his mouth go dry. "Genes." He didn't know what else to say, but he could feel a wave of panic unfolding in his stomach.

"I don't intend to marry, of course. There's no need for that at this point."

"I see."

"But I will certainly expect to pay well for the services of a good father. I want the best, Zac. I can afford the best."

Zac took a step backward and found himself up against a wall. His tie was suddenly much too tight around his throat, and it seemed to him that the night air had become almost unbearably warm. Behind him he could hear the laughter and the careless conversation floating through the French doors, but safety was a million miles away. "Elizabeth, I think I'd better go find Gwen. She doesn't know too many people here tonight, and I shouldn't leave her on her own."

Elizabeth stepped closer. Her perfume was filling the air, making it difficult for Zac to breathe. He hated perfume. One of the things he liked about Guinevere was that she never wore any.

"You needn't worry about your relationship with Miss Jones," Elizabeth said soothingly. "I only need you in one capacity. It can be our little secret. Once the job of impregnating me has been done, I won't have any further need for you."

Images of black widow spiders popped into Zac's head. He was aware of a definite dampness under his armpits. Hastily he downed the last of the tequila. In his lifetime he'd faced armed men, scheming swindlers, and fanatic terrorists. But Elizabeth Gallinger was a first. He was almost immobilized by the experience. Gwen, he yelled silently. Gwen, do something! Aloud he said in as cool a tone as possible, "Miss Gallinger, I believe there's been a misunderstanding here."

"Would it be so unpleasant, Zac?" she asked with the confidence of a woman who knows she can have any man she wants. "I'd want to do it the natural way, of course. I don't like the idea of artificial insemination. My attorney will handle all the details, including the cost for your services. I assure you, you won't have any complaints." She took another step closer and raised her face invitingly.

And then, just when Zac assumed all was lost, Guinevere's voice came liltingly across the patio.

"There you are, Zac! I was wondering what had happened to you. I've been looking everywhere." She came forward easily, smiling at Elizabeth. But Zac could see the unnatural glitter in her eyes. "Have you forgotten we have to be home by eleven? Elizabeth, it's been a wonderful party. Thank you so much for letting Zac bring me along. Fabulous view from up here," she added, waving at the lights that ringed the lake. As she reached Zac's side she put a hand possessively on his arm.

Zac rushed to accept rescue with the same alacrity with which wagon trains used to greet the cavalry. "Of course, Gwen. I was just saying good night to Elizabeth. The security work I'm doing for her firm is almost finished, you know. It's been quite a project." He put his arm around Guinevere's waist and turned to smile politely at Elizabeth Gallinger. "It's been a great party. I'll see that the final report on Gallinger Industries' security needs is on your desk by Friday. Have your secretary contact me if there are any questions. Ready, Gwen?"

"Ready. Good night, Elizabeth."

"I'm so glad you both were able to come," Elizabeth was saying with automatic graciousness. But she didn't get a chance to finish the farewell. Zac and Guinevere were already halfway back to the French doors. A moment later they disappeared inside the elegant living room.

Five minutes later they were climbing into Zac's aging Buick and heading toward the floating bridge that linked Mercer Island with the city of Seattle. Nothing was said until he was parking the car in front of Guinevere's apartment house. It was obvious, Zac realized, that if he didn't break the fraught silence, no one would.

"I have never," he growled as he opened the security door, "been so embarrassed in my entire life. I couldn't believe what I was hearing, Gwen. I couldn't believe it. From a *client*, no less."

Guinevere said nothing. She was already on the second-floor landing, inserting her key into her lock. Zac reached out and took it from her to finish the job.

"She wanted me to stand at stud for her, Gwen."

"Can you do it standing up? You must show me sometime."

"Gwen! Listen to me. This has been one of the most unnerving nights of my entire life. You have no idea what it was like. The woman assumed she could buy my *genes*."

"Are they for sale?" Guinevere marched through the open door, her back ramrod straight.

"Gwen, don't do this to me. You've got to understand what happened back there." Zac hurried through the door, closing it quickly behind him as he struggled for words to explain the ordeal he had just lived through. But whatever words he might have found, died forgotten as he saw Gwen's sudden stillness. She was staring across the room at a blank wall. "Gwen? What the hell . . ." Instantly he was moving forward, looking for the source of her shock.

Abruptly Zac remembered that there had been a large mirror hanging on that wall. It lay now in huge, jagged shards on the floor.

Someone had pushed the broken pieces back into a semblance of the original shape of the mirror. And after that had been done, a black pentagram had been painted on the shards, a pentagram with a crude bolt of lightning in the center.

CHAPTER 5

"Get out of here. *Now.*" Zac's large hand was already closing around Guinevere's arm, crushing the delicate red silk. In this mood one didn't argue with him. Guinevere had seen him like this once or twice, and she knew it wasn't the moment to have a rational discussion.

An instant later she was out in the hallway while Zac meticulously walked through the apartment. By the time he reappeared a few minutes later, she'd had a chance to do some thinking.

"All right," he said quietly, "there's no one here now. Come on back inside." His face was set in hard, cold lines. "Take a good look at that mirror. It's the same kind of pentagram drawing that someone made on Adair's painting, isn't it?"

Guinevere nodded, staring down at the broken mirror. There was something unnaturally menacing about the simple damage, as if the shards of mirror were somehow more threatening than a broken vase would have been, perhaps because of the eerie effect the pieces caused when one looked into them. Guinevere gazed at her shattered reflection and shivered. "It's the same sketch. Someone must have taken the mirror down from the wall and dropped something on it to make it break like this. Then whoever it was drew the pentagram." She lifted her head, her gaze anxious. "Zac, I don't understand."

"Neither do I, but we're going to get some answers tonight." He was already heading toward the door. "This has gone far enough."

"Zac, where are you going?" She didn't like the grimness that enveloped him. In its own way it seemed as threatening as the mirror.

"I'm not going anywhere. *We*, however, are going to have an informative little chat with Mason Adair. His problems seem to have become yours. And that makes them mine."

"But, Zac, it's the middle of the night."

"I don't really give a damn what time it is. Move, Gwen. I want those answers and I want them now."

"I don't think Mason's going to know any more about what's going on than we do," she protested, but she obeyed his summons, hurrying forward as he stepped out into the corridor.

"Believe me, he knows a great deal more than we do."

"How do you know?" she demanded as he herded her quickly back down the stairs and out onto the sidewalk.

"Trust me."

"Uh-huh." Guinevere stifled the remainder of her skepticism. Zac was hurrying her along at a brisk pace. She wished she'd had a moment to change into more comfortable shoes. Trotting along a city sidewalk in three-inch heels made one conscious of the social restraints imposed on females in this society, she reflected. "What if he's not home?"

"For his sake he'd better be home. I'm in no mood to wait around for him."

"Zac, you're acting as if this is all Mason's fault."

"As far as I'm concerned, it is. Whatever part of it he's not responsible for, you are. I told you to stay clear of him and this whole mess, didn't I?"

"You're slipping into one of your unreasonable moods, Zac. When you get like this, you're impossible."

"I'll probably get worse as the evening wears on. All in all, it's been a hell of a night."

She found out how he'd gotten into Adair's apartment building the previous evening. When Zac reached the door now, he slipped a small wire out of his jacket pocket and in less than a minute had the security door open. Zac was good with his hands.

He urged her up the stairs and at the top turned her down the hall toward Mason's closed apartment door. In front of it Zac raised his fist and pounded imperiously.

Embarrassed, Guinevere shot a look at the nearest apartment doors, afraid they would spring open to reveal irate tenants. "Zac, don't do that, you'll cause a scene with the neighbors. Try the door bell."

"Pounding on his door is infinitely more satisfying." He raised his hand and slammed the wooden panel once more. It swung open before Zac could strike it again. Mason stood there dressed in only a pair of jeans. He blinked sleepily.

"What the hell? Oh, it's you, Zac. What are you and Gwen doing here at this time of night?"

"We're here to ask you a few questions." Zac was already pushing his way inside, tugging Guinevere after him.

"Well, sure, but why now?" Mason backed obligingly out of the way, his questioning gaze going from Zac's implacable features to Guinevere's apologetic expression.

"I'm sorry about this, Mason," she said. "But I'm afraid there's been a slight, uh, incident over at my apartment, and Zac felt that perhaps you could shed some light on the situation."

"Shed some light?" Mason looked even more perplexed. "I don't understand."

"Neither do I, and Gwen's polite way of phrasing things isn't helping to clarify the situation. Shut up, Gwen. I'll do the talking."

Guinevere raised her eyes ceilingward in silent exasperation but said nothing.

"All right, Adair," Zac said, "I'll lay this out in words even an artist should be able to follow. Gwen and I got back to her apartment tonight and found that someone had been inside. Whoever it was took great pains to crack a mirror and then draw one of those damn pentagram symbols on the broken pieces. The damage looked a lot like what was done to your painting the other night, and after what happened to you last night, I'm finding tonight's little 'incident' too much of a coincidence. Whatever is going on comes under the heading of weird. You are the only one around who's had some connection with weirdness. I want the whole story, including the rundown on that crazy group of witches you supposedly hung out with a couple of years ago."

Mason glanced helplessly at Guinevere. "Witches?"

"I'm sorry, Mason," she said softly. "I told Zac a little about that crowd you were involved with. I thought he might see some connection between them and what's been happening to you."

"Don't apologize, Gwen. I'm the one who should be sorry. I had no idea anything like this would happen."

"What exactly is happening, Mason?" she asked gently.

He swung away in obvious frustration, starting to pace the floor in front of the arching studio window. Across the way there was a glow through closed mini blinds, reminding Guinevere that she must have left the lights on earlier in her kitchen. She didn't recall doing so. Perhaps the intruder had switched them on while prowling through her apartment. It gave her chills to think of someone invading her privacy that way.

"I'm sorry," Mason said again, sounding shaken. "I'm really sorry, Gwen."

"Sorry isn't going to get us anywhere." Zac sounded completely untouched by Mason's obvious distress. "Talk, Adair."

Mason stopped in front of a half-finished canvas, shoving his hands dejectedly into his back pockets. He shook his head. "Zac, I honestly don't know what this is all about. That group I was involved with two years ago doesn't exist anymore. At least none of the people who were my friends are still in it."

Guinevere thought back to something Mason had told her on the way back from the art gallery. "You said something about leaving it when some of the members started getting too serious."

Mason nodded. "I did leave it. So did just about everyone else."

"But there were some left in it?" Zac demanded.

Mason hesitated. "Possibly."

"Possibly? Come on, Adair, you can be a little more specific than that. I'm not going to play twenty questions with you. I don't have much patience left this evening. I want to know everything you know and I want to know it now."

Guinevere opened her mouth to urge Zac to lay off but changed her mind when she saw the relentless expression in his eyes. Nothing she could do or say at this point would deflect him. There was no point in trying. Mason looked at his canvas as if studying it in great detail. Slowly he began to explain.

"I'll tell you what I know, Zac, but it isn't much. A couple of years ago some friends of mine got off on this occult kick. It was just a joke, an excuse to roll a few joints and drink a little booze, read some poetry, and, well, party. We were all struggling to make it with our art. Most of us were just barely scraping by, waiting tables or working in bookstores. We were a group with a lot of things in common."

"What did you have in common besides art?" Guinevere asked.

"Oh, the usual. None of our families approved of either our career goals or our lifestyles. We were all living at the poverty level, and we kind of supported each other emotionally. When times got really tough, we supported each other financially. It was a close-knit group for a while."

"And then some of you started selling your art?" Zac leaned against one high-ceilinged wall, folding his arms across his chest. His penetrating gaze never left Mason.

Mason nodded. "Yeah. Patty started finding a market for her ceramics, and then Walt sold a few pictures. Sylvia got lucky with her prints. Nothing big, but enough to give everyone hope."

"And make a few people envious?" Zac didn't stir from his position against the wall.

"I didn't think so at the time," Mason said slowly. "I honestly didn't think so. We were too close for that."

"Don't feed yourself that line," Zac told him. "Whenever a tight-knit group of struggling nonsuccesses suddenly starts producing a few successes, someone is going to get mad. Believe me. It's human nature."

Mason glared at his painting. "As far as I know, none of the others ever had anything like this happen to them during the past couple of years. I was one of the last of the group to get lucky with my art. Why should someone wait until now to pick on me?"

Zac shrugged. "Maybe because you're getting lucky in such a big way. One of your paintings was hanging in Elizabeth Gallinger's home tonight. Gwen tells me that's the big time, Mason. A real sign of success. Maybe one of your ex-buddies resents one of the group breaking out in such a showy style. Who knows? We'll get to that part later. Go on with your story about this cheerful little party club."

"Well, there isn't much to tell. We got together on Saturday evenings at Ron Sandwick's house."

"Where's that?" Zac interrupted.

"Up on Capitol Hill. One of those old-style places." Mason grimaced. "Run-down neighborhood. Lots of atmosphere."

"Is that why you chose it?"

Mason shook his head. "No. We used it because it was available. Sandwick had inherited it. But he couldn't afford to keep up the payments for long. Not on a starving artist's income. He put it up for sale almost as soon as it was his. But it didn't move very quickly. The real estate market had been flat for ages, and that old place would have been a real millstone around anyone's neck. All the old plumbing and electrical wiring needed repair, not to mention the decaying basement. Sandwick finally unloaded it through a real estate agent about six months ago. An all-cash deal, he said. He took the money and split for the South Seas to play Gauguin. He still owes me fifty bucks," Mason added reflectively.

Zac assimilated that. "Tell me exactly why the group drifted apart."

"A couple of new people joined," Mason said quietly.

"Who brought them into the group?"

"I'm not sure, exactly. I think they were friends of Sandwick, but to tell you the truth, it was never really clear. All I knew was that these two started showing up on Saturday nights and they were really into the occult bit. For them it was more than a joke."

Guinevere shot a glance at Zac, who was obviously about to ask another question. She slipped one in instead. "How do you know they were taking it seriously, Mason?"

"Oh, they started insisting on the accuracy of the stupid little rituals we played with when we wanted to pretend we were reaching into the next dimension. They brought in old books that had specific rules for the way things should be done. Until those two came along we just lit a few candles in the basement, poured some wine, and did a little chanting. But they insisted on black candles and chants they got out of one of their nutty books."

"Did anything supernatural ever happen?" Guinevere asked, fascinated.

Mason smiled wryly. "Of course nothing ever happened. How could it? Don't tell me you actually believe in that kind of thing?"

Guinevere shook her head hastily, aware of Zac's derisive glance. "Absolutely not. I just wondered if anything, well, abnormal ever occurred during these ceremonies."

"Valonia and Baldric sometimes claimed they could see into the next dimension and claimed they were 'feeding' on power from it, but it was all a bunch of cow fertilizer."

Zac cocked a brow. "Valonia and Baldric?"

"Those were the two who started demanding the proper rituals."

"Were they artists, too?"

Mason paused, considering. "You know, I was never real sure what they did for a living. But I don't think they were part of the Seattle art world, either the low end or the high end. I've never run into them since those Saturday-night gatherings at Sandwick's."

Zac took a small pad of paper out of his pocket and started making notes. "Are they still living in Sandwick's place?"

"No. They never did live there as far as I know. Like I said, Sandwick sold the old house six months ago, anyway. Whoever Valonia and Baldric were, they couldn't have afforded to buy it. They definitely didn't have that kind of money."

"You're sure?"

"Positive. They were one step off the streets. Maybe not even that far. Baldric always wore a huge backpack, and Valonia carried a big satchel. I got the feeling that they lived out of both. They were pretty scruffy and sometimes a little hungry, too. The Saturday-night group broke up, and I never saw or heard from those two again."

"But you did keep in touch with the others?" Guinevere asked.

"Oh, sure. To some extent. I know where most of them are. One or two moved down to Southern California. Sandwick left the country. A couple bought a house in the woods down in Oregon as soon as they started selling their stuff. And the other two are here in town. They're doing okay. I was the last of them to start selling."

"The pentagram," Zac said musingly. "Was that part of the Saturday-night rituals?"

"Sometimes," Mason admitted. "Pentagrams are a very common magical symbol. Traditional, even. But the ones our group used in the beginning didn't have that jag of lightning in it. Valonia and Baldric added that little nuance."

"I assume Valonia and Baldric are the only names you knew them by?" Zac asked.

"Yeah, and I'd be willing to bet that they made them up or got them out of one of their damn books on witchcraft. Who ever heard of anyone being named Valonia and Baldric?"

Zac nodded and fell into a remote silence. Guinevere peered at him expectantly. She knew what was happening. He was slipping into one of his private trances during which odd little connections would be made inside his careful, methodical brain. When he came out of the contemplation, he would be aimed in the same way a glacier was aimed down a mountainside, and he'd be just as unstoppable. In the meantime Zac might stay in this disengaged mood for a very long time.

"Zac?" she prompted, aware of Mason's curious stare. "Zac? We'd better be going. It's late and Mason's told you everything he knows." She touched his arm. She thought he was at least minimally aware of her.

"The cops," he said distinctly.

Mason looked alarmed, and Guinevere understood instantly. "No," she said. "We can't call the police again, Zac."

"The hell we can't."

"Zac, listen to me, if we call the cops again, news of this weird stuff is going to leak out. We both know that. Some sharp-eyed reporter is going to have a great time with hints of witchcraft surrounding a young new artist who's exploding on the local art scene. Mason's career is just getting launched. This sort of thing could ruin him before he's gotten established. Do you think people like Elizabeth Gallinger will want to be associated with anything that even hints of the occult?"

"Mason is free to do what he wants," Zac said. "It's you I'm worried about."

"Well, let me assure you that any publicity linking me to some occult group isn't going to do me a damn bit of good, either," she reminded him forcefully. "Zac, please, you've got to treat this just as you would any other business case. Your clients call on you precisely because they want to avoid awkward publicity. Think of Mason and me as being clients who want this handled discreetly."

Zac's mouth twitched. "You and Mason can't afford my usual fees."

"Zac!" Guinevere was shocked.

He came away from the wall. "Forget it. A small joke. Stop worrying for now, both of you. I'm not going to call in the cops, but only because I don't think they'd get very far at this point. There just isn't enough here to go on. We need more information before we can turn it over to them. And I don't want Guinevere's name dragged into this mess, Adair."

The younger man nodded. "I understand. I don't particularly want my own name dragged into it. I swear, Zac, I don't have the slightest idea what's going on here. I just can't believe one of my old buddies has gone crazy with envy. And Baldric and Valonia weren't into art, so why should they be envious? I doubt if they would even know I've started selling."

Guinevere recalled something Carla had said. "My sister thought that some of the freeloaders who showed up at the gallery the other night weren't all that happy to see you making it so big. And that Henry Thorpe person sounded as if he might have a back-stabbing sort of nature."

"Forget Thorpe. He had nothing to do with that group," Mason said firmly.

"But he knew about it. He's the one who first mentioned it to me."

"He might have been aware that a few of us hung around together and got up to some weird things, but he was never close to any of the members. He wouldn't have been aware of the pentagram with the bolt of lightning in it, for example."

Zac shook his head. "Maybe. Maybe not. I want both of you to understand something here. My main concern is Gwen. I don't want her business reputation tarnished by having people gossiping about an association with witchcraft. But more importantly, I don't want her physically threatened or hurt. From now on I'll be staying with her at night, either next door or at my place. During the daytime, Mason, I want you to put your window to good use. We'll leave the blinds in Gwen's kitchen window open all the time. If you ever see them closed or if you see anyone moving around inside whom you don't recognize, call me. Call Gwen, too, and tell her not to go into her apartment until I'm around."

Mason nodded. "Got it. I spend a lot of time right here in the studio during the day. I'll keep an eye on things. Gwen says you investigate security problems for people. Does this mean you're taking me on as a client?"

"I don't seem to have much choice." Zac took Guinevere's arm again and led her toward the door. "Why is it," he complained to her, "that you always manage to get me into these situations?"

"You're not so good on your own," she told him cheerfully, as the door closed behind them. "Just remember what happened to you tonight at Queen Elizabeth's party. Your genes were about to be summoned for royal service."

Zac went a dull red in the dim hall light. "If you had a charitable bone in your body, woman, you wouldn't remind me of that incident. It was one of the worst moments of my entire life. I had no idea that all that talk of biological clocks was leading up to that . . . that proposition she made."

"Poor Zac. Now you know how a woman feels when her boss gives her all sorts of encouragement and support and then expects her to pay him back with a few bouts in bed. You've just been the victim of job harassment."

"I still can't believe it," Zac muttered as they walked down the street to Gwen's apartment.

"If I were you, I'd finish up the Gallinger project very quickly and get your fee. That woman didn't get where she is today by being anything less than tenacious."

"It was probably just a terrible misunderstanding."

"The hell it was," Guinevere retorted spiritedly. "That woman wants a stud, and you're the chosen male."

"Do all women become that . . . that forceful when they decide they have to have a baby?" Zac asked in subdued tones.

"I don't know."

Zac slid an assessing glance at her as he walked beside her up the stairs. "Are you sure, Gwen?"

She heard the genuine concern in his voice and wasn't certain how to interpret it. What was Zac trying to say? That he might be looking for a woman who was interested in having babies? Someone other than Elizabeth Gallinger? She wished desperately that she knew more about his feelings for her. The desire to be a father might be as sudden and strong in some men as the need to be a mother was in some women. Guinevere felt as if she were walking on eggs. One misstep and she might crush the fragile relationship that existed between herself and Zac.

"I'll let you know if I ever change my mind," she tried to say lightly as she opened her door.

"You do that," he said behind her. "You make sure you do that. I don't want you going hunting the way Elizabeth Gallinger is hunting."

Fortunately the shattered mirror provided a timely distraction. Guinevere walked across the floor and looked at it once again. "What now, Zac?"

He tugged at his tie. "First we pick up the pieces and then we go to bed."

"No, I mean, what happens next in this case?"

"I don't think of this as a *case* exactly," he told her as he unbuttoned the first button of his shirt. "I see it as more in the nature of a damned nuisance."

"But what are we going to do next?"

"I think," Zac said thoughtfully, "that I'll go take a look at that old house on Capitol Hill for starters."

"But Mason said it had been sold six months ago," Guinevere protested impatiently.

"We'll see."

"Now, Zac, don't go all enigmatic and cryptic on me. Tell me why you want to take a look at that old place."

"Simple curiosity. And because it's a starting point. Probably a dead end, but you never know."

Guinevere eyed him thoughtfully, aware of the first faint ripple of excitement she always got when she was involved in one of Zac's more exciting investigations. He claimed he didn't like this kind of thing, and she was inclined to believe him. He was cut out to be a staid, plodding, methodical analyzer of other people's security problems. But occasionally other people's security problems had a way of blowing up into intriguing, sometimes dangerous situations. And Zac coped. Very well.

"When do we go take this look?" Guinevere demanded.

"Don't look so excited. You're not going with me."

"But, Zac—"

"I mean it, Gwen. I'm not taking you along. I have no way of knowing what I'll run into, and whoever clobbered Mason last night might have gotten a good look at you through the window. If there is someone interesting still hanging around that old house, I don't want him to see you. It would only tip him off."

"But you said that going to the old place is probably just a dead end," she reminded him as she scooped up broken bits of mirror and put them in a paper sack.

"I'm not taking any chances. Not where you're involved."

She heard the steel in his voice and reluctantly stopped trying to argue. There were times when you had to go around Zac because you certainly couldn't go through him. "So when are you going to take this look?"

"In a few hours. I'll set the alarm for three."

"Three in the morning? Isn't that a little early?"

Zac shrugged, taking the paper bag from her and putting it carefully into the hall closet instead of into the garbage. "It's a good time to have a look around. Not many people up and about at three in the morning."

Guinevere went toward him, aware of a growing sense of anxiety. "I'd feel better if I went along."

"No, Gwen. Not this time."

She sighed as her arms went around his neck. "Sometimes you can be a very stubborn man."

"We all have some strong points," he agreed philosophically. His hands wrapped around her waist. "Have I thanked you for coming to my rescue tonight at Gallinger's house?"

"I wasn't sure for a while if you wanted to be rescued."

"Believe me, I wanted rescue."

"She's very beautiful and very rich, Zac."

"I want to be loved for myself, not my genes," he said as he began undoing the fastenings of the red silk dress.

Did he mean it? Guinevere asked herself silently as the red dress slipped to the floor. Did he really want to be loved, or was it only one of those throwaway remarks people make when they want to lighten a situation? She wished she knew for certain. There was a great deal she did not yet know about Zachariah Justis. Some things she might never know. But he was here tonight, and that would do for now. She lifted her face for his kiss and closed her eyes as she felt the familiar male hunger reach out to enclose her.

Zac felt the soft swell of her breasts against his chest and forgot about biological clocks and embarrassing confrontations with clients. When Guinevere was in his arms, she was all that mattered. The extent of her response to him filled him with a heady satisfaction that wiped out everything else in the vicinity. This was one element of her nature that he could read with certainty. She was the most responsive, the most honest woman he had ever held.

"If you ever want my genes," he told her thickly as he put her down on the bed and came down beside her, "you can have them for free."

"I'll remember that." Her eyes gleamed up at him in the shadows as she took him into her waiting softness.

Three hours and fifteen minutes later Zac awoke with the alertness he felt only when things were getting nasty. He didn't like the feeling, but he had learned to respect it over the years. He was ahead of the alarm clock and reached out carefully to switch it off before it could ring. Five minutes to three.

Quietly he got out of bed, hoping not to wake Guinevere. But as he pulled on his slacks he realized that she was watching him.

"I'll have coffee waiting for you when you get back," she promised.

He grinned in spite of himself. "If you're planning to use that red-and-black monstrosity to make it, you'd better start early." He leaned over her, planting a hand on each side of her on the bedding. Then he kissed her. "See you by five."

Guinevere wanted to say something else, but there wasn't time. He vanished silently through her bedroom door.

Her staid, plodding, methodical Zac was once again on the hunt.

CHAPTER 6

The house had once been a stately, if rather overwrought, home for a successful businessman during the first part of the century. Now it was what real estate people liked to call a fixer-upper. The streetlight directly in front of the sagging porch was out, but with the fretful moonlight Zac could see that the plump wooden columns that flanked the steps were badly chipped, as if someone had idly carved on them with a pocketknife. The place had once been painted gray, if one could judge by what remained of the old paint. The porch wrapped most of the way around the aging two-story structure, and the weeds in the uncared-for garden were as high as the railing in some places. The screen door appeared to have given up the ghost long ago. It hung lethargically on its hinges. Someone or something had kicked a hole in the bottom part of the screen. No one had bothered to repair it. There was no light in any of the windows.

Zac quietly walked through the backyard of a vacant house next door to what had once been the Sandwick place. He assumed the house was vacant because of the FOR SALE sign in the front yard, but he didn't take any chances. About half the houses in the neighbor-hood had FOR SALE signs in the front yards. So far he had been lucky enough not to arouse any dogs in the area, and he was hoping to keep it that way.

The neighborhood was one of the streets near Capitol Hill that had not yet been rehabilitated by the upwardly mobile types who had been moving into the district in droves during the past few years. The Sandwick house was slightly more run-down looking than its neighbors but not significantly so. Whoever had paid cash for it sev-eral months ago had obviously not had a lot left over to effect even minor repairs.

Moving quietly and without the aid of a flashlight, Zac made his way around to the rear of the house Adair and his friends had once used for their occult games. When he reached the back steps, he paused and glanced up at the unlit windows with a certain morose resignation.

This wasn't, Zac decided, the kind of investigation he thought appropriate to the newly emerging image of Free Enterprise Secu-rity, Inc. It was his firm's mission to cater to the security needs of sophisticated businesses. He was supposed to be a consultant, for God's sake. One who charged very large fees in return for reports bound in genuine simulated-leather binders. This business of sneak-ing through decaying neighborhoods to spy on an old house that once might or might not have been used for witchcraft definitely came under the heading of tacky. Very low class. And it was all Guine-vere's fault.

He thought of Guinevere as he had left her over half an hour ago. She had been lying in the tousled bed, her dark hair tumbling around her bare shoulders, eyes wide and a little worried in the shadows. Zac admitted to himself that he rather liked it when she became anxious on his behalf. He couldn't remember anyone else in recent history who had ever really worried about him. Already he was looking forward to the coffee and concern that would be waiting for him when he returned from this sortie into the wilds of Capitol Hill. A man could get used to the idea of someone waiting for him.

No use putting off the inevitable. The sooner he was finished here, the sooner he could collect both the coffee and Guinevere. Silently Zac started up the back steps of the house. At the rear door he paused and let the tiny sounds and nuances of the night infiltrate his heightened sense of awareness.

Zac could usually tell when a place was occupied. There was a sense of presence about a room or a house or a building that made itself felt. It wasn't anything concrete, just a kind of instinctive awareness. There had been times in the past when that kind of awareness had kept him alive. There had also been occasions when it had let him down at awkward moments. He hoped this wasn't going to be one of those moments. Zac didn't fool himself. He wasn't psychic; he simply had fairly well-developed survival instincts. But they weren't infallible.

Still, there was nothing to indicate that anyone was at home here tonight. Zac slipped into the deeper shadows of the porch and examined the lock on the back door. Piece of cake. He pulled the small twist of metal out of his pocket and, a moment later, let himself into what proved to be the kitchen.

As he eased the door shut behind him, he stood still for another few seconds, trying to pick up any new vibrations that might indicate the presence of another person.

The house was silent. Perhaps too silent. Zac frowned thoughtfully and walked through the kitchen. The refrigerator was turned off, and there were no dishes standing in the chipped sink. He was about to make his way into the next room when he saw the Styrofoam hamburger containers in a paper sack by the stove. Someone had made a recent foray to a fast-food restaurant and brought the results back here to eat.

Zac considered the possibilities. A transient might be using the place to bed down at night. A workman might have been commissioned to do some repairs and had brought a fast-food lunch with him. Neighborhood kids might have been using the old house as a hangout. There were a variety of potential answers to the questions raised by the burger container. Zac didn't like most of them.

The floor beneath his feet was hardwood, and it was in better condition than most of the rest of the house. Zac was cautious as he moved into the breakfast room, but there were no squeaks or groans.

There were a few pieces of furniture in the breakfast room and also in the parlor he found on the other side. None of them were in decent condition. No one had even bothered to cover the few chairs, tables, and the sofa. Zac could smell the damp, dusty odor emitted by disintegrating fabric in every room. The only reason he could see at all was because the drapes were in such tatters that the vague streetlight could filter in through the large windows.

He found the staircase in the front hall. It was broad, heavily banistered, and still sturdy. The shadows were thicker on the second floor because the windows were smaller and allowed less moonlight and light from the street to enter. There was no more evidence of recent habitation, but Zac found himself using more caution than should have been necessary under the circumstances. It was a good thing he'd had the sense to make Guinevere stay behind. She would have been running around, exploring and investigating like an eager puppy. Guinevere tended to be both impulsive and a little reckless, Zac thought with indulgent disapproval. He wondered if he was going to spend the rest of his life getting himself dragged into a series of adventures such as this one.

The odd part was that in the beginning, when he had first contacted her, he'd entertained a few notions of using Guinevere on certain kinds of cases. Her temporary-help business provided an ideal cover for planting an observer in almost any sort of firm. Everyone needed secretaries and clerks, and no one paid much attention to them, not even when they were temporary replacements. But lately, Zac noted wryly, he seemed to be the one getting involved in Guinevere's adventures, rather than vice versa.

The upper floor was as empty as the first. There was an old, tilted bed in one room with a lumpy, stained mattress. Zac didn't get the feeling it had been used in the past several years. If some transient was using the house at night, he wasn't sleeping in the bedrooms.

Getting up at three this morning had probably been a waste of time and energy. He could just as easily have stayed in bed with Guinevere and learned as much. Zac headed back downstairs, still moving cautiously.

In the kitchen he glanced around once more and idly opened a few cupboard doors. Most of the shelves were empty, although there were a couple of grungy mugs in one cupboard.

He was hunting for the broom closet when he opened the door that revealed a flight of stairs down to a basement. The door had a key-activated bolt on it, but no one had locked it that night. Perhaps not for a long time.

Zac paused on the threshold and tried to analyze what it was that seemed different about the dank odor wafting up from the dark pit at the bottom of the steps. He couldn't see a thing past the first two or three treads.

For the first time he removed the small, pencil-slim flashlight from the pocket of his Windbreaker. Closing the basement door behind him so that light wouldn't escape back into the kitchen, he flicked on the narrow beam.

At first he could see nothing but a few more steps. The utter darkness of the basement seemed to crowd in on the small band of light as if trying to devour it. For the first time since he had entered the house, Zac felt a tiny frisson of awareness. Grimly he shook it off. He was letting his imagination take over. Not a common state of affairs. Once again he thanked his lucky stars he'd held the line with Gwen and refused to let her accompany him. *Her* imagination would be having a field day down here.

Slowly he started down the steps. The flashlight fought back bravely against the overpowering darkness, and Zac followed in its wake. It seemed a long way down to the concrete floor, but eventually he reached the last step. His imagination was not settling down, he noticed.

Methodically he turned to the right at the bottom of the steps, prowling along one wall. He didn't see the heavy black drapes until he nearly blundered into them. One moment he was feeling his way along a cold, damp surface, and the next his hand tangled with thick velvet cascading from the low ceiling all the way to the floor. Startled, Zac stopped and shone the light along the entire surface of the black drapes.

As far as he could tell, there was nothing but basement wall behind the wide expanse of fabric. Certainly there was no window to be shielded. It didn't take much investigative talent to realize that, unlike the torn and rotting fabric on the windows upstairs, these drapes were in good condition.

Zac edged back, playing the light on the fabric as he studied it. He had to move back quite a ways to see the full extent of the velvet wall coverings. The velvet hung in heavy folds along most of one entire wall. Who the hell would drape a basement in black velvet?

Zac didn't like the possible answers to his questions. Perhaps this was a leftover from the days when Adair and his friends had held their little parties here. The new owners of the house might not have bothered to take down the drapes. They certainly hadn't bothered to make any repairs or modifications. Perhaps they hadn't even seen their new acquisition. Zac made a note to find out who the legal owner was as soon as the appropriate county offices opened for business that day. The information probably wouldn't do him any good, but Zac liked to have all the loose ends accounted for.

He took another step backward, marveling over the extent of what must have been very expensive, if very ugly, drapery, and promptly collided with a cold, unyielding surface. Zac swung around and let the flashlight beam run along the edge of a long, high table.

It wasn't, Zac decided grimly, exactly a Formica-topped dining-room table. This monstrosity was at least six feet long and appeared to be made out of some sort of black stone. It was supported by three squat columns that had clawed feet.

The uneasy flicker of awareness sizzled lightly over his nerve endings once more. This time Zac decided not to ignore it. He switched off the flashlight in the same instant that he felt the small disturbance in the air behind him. Zac threw himself to one side, but the heavy metal object that had been descending toward his head didn't miss him entirely. It glanced along the side of his skull and landed with numbing force on his left shoulder.

Zac spun around, his body automatically following the direction of the blow in an effort to lessen the impact. There was a stifled grunt as his right fist landed in the center of a man's chest. It was pure luck as far as Zac was concerned. The impetus of the man's rush had carried him straight into Zac's instinctively raised hand.

The thing about luck was that it didn't do you any good unless you took advantage of it. With no feeling at all in his left shoulder Zac had to rely entirely on his right arm. In the utter darkness he could see nothing of his attacker, but the man's heavy, scrabbling body was easy enough to locate. It was all over Zac.

Whoever he was, he still had the metal object he'd used a few seconds earlier. Zac struggled to land a decent, chopping blow before the other man could swing again. There was another grunt as Zac found a solid, if slightly soft, target in the stomach region. He brought his knee up, hoping for a more vulnerable area.

But the attacker was staggering backward, blundering into the table. Zac's maneuver landed slightly off target. There was a vicious curse as the other man hit the stone, and Zac followed the direction of the sound. He aimed another chopping blow at what should have been the neck region and connected with what must have been a shoulder. Then a wild, swinging kick from a booted foot caught Zac on the thigh, sending him staggering against the curtained wall.

When his left shoulder struck the wall, Zac realized that the numbing effect of the blow was wearing off. Streaks of agony laced through his arm and shoulder, making him suck in his breath and struggle to keep his senses from reeling into a darkness that was greater than that of the basement.

The shock of the pain drove him to his knees. Through the daze he could hear frantic shuffling sounds from his attacker and braced himself for another assault. If the man rushed him, Zac decided the only thing he could do was hit the floor and hope the other guy crashed into the wall.

But the other basement denizen wasn't planning any more heroic attacks. The shuffling sounds sorted themselves out into footsteps, and a few seconds later Zac heard the man on the stairs. Apparently whoever it was knew his way around the basement far better than Zac. The door at the top of the stairs opened briefly, revealing a rectangle of lighter shadow, and then it slammed shut again. There was no sound of a key in the lock. Perhaps the escaping man didn't have the key, or maybe he just didn't want to take the extra time it would take to lock the door to the basement.

Zac struggled awkwardly to his feet, listening for the sounds that would tell him whether his assailant was escaping or merely going for bigger and better weapons. With a small sense of relief Zac heard the back door slamming shut. It was a very distant echo. The heavy wooden flooring upstairs covered almost all the noise.

His senses swam as Zac managed to straighten into a more or less standing position. Gingerly he touched his left shoulder with his right hand and winced. But as far as he could tell, nothing was broken. One had to be thankful for small mercies in this sort of situation.

He found the flashlight when he accidentally kicked it with his foot. The frail beam shone listlessly across the dusty basement floor. Bending down, Zac retrieved it and swung it around in an arc. Light fell on the object that had been used to nearly brain him. It was a black metal candlestick, heavy and tall, almost as good as a length of pipe for cracking skulls. Zac left it where it was. All he wanted now was to get out of the basement before whoever he had tangled with returned with assistance. This sort of thing could be potentially embarrassing to an upwardly mobile executive in the security business.

He was starting up the steps when the flashlight beam skimmed along the surface of a long object propped against one side of the staircase. Pausing, Zac ran the beam along the surface and realized that he was looking at a framed painting. A framed Mason Adair painting. There could be no mistaking the brilliant light and clear, vibrant colors. Even here, in a pitch-dark basement, illuminated only by a flashlight, the effect of Adair's work made itself felt. Maybe the guy really had some talent, Zac admitted reluctantly to himself.

Tentatively Zac leaned over the wooden stair rail and tried to lift the framed canvas. It was heavier than he'd expected. There was no question that it would take two hands, and just then Zac didn't have two working hands available. Regretfully he left the canvas where it was and finished the trek up the steps.

The kitchen seemed almost flooded with light compared to the oppressive darkness of the basement. Zac stood blinking in the shadows for a few seconds, letting his eyes adjust as he switched off the flashlight. Then he let himself out the back door.

It seemed a long way back to where he'd parked the Buick. He couldn't risk the sidewalks, so he stuck to backyards and gardens. He briefly noted one particularly thriving crop of an agricultural product generally characterized as an illegal substance. He finally emerged on the street where he'd left the car. It was still there, complete with hubcaps. No one went out of his way to steal three-year-old Buick hubcaps.

He had some movement back in his left arm but no real strength. Using his right hand for everything, Zac fished the car keys out of his pocket and got the reliable engine started. A moment later he was driving sedately out of the area, keeping his headlights off for a couple of blocks until he was sure he wouldn't be observed by anyone who might feel obliged to notice a strange vehicle in the neighborhood and report it. Not that the neighborhood was likely to have a Block Watch Program. This wasn't the sort of district where people went out of their way to keep an eye on strangers, but there was no point in taking any more chances. Life had been adventurous enough tonight.

Guinevere was pacing the floor at four thirty when she heard Zac's key in the lock. With a strangled little cry of relief she raced forward, throwing herself into his arms as he opened the door.

"For God's sake, don't do that," Zac hissed painfully as her arms closed tightly around him.

Startled at the distinct lack of welcome in his greeting, Guinevere drew back and eyed him anxiously. "What's wrong?"

"A great deal. My left arm feels as if it may fall off at any moment." He stepped into the room and shut the door behind him.

"Your arm! Zac, what happened? Are you all right?"

"I think I'm going to survive, but I can tell you, Gwen, that this little investigation you've sicced me onto isn't the type of thing I had in mind when I incorporated in the State of Washington. Did you get the coffee made?"

"It's ready. I've been worried, Zac. What on earth happened to your arm? Did you fall?"

"Some joker got me with a candlestick. I'll take a few aspirin with the coffee, if you don't mind."

Guinevere stared at him, appalled. The grimly etched lines around his mouth told their own story, as did the careful way Zac was cradling his left arm. "Maybe we should get you to a doctor."

"No."

"But, Zac . . ."

He gave her a disgusted glance. "Nothing's broken. I'll be all right eventually, although I may not be my usual athletic self in bed for a while."

"This is not the time for sexual humor, Zachariah Justis. Come into the kitchen and sit down. I'll get your coffee and aspirin. Then I want to take a look at that shoulder."

"You can look but don't touch. It's going to be a while before I let anyone touch it. Christ. If I weren't such a macho type, I'd admit that it hurts like hell."

"Oh, Zac . . ."

"I love it when you go all dithering and feminine on me."

"I am not dithering." She urged him into a chair and poured coffee.

"When did you put the coffee on?" he asked, accepting the mug. "The minute I left?"

"Forget the nasty comments on my coffee machine and tell me what happened."

"First the aspirin."

Guinevere hurried into the bathroom and returned a few seconds later with a bottle of tablets. "Here you are. Zac, really, I think you should take off your jacket and shirt and let me see that shoulder."

"Getting out of this jacket right now would put an end to my macho facade. Give me a little time, okay?"

"All right, but I'm worried, Zac."

"So am I. But not about my shoulder."

"Zac, tell me what went on in that house tonight." Guinevere shook her head mournfully. "I knew I should have gone with you."

"Oh, you'd have had a field day. The place would have inspired your imagination." Gratefully he sipped the hot brew.

"Is it haunted?" she demanded.

"If it is, the ghosts aren't the ones causing the problems. The guy who got me with the candlestick was very much alive."

In succinct, unadorned sentences Zac gave her a quick rundown on what had happened in the old Sandwick house, concluding with the discovery of the Mason Adair painting.

"Someone is storing a Mason Adair painting in that awful basement? But why? And what's with the altar and the black velvet drapes?" Guinevere wondered aloud.

"An altar." Zac thought about the stone table. "Yeah, that's a good way to describe it. A black altar."

Guinevere shuddered. "Your description alone is enough to give me the creeps. It must have been horrible going through that basement. Zac, you could have been killed."

"I'm not sure the guy was out to kill me. I think I surprised him, and he struck out with the first thing he could find, namely a candlestick. Could have been a transient, someone bedding down illegally in an empty house. I was probably as big a surprise to him as he was to me."

"But you said the black drapes looked in good condition?"

"They were a lot newer than the rest of the furnishings upstairs."

Guinevere chewed on her lower lip, thinking. "Was there a lot of dust on that altar?"

"Good point." Zac closed his eyes, trying to recapture the image of the black stone. "No."

"So someone's taking care of the basement while the rest of the house rots away? Zac, it doesn't make any sense."

"Maybe it will when we find out who bought the place from Sandwick." Zac glanced at the kitchen clock. "In a few more hours I'll go down to the county courthouse and take a look at the land records."

"What about the painting?"

"Describe it to Adair and see if he can remember whether he sold it or gave it to anyone."

Guinevere nodded. "Maybe Theresa, the gallery owner, will know if it was one she sold. Mason hasn't sold too many pictures yet. It shouldn't be hard to figure out who bought a particular one. What did it look like?"

Zac gazed into the depths of his coffee, remembering. "Lots of turquoise and purple. A water scene with lots of glare on the surface of the sea. But the effect was reversed, as if you were under the water looking up at the sun, if you know what I mean."

"Um. I recall that one from the night of Mason's show although I can't remember the title. Why don't I contact both of them and see what I can find out while you check the land records?"

"I knew it," Zac said ruefully.

"Knew what?"

"You're taking charge already. I go out and do the dirty work, and then you get to do the executive stuff. It always happens like this."

Guinevere leaned forward, her chin resting on her propped hands. Her eyes were light with warm amusement. "You know what they say about brains and brawn. Besides, it was your idea to do the dirty work alone. I offered to come along and help."

"So you did."

Her amusement disappeared. "Zac, what do you think is going on? None of this makes any sense."

"I'm aware of that. At the moment your guess is as good as mine."

"I keep thinking about the possibility of professional jealousy," Guinevere said slowly. "This all seems a little bizarre for that."

"We live in a bizarre world. People have been known to do ruthless things in the name of professional jealousy. But it's this connection with that occult group that's got me nervous, Gwen. I don't like it. Give me a nice, clean, financially motivated thief or swindler every time. I can understand financial motivation."

Guinevere watched his hand go probingly to his left shoulder. "I'm worried about that shoulder, Zac."

He smiled cryptically. "I like it when you're worried about me."

"Zac, I'm serious."

"So am I."

Mason Adair recognized the description of the painting immediately. He listened as Guinevere stood in his studio later that morning and told him what Zac had seen in the basement of the old house. Slowly he walked to the window and stood looking down onto the street.

"*Glare,*" he said.

"I beg your pardon?" Guinevere countered.

"The name of the picture is *Glare*. It's supposed to be hanging in the Midnight Light gallery. As far as I know, Theresa hasn't sold it."

"Then I think," Guinevere announced firmly, "that we'd better contact Theresa."

"I'll call her now." Mason picked up the phone. Theresa came on the line at once, and even from across the room Guinevere could hear the agitation in the woman's voice. When Mason finished talking and replaced the receiver, Guinevere was already half prepared for the answer.

"Stolen?" she asked softly.

Mason nodded. "Sometime late yesterday or early last night, Theresa thinks. She was waiting until her assistant got in this morning to make sure it hadn't been sold, but the assistant just arrived and swears it was hanging on the wall until at least four o'clock yesterday."

"Could somebody have just walked out with it?" Guinevere asked. "Or was there some sign of forced entry?"

"No evidence of anyone having tried to break into the gallery. And, yes, someone could have walked out with it. It happens. Security isn't exactly tight around most of the Pioneer Square galleries. There have been a few instances of paintings having disappeared during working hours. Theresa was going to report the theft to the cops. I told her to wait."

"I heard you. Zac's going to find this interesting."

But Zac had news of his own by the time Guinevere called him and told him what she'd learned.

"The house was bought for fifty-five thousand in cash by a Barry Hodges. All the taxes are being kept up-to-date." Zac glanced at his notes as he spoke into the phone. "I talked to some real estate people who checked their multiple listings. They say the house isn't for sale, and no one's got it on the market to rent. The agent who handled the deal said it was a very quick sale, with no real negotiation. Sandwick wanted the money and took the first offer he got."

"Does the agent remember this Barry Hodges?" Guinevere asked.

"She remembers that he didn't look like the type who could come up with fifty-five thousand in cash. I gather he was kind of scruffy, long-haired, and overweight. Said he wanted a fixer-upper and had already picked out the Sandwick place. But so far he hasn't done any fixing. The agent hasn't seen him since he signed the last of the papers."

"How did you get all that information out of her?" Guinevere demanded.

"Innate charm."

"The same sort of charm you seem to have been using lately on Elizabeth Gallinger?" Guinevere kept her tone light, but Zac's lack of response on the other end of the line told her that he didn't appreciate the joke. She rushed to fill the unpleasant silence, wishing she'd kept her mouth shut. "Theresa says the painting probably disappeared late yesterday afternoon, by the way. Mason asked her not to report it to the police."

"That figures. Mason's definitely running scared about jeopardizing his newfound fame and fortune, isn't he?"

"Wouldn't you be, in his shoes? Painting is his business, the same way security work is yours and mine is providing temporary help. He's just as concerned about protecting his image and reputation as any businessman, Zac. Just think of him as a *client*. You're always helping your clients avoid embarrassing publicity."

"Gwen, let's get this straight, once and for all. I am not wasting my time in dark basements for the sake of an artist who might one day be rich but who presently couldn't possibly afford me."

"I know, Zac. You're doing this for me. And I want you to know I really do appreciate it," Guinevere assured him earnestly.

"Good. Because when this is all over, I intend to collect my fee one way or the other. Now, back to business. I think it's time you and I played house."

Guinevere nearly fell out of her office chair. "What?" she got out weakly.

"I may have misstated that. We're going to pretend we're looking for a house."

"To buy?"

"Uh-huh. A fixer-upper in the same neighborhood where the Sandwick house is located. Or maybe I should start calling it the Barry Hodges house. I want an excuse to talk to the neighbors, and people always seem to talk a lot more freely to you than they do to me."

"My innate charm," Guinevere explained loftily.

CHAPTER 7

It *was* partly Gwen's charm that people usually responded to so easily, Zac thought as he parked the Buick a block down the street from the Sandwick house. But it was more than that. She had a curiously empathic ability that he knew he lacked completely. It was the empathy that really broke down the barriers, even those of strangers. People would talk freely to Guinevere when they wouldn't have given him the time of day. He glanced at her appraisingly as they started up the weed-strewn sidewalk.

"I'm seeing a whole new you," Zac remarked, eyeing the tight curve of her derriere in her faded blue jeans. With the jeans she wore a sporty plaid shirt. "Do you realize how different you look this afternoon?"

"This is my country-western look," Guinevere explained, patting her hair, which was worn long and anchored with a clip. "From what you told me about the neighborhood, I didn't think I should show up here in my new suit from Nordstrom's. We're supposed to be a struggling young couple trying to buy a first house, right?"

"We *are* a struggling young couple," Zac told her.

"Not so young, I'm afraid."

Zac shot her another sidelong glance. "Is that worrying you?"

"Everyone worries about getting older."

"Yeah, but women have to worry about that biological clock thing on top of everything else."

Guinevere wished she'd kept her mouth shut. "Back to clocks, are we? What is it with you lately, Zac? I thought you'd learned your lesson the hard way last night at Elizabeth Gallinger's house."

"Forget it. Now listen to me. I don't want you saying too much or letting anyone know we might be anything other than just prospective home buyers checking out the neighborhood. Act like we're engaged."

Guinevere considered that. "First marriage or second?"

"For Pete's sake, Gwen, you don't have to get that detailed about the story."

"This is my first time as an undercover agent. I want to be a success."

Zac muttered something she didn't quite catch and then said firmly, "We'll try that lady in her garden across the street."

Guinevere glanced around at the seedy front lawn of the house they were passing. "I think there are a couple of people working in the backyard of this place. Why not start here?"

"I don't think those two will be too chatty."

"Why not?"

Zac took her arm to help her across the quiet street. "I went through their backyard last night. They've got a very healthy crop of marijuana growing back there."

"No kidding? You don't think they'll want to share some gardening tips?" Guinevere grinned up at him. "What on earth were you doing wandering around their backyard?"

"I was hoping I'd be less conspicuous that way. People walking through quiet neighborhoods such as this at three in the morning tend to cause comment."

"Last night must have been exciting for you," Guinevere observed.

"Oh, it was."

They ambled along the sidewalk with a deliberately casual air, talking in low tones. When they reached the house Zac had selected, a fat gray cat strode into their path, meowing authoritatively. Guinevere went down on her haunches and held out her hand. The cat regarded it arrogantly for a few seconds and then trotted forward to investigate.

"Hope you don't mind cats," said a surprisingly husky, female voice. "Old Jumper there is my guard cat." The comment was followed by a hoarse chuckle that ended up in a smoker's cough.

Zac smiled blandly at the small elderly woman on the other side of the sagging picket fence. "My fiancée loves animals. When we get a house of our own, she's hoping to get a couple of cats."

Guinevere glanced up, smiling, as she stroked Jumper's ears. "How do you do? I'm Guinevere Jones. This is my, uh, fiancé, Zac Justis. We were having a look around the neighborhood. Our real estate agent said there were a couple of places for sale here that might be in our price range."

"Abby Kettering," the older woman offered cheerfully enough as she withdrew a pack of unfiltered cigarettes from the pocket of her gardening apron. She lit one and inhaled vigorously. Abby Kettering was probably close to eighty, her thin hair a wispy white cloud around heavily lined features. Sharp brown eyes shone like buttons in her face. She let out the smoky breath in a long sigh of satisfaction and regarded the tip of her cigarette. "Doctor says I shoulda quit these things forty years ago. I told him there wasn't much point in quitting now. Aren't that many fun things to do when you get to be my age. House hunting, huh?"

Guinevere nodded, straightening. "That's right. Something afford-able. A place we could fix up on our own as the money comes in. Prices here in Seattle are pretty steep, we've found. You like this neighborhood?"

Abby gazed speculatively up and down the run-down block. "Let's just say I own this place free and clear. That puts a rosy glow on the whole neighborhood as far as I'm concerned."

Guinevere laughed. "I understand completely."

"Who knows," Abby went on philosophically, inhaling on her cig-arette, "maybe one of these days we'll get selected for one of those big rehabilitation grants. Or maybe some developer will come in and want to buy up the whole block for a hotel or something." She leaned against the fence, which gave a little beneath her weight. "This used to be a pretty nice area, you know," she went on wistfully. "Back when my husband was alive, all these houses were full of families. People took care of their gardens. Didn't let 'em run to pot the way that bunch down the street has." She broke out in another hoarse chuckle. "Pot. Get it? They got a bunch of marijuana growing in the backyard."

"Good grief," said Zac, looking appropriately appalled.

"Stingy as all get-out, too," Abby continued. "Not at all neigh-borly. I asked 'em for a little bit just for my own personal use, and they wouldn't give me a single leaf. And after all the zucchini bread I've taken over to 'em." She shook her head. "Young people these days. They just don't understand the meaning of neighborliness."

"I suppose you're right," Guinevere agreed sadly.

Abby opened the creaky gate. "Long as you're just casing the area, why don't you come out back for a glass of iced tea? Wouldn't want you to get too bad an impression of the folks around here."

"That's very kind of you, Mrs. Kettering," Guinevere said as Zac immediately propelled her through the gate.

"Call me Abby." Abby Kettering led the way around to the backyard and seated Zac and Guinevere in an old porch swing while she went into the kitchen to pour three glasses of iced tea. When she reappeared a few minutes later, she smiled. "So you two are gonna get married, huh?"

"That's right," Zac said, lightly touching Guinevere's hand.

"Neither one of you looks like you're just outta high school. This gonna be a first or second marriage?"

"First," said Zac.

"Second," said Guinevere simultaneously.

Abby wrinkled her nose. "You ain't sure?"

"Well," said Guinevere, lowering her eyes demurely, "it's my first. Zac's second." She ignored Zac's irritated movement beside her.

"Gotcha." Abby leaned back in her lawn chair, nodding to herself. "You got some pretty heavy-duty alimony and child support to pay from that first marriage, Zac?"

"Uh . . ."

Guinevere moved to cover Zac's floundering response. "It's one of the reasons we have to find an inexpensive house, Abby. What with all the money that has to go to Zac's ex-wife and four kids, there just isn't a lot left over at the end of the month." There was a choking sound from Zac that turned into a cough. "We've spotted a couple of places on this street that might do for us. There's one two doors down that has a for-sale sign in front of it."

Abby nodded complacently. "The Comstock place. Comstocks moved out a few months ago when they split up. Put the house on the market, but it's been damn tough to sell houses in this area for the past few years. They're probably getting desperate. You might get a real good deal on it."

"Actually, I like the one next to it better," Guinevere said musingly. "The old two-story place with the wraparound porch? I just love those huge, old-fashioned porches."

Abby frowned, thinking. "Oh, I expect you mean the Sandwick place. It was for sale for a long time, but that Sandwick boy finally found a buyer a few months ago. Far as I know, it ain't for sale now."

"Is that right?" Zac frowned. "But there doesn't appear to be anyone living there. We just assumed it was up for sale. Are you sure it was sold a few months ago?"

"Sure as hell. I talked to the guy who was scouting it out for some big-time investor back East. He was just like you two. Asked a lot of questions about the area. Said the hotshot he represented wanted to invest in some low-income fixer-uppers out here in Seattle, but he was a little uncertain about the neighborhood. I told him I thought the place had real potential 'cause we're so close to Capitol Hill, and Lord knows Capitol Hill has gotten downright trendy in the past few years. One of these days we might get trendy, too."

Zac leaned forward to set down his tea glass, his movements deliberate. "So this investor's representative went ahead and bought the Sandwick place?"

Abby shrugged. "I guess so. Next thing I knew, the for sale sign was down."

"He certainly hasn't put any work into the place," Guinevere said disapprovingly. "It's quite run-down."

"Maybe he's just sitting on it until the market picks up," Zac suggested.

Abby lit another cigarette. "Don't know about that. Once in a while I've seen a couple of rough types hanging around the place. Usually late at night. Sometimes these days I don't sleep too good, you know? Ever since my Hank died . . . Well, anyhow, I think I've seen a man and a woman comin' and goin' from there. Sometimes others. Thought at first they might be new tenants. But they just come and go occasionally, mostly at night. Don't appear to live there. Maybe just some street people who've found a vacant house to sleep in when the weather's bad." Abby exhaled a ring of smoke. "Street people. Funny how words change, ain't it? I can remember when we used to call that type bums."

Guinevere summoned up a startled expression. "Bums? There are bums staying in the Sandwick house?"

"They're not so bad," Abby told her reassuringly. "Leastways they're quiet. Not like that rowdy group that used to hold parties there back when the Sandwick boy owned the place. Bunch of beatnik types."

Zac blinked. "Beatniks?"

Abby waved the hand holding the cigarette. "Don't know what they call 'em now. You know, artsy types. Think they're all red-hot painters who are gonna set the world on fire someday. They used to show up over there on Saturday nights and have themselves a good time. Never invited me. Anyways, they're all gone now. They used to be there on a regular basis, but then they stopped holding those wild parties, and next thing I knew, that guy from back East was buying the place for his investor friend. That Sandwick boy owes me something, although he doesn't know it."

"How's that?" Zac asked.

"Well," Abby confided, "if it hadn't been for me talkin' up the potential of the neighborhood, so to speak, I'm not sure that representative feller would have recommended that his pal buy the place. The rep had heard all sorts of rumors about weird things happening over there at the Sandwick place. Asked me a lot of questions about 'em. I reassured him."

"Is that right?" Guinevere tried to look vaguely alarmed. "What sort of weird things, Abby? The place isn't haunted or anything, is it?"

"Good Lord, no!" Abby's laughter dissolved into another wave of coughing. When she recovered, she took a long swallow of tea and shook her head. "No ghosts as far as I know. Seems like that representative guy had heard the parties goin' on were connected with some spooky occult-type stuff. I told him that was most likely a load of nonsense. Just a bunch of young folks having fun. So what if they played a few games? It wasn't anything serious."

"Were they playing occult games there, Abby?" Zac asked with deep concern.

Abby lifted one thin shoulder. "Maybe. A time or two I'd look out late at night and see all the lights go off. Then the house would stay dark for a long time. Sometimes I could see some lights flickering. Maybe candles. But that was the extent of it. Who knows what was going on? My guess is that they were all sitting happily in the parlor getting rocked out of their tiny little minds."

Guinevere frowned. "Rocked?"

"Stoned. Whatever. I forget the word they use. All I know is the young folks get to have all the fun these days." Abby sighed. "Then again, maybe it was always that way. So. When you two gettin' married?"

"We haven't set the date," Zac said clearly, crushing Guinevere's hand as she opened her mouth to respond. "It sort of depends."

"On what?" Abby demanded. "On whether or not Gwen here is pregnant?"

Guinevere choked on her iced tea. Zac pounded her obligingly on the back until she recovered. "Strange you should mention the subject of babies, Abby," Zac went on as he assisted Guinevere. "Gwen and I have been discussing the matter a lot lately."

"If you're gonna have 'em," Abby advised Guinevere, "better start soon. Got to have babies while you're young. How old are you, anyway? Look like you're hoverin' around thirty."

"As a matter of fact, I am," Guinevere admitted, glaring at an innocent-looking Zac. "But it's Zac I'm worried about. He's getting very close to forty, you see."

Abby grinned. "Don't you worry too much about him slowin' down just 'cause he's gettin' near forty. It's not necessarily true that men are over the hill after forty. Lots of 'em keep goin' strong. Take my husband, for instance—"

"Uh, maybe we'd better be on our way," Zac said, interrupting his hostess as gently as possible. "Gwen and I still have a lot to do today. There are a couple of other neighborhoods we're supposed to check out before we make a decision on a house. We certainly do appreciate your advice, Abby. Maybe we'll be neighbors someday." He was urging Guinevere out of the backyard. "Thanks for the iced tea."

"Anytime," Abby called after them. "Anytime at all. Maybe next time you drop in I'll have some of my neighbor's pot to offer you. I'm thinking of offering them something more interesting than zucchini bread by way of a trade. Got some really beautiful beefsteak tomatoes coming along back here. They might go for 'em."

"Good luck, Abby," Guinevere called back. Then she found herself out on the sidewalk in front of the house. Plaintively she looked up at Zac, whose face was set in frozen lines. "What's the rush? The conversation was just getting interesting."

"We got all the useful information we were likely to get."

"Concerning the Sandwick house, maybe, but what about all those pearls of wisdom she was giving me about aging males?"

"Anything you want to know about aging males, you ask me. I'm becoming an authority. I seem to be aging rapidly around you. Ex-wife and four kids. Jesus, Gwen, your sense of humor is weird, you know that?"

"Probably the company I keep. Where to now?"

"Back to the office. Believe it or not, I do have other projects besides this one that require my attention. *Paying* projects."

"Aha. The Gallinger analysis."

"I want to get that final report in and collect my fee." Zac opened the Buick door for her.

"You're certainly in a hurry to wind that business up," Guinevere noted sweetly.

Zac shot her a quelling look as he guided the Buick away from the curb. "When I've finished with the report, I want to have another talk with Adair. Set up a time this evening, will you?"

"Sure. What do you think that 'investor's representative' business is all about? Who do you think it was who asked Abby about the Sandwick house parties?"

"I don't know, but it sure doesn't sound like the same guy who bought the house through the real estate agent. The agent said the client was scruffy and didn't look like he possibly could have put fifty-five grand together. The agent's client sounds more like one of the 'street people' Abby thought might be staying in the place from time to time. I'm hoping Mason might have some more information. Maybe he knows more than he realizes. Give me a call this afternoon after you've set up a time to meet with him."

"You'll be in your office?"

"Either there or over at Gallinger's."

"Keep an eye on your genes."

"I appreciate your concern."

Carla was busy handling a client call when Guinevere returned to the office that afternoon. She had a terrific telephone voice, Guinevere thought as she listened to her sister promise a temporary secretary to one of Camelot Services' better clients. Maybe she should think twice about pushing Carla out on her own. There were times when it was extremely convenient to leave the office in good hands.

"Find out anything useful?" Carla asked expectantly as she hung up the phone.

"Maybe. Zac's not sure. One of the neighbors said she thought the Sandwick house had been sold to a big-time East Coast investor. Yet the real estate agent says the buyer was a grungy, long-haired local. Zac wants to talk to Mason again. I'm supposed to set up an appointment for all of us this evening."

"I'll do it," Carla said, reaching for the phone immediately.

Guinevere raised one brow but said nothing. Her sister's eagerness to talk to Mason Adair was almost amusing.

"Mason? It's Carla. Zac and Gwen want to get together to talk about the problem this evening. Are you free? Great. Why don't we meet down at one of the taverns in Pioneer Square?" There was a pause while Carla listened. "Okay, that sounds fine. I'll tell Gwen. See you later, Mason. Oh, by the way, I talked to a columnist from the *Review-Times* today. He covers art for the paper, and I got him interested in doing an interview with you. I think it could be a really nice piece of publicity, Mason. I'll let you know the details later. I think I'll have a chat with Theresa this afternoon, too. I want to speak to her about putting *Frost* and *Mission* up front in the gallery. She's got them too far back. You need to lure people in with a flashy display. This is a competitive world, Mason. You can't run an art gallery the old-fashioned way. You need to catch people's attention. Yes, all right. See you then. Bye, Mason."

Guinevere took over her seat at her desk as her sister vacated it. "Does Mason mind the fact that you're beginning to run his career?"

"Not at all. He's grateful. He hates the business side of art."

"You don't seem to hate it."

"No," said Carla thoughtfully, "I love it. I think I could be very good at managing artists' careers, Gwen. I can see me now with my own little gallery in Pioneer Square. What do you think?"

"A fascinating idea. When do we meet Mason?"

"At five thirty. Bouncer's. Know it? It's that little sidewalk tavern near the Midnight Light gallery."

"I know it. I'll tell Zac."

Carla was studying the tip of her pencil. "Why don't you and I leave a little early, Gwen? I want to talk to Theresa. We could go to the gallery first and then meet Mason and Zac."

"I don't know, Carla. I'm not sure I want to be around when you start lecturing Theresa on how to display Mason's art."

Carla smiled. "Leave it to me. I know what I'm doing."

"I wish I did." Guinevere picked up the phone to dial Zac's office.

As it happened, Guinevere was not obliged to go with Carla when she talked to Theresa that evening. The two sisters left Camelot Services and started walking up First Avenue toward Pioneer Square shortly before five. The street was full of commuters heading toward the ferry docks. In the mornings people who lived on Bainbridge Island or over in Bremerton frequently walked onboard a ferry at one end and walked off to work in downtown Seattle at the other. In the evenings they reversed the procedure. The bars and pubs sprinkled along First Avenue catered to the people waiting for ferries or buses or those who simply wanted a little happy hour time before heading back to the suburbs. During the spring and summer many of the small taverns put tables out in front on the sidewalks.

Guinevere and Carla had crossed Yesler and were heading toward the Midnight Light gallery when someone hailed them from a sidewalk table. At first Guinevere didn't recognize the thin-faced man who was raising his hand to beckon them. Then something about his nervous, high-strung manner jolted her memory. She smiled aloofly at Henry Thorpe and was about to ignore his invitation when she thought better of the idea. She paused in front of his table.

"Hello, Henry. Carla, did you meet Henry Thorpe the other evening at Mason's show?"

"Yes, I believe I did," Carla said politely, waiting for her sister to continue down the street with her.

"Sit down, sit down," Thorpe commanded genially. He had obviously started happy hour early. The glass in front of him was half empty, and Guinevere was willing to bet it wasn't his first drink of the day. "Plenty of room. Let me buy you both a drink."

"We're in a hurry," Carla began austerely.

Guinevere looked at her. "Why don't you run along to the gallery, Carla? I'll have a quick drink with Henry and join you later."

"But, Gwen . . ." Carla paused, trying to read her sister's face. She seemed to realize that there was something going on and was shrewd enough not to interfere. With a smile for Henry she nodded and walked off.

"That sister of yours is nice looking," Henry said, gazing after Carla with regret. "She ever do any modeling?"

"No." Guinevere ignored the fact that Henry had been hoping Carla would join him. She plunked herself down in the seat opposite him and smiled blandly. "I'll have a glass of white wine, please."

"What?" Henry was still gazing mournfully after Carla. "Oh, sure. White wine." After a couple of attempts he managed to catch the waitress's eye and give the order. Then he sat back, obviously resigning himself to a drink with the less-attractive sister. "So. How goes the war?"

"What war?"

"Just an expression." Henry looked petulant. "Is Mason still riding high on his big success the other night?"

"He seems to be anxious to get back to work."

Thorpe's eyes narrowed. "It'll be interesting to see if he can get back to work. Lots of artists do great up until they start to make it big and then *phfft*. Up in smoke."

"I beg your pardon?" Guinevere sipped cautiously at her wine.

"They blow up. Dry up. Can't work anymore. Can't handle success. It's a common story," Thorpe explained knowledgeably.

"I hadn't realized." Perhaps this was the excuse Henry Thorpe had been trying to use for himself during the past few months, Guinevere thought. She remembered Mason saying that the thin, nervous man hadn't done any worthwhile painting for quite some time.

"Yeah. Some turn to coke, some head for the South Seas. Some just drink too much. Be interesting to see which route Adair uses."

"You're assuming he won't be able to handle his success. Perhaps you're wrong." Guinevere wasn't sure just why she had sat down with Henry Thorpe. Some vague instinct had suggested that she do so. Now she wondered if she hadn't wasted her time. Henry Thorpe was an embittered man who could only offer caustic comments about Mason Adair. It was a good thing Carla hadn't stayed.

"I'm not wrong," Thorpe said irritably. "You just wait and see. It's just like I told that guy a few months ago. Adair's a flash in the pan. Here today, gone tomorrow. By this time next year no one will remember him."

Guinevere caught her breath. "You told someone else that Mason probably wouldn't make it?"

Thorpe frowned and took a gulp of his drink. "Forget it. It was just some jerk hanging around the galleries looking to make a *discovery*. Thought he'd found one when he saw some of Adair's stuff hanging in the Midnight Light gallery. He happened to wander into the gallery next door where I had one of my pictures." Thorpe's mouth tightened. "One I did a while back. Still hasn't sold. Some fools don't know art when it hits them in the face. I thought for a while that this guy was going to buy it. But then he started talking about Adair's stuff."

Guinevere paused, trying to pick her words carefully. "But you set him straight on Mason Adair? Told him Mason wouldn't be important in the long run?"

Thorpe moved uneasily in his chair. "I just told him the truth, that's all. Said if he wanted to buy something worthwhile for his backer, he should be looking at someone else's pictures. Not Adair's."

"I see." Guinevere wished she'd had more experience trying to pump people. She would just have to rely on the empathic charm Zac claimed she had. "This man was buying for a backer? How interesting. Is a lot of art sold that way?"

"Oh, sure. People who don't trust their own taste use professionals to do their collecting for them." Thorpe was scathing.

"It does sound a little remote," Guinevere observed. "I'd certainly want to see what I was buying before making a purchase."

"Yeah, but a lot of people don't know one goddamn thing about art. They just want to *collect*."

"I suppose so. Did this man end up buying anything by Adair?"

"I don't know. We talked for a while. Had a few drinks. He told me he thought he'd buy that picture I've got in the gallery next to Midnight Light. But he never did. I didn't see him after the night we had our drinks."

Guinevere wondered just how many drinks Henry Thorpe had put away while chatting with the art buyer's representative. She doubted whether Thorpe himself could remember, much less recall just how much he'd talked about Mason Adair to the man buying the drinks. "This happened a few months ago, you say?"

"Yeah. Six, maybe seven months. Say, you want another glass of wine?"

Guinevere smiled regretfully. "I wish I could stay, but I have an appointment."

"Oh." Thorpe looked disappointed.

"I think I'll stop in at the gallery next to Midnight Light and take a look at your painting," Guinevere said gently.

Thorpe brightened. "You do that. Who knows? Maybe you'll be the one to see the real depth in it." The momentary dash of hope died as he swallowed the last of his drink. "God knows no one else has. Everyone these days wants art to be *pretty*."

"Thank you for the drink, Henry." Quietly Guinevere got up and left. She knew now why she had followed her instincts and let Henry Thorpe buy her a drink.

Farther down the block a sense of guilt made her drop in at the gallery next door to the Midnight Light gallery. She inquired about the Henry Thorpe painting and was shown a medium-size canvas hanging on the back wall.

The canvas was a ceremonial mask of rage and pain. It was done in harsh reds and browns, and it had a kind of raw energy that couldn't be denied. But Guinevere knew she certainly wouldn't want it hanging in her home. It was far too depressing.

With a sigh for the inner fury that must be driving Henry Thorpe, she walked back out onto the street. Zac would be waiting together with Carla and Mason at the tavern.

Zac was going to be fascinated to learn that not only had a big-time East Coast investor's representative been making inquiries about the people who used the Sandwick house for parties, but that an art buyer's representative had been making inquiries about Mason Adair. All at about the same time. Six or seven months ago.

Zac was highly suspicious of coincidences.

CHAPTER 8

Clutching the simulated-leather-bound document labeled *Analysis of Security Systems of Gallinger Industries by Free Enterprise Security, Inc.,* Zac sat outside Elizabeth Gallinger's office door and awaited the summons.

He had been sitting in the plush outer office for only a few minutes, but he had already used up his entire stock of bracing sayings and encouraging words. He was down to "A man's gotta do what a man's gotta do" and "No guts, no glory."

But the constant pep talk he had been feeding himself since he'd left his office fifteen minutes ago was not doing much to stem the tide of masculine nerves. He still wished he were anywhere but in Elizabeth Gallinger's outer office. The thought of facing her after the excruciatingly embarrassing scene on the terrace of her home last night was anathema. The thought of abandoning the potential fee he was about to receive for his security analysis services, however, was unthinkable. So: A man's gotta do what a man's gotta do.

He still wasn't quite ready when Elizabeth's private secretary smiled and showed him into the inner office, but he got another tiny reprieve. Elizabeth Gallinger was still on the phone.

"No, I don't think that's such a good idea. I want all four houses or none of them. See what you can do, Hal. Yes, the usual financing arrangements. All right, that will be fine. Give me a call in the morning. Good-bye, Hal."

She hung up the phone and smiled brilliantly at Zac. "Sorry about that. Just finishing up some business with someone who handles my real estate investments for me. Do sit down, Zac. I see you have your report. I'm anxious to read it."

Zac breathed a sigh of relief. She was all business today. Maybe they could both just pretend last night's scene on the terrace hadn't happened. He took the leather chair across from her and handed her the genuine simulated-leather binder. He could be all business, too.

"I think you'll find that everything's been covered. I'll be glad to go over any of the details with the people in your security department, but in general they will concur with almost all the recommendations. I've already spoken to them. Your main areas of concern are the shipping docks and the computer operations. That's typical for companies the size of Gallinger Industries. But there are steps that can be taken to tighten up both departments. In addition, I've outlined some ways of limiting the kind of casual employee theft that takes place in large organizations."

Elizabeth opened the binder and glanced through the table of contents. Zac was enormously glad he'd taken Guinevere's advice and hired one of her temporary secretaries to type the final draft. At least he knew the document looked polished and professional. Of course, Guinevere had charged him a fortune for the afternoon's work, and it had been disconcerting to discover that the temporary secretary she had assigned him was male, but now it all seemed worthwhile. He waited while Elizabeth perused the opening remarks. Then she looked up with another smile.

"It looks fine, Zac. I certainly appreciate your efficiency. I thought this sort of thing would take months to produce."

Not when you're inspired the way I was, Zac thought ruefully. "I gave it my top priority, Elizabeth."

"I see. Well, I suppose that concludes our association, doesn't it?" she asked with just the smallest touch of wistfulness.

Zac decided to steer clear of the direction in which she was heading. "I don't mean to pry, Elizabeth, but have you had a lot of experience in real estate investment? You said a moment ago that you were talking to your agent. I've, uh, been thinking of picking up a fixer-upper myself."

"Have you? It can be very time-consuming if you don't have someone like Hal to ride herd on the properties and financing for you."

"Financing? You don't just pay cash?"

Elizabeth shook her head. "Of course not. When you're investing, the whole point is to use other people's money as much as possible. Never tie up your own capital. If I can't work out a good financing arrangement with the owners or my bank, I don't buy."

"I see. I certainly appreciate the advice."

"Let me give you Hal's phone number. If you're really interested in picking up some choice properties, give him a call. He's a wonderful negotiator. Knows all the ins and outs of financing."

"Thank you, Elizabeth." Dutifully he accepted the phone number and inserted the slip of paper into his wallet. Then Zac got to his feet. "I've enjoyed working with you. I hope the analysis answers all your questions. As I said, give me a call if your people have any questions."

He was halfway to the door when Elizabeth's voice caught him. "Zac?"

His hand froze on the doorknob. "Yes, Elizabeth?" He glanced back over his shoulder.

"You won't reconsider the offer I made last night?"

Zac cleared his throat. "I'm afraid I can't. I've more or less committed my genes elsewhere."

There was a small hesitation, and then Elizabeth nodded soberly. "I understand. I envy her. Good-bye, Zac. And thank you." Regally gracious to the last.

"Good-bye, Elizabeth." He escaped into the outer office. Nodding politely to the secretary, he forced himself to walk calmly down the hall to the elevators. It seemed forever before the elevator doors hissed shut behind him and he was swept downstairs to safety.

Out on the street he breathed the air of freedom and glanced at his watch. He realized he was going to be a few minutes late to the rendezvous he'd arranged with Guinevere and Mason. He decided to grab one of the free buses that ran through the core of the city.

The bus was jammed because of rush hour, and Zac nearly missed the stop he wanted in Pioneer Square. He emerged at last, straightening his jacket, and tried to look as if he'd just parked his Ferrari down the block. Hot-shot security consultants probably didn't ride buses, free or otherwise. Image.

Guinevere saw Zac approaching from the table she was sharing with Mason and Carla. The warm afternoon had attracted a good-size after-work crowd, and the sidewalk seating was nearly filled. She and Mason and Carla had been lucky to get a table.

"Over here, Zac." She waved encouragingly. "You're late."

"Sorry. Got held up at the office." He sat down beside her, nodding at Carla and Mason.

Guinevere waited impatiently while he ordered his tequila from the busy waiter, and then she leaned forward. "Okay, Zac. What's up? Have you made some major breakthroughs?"

He gave her a disparaging glance. "I called this little meeting to give us all a chance to hash over everything we've learned. No major breakthroughs. At least not from my end." He regarded the others with mild interest. "Has anyone else had any brilliant thoughts on the matter?"

Mason and Carla shook their heads unhappily. Guinevere smiled with smug expectancy. Zac eyed her warily. "Okay, Gwen. Why the cat-with-the-canary look?"

"Just a minor detail I picked up a little while ago from Henry Thorpe," she said easily.

"Who's Henry Thorpe?"

Quickly Guinevere explained.

"Thank you," Zac said gravely. "Always nice to be kept informed."

"You're welcome. Now to get on with this. He said that someone posing as an art dealer was hanging around the galleries a few months ago. He was asking questions about Mason Adair."

Zac was silent for a long moment while the others stared at Guinevere. "A few months ago," he finally repeated. "Would that have been at about the same time someone was posing as a real estate investor's representative and asking questions about the neighborhood where the Sandwick house is located?"

"You got it." Guinevere waited for praise and admiring comments on her brilliant detective work.

"Well, shit," Zac said.

Guinevere glared at him. "That wasn't quite what I expected."

Mason sighed. "I don't think that's such a big deal, Gwen. We know my cousin Dane has been trying to locate me for months. He must have hired private detectives, and they were probably the ones asking the questions."

Guinevere did a quick staccato drumroll of impatience with her crimson nails. "I suppose you're right."

Zac took over control of the discussion. "All right, we'll file that info for now. Mason, I've got a couple of questions. When you and your friends were sharing the good times at the Sandwick house, did you install a big stone table and a wall of black velvet drapes in the basement?"

Mason looked startled. "Hell, no. Have you any idea what that would cost? Besides, we were into partying, not redecorating the basement. Did you say black velvet drapes?"

"Uh-huh."

"And a *stone* table?"

Zac nodded. "Looks something like an altar. A black altar."

Carla shivered. "It sounds gross."

Mason grimaced. "Actually, it sounds like something Baldric and Valonia might have installed. But where would they have gotten the cash? Real stone tables are incredibly expensive. Just ask in any good furniture store."

"They probably got the money for the table from the same place they got the cash to buy the house," Guinevere offered.

"I don't know," Mason said slowly. "They just didn't have that kind of cash. Not when I knew them."

"Perhaps they're into more profitable things these days," Zac suggested. "Drug dealing, maybe."

Mason thought about it. "I suppose it's a possibility. It would explain the sudden infusion of money. But you said there's no sign of them living in the house?"

"No," Zac admitted.

"Why would they buy a place and not live in it?" Carla wondered.

Guinevere shrugged. "They might have bought more than one house. Maybe they use one for their weird occult ceremonies and live elsewhere."

"The point is," Carla injected, "why are they hounding Mason?"

"Excellent point," Mason growled, taking a swallow of beer. "And what the hell are they doing with *Glare* stashed in the basement of that house?"

"You're sure neither one of them has any reason to hate you personally or to be professionally jealous?" Zac asked Mason.

The younger man shook his head dolefully. "Well, the group of us who were using the house originally refused to take their stupid ceremonies seriously. I suppose they could be resentful on that score. But why take it out on me?"

Guinevere frowned thoughtfully. "Because you're the only one they can find? Most of the others seem to have split for parts unknown."

"But there are a couple left in the area, and I haven't heard any gossip about them having the kind of trouble I'm having," Mason pointed out.

"Personally," declared Carla, "I still like the jealousy motive."

Zac shook his head. "It doesn't make any sense in this case, Carla. But your instincts are good."

"How's that?" she asked.

"You're looking for a rational motive. So am I. I would prefer one I could understand."

Guinevere said calmly, "I think the witchcraft is a potentially genuine motive. There have been occasional newspaper articles about occult groups living in the Northwest. This wouldn't be a first. There are some strange people in this world, Zac."

"I know," he agreed. "But, like Carla, I guess I would prefer a more rational motive."

"If someone were after money, why haven't they tried to blackmail me or tell me the vandalism will stop if I pay them off?" Mason asked, wrinkling his brow.

"How could you pay them off?" Guinevere asked bluntly. "You've been living at borderline poverty level for over two years. A couple of sales at the gallery show the other night aren't enough to put you on easy street."

The question hung in the air. In silence the four people sitting around the table finished their drinks as the after-work crowd began to thin. Finally Zac got to his feet with an abrupt movement.

"Let's go home, Gwen. I've got some thinking to do." He turned around and started making his way between tables.

Guinevere threw the other two an apologetic look as she got hurriedly to her feet. "Sorry. He gets this way sometimes when he goes into Deep Think."

"Deep Think?" Mason stared after the departing Zac. "He's thinking?"

"Uh-huh. See you later, both of you. I'll let you know if he comes up with any brilliant ideas this evening."

Guinevere trotted after Zac, catching up with him as he started down the sidewalk toward her apartment. He had his hands shoved into his jacket pockets, his shoulders slightly hunched, and the remote, miles-away look in his eyes that Guinevere had come to associate with times such as this. She didn't bother trying to ask any questions. Zac would talk when he was ready. Silently she walked beside him until they reached her apartment building.

Upstairs she poured him another shot of tequila and sat beside him on the sofa while he cradled the drink in both hands and stared unseeingly out of one of her vaulted windows.

This mood could last for hours, Guinevere reminded herself. She might as well fix something to eat. Rising to her feet again, she traipsed back into the kitchen to make a sandwich. No sense wasting gourmet cooking on Zac when he was in Deep Think.

Three more hours passed before Zac finally spoke. Guinevere, deep into a mystery at the time, was startled. She had gotten accustomed to the silence.

"Those private investigators were asking their questions several months ago," he began slowly, just as if there had been no break in the conversation.

"About six or seven months ago," Guinevere agreed.

"Yet cousin Dane didn't contact Adair until this week."

Guinevere closed her book. "That's true."

"Why the delay?" Zac asked softly. "Those investigators must have gotten their answers six months ago. They must have located Adair then. He wasn't trying to hide. He hadn't even changed his name. Once someone had realized he was in Seattle and was part of the local art scene, the rest would have been easy. Cousin Dane and the rest of the family must have known where he was six months ago."

"Zac, what has Dane Fitzpatrick's search for Mason got to do with the Sandwick house and the vandalism?"

Zac picked up one of the sandwiches that had been sitting on a plate in front of him for the past three hours. "I told you earlier that given a choice, I prefer a rational motive. Money is the most rational of all motives. There's money in this mess, Gwen. It's all over the place. Fifty-five thousand in cash to buy a run-down house on Capitol Hill with virtually no negotiation. Real estate wheeler-dealers always negotiate, and they don't use their own cash if they can avoid it."

Guinevere eyed him curiously. "You're an authority on the subject?"

"No, but I talked to an authority this afternoon."

"Who?"

"Elizabeth Gallinger. She was on the phone to the guy who handles her real estate investments when I walked into her office."

"I see." Guinevere decided this wasn't the time to discuss Queen Elizabeth in greater detail. "Okay, so there's money in this mess. It could be drug money, as you suggested earlier, Zac. Drug dealers with a lot of excess cash on their hands might not quibble over the price of a house they want to buy."

Zac nodded. "True. But that isn't the only money involved here. There's East Coast preppy money, too."

"Adair family money? But that doesn't make any sense. Mason's out of his father's will. And how would Baldric and Valonia know about his family connections, anyway?"

"An interesting question."

"Zac, what's going on? What are you thinking?"

"Nothing solid yet. But there are some things I'm going to have to check on tomorrow. Things I probably should have checked out much earlier." He munched his sandwich and then looked at Guinevere. "Let's go to bed, honey. I've got a lot to do in the morning."

On the way into the bedroom Zac yawned hugely and said, "This isn't so bad, is it?"

"What isn't so bad?"

"Living together."

She slid him a speculative glance. "We haven't exactly given it a long run," she reminded him cautiously. "This was just a short-term arrangement until you solve Mason's problem."

"I know." Complacently he walked into the bedroom and started unbuttoning his shirt. "But the concept has potential, don't you think? Of course, if we did this on a full-time basis, you'd have to get rid of that lousy coffee machine."

Guinevere, not knowing how to respond to the hint that Zac might actually want to move in with her, sought refuge in humor. "I hope you won't force me to choose between that beautiful machine and you, Zac. It would be a tough choice. The coffee machine is color-coordinated with my apartment, don't forget."

"And I'm not?" He finished undressing and crawled into bed beside her.

She touched his broad shoulder as he turned out the light beside the bed. Then she smiled. "Not exactly. But you do have your uses."

His feet tangled with hers as Zac pulled her close. "I'm damn well more useful than that imported coffeemaker. Come here and use me."

Guinevere went into his arms the way she always did, with a sensual abandon that forever surprised her and which Zac inevitably accepted with deep hunger.

It wasn't just the money and the motive that raised questions, Zac told himself the next morning as he sat in his office and went over his notes on the Mason Adair situation. There was also the curious matter of timing. The Sandwick house had been sold at about the same time that an unknown investigator or investigators were asking for information on Adair. At least one of those phantom private detectives had said he was representing an East Coast real estate investor and had specifically asked about the Sandwick house.

Money and timing. In the security business those two issues often went together. One was usually related to the other. Zac stared at his notepad a while longer, and then he reached out and picked up the phone.

"Camelot Services." The professionally cheerful voice on the other end of the line was not Guinevere's.

"Hi, Carla, it's Zac. Is your sister there?"

"Nope. She's out drumming up business with a new client. What can I do for you?"

"Since when does she have to leave the office to drum up business?" He glanced at his watch. "I was going to take her to lunch."

"Well, you'll have to get in line. The new client is taking her to lunch. I think he intends to set up a contract with Camelot Services to provide his firm with all the temps he needs. He'll get priority service that way."

"I don't see why Gwen has to have lunch with him in order to settle the deal." Zac was aware of the fact that he was growling.

"You know how it is with these executives," Carla said vaguely. "They do everything over lunch."

Zac had a sudden jolting image of what "everything" might include and immediately shoved it out of his mind. Guinevere had a business to run, after all. He couldn't afford to get nervous every time she had lunch with a client. "All right, Carla. Tell her I called. In the meantime can you do me a favor?"

"You want another typist?"

"At the prices Camelot Services charges? Not on your life. It will take me six months to pay the bill on the last one I got from your sister."

"Gwen believes in turning a profit whenever possible," Carla admitted blandly.

"And after all I've done for that woman," Zac intoned.

"I'll let you two settle the matter of the bill for the typist we sent over. What was the favor?"

"I need Mason's father's phone number back East."

Carla sucked in her breath. "His father's phone number? But, Zac, why?"

"I don't know why. Not yet. I'm just trying to tie some loose ends together. Can you get it from him for me?"

"Possibly. But he'll ask a hundred questions, and I can't blame him. What shall I tell him?"

"Tell him I need it to pursue his case," Zac said, irritated at the delay. "If he wants me to stay on it, he'd better cooperate."

"Okay, okay, don't get huffy. I'll contact him now." Carla hung up the phone.

Zac sat with his feet propped on his desk, leaned back in his swivel chair, and waited. While he waited, he stared into the office across the hall. The sales rep who was using the other cubicle as a base for his operations finally sensed the steady gaze and glanced up questioningly. Zac looked away, wishing he had a real window. One of these days he was going to have to move up in the world. He needed a bigger and better office. A few more accounts like the Gallinger account and maybe he'd be able to afford one.

The phone rang five minutes later. It was Carla. "All right, Zac, I've got it for you." She rattled it off while he copied it down. "Mason wanted to know what you were going to do. I told him not to worry, that you would be discreet and not become involved in what was obviously a private family matter."

"You told him all that?"

"I certainly did. Mason's very touchy on the subject of his family. It's a very unhappy situation, you know. I reassured him that you would be very careful about what you said to his father. Don't make a liar out of me, Zac."

Carla hung up the phone before he could ask if Guinevere had returned yet from her client lunch. He looked down at the phone number he had written in his notebook and wondered if he could wait until after five o'clock to make the call. He hated to pay daytime long-distance rates when there wasn't a client footing the expense tab. With a resigned sigh he picked up the phone and dialed.

It took a great deal of talking to get Julius Edward Adair on the telephone. Apparently Mr. Adair was not the sort of man who took phone calls from strangers, especially strangers on the West Coast. But after Zac mentioned Mason's name a few times, the senior Adair came on the line. The rich, deep voice was full of East Coast prep-school breeding. Zac ignored his own annoyed reaction. It wasn't Adair's fault that he came from a family that could trace its lineage and its money back a couple of centuries. Everyone had a cross to bear.

"Mr. Adair? This is Zachariah Justis. I'm president of a firm called Free Enterprise Security, Inc. We have been asked to make some inquiries on behalf of your son, Mason."

There was a moment of shocked silence. "Mason? What do you know about my son? Where is he? Where did you say you were calling from? Oregon?"

"Washington, sir."

"My son is in Washington, D.C.?"

"No, sir, State of."

"The State of Washington? Good Lord. Whatever made him go there?"

"This may come as a jolt, Mr. Adair, but out here we really don't think of Washington as being just the last stop for the wagon trains any longer. We've even got flush toilets in a few of the more progressive homes now."

"There is no need for sarcasm, Mr. . . . What did you say your name was?"

Zac took a deep breath. "Justis. Zachariah Justis."

"And you say you're working for my son?"

"I'm making a few inquiries on his behalf, yes, sir."

"May I talk to him?" Adair asked carefully.

"I'm sorry, he's not here at the moment."

"Will you give me his phone number, please," Adair said imperiously.

"I can't do that," Zac said with sudden gentleness. "He hasn't authorized me to do so. But I would have thought you had that information already. Or at least his address."

"How on earth would I have that? We haven't been able to locate

Mason for quite some time. I've had men working on the problem for almost a year."

Zac cleared his throat, hunching a little over the phone while he reached for his notepad. "Have you, sir? You, personally, commissioned a firm of private investigators to find him?"

"I had my nephew handle the details, but, yes, we've been trying to locate him. Now, if you have information on the matter, Mr. Justis, I will be more than happy to pay for it."

Zac winced at the cold condescension in the words. "Sir, there would be a slight conflict of interest at the moment. I'm already working for your son."

"What are you doing for him? Is he in trouble? What does he need?" There was a father's genuine concern beneath the cultured, aloof exterior.

"What he needs and what I need in order to help him are some answers, Mr. Adair."

"I don't know who you are, Mr. Justis, but I can find out. In the meantime, if you have made contact with my son, I don't want to lose contact with you. Ask your questions."

"I'm afraid I will be making some extremely personal inquiries, sir."

"Just ask, damn it!"

"All right. I understand that you struck Mason out of your will a couple of years ago when the two of you quarreled."

"That is correct," Adair said austerely. "I assumed it would bring him to his senses. Mason had been born and bred with a silver spoon in his mouth. Frankly, I didn't think he'd last more than three or four months without access to the kind of money and connections he had always taken for granted. I have realized during the past couple of years that I was mistaken. That boy turned out to be every damn bit as stubborn as I am. In some ways it made me realize that he was a throwback to his grandfather and his great-grandfather. Mason has lived a soft life, but it seems my son is not soft because of it." Pride laced the comment.

"You say Mason had always lived in relative luxury?"

"It was his heritage. In return he had an obligation to that heritage. We . . . disagreed on the subject."

"I understand." Zac paused and then asked his next question. "You say you've been trying to contact him for some time now."

"That is correct."

"Did you intend to put Mason back in your will in the event that you located him?"

"Yes, Mr. Justis. I did."

Zac exhaled slowly. "I think that answers most of my questions, Mr. Adair."

"Wait, don't hang up, Justis," Adair said urgently. "What about Mason?"

"I'll tell him I talked to you and that you've been trying to reach him," Zac said, searching for a way to leave the older man some hope without building those hopes too high.

"May I have your number, Mr. Justis?"

"Yes." Zac gave it to him and then eased himself off the phone. He sat for a long while after that, contemplating what he had learned. He had been right about this mess. There was money involved. A lot of it. Adair money.

Things finally began to jell. It didn't take any great intuition to realize that there was more at stake than a bit of malicious mischief.

Dane Fitzpatrick had located Mason several months ago, but he not only hadn't contacted the artist, he also hadn't bothered to tell Mason's father. Furthermore, Dane had made a trip to the West Coast and actually talked to Mason. Then he'd returned home and still not mentioned the fact to the senior Adair. Was it because Mason was still being stubborn and refused to talk to his father?

Or because once contact was made, Mason would be back in the will, and Dane would be out in the cold?

And what the hell did all this have to do with Baldric, Valonia, and the Sandwick house?

Zac dialed Guinevere's number again, but Carla assured him that she was still engaged at lunch. Zac frowned as he glanced at his watch. It was already after two. How long was the business lunch going to last? He had another appointment himself that afternoon, one that would take him out of the office. "Carla, tell her to call me as soon as she walks in the door, understand? I want to talk to her."

"I'll tell her, Zac."

The phone was ringing as Guinevere walked into her office much later that afternoon. Carla had already left for the day, she noted, glancing at her sister's messages on the desk. Apparently she'd scheduled a meeting with Theresa at the Midnight Light gallery. Guinevere picked up the receiver.

"Camelot Services."

"Gwen, is that you? I've got to talk to you." Mason Adair's voice was hoarse with tension.

"Mason? What's the problem?"

"I'll tell you when I see you. I'm in my studio. Please come quickly. Something else has happened. I can't reach Zac." He replaced the receiver on his end.

The phone hummed in Guinevere's ear. She stared at it, frowning. The urgency in Mason's voice had been real. Guinevere paused long enough to dial Zac's number, but when Gertie answered, she just said to tell Zac she'd called and then hung up. Guinevere grabbed her shoulder bag and hurried out the door.

CHAPTER 9

Guinevere had almost reached Mason's apartment building when a hunch made her hesitate beside her own door. The urgency in Mason's voice had alarmed her. She had a feeling that whatever had happened was something Zac would want to know about.

Digging her key out of her purse, she let herself inside her own building, determined to try to reach Zac by telephone before going on to Mason's apartment. The call from her phone would only delay her another minute or two.

She opened her door, intent only on calling from the kitchen phone. The mini blinds on her kitchen window were open, and she peered through them, trying to see if she could spot Mason across the street. There was no sign of him.

Zac's phone was once more answered by his service.

"I'm sorry, Mr. Justis is not available at the moment. May I take a message?"

"Gertie, this is Guinevere Jones. Just tell him I called again and that I'd like him to contact me or Mason Adair as soon as he gets back."

"I'll tell him, Gwen. Listen, are you all right? You sound a little upset."

"No, I'm fine, Gertie. Just fine. Be sure to give Zac my message."

"I will."

"Thanks." Guinevere hung up the phone and heard the faint noise in the hall at the same time. Belatedly she realized that she hadn't locked the door behind her when she entered the apartment. She had only intended to stay a moment or two.

Nerves. Gertie was right. She was a little upset and there was no good reason. The worst Mason might have to tell her about was another incident of vandalism.

Hoisting her purse over her shoulder again, she swung around . . . and came to a dead halt as she found herself facing a thick, heavily built man with a gun clutched in his right fist. Shock held her paralyzed for about three taut seconds. It hit her quite forcibly that this was the man she had seen through Mason's window the night he had been attacked. He wasn't wearing a hood this time, and his scraggly, limp brown hair hung almost to his shoulders. There was a flat, aggressive bluntness in his features that reminded her of a pit bulldog. But it was the wild, alien look in his washed-out eyes that truly frightened her.

"Don't say a word. Not one single word. I can kill you and be out of this building before any of your neighbors realizes what's happened. In fact, most of them aren't even home at this time of day. I already checked. You understand me, Guinevere Jones?"

"I understand." She stood very still. There was something abnormal about the way her blood was moving in her veins. Her pulse seemed too fast all of a sudden. Her fingers were tightly clenched around the strap of her shoulder bag. "What do you want?"

"We've already got what we want, don't we, Valonia?"

"Yes." The woman who materialized behind the heavy man had

a ghostlike paleness about her that was unnerving under the circumstances. In contrast to the man, she was very thin with pale skin, pale eyes, colorless lips, and wispy, almost red hair that hung nearly to her waist. She stared at Guinevere with an unblinking, intent gaze. She held a small package in one hand. "So. We were right to keep an eye on this building, too. You were correct in assuming she might stop here before going over to *his* place."

Guinevere forced her tongue to work again. "His place? Mason's? What have you done with him? What's going on here? Look, I don't know what this is all about, but it's obvious you two are playing some pretty serious games; games that have gone much too far. If you had any sense, you'd get out of here. Now."

"Games?" The man, who must have been Baldric, smiled without any humor. "You think we're playing games? You're a fool. But that's not very strange, considering the fact that most people are fools. You should never have gotten involved, Guinevere Jones. Your foolishness is going to cost you. Come here."

Guinevere didn't move. For some reason her attention was on the thin woman. She was holding the small package in her hand with a tension that Guinevere could feel across the width of the kitchen. Even as Guinevere watched, Valonia raised her hand slightly. A strange scent wafted through the air.

"I'm not going anywhere, and if you try to drag a struggling woman down the stairs and out the front door, you're going to be asking for trouble. Someone's going to notice and you know it."

"We do not intend to drag a struggling woman out onto the street," Valonia assured her, stepping closer and raising the oddly scented package. It appeared to be a folded cloth, part of which was dangling into a jar fashioned of cobalt-blue glass. Liquid from the glass was climbing the trail of fabric, permeating it. "You will not be struggling at all. And we will be certain to take you down the back stairs. No one will see you, Guinevere Jones. Do not deceive yourself with false hope. There is no hope."

The acrid smell emanating from the cloth and the glass in Valonia's hand was stronger now. Guinevere was suddenly more afraid of it than she was of the weapon Baldric was holding. She edged backward and found herself up against the counter. The handsome red-and-black coffee machine was immediately behind her.

"Don't touch me," Guinevere hissed. "Don't you dare touch me, you little witch."

Valonia smiled evilly. "How very astute of you." She lunged forward, trying to slap the package against Guinevere's nose and mouth. Guinevere gasped and tried to dodge. Her arm swept out in a wide, desperate arc in an attempt to ward off Valonia.

"Stand still or I'll shoot!" Baldric issued the warning as he leapt toward Guinevere.

Guinevere's hand missed Valonia but struck the coffee machine. Her fingers closed around the handle of the glass pot just as Baldric clamped a hand around her mouth and shoved the snout of the gun into her ribs. The smell of the object in Valonia's hand was overpowering. The damp cloth was forced against Guinevere's nose. Almost instantly her senses reeled.

"Hold her still!" Valonia shoved the cloth more tightly into position.

"Watch out for that coffeepot," Baldric snarled as Guinevere swung her arm in a frantic, awkward movement.

From a great distance Guinevere heard the sound of shattering glass and Baldric's furious oath. She wasn't sure if she had hit either of them. Already she was slumping to the floor, her mind spinning away into darkness as the fumes from the cloth invaded her consciousness. She was aware of a great deal of scrambling movement and crude oaths from both Baldric and Valonia as they tried to follow her to the floor. Guinevere lost her frail grip on the handle of the pot.

She scrambled about in useless protest as she tried to evade Baldric's grasp. Both Baldric and Valonia were concentrating on keeping the cloth pressed against her face. They didn't pay any attention to Guinevere's futile struggles. When her hand closed around a shard of heavy coffeepot glass, Guinevere was too far gone even to be sure of what she was holding. Some vague, rapidly receding instinct made her fumble the piece of glass into the pocket of her skirt. She wondered fleetingly if it would fall out when Baldric and Valonia carried her down the fire escape stairs, and then she wondered what she could possibly do with a piece of glass in any event. Useless effort.

"Clean up that mess." Baldric's order seemed to come from a million miles away. "We don't want anyone to guess what happened here. Get rid of the glass. Hurry!"

It occurred to Guinevere as she slipped into unconsciousness that Zac, for one, would be glad to know that the stylish coffee machine was out of commission, at least temporarily.

Zac sat brooding in Guinevere's apartment, a glass of tequila in front of him. It was nearly eight o'clock. He knew that beyond a shadow of a doubt because he'd been glancing at his watch every couple of minutes for the past two hours. He was not in a good mood. The only explanation he could come up with for Guinevere's absence was that lunch with the client had turned into dinner. That explanation did not please him.

In fact, Zac decided, staring at the half-empty tequila glass, the explanation infuriated him. He sat alone on the black leather sofa and faced the extent of his jealousy. This was what came of not pushing her for some formal commitment. Declaring to each other that they were in the midst of a genuine affair was not enough. Something more was needed in this relationship. Zac vowed that when Guinevere finally came through the front door, he would point that out to her in no uncertain terms.

Grand, masculine wisdom told him that women had become unmanageable during the twentieth century. Somehow, somewhere, sometime, men were going to have to put their feet down again and exert a little male authority. It was ridiculous that a woman, even a businesswoman, could take an extended lunch with a client and then turn around and take an extended dinner with him, too.

The phone rang as Zac was mentally listing his grievances. Irritated, he stood up, scooped up the glass of tequila, and went into the kitchen to answer it. The voice on the other end was Carla's.

"Hi, Zac. Is Guinevere there?"

"No, she is not. Apparently lunch turned into dinner."

"What does that mean?"

"I haven't seen her since this morning. Every time I called Camelot Services today, you informed me she was at lunch with a prime client. Remember?"

"I remember. You sound annoyed, Zac."

"Possibly because I am annoyed. It is eight o'clock at night and I still haven't seen your sister."

"Hmmm. She should have been home by now."

"Tell me about it." He took a swallow of tequila.

"Well, we can commiserate together," Carla said with an air of resignation. "I can't locate Mason, either. We were supposed to have dinner together. I was going to coach him on how to handle the interview with the reporter from the *Review-Times*. Maybe he got caught up in his work."

Zac's brows came together in a heavy line as he considered that bit of information. Automatically he glanced through the mini blinds to check Mason's studio. The window was unlit, but there was still enough lingering daylight to let him see that the apartment across the street was empty. "He's not working. I can see the studio from here."

There was a pause from Carla's end of the phone. "Interesting. I wonder where he could be? Do you suppose he and Guinevere have, uh, gone out to dinner together?"

"Why would they do that? Especially if Mason had a date with you?"

"I don't know," Carla admitted.

There was another long pause as they both considered the various possibilities. Zac's frown deepened. "Hang up, Carla. I want to call my answering service. I didn't do it earlier because I got back to the office late this afternoon and I didn't want to deal with any business until tomorrow morning."

"Doesn't Gertie have Gwen's number?"

"Yes, but she wouldn't necessarily try to contact me here unless I gave her specific instructions to do so. Hang up. I want to check."

"Okay. Zac, let me know if you find either of them."

"I will." Zac cut the connection and redialed. "Gertie? This is Zac. Any messages?"

"Gwen called around five o'clock. Said to tell you to contact either her or Mason Adair when you got back to the office. I tried your office around five fifteen and again at five thirty. You weren't there. I thought you would call in before now." Gertie sounded defensive.

Zac rubbed the back of his neck while he contemplated Mason's empty studio. "Don't worry about it, Gertie. Did she say where she was when she called?"

"I'm afraid not, Mr. Justis."

"All right. Thanks for the message." He let the receiver drop into the cradle. If Gwen hadn't stipulated where he was supposed to call, then he had to assume that she had been calling from either her office or her apartment. She was in neither of those locations now. And Mason Adair was not in his studio.

Uneasily Zac gazed around the kitchen, wondering if Gwen had been standing here when she made the call. It was a possibility. He stood silently, aware of the utter lack of Gwen's presence. Where the hell could she be at this hour of the night? Surely she and Adair hadn't decided that they were more than two ships passing in the night, after all. It didn't make any sense. There was no way on earth Gwen could respond in bed the way she did to him, Zac told himself, and then turn around and jump into Mason Adair's arms.

Besides, he'd seen the way Adair had looked at Carla the last time they were together. The artist definitely had his eye on the younger Jones sister.

Damn it, Zac thought, *I'm letting my imagination run wild.* Maybe what he needed was another shot of tequila. His eyes went to the cupboard that held the Jose Cuervo, and for some reason he noticed that the coffee machine was minus its pot.

No loss, Zac told himself as he glanced around the small room, looking for it. With any luck the sucker was broken and Gwen wouldn't be able to replace it. It would be tough to find a replacement for that idiotically designed pot. Out of curiosity he opened the cupboard under the sink and saw the broken pieces of glass in the trash can. He could imagine Gwen's irritation. She had really liked the looks of that coffee machine.

He sniffed and wrinkled his nose. He could do Gwen a favor and empty her trash. It was getting a little strong. Zac reached down and pulled the plastic sack out of the can. Another unpleasant whiff made him turn his head the other way and twist the top of the bag firmly shut.

Zac was halfway to the door when he realized that, as unpleasant as the smell was, it didn't remind him in any way of garbage. He paused and cautiously opened the sack. He couldn't identify the odor, and that was beginning to bother him. It seemed to cling most strongly to a couple of pieces of paper towel. Perhaps Guinevere had spilled something and used the paper towels to wipe up the mess or clean her hands. But Zac couldn't think of anything she had around the apartment that would give off this acrid, penetrating odor. Thoughtfully he closed the bag and went out into the hall to dump it down the garbage chute.

When he was finished, he locked Guinevere's door and headed for Mason's apartment. There might be something there that would give him a hint of where Mason, at least, had gone.

But Adair's apartment was as empty as it had looked from Guinevere's window. After letting himself inside Zac spent a few minutes wandering around, trying to understand the new sense of tension he was feeling. He was near Adair's worktable when he caught the faint trace of the same smell he had discovered in Gwen's trash can.

Zac came to an abrupt halt, a painful sense of alertness jolting through him. For a few seconds he stood quite still. Then he went to work, looking for the source of the smell. A few minutes later he realized it was lingering around the workbench itself, as though something had been spilled on the paint-stained wood and had dried. He leaned closer and inhaled carefully.

His head swam sickeningly for a few seconds. Stepping back, Zac turned and went through the apartment with quick, long steps. Nothing. Absolutely nothing except that damned odor.

Guinevere and Mason had disappeared, and both had probably been in their own apartments as recently as late this afternoon. The lingering odor was the only link.

Zac closed his eyes briefly, trying to fight back the knowledge that he knew he couldn't avoid. Then he reached for Adair's phone to call Carla's Capitol Hill apartment.

"Carla? Any word?"

"You mean from Mason? No. Zac, what's wrong?"

"I don't know. Look, I'm going to call Gertie and tell her to ring your number if she gets any more messages."

"All right, but why, Zac?"

"I'm not sure yet," he said honestly. "But I want to do some looking around. If you don't hear from me by midnight, I want you to contact the police. Tell them everything you know about the mess Adair's in and have them check out the Sandwick place. Got that?"

"Yes, but, Zac, what's *wrong*?"

"Nothing, I hope."

But he wasn't feeling so hopeful as he placed the call to Gertie and then loped downstairs to where he'd parked the Buick. He drove first to his own apartment in a tower of condominiums that overlooked Elliott Bay. Leaving the Buick in the loading zone, he took the elevator to the ninth floor.

He was getting accustomed to living with Guinevere's bright color scheme, Zac realized absently as he retrieved his small Beretta from under the bathroom sink. The subdued browns and grays of his own apartment seemed dull to him now. Then, again, life in general would seem very dull without Guinevere Jones.

On the other hand, he decided grimly, going swiftly down the hall to the elevators, she didn't have to go to these lengths to liven things up for him.

The decision to check out the Sandwick house was based as much on guesses and a hunch as on anything else. But Zac had relied on such a nonscientific approach often enough in the past. He just wished to hell he'd started putting the guesses together into a hunch before now. As usual he'd been a little slow getting to the final conclusion. Now he had to make certain Guinevere didn't pay for his slowness.

During the drive to the house on Capitol Hill, Zac was aware of two things. One was that it was almost dark now. The other was that he was calming down as his mind and body slipped into the familiar, cold, savagely alert state. He knew this condition, and he didn't like it. It was almost painful. He'd experienced it too often in the past. He'd assumed that when he'd left his job with the international security firm and started his own business, he would never again know this kind of acute awareness. What could be so dangerous about analyzing white-collar-business security problems?

It only went to show, Zac decided, that life was full of surprises.

Guinevere wasn't sure she had regained consciousness. She knew she had her eyes open, but the oppressive darkness surrounding her was as thick and menacing as that which she had known when she'd passed out.

She was aware of an uncomfortable, binding feeling on her wrists and ankles and finally decided she must have been tied hand and foot. The floor on which she lay was cold and damp.

At least there wasn't a gag across her mouth. But that was probably because no one would hear if she chose to scream. She lay still for a moment, listening. She thought she heard someone else's steady breathing.

"Is anyone there?" Her throat felt dry and raspy.

"Gwen? Are you awake?"

"Mason. My God, where are you?"

"A few feet away from you, I think. I can't move. They've got me tied up."

"Are you all right?"

"Yeah, I think so. What a fool I was. Zac was right. I should have let him go to the cops."

"I'm not sure it would have done much good. Who could have predicted things would turn this nasty? We all assumed it was just a case of harassment and vandalism." She struggled to find a slightly more comfortable position and felt something scrape against her thigh. "My head hurts."

"Mine, too. Probably from that stuff they used to knock us out."

"We're talking about Valonia and Baldric, right?"

"Afraid so," Mason agreed wearily. "I got back to my studio this afternoon and found another painting defaced. I called Zac, and when there was no answer, I called you. As soon as I hung up the phone, they jumped me. They must have been hiding in the bathroom."

"Have they gone crazy?"

"Looks like it. I told you, they always did take that damned occult stuff too seriously. I think they've gone absolutely bonkers."

"Where are we?"

"I'm not sure," Mason admitted, "but at a guess, I'd say it's the basement of the Sandwick house."

"Good grief." The object in her skirt pocket poked through the fabric, making Guinevere wince. She tugged at the skirt with her bound hands, trying to pull the pocket out of the way. When she got a grip on the fabric, she suddenly remembered that she had put something in that pocket just before she'd gone unconscious. Laboriously she inched the skirt around her waist until she could get her fingers into the pocket. She touched the heavy shard of glass. "Hmmm."

"What's wrong?"

"Everything. But I just found a piece of glass. In the movies people always seem able to cut through their bonds with handy little things such as this."

"Maybe if I can get closer to you, I can help. It's damn sure worth a try."

Guinevere heard him shift about in the darkness, trying to maneuver himself toward the sound of her voice. "Over here," she whispered.

"Keep talking. I can't see a thing."

Guinevere turned on her side, trying for a better angle of attack against the ropes that bound her. Her face brushed fabric, and she sucked in her breath in alarm.

"What is it?"

"Just fabric. Feels like velvet. Must be the drapes Zac told us about." She went to work on the ropes again. It didn't take long before she realized that in spite of what happened in the movies, cutting through tough rope with a piece of glass was neither a speedy nor a simple proposition.

"What do you think they're going to do with us, Gwen?"

"That," answered Guinevere with great depth of feeling, "is something I don't want to think about. The real question is how long it's going to take Zac to realize something's wrong."

"Even if he does realize it, how can he put two and two together and figure out where we are?"

"Zac is very good at putting two and two together. Eventually."

Zac took his usual route through the weed-strewn, languishing backyards that were such a prominent feature on the dilapidated block of old houses. There were lights on in one or two of the structures, but for the most part everything looked as vacant at this hour of the evening as it did at three in the morning. A fat gray cat meowed questioningly at him, and he thought he recognized the animal as belonging to Abby Kettering, but he couldn't be sure. It disappeared in search of more interesting night prey.

From the shelter of the precariously tilting garage of the house next door to the Sandwick place, Zac stood watching for a time. There were no lights on in the Sandwick house, even though it was dark, but there was activity. Occasionally he thought he caught the brief flicker of a flashlight. It never lasted long. Whoever was in the house was depending mainly on the limited light from the street. They obviously did not want to attract attention.

Of course, Zac reminded himself, down in the basement they could have all the light they wanted. No one would ever be aware of it. No one would be aware of anything that went on in that basement. Not for a long time.

As he watched, a long-haired, burly figure dressed in pants and what appeared to be a sweatshirt moved along the side of the house, heading toward the kitchen door. With that long stride it was probably a man. The kitchen door opened and closed behind him.

Zac waited a few more minutes and then eased forward, hugging what cover he could find. When he reached the Sandwick house, he stayed in the shadows near the kitchen door and paused again, listening. The faint sound of voices came from inside the darkened kitchen, but he couldn't make out the words.

He waited until the voices stopped. The next sound was of a heavy door being opened and closed inside the kitchen. Zac knew it had to be the door to the basement. Silence reigned.

Zac was about to let himself into the kitchen and deal with whatever he found there when a faint scraping sound made him halt. The kitchen door swung open, and a man stepped out to look around. The figure was dressed in a dark robe, the cowl of which was pulled forward, almost completely concealing the face. The hem of the garment fell to his sandaled feet.

Zac didn't hesitate. He stepped forward quickly as the hooded figure glanced in the other direction. The other man never made a sound as Zac snapped the heel of his hand against his throat. Zac caught his victim as the dazed man sank slowly toward the ground. With any luck he wasn't unconscious, just temporarily voiceless.

The robed figure was heavy, but when Zac dragged him into the concealment provided by a tree at the back of the yard, he knew the guy wasn't heavy enough to be the same man as the one who had surprised him in the basement. Zac twisted his arm around the dazed man's throat and held the nose of the Beretta against his neck, making sure his victim felt the cold steel as he groaned and opened his eyes.

"What the hell . . . ? Who are you?"

Zac reached out and shoved back the hood. "Strangely enough, I was going to ask you the same question. But not now."

"If you're police, you got no business here. This is a private religious ceremony. We aren't doing anything wrong."

"Sure. Unfortunately for you, I'm not from the police. Now tell me exactly what is going on in that place and tell me quickly. Start with your job. What the hell are you supposed to be doing all dressed up like something out of the Middle Ages?"

"I don't have to tell you a damned thing!"

"True, but if you don't, I'll slit your throat and try someone else who might be a little more cooperative." Zac kept the gun in place while he flicked open the pocketknife he held in his other hand. He sensed the man's startled reaction. A knife against the throat sometimes had more impact than a gun. Zac wasn't sure why this should be so, but he'd seen the phenomenon before this.

"You wouldn't . . . you can't . . . Look, I don't know what you want, but you got no business here. We aren't hurtin' anything."

Zac let the tip of the blade sink into a few layers of skin. He knew he drew a little blood. "One more time. Like I said, if you're not feeling chatty, I'll get rid of you and try someone else."

Something about his voice must have gotten through to the man.

Zac had seen that phenomenon before, too. Perhaps it was because the utter lack of emotion in the words told the victim very clearly that Zac would carry out the threat. Zac knew he lacked Guinevere's empathic charm, but there were other ways to communicate.

"Look, I'm just the doorman, you know? I keep watch on the door before the ceremony starts. Make sure only members get inside. That's all."

"And that's what you're supposed to do tonight?"

"Well, yeah. This is just another meeting tonight." The man sounded shaken. He also sounded as if he were lying. Zac had heard a lot of people lie.

"And you're assigned to watch the door. How many people are due tonight?"

"The usual."

Zac let the knife sink in a little deeper. "How many?" he repeated very calmly.

"Seven in all, counting me and the honcho who's supposed to show up. I swear it. Seven."

"And how many are already in the house?"

"Five. The special guy isn't here yet."

"Fine," said Zac. "I think I'm beginning to get the picture. A few more questions and this will all be over."

"But I don't know anything else," the man protested. "I keep telling you, I'm just the doorman, and this is just a private religious thing."

"You'd be surprised at how much inside information your average doorman picks up in the course of his nightly work."

Guinevere was making slow but steady progress on the ropes. Mason was huddled next to her in the darkness, unable to be of any real assistance but doing his best to provide moral support when the door above the basement stairs opened. Instantly Guinevere froze as a nameless dread went through her. From sheer instinct both she and Mason pretended to be still unconscious.

In the oblong patch of dim light above the stairs she could see the shadowed outline of a figure in a cowled robe. The man's face was in total darkness. He paused to light the candle he held in his hand, and then he came slowly, majestically, down the steps. He was followed by a smaller figure, also dressed in a robe, and then the door closed again.

The flickering flames of the candle guided the two newcomers down the steps and over to the altar. Guinevere wondered why no one was using a flashlight. Maybe it didn't fit the image.

The figures talked in subdued tones to each other as they moved around the altar, setting up two more candles in tall black candlesticks. They paid no attention to Guinevere or Mason, who huddled, unmoving, on the floor a few feet away. The light of the candles was barely enough to reach their feet.

A heavy metal bowl was set at the head of the long stone table. Beside it a huge knife with a curved blade was set. Guinevere shivered. She felt rather than heard Mason catch his breath.

"All is ready?" The voice was definitely Baldric's. There was an unnatural formality about the words.

"It is ready. Soon the ceremony may begin," responded Valonia in oddly serene tones. "We will start when the last of them arrives."

"He will be here tonight," Baldric told her. "He says it is time he revealed himself to us. The hour has arrived."

"Excellent. We owe him much. His guidance has been invaluable. It has made all the difference. The Dark Power will be pleased."

"It is especially fitting tonight. The ultimate sacrifice is finally ready. We have been a long time preparing."

Baldric turned his cowled head toward Guinevere and Mason. The flame of the candle cast a long, evil light over his features for a brief moment. In that moment Guinevere was certain she saw madness on the face of another human being. She was assimilating the horror of it when both Valonia and Baldric turned away to fetch a large canvas out of the shadows near the staircase. She couldn't see the painting, but it didn't take much effort to guess that it was *Glare*. The painting was hauled over near the altar. It was obviously scheduled to be part of the ceremony.

The door at the top of the stairs opened again. Slowly a parade of three cowled figures came down the steps. They filed into the basement in eerie silence, guided by the candles on the stone table. The door closed with awful finality. The robed figures moved to stand in a small semicircle, and then they began to hum.

For some reason Guinevere thought the tuneless humming was the worst of all. It made no sense. It grated on the ears. It rasped against her nerves. And it never stopped. She wanted to scream. Instead she went back to work with the glass shard. At least the cowled figures were ignoring her and Mason for the time being. The black shadows hid her efforts. She was almost through the rope now. She didn't want to think of how little good all the effort might do. The odds of her and Mason getting out of this room alive were depressingly slim. She wondered what Zac was thinking about her long absence. More importantly, what was he doing about it?

The humming continued for what seemed an endless length of time, and then the door at the top of the stairs opened once more. The noise of the humming rose several notches as another robed figure appeared above the small crowd in the basement. Slowly the other figure started down. Behind him another cowled figure closed the door and came down the steps.

Baldric's voice rose above the humming. "Welcome, my lord," he said gravely to the first man as he reached the bottom of the steps. Baldric didn't pay any attention to the last figure, who took a place at the edge of the circle.

The new figure did not respond, but he inclined his head in regal acceptance of Baldric's words.

"We would have you stand at the head of the altar, my lord." Baldric lifted his arms, and the humming crowd parted to allow the honored figure to move toward the far end of the stone table.

Then Valonia stepped toward the heavy metal bowl and dipped a flaming candle into the center. With a flash of light and a sharp, crackling sound, flames leapt into existence in the bowl.

Guinevere felt her hands come free at that moment. A sob of relief almost escaped her. She touched Mason's arm. He started and then moved his bound arms slightly so that she could reach his ropes.

Around the altar the ceremony began. The humming ceased as Baldric led his small audience in a chorus of strange phrases repeated in an even stranger language. It was obvious that the silent man who stood at the far end of the altar was a special participant. Guinevere remembered what Baldric and Valonia had said earlier about his arrival. This was someone they had never met in person and who was here tonight to reveal himself for the first time.

The dark proceedings continued. The responses of the cowled figures grew louder and a fierce, morbid excitement filled the air. Someone struck a harsh note on a brass gong. At one point *Glare* was lifted up onto the altar and slashed with ritualistic motions.

Guinevere didn't want to think about what was going to be put on the altar after the painting had been dealt with. She was going to have to do something quickly. These people were working themselves up into a frenzy of some sort. Given the presence of the naked blade near the bowl of fire, she could just imagine what was scheduled to happen. The bonds around Mason's wrists came free just as

Valonia lifted the knife and passed it through the fire. Baldric started a new, more menacing litany. Guinevere's hands closed around the hem of the black velvet curtain. Silently she guided Mason's fingers to the fabric. When she tugged suggestively at the velvet a few times, he got the message.

Baldric lifted his arms high into the air and called out something totally incomprehensible. Then he whirled and pointed at Guinevere and Mason.

"We will begin with the woman. Bring her forth!"

Two cowled figures detached themselves from the circle and moved forward. Guinevere's hands tightened around the hem of the drape. It would have to be now or never.

"Freeze." Zac's voice cut through the horrifying scene with the impact of a grenade, shattering the awful illusion. "I will shoot whoever moves. And then I will kill your honorable guest attendee. Is that very clear to each and every one present?"

Every cowled head in the room swung around to stare at Zac, who had thrown back his hood. He had his arm around the guest's throat, and even in the flickering firelight it was quite possible to see the wicked looking Beretta in his other hand. For the span of a few seconds stunned silence prevailed. Zac took command, pointing the Beretta at Baldric. "Back against the wall. First you, Baldric, and then the others. Move."

"This is impossible. You can do nothing. You'll never get out of here alive." But Baldric inched slowly backward.

Guinevere, her feet still tied, struggled frantically with her remaining bonds. Mason was doing the same.

"Zac," Guinevere called in breathless relief, "I'm almost out of these ropes. Just a few more seconds."

"As soon as you and Adair are free, get over here."

"We're on our way, Zac." She tugged violently at the ropes.

"No! I will not allow this. You insult and mock the Dark Powers, and you shall not escape!" Valonia's voice was a scream of rage.

"Wait, don't do anything," yelled a new voice. It was the man Zac was holding hostage. "Let them all go. He'll kill me. He means it."

"The Dark Powers will protect you if you have served them as faithfully as you claim!" Valonia yelled back. She lifted the knife in her hand.

"She's right!" Baldric screamed. "Take him. Rush the fool. He cannot stand against all of you at once. *Take him*."

There was a stumbling, awkward movement from the other figures, a couple of which had been trying to sidle toward the steps.

"I mean it," Zac said with startling calm. "I will kill the first one who tries."

It was Valonia who moved. Seizing the long, curved knife, she whirled toward Mason, who was still struggling with his ropes. In that moment the others seemed to gather their courage. There was a concerted rush, not toward Zac but toward the door. In the resulting confusion Zac was denied a clear shot at Valonia. But Baldric's hand came out of the depths of his robe holding an automatic. Firelight flickered on the short barrel, and Zac caught sight of the gleaming metal. He fired. Baldric screamed and fell backward.

The man Zac was holding tried to dart away in the chaos. Zac used the heel of his hand on the man's jaw, and the figure crumpled to the floor.

Even as she heard Baldric's scream, Guinevere saw Mason twist away in an effort to protect himself, his face a mask of shock and fear. She couldn't reach Valonia in time, and neither could Zac.

"Valonia, stop!" Guinevere pulled furiously on the heavy velvet drapes. They tumbled down in a cascade of thick, smothering fabric, blanketing Valonia, Guinevere, and Mason in a dusty shroud.

"Gwen!"

"In here, Zac." Guinevere shoved at the heavy drapes, emerging at last just as Zac reached her. There was a steady, thudding sound on the stairs as the escaping ceremony attendees made for the only exit.

Zac threw Guinevere a quick glance as he hauled the drapes off Mason and Valonia. She looked all right, and so did Mason. Valonia lay on the cold floor, screaming curses. The knife was not in sight. It had apparently been knocked from her grasp by the falling weight of the drapes.

"Hurry," Zac muttered as he cut Mason's ropes. "For Pete's sake, Gwen, get moving!"

"What's that smell? Zac! Something's on fire."

"The drapes."

Guinevere glanced around and saw the flames from the metal bowl licking hungrily at the edge of the fabric. Already they were throwing huge shadows across the room. In the fiery light she could see two still figures besides Valonia's on the floor.

"Mason, you and Gwen see if you can get Valonia up the steps. If you can't, don't worry about her. I'll see if these other two are in any shape for a little exercise. Hurry, damn it. We haven't got much time."

Guinevere and Mason grabbed Valonia. She didn't fight them. She was too busy sobbing and cursing unseen powers who had clearly let her down severely.

"It's all right," Guinevere said to Mason. "I can handle her. Help Zac."

"Right." He turned away to give Zac a hand with Baldric and the other robed man.

A few seconds later, smoke licking at their heels in choking, billowing clouds, Guinevere, Mason, and Zac made it safely up the steps and into the kitchen with their prisoners. Even as they raced out the back door the flames found the wooden steps.

By the time Zac had pounded on Abby Kettering's door and gotten her to call the fire department and the police, the Sandwick house was engulfed in flames.

In the violent glare of the burning house Mason Adair stared in stunned amazement at the face of the man who had been the honored guest at the ugly ceremony. It was his cousin, Dane Fitzpatrick.

CHAPTER 10

The postmortem was held the following afternoon at one of Pioneer Square's sidewalk taverns. Two glasses of white wine, one beer, and one tequila were ordered. Guinevere, Zac, Carla, and Mason faced each other around the table. Mason still looked dazed.

"I still can't believe Dane flipped out like that," Mason said for about the hundredth time. "I mean, I never really liked the guy, but I didn't know he was nutty."

Zac wrapped his large hand around the tiny tequila glass. "People tend to flip out and get very nutty when big money is at stake."

"But how did you realize Dane was behind the whole thing?" Mason demanded.

"Partly the timing and partly the fact that there was too much money floating around. It was just too damn much of a coincidence that someone was shelling out fifty-five grand in cash for the old Sandwick place right around the time private investigators were asking questions about it and you. Add to that the fact that Dane knew where you were at least six months ago but didn't bother to contact you until this week." Zac paused for another swallow of his drink. "The way I figure it, he couldn't believe his lucky stars when you and your father quarreled and you got yourself stricken from the will. All of a sudden Fitzpatrick was your father's heir, potentially several times richer than he ever dreamed he'd be."

"But," said Guinevere, "that money was going to come to him only if your father died before you and he reconciled. Dane had to live with the knowledge that there was always the possibility that you and your father would repair the breech. It must have made him very nervous."

Zac nodded. "And then one day your father said he was going to try to find you. Dane knew disaster had struck. He decided the only thing he could do was find you himself and see that you suffered an unfortunate accident. He very graciously told your father that he would handle the details of hiring a private detective agency and putting them on your trail. Which he did. You weren't hard to find."

Mason shrugged. "I wasn't trying to hide. I just hadn't contacted Dad or the family."

"Fitzpatrick located you about six or seven months ago. In the course of their investigations the agency Dane had hired found out about the Sandwick house and the group you were associating with when you were holding your parties there. They probably pursued that route a while just to see if you were still involved. It would have been mentioned in the report to Fitzpatrick. Later they came up with an address for you. They probably also gave your cousin the incidental information on Barry Hodges, alias Baldric."

Mason sipped his beer thoughtfully. "They turned all the information over to my cousin, who didn't bother to tell my father."

"Exactly," Zac said. "Then he started wondering what sort of accident you might be inclined to suffer out here on the wild and wooly West Coast. Everyone back East knows we're only partially civilized here. The idea of having you perish during some grim occult ceremony appealed to him. For one thing your death couldn't be traced back to him. You had been a member of the group at one time, and as far as anyone might know, you still were. After all, it was a very secret organization. Furthermore, if you were to die because of being associated with a group like that, it would prove to your father that you really had gone off the deep end. It would strengthen Fitzpatrick's position as sole heir."

"But how did he know that the new members of the group were for real?" Carla asked quickly. "There are a lot of strange societies with odd rituals. Most of them harmless. How could Fitzpatrick have found out that Baldric and Valonia really believed in their idiotic rituals and might go in for something like human sacrifice?"

"He didn't at first. He was simply checking out various possibilities. With the information the investigators dug up for him, he was able to contact Barry Hodges, or Baldric as he calls himself. The cops told me that he and Valonia, or Valerie Martin, which is her real name, were living in a downtown flophouse at the time. After they started taking cash from your cousin, they moved out and covered their tracks."

"So Dane offered them money and they went for it?" Mason asked.

"Even leaders of insane occult societies need cash. Stone altars and private, soundproof basements don't come cheap," Zac reminded him. "As soon as Fitzpatrick contacted them, he knew he could manipulate them. He took precautions, of course. He was always just a voice on the phone who claimed to be an even more powerful witch or warlock or whatever than either Baldric or Valonia. When he told them the money was being provided by the Dark Powers, they were happy enough to believe him. After your friends split, Baldric and Valonia had picked up new members for their little club.

Barry Hodges told Fitzpatrick that they were illegally using the Sandwick house for their ceremonies and were afraid of being caught and kicked out. Once he'd heard about the house and the basement, Fitzpatrick knew it would be perfect for what he had in mind. It was worth fifty-five grand in cash. He saw the purchase as an investment in his own future, so he bought the place for them. But he didn't want Baldric and Valonia living there until after his goal was accomplished. They might have drawn too much attention to themselves and ruined everything. So Fitzpatrick made it a condition that Baldric and Valonia and their cute little group had to remain as anonymous and mysterious as possible. After six months of taking his money they were ready to go along with Fitzpatrick when he suggested that the way to become as rich and powerful as he was—"

"Was to have a human sacrifice," Carla concluded with a shudder.

"Something like that," Zac agreed. "If it hadn't worked, Fitzpatrick would have arranged some other kind of accident for Mason."

"But why did he attend the ceremony last night?" Mason asked. "Why not stay safely on the East Coast?"

"As far as your family is concerned, he was on the East Coast, supposedly vacationing briefly at his country home." Zac gave Mason a level glance. "He came to the ceremony because he wanted to make absolutely certain that the whole plan had worked. He wanted you dead, and he didn't want any slipups or surprises. Murderers tend to be obsessively thorough about the job. They might make a hundred other mistakes in the course of the crime, but they don't want to screw up the act of murder itself. He never intended to reveal himself after the ceremony, of course. He was simply going to disappear, leaving his little gang to figure out how to get rid of the body and what to do next. They were stupid enough, so they probably would have been caught eventually. But they couldn't point the finger at him. The cops would assume that the mysterious 'voice' that had told them to perform the sacrifice was just another manifestation of their craziness. But Fitzpatrick had told Baldric and Valonia that he would reveal himself after the ceremony. He had promised them that afterward they would be part of the Inner Circle or some such nonsense."

"Why did they grab Gwen?" Carla demanded, glancing worriedly at her sister.

"Because she was getting too involved in the things that were happening to Mason. And she actually saw Baldric that night Mason walked in on him in the studio. Baldric had gone there to deface another painting. He saw it as part of the ritual of preparation for the sacrifice. Baldric's one talent seems to be a certain ability with locks. Mason surprised him. Baldric panicked and slugged him. Then he looked out through the studio window and saw Gwen staring at him from her kitchen window. He and Valonia tried to warn her off—"

"The broken mirror!" Guinevere stared at Zac.

He nodded once, very grimly. "Exactly. The broken mirror. But she was a witness and appeared to be close to Mason. So in the end Baldric and Valonia convinced themselves that she had to be part of the sacrifice. I don't think Fitzpatrick knew until he showed up in the Sandwick basement last night that she was on the agenda, along with Mason. Baldric and I tangled because I surprised him while he was trying to hide *Glare*."

"Why did Dane bother to look me up at all this past week?" Mason asked curiously.

Zac shrugged. "It was a stupid move on his part and was probably connected with the obsession that made him want to be present at the ceremony. Something to do with the hunter playing with his prey. It's hard to explain, but I've seen people do it on more than one occasion." Zac paused and then said very quietly, "I've done it myself."

"Last night when you realized we'd been kidnapped, what made you head first for the Sandwick place?" Mason asked.

"It was the logical point at which to start. If there had been no sign of you there, I would have called in the cops and anyone else I could think of because, frankly, there was no other place to start looking." Zac finished the tequila in one long, heartfelt gulp. "It shouldn't be tough for the cops to find the ones who got away last night. Baldric and Valonia will talk their heads off."

"While my cousin hires the best lawyer money can buy. Probably someone from the family firm," Mason finished wryly.

"That reminds me," Carla said slowly. "The first stories have already appeared in this morning's paper. So far I've kept Mason under wraps. The press hasn't located him yet, but it won't be long. The same goes for Gwen. I think we should hold a little war council to decide how we're going to handle this. There's no way to keep it quiet."

"So much for trying to prevent gossip and scandal," Guinevere said with a sigh. "I'm sorry, Mason."

Carla lifted her chin, the light of excitement in her eyes. "Don't worry about it. The way I have it figured, we can work the whole mess to the advantage of Mason's career. I've already contacted that reporter from the *Review-Times* who wanted to talk to Mason about his art. I've promised him the inside scoop on this sacrifice story. He's thrilled. Art and music always get pushed to the second or third section of the paper. They're almost never considered front-page material. This is his chance at the big time. He's never gotten to do a front-page story before. Don't worry about the publicity. In this day and age any publicity is good publicity, if it's handled correctly. By the time I get finished handling this, Mason's going to be the hottest artist in the state. Maybe on the whole West Coast. We can generate all kinds of excitement."

Guinevere, Zac, and Mason stared at her. Finally Guinevere asked hesitantly, "Carla, are you sure you know what you're doing?"

"Positive." She jumped to her feet and reached for Mason's arm. "Come on, Mason. We need to go practice exactly what you're going to say to the reporter."

Mason grinned, obviously willing to let her take the lead. "What about Gwen?"

"Oh, I think we can keep Gwen out of this," Carla said easily. "You're the main story. Gwen will just show up as a small footnote if we handle this right."

"Mason," Guinevere said urgently as the other two prepared to depart, "did you . . . did you call your father?"

His grin faded. "This morning. I had to tell him about Dane first. I didn't want him finding out secondhand."

"How did it go? The conversation with your father, I mean," she pressed.

Mason's mouth curved faintly. "Let's just say I'm flying back East in a week or so to renew my acquaintance with my family. We'll take it from there."

"Take them one of your paintings," Zac suggested mildly.

"I'll do that. Oh, and by the way, I don't want you to think I'm not going to pay my tab. I owe Free Enterprise Security, Inc., my life. I haven't got a lot of cash on hand yet, but I've got a couple of paintings you might like. Theresa tells me that in the current market they're probably worth fifteen hundred apiece. Will that cover the bill?"

"More than cover it," Zac said with a grin. "I'll hang them in my office. I need a better view."

Zac and Guinevere watched the other two walk arm in arm down the street. For a long time silence hovered over the table. Then Zac pushed aside his empty glass.

"Ready to go home?"

"Yes."

Neither said anything else during the short walk up the street to
Guinevere's apartment. But when Zac opened the door, he said quietly, "You know, I've kind of gotten used to this place."

"Have you?" Guinevere walked into her brightly colored living
room and tossed down her shoulder bag. "I've kind of gotten used to
having you around." She smiled tremulously and turned away to
gaze out the window at the street below. A mother and two toddlers
were waiting for the bus. Zac came to stand behind Guinevere, one
hand on her shoulder. He looked down at the small family.

"Cute kids." His voice was perfectly neutral.

Guinevere took a deep breath. It was time to ask. "Zac, have you
been trying to tell me something lately?"

He frowned. "About what?"

"About children." She stood very still. "I need to know, Zac. Are
you . . . have you decided you want a family? Is that why you've
been worrying about biological clocks and babies?"

"What I want," Zac said quietly, "is you."

She let out a long sigh and leaned her neat head back against his
shoulder. "But the baby talk . . ."

"I started worrying that you might be thinking about having
kids. Every other woman I've run into lately seems to be getting
anxious. But you never said anything. I tried to get you to talk about
it. I was afraid you'd decide you want them and that I wasn't the right
man to be the father." His fingers tightened around her shoulder. "I
couldn't stand it if you went out looking for another man to be the
father."

"You don't have to worry about that, Zac," she said simply.
"Never worry about that."

"Because you don't want kids?"

"I don't have any particular desire for children. Not now. But if I ever do want them . . ." She turned into his arms and lifted her face. "Your genes are the ones I'd go after. I promise."

He relaxed, holding her close. "I'm glad to hear it."

"What about you, Zac?"

"I've told you. What I want is you."

"You don't feel any pressing need to become a father?"

He shook his head, smiling faintly. "No. But if I ever do, your genes are the ones I'll go after."

"Promise?" she asked, nestling against him.

"I swear it. No one else's would do."

"Thank you. I feel much better," she admitted honestly.

"I think," Zac said carefully, "that we've both been a little insecure lately."

"You mean, we've been jealous of each other and worrying that the other person was planning to run off and start a family with someone else."

"Like I said. Insecure." He framed her face between his hands. "Gwen . . ."

"I know, Zac. I love you."

He kissed her, all his own special needs and longing pouring over her. "That's what I've been needing to hear. I love you, Guinevere."

For a few seconds they stood there as the evening sun faded outside the window. Then Guinevere said softly, "I'd better shop for a new coffeepot tomorrow."

"New coffeepot, hell. We'll shop for a whole new machine. We'll give the other one to a thrift shop."

"But, Zac, a new machine will cost a lot of money."

"We'll take the money from the petty cash fund of Free Enterprise Security and Camelot Services. The way you use coffee machines and pots, I figure it's a business expense."

Guinevere thought about going shopping for a household appliance with Zac. There was something very pleasantly committed about the whole project. When she looked up at him, she knew Zac was thinking the same thing.

Without another word of protest, she put her arms around his neck and kissed him.

THE
FATAL
FORTUNE

CHAPTER 1

Guinevere Jones handed the sniffling young woman another tissue and waited for the newest spate of tears to halt. As she waited, she pushed the cup of tea closer to her companion's elbow, silently urging her to take another sip.

Tea and sympathy. It wasn't much to offer, under the circumstances, but until Sally Evenson had composed herself, there wasn't much else Guinevere could do. The two women were seated at the corner table in a small restaurant just off First Avenue in downtown Seattle. It was the middle of August and the temperature outside was in the mid seventies. The weather was perfect for dining at one of the outside tables, but that would be much too public for poor Sally in her present mood.

Sally Evenson had worked for Camelot Services as a temporary secretary for several months. Guinevere had sent her out on a number of jobs, and the frail-looking Sally had gained confidence and skill with each new assignment. She had been turning into one of Guinevere's most reliable temps, until disaster struck on the latest assignment. Guinevere still wasn't certain just what shape disaster had taken, because all Sally had been able to do for the past half hour was cry. Perhaps it was time to take a firm hand.

"All right, Sally, finish your tea and tell me exactly what's going on at Gage and Watson."

Sally raised her head, her eyes swollen and red. She was a young woman, twenty-three to be exact, painfully thin, and rather nervous in even the most serene situations. Some of that nervousness had been fading lately as Sally's job performance had improved. There had been a direct correlation between confidence and composure. Guinevere had been pleased at the transformation, but now it seemed all the progress had been undone.

"I can't talk about it, Miss Jones. You wouldn't understand. No one would understand. I'm sorry to bother you like this. I don't know what got into me. It's just that lately everything seems so . . . so impossible." Sally ducked her head again and blew her nose. Whatever claim to attractiveness the young woman had was submerged beneath the mournful wariness in her pale blue-green eyes and tautly drawn features. Her hair was an indeterminate shade of brown, worn in a short bob that badly needed a professional stylist's touch. She still wore her Camelot Services blazer, a smartly cut jacket of royal blue with the new Camelot Services crest on the left pocket.

Sally had fallen in love with the blazer the day Guinevere had given it to her. It was probably the most expensive garment she had ever had. Two months ago, Guinevere had hit on the idea of giving all her skilled, long-term employees jackets as a symbol of their elite status in the temporary-service field. The blazers were slowly but surely becoming an emblem of the best in temporary help in the Seattle business community. Camelot Services employees wore them with pride. It was good advertising, Guinevere told herself each time she wrote out a corporate check for another of the expensive blazers.

Guinevere took a sip of coffee and set the cup down gently but firmly. "Sally, I can't help you if you don't tell me what's going on. Now, it's been obvious for the past couple of weeks that you've developed personal problems. I do not believe in getting involved in my employees' problems—unless they affect job performance. Unfortunately, your problem has gotten to that stage. If you don't pull yourself together, I'm going to have to take you off the Gage and Watson job. You know it and I know it."

Sally stared at her with horror. "Oh, please, Miss Jones, don't do that. I love the job, and my manager at Gage and Watson says it could go on for a couple more months. I need the money. I've moved into a new apartment, and I was going to go shopping for some clothes and I wanted to buy a new stereo—"

"All right, all right," Guinevere said gently, holding up a hand to stem the flow of protest. "I realize you need the job. And I need you on it. You've been doing excellent work. Gage and Watson assures me they're very pleased. I wouldn't be surprised if when this assignment is over they offer you full-time employment."

Sally's face lit up. "Do you really think so? Oh, Miss Jones, that would be fabulous. A real, full-time job. A *career*." For a moment she was lost in blissful contemplation of a future in which she had a career.

Guinevere smiled wryly. "Gage and Watson's gain will be my loss."

Sally's excitement dissolved on the spot. Guiltily she dabbed at her eyes. "Of course. I forgot. If I were to get a full-time job at Gage and Watson I'd no longer be able to work for you on a temporary basis, would I? I'm sorry, Miss Jones, I didn't stop to think. I owe everything to you. I wouldn't dream of leaving you, after all you've done for me."

Guinevere grinned. "You most certainly will leave me, when the right full-time position comes along. It's called 'career advancement,' Sally, and, although I'll hate to lose you, I have absolutely no intention of holding you back. Don't worry. Happens all the time in the temporary-help field. I'm used to it." Which didn't mean she liked it, but she was businesswoman enough to accept the inevitable. Besides, sending out temps who were good enough to hire on permanently at the offices where they had been assigned was just another example of sound advertising. As she was always telling Zac, you had to look on the positive side.

Sally smiled tremulously. "You're so understanding, Miss Jones."

"I'm trying to be, Sally. I'm trying. Now, tell me what's gone wrong at Gage and Watson."

The young woman hesitated and then confided in a rush, "It's got nothing to do with Gage and Watson. Gage and Watson is a wonderful company, Miss Jones."

"Is it the people you're working with? Is some man hassling you on the job? There are laws against that, you know," Guinevere said bluntly.

"Oh, no, nothing like that." Sally gave her a pathetic glance. "I'm not exactly the sort of woman men would hassle on the job, you know."

"No, I do not know. You're an attractive, single woman. Unfortunately, job harrassment occurs even at the best firms. But if it's not the people at Gage and Watson who are causing you trouble, what is it? If it's something too personal to talk about to me, then maybe you should consider some counseling, Sally, because whatever it is, it's starting to ruin everything you've been working so hard on for the past few months."

Sally bit her lip. "I . . . I am getting counseling, Miss Jones."

Guinevere's eyebrows went up. "You are?"

"Well, of a sort. I mean, Madame Zoltana is a kind of counselor.

She's very intelligent, and she . . . she sees things, you know? But she's kind of expensive, and lately I've been having to see her a lot." Sally reached for a few more tissues to blot the new flow of tears.

"Madame Zoltana?" Guinevere stared at Sally. "That doesn't sound like a counselor's name or title. Who on earth is Madame Zoltana?"

"She's a psychic," Sally explained uneasily, not looking at Guinevere. "Several people at Gage and Watson go to her. Francine Bates introduced me to her a few weeks ago. She has a great gift—Madame Zoltana, that is, not Francine. It's absolutely incredible what she can see. She can tell you so many things about your past that sometimes it's frightening."

Sally looked frightened, all right, Guinevere decided abruptly. Frightened and alone in the world. A very scared young woman. "Tell me, Sally, exactly what Madame Zoltana does when you go to see her."

Sally's lower lip trembled. She stared down into her teacup. "She sees things. She warns you about things that might happen if you aren't careful. Then she . . . she helps you."

"Helps you?"

The young woman nodded bleakly. "She can sometimes change things for you. Things that . . . that might go wrong."

Guinevere swore silently to herself. "And she'll help you avoid these things that might go wrong, as long as you continue seeing her on a regular basis, I suppose?"

Sally nodded, looking up with a kind of sad fear in her tear-filled eyes. "I do try to see her regularly, Miss Jones. But as I said, she's very expensive, and last week when I explained to her that I might not be able to pay her fees, she said that unless I did, the most awful thing would happen."

"What did she say would happen, Sally?"

Sally Evenson collapsed into fresh tears. When she finally stopped crying, she told Guinevere exactly what threat hung over her frail, young head.

Guinevere was still fuming when she got back to the office an hour later. Trina Hood, the temp Guinevere used to help out in Camelot Services' own offices, looked up with a cheerful smile.

"Mr. Justis called. He said to remind you that you promised to help him deal with the caterer tonight after work. I think he's getting nervous, Miss Jones."

"Zac hasn't ever given an office reception," Guinevere explained mildly as she sat down at her desk and sifted through a small stack of messages. "He's going through the usual party-giver's panic, wondering if he'll wind up spending a fortune on food and champagne and have no one show up. Did he say what time he wanted to meet me?"

Trina nodded. "He said he'll come by to collect you around five."

"Collect me?"

"I think that was the word he used. He instructed me not to let you get away."

Guinevere smiled fondly. "Poor Zac. Amazing how a man with all his talents is reduced to fear and trembling by the mere thought of giving a party. Anything else crucial happen while I was gone?"

"Two more calls for clerks needed for vacation fillins. I've already contacted two people in our files. Both said they'd report to work at the firms tomorrow morning."

"Great." Guinevere smiled approvingly at Trina. She had used a handful of different people from her own staff during the past few weeks, in an attempt to find someone who would work out on a full-time basis. After her sister Carla had left to set up her own art gallery in Pioneer Square, Guinevere had discovered just how much she had come to rely on full-time office help at Camelot Services.

Trina Hood was showing definite potential. She was a pleasant woman in her mid-forties who had recently been divorced and now had two children to raise alone. There was a certain comfortable plumpness about her, and she had an excellent telephone voice. She was also a hard worker and anxious to please. As she had explained to Guinevere, she had been out of the work force for almost ten years, and she had been terrified of the prospect of having to find a job. She had decided to start out as a Camelot temp, to get her feet wet in the business world. She had walked through the doors of Camelot Services on the very day Guinevere had acknowledged to herself that she wasn't going to be able to get by with part-time help. Guinevere had grabbed her.

"What about Gage and Watson, Gwen? Want me to find someone to replace Sally Evenson?" Trina asked quietly. She was well aware that things were shaky.

Guinevere thought for a moment. "No," she said finally, "I think I'll go over to Gage and Watson myself for a few days. Something is bothering Sally, and I want to check out the situation there. Can you find her another short-term assignment? She needs to work."

Trina nodded. "Gallinger Industries needs a typist for a few days."

"Put Sally on it."

"I don't get it. You're going to go into Gage and Watson yourself?"

"That's right. I'll tell Gage and Watson that Sally is ill and that I'm her replacement."

"Well, all right, but I don't understand why you want to take one of your own temporary assignments. What about running things here?"

"For that I'll rely on you, Trina."

Zac showed up in the doorway of Camelot Services at five minutes after five. It was obvious he had walked straight down the hill from his own small office in a Fourth Avenue high-rise. He had his conservatively tailored jacket hooked over one shoulder. His crisp, white shirt fit him well, emphasizing the solid, compact strength of his shoulders and the flat planes of his stomach.

Zachariah Justis, president and sole employee of Free Enterprise Security, Inc., would never win any male beauty contests. The first time Guinevere met him, she had labeled him a frog. It wasn't that he was as ugly as a frog, it was just that he had been surrounded at the time by a bar full of young, beautiful, upwardly mobile types, and in their midst he had stood out quite prominently. Add to that the fact that shortly after he'd introduced himself to Guinevere, he'd coerced her into helping him in an investigation, and one could understand why she had been less than enthusiastic about Zac Justis.

Zac was just under six feet tall, a compactly built man with short, almost military-style night-dark hair and cool, ghost-gray eyes. He was thirty-six years old, but it had struck Guinevere on occasion that those years must have been years of hard-fought experience. Sometimes she wanted to ask him more about his past, but he usually showed no interest in discussing it, so she tended to back off the subject. Among the few facts she did know was that Zac had spent several years working for a large multinational security firm before starting his own small business in Seattle.

She could guess at some aspects of his past, because she had witnessed some of his more unique skills. She had, for example, seen him make the transition from businessman to cold, lethal hunter on more than one occasion, and it gave her chills to think of the kind of life he must have led before settling down in Seattle. Guinevere still wasn't certain why she had fallen in love with the man. She only knew that her life was never going to be the same now that Zachariah Justis was in it.

They had begun their relationship as adversaries, but the tension between them had quickly exploded into passion. Passion had led to an affair and then to love. It was a very new, cautiously admitted love, something that they had both finally acknowledged only a couple months previously. They didn't talk about it very much. There was still a sense of wonder and uncertainty about the relationship, as far as she was concerned. In true male fashion, however, Zac seemed to take everything for granted now. That was typical of Zac. He had a blunt, straightforward approach to most things—including, apparently, falling in love.

Guinevere reminded herself on occasion that there was much she didn't know about Zachariah Justis. The reverse was true, too, but Guinevere doubted that a complete résumé of her past would contain any earthshaking surprises for Zac. However, she wondered what she would learn if she were to see a detailed résumé of *his* past. She told herself philosophically that the early stages of love were a time of discovery. It was not a time to be rushed. She would continue feeling her way, learning what she could about Zachariah Justis.

"The caterer said he'd see us at five thirty," Zac announced as he came through the door. "Let's get going."

"Relax, Zac. He's only a couple of blocks away. We'll get there in plenty of time." Guinevere picked up her shoulder bag and glanced around the office. "Besides, I want to talk to you. I need some professional advice."

Zac waited impatiently by the door, his eyes turning suddenly suspicious. "Professional advice? What sort of advice? Gwen, I don't want you getting mixed up in any more crazy investigations. I can find my own clients. I don't need you to dig up more work for me."

She smiled in what she hoped was a reassuring way. "Calm down. I'm not asking you to take on any investigations. This one I'm going to handle on my own. I just want some advice from you, that's all." She playfully pushed him out into the hall and locked the office door.

"Gwen, I mean it, I've got enough to do during the next couple of weeks without having to chase after you trying to keep you out of trouble. I've got this damn reception to plan, and the move to my new office to supervise. On top of everything else, I'm supposed to be interviewing for a secretary. That reminds me—why haven't you sent anyone over for me to talk to?"

"I'm still selecting the final candidates. A good secretary is hard to find, Zac. It takes time. Trust me."

"Uh-huh. Are you sure you're not being a little too picky?" He took her arm and steered her forcefully down the stairs and out onto the sidewalk.

"Zac, I have to be picky. You're not going to be the easiest man to work for, you know. You need someone calm and unflappable. Someone with a good personality, so that she can handle your important clients properly. You also need someone who can do your typing, handle your accounts, and present a good image."

"Damn it, Gwen, I just want a secretary, not a presidential aide."

"Don't worry, Zac, I'll send someone over soon. Now, about my little problem—"

"Guinevere, I have learned through hard experience that your problems are rarely *little*."

"Don't sound so abused. I'm not going to involve you in this. I've told you, I just want some advice. Now, here's the situation: I think one of my employees has become the victim of a very subtle, very cruel protection racket."

Zac slid her a sidelong glance. "Are you kidding?"

"No. Listen to this and tell me what you think. I sent a young woman over to Gage and Watson a few weeks ago."

"The electronics firm?"

Guinevere nodded. "Someone in her office turned her on to a psychic, a character who goes by the name of Madame Zoltana. Madame Zoltana agreed to see her initially for a small consulting fee, but after a couple of visits she revealed to poor little Sally that she knew Sally had gotten pregnant when she was seventeen."

"Oh, hell." Zac sounded as if he knew what was coming.

"Sally was flabbergasted. It seemed to prove that Madame Zoltana really knew her stuff. But it didn't stop there. Zoltana also knew that Sally had given the baby up for adoption. You have to understand, Zac, that the experience nearly devastated Sally. She's a fragile person in the first place. Finding herself pregnant and abandoned at seventeen nearly caused her to commit suicide. She was talked into having the baby by one of those antiabortion groups. They promised her that once she gave the baby away she would be free to rebuild her own life. Sally did exactly that. It's been a long, slow process. Because of the baby, she was forced to drop out of school. She had to complete high school through a GED program. Her parents disowned her, and she was left destitute. It's a sad story. Suffice it to say that she's gradually pulled herself back together. A few months ago she came to work for me, and she's shown remarkable improvement on the job. She's starting to come into her own at last."

"Guinevere, the social worker," Zac commented dryly.

"I'm serious, Zac. That young woman really started to get her act together during the past few months. For the first time since she was seventeen, she's beginning to see a future for herself. But she's still very fragile, Zac. Now along comes this screwy Madame Zoltana and warns her that her whole world is about to fall apart again."

"How?"

Guinevere drew a deep breath. "She told Sally that unless Sally kept coming to her on a regular basis, the baby she gave away when she was seventeen would someday learn who its natural mother is, come looking for her, and ruin Sally's life. For the right price, Madame Zoltana says, she can prevent that from happening with her psychic powers. Poor little Sally is absolutely terrified."

Zac whistled softly. "I'll be damned. That's pretty grim, all right. What a racket."

"That's exactly what it sounds like to me, a sleazy sort of protection racket. Madame Zoltana finds some useful secret in a person's past and then offers 'protection'—for a price."

"And the price is continued visits to Madame Zoltana at very high fees."

"Exactly." Guinevere lifted her chin determinedly. "I can't allow that sort of thing to happen to one of my employees on the job, Zac. I'm going to find out what's going on and expose the whole sordid mess. That Madame Zoltana deserves to be hung."

Zac sighed. "Gwen, if people are stupid enough to believe in psychics and dumb enough to pay them, there's just not much you can do about it. About all you can do is explain to Sally what's going on, and hope she'll be smart enough to believe you."

"Poor Sally is too distraught to know what to believe. I've got to prove Zoltana is a fraud."

"Be reasonable, Gwen. How are you going to do that?"

"The way I figure it," Guinevere said thoughtfully, "Zoltana must have some inside help at Gage and Watson. Sally's not the only G and W employee who's seeing her, and from what I can gather, a couple of the others have been getting the same treatment. Somehow, Zoltana spots the gullible ones and then finds out something she can use against them."

Zac lifted one eyebrow. "Inside help?"

"Yeah. You know, someone who works at Gage and Watson, someone who potential victims might confide in. Whoever it is then passes the information along to Zoltana. From what Sally told me today, that would seem to be the way things work."

"Gwen, do you mind if I point out that you've got a company to run? You can't make a career out of exposing fraudulent psychics, believe me. Houdini tried, and it didn't do much good. There are always going to be some people who *want* to believe in charlatans like Zoltana. As long as there are believers, there will be frauds."

"All I want is a little advice from you, Zac. I thought you could give me some pointers on how to go about exposing a fraud."

"As usual," Zac said with a long-suffering sigh, "my advice to you is to *stay out of it*. But, as usual, I suppose you won't pay any attention."

Guinevere smiled contentedly. "I knew you'd help me."

"Wait a minute. I never said I'd help."

"Now, Zac, I'm approaching you in a professional capacity here."

"The hell you are. You're just trying to get some free assistance," he shot back.

"Well, you owe me something for all the help I'm giving you planning your reception," Guinevere informed him as they reached the entrance of a trendy delicatessen-restaurant on Western Avenue. "Here we are. We can discuss my case later. Now, remember what I told you about dealing with this caterer, Zac. I don't want you making a fuss every time I mention French champagne or good pâté. If you're going to have a proper reception for your clients, you have to do it right. You must go first class."

"Easy for you to say. It's not your money."

"Quit complaining. This is going to be a wonderful party. Great PR for Free Enterprise Security."

"What if no one shows up?" he demanded, holding open the door for her.

"Then you and I will have a lot of food and champagne to take care of. Might take us the rest of the year!"

"Gwen!" Horrified, he hurried after her, catching up just as she hailed the young chef with whom they had an appointment.

"Hello, Charles," Guinevere said cordially. "I think we're ready to make the final decisions. Zac has made it clear he wants everything to be just right, so please feel free to advise us." She ignored Zac's groan of despair and led the two men toward a vacant table.

"I am sure you will be quite pleased, Mr. Justis," Charles assured him, taking out a pen and a long pad of paper. "Shall we deal with the canapés and pâtés first? We have an excellent lobster pâté I would like to suggest. It's a specialty of the restaurant, and we do it exceedingly well."

"Lobster?" Zac's voice sounded strained. *"Lobster?"*

"I think the lobster is a wonderful suggestion, Charles," Guinevere offered swiftly. "I also think we should feature some salmon, don't you?"

"Salmon is always popular," Charles agreed, scribbling rapidly. "And we do a truly superior salmon hors d'oeuvre, which features just a touch of dill and caper. I'm sure you'll like it."

Zac knew there was no room in this conversation for him. He sat back in his chair, watching dolefully as Guinevere blithely ran up the tab for the reception he was planning. Hard to believe that initially it was just an off-the-cuff suggestion he'd made, when he'd decided to move the offices of Free Enterprise Security into a suite higher up in his office building. Business had been improving for his firm lately, and Zac was anxious to move up in the world. Time to get a real office, a view, and a secretary. One had to think of the image. And wouldn't it be nice maybe to invite some of his clients to a little reception to celebrate?

Guinevere had assured him it was a brilliant notion. The next thing Zac knew he was planning a no-expense-spared party. The formal announcements had gone out last week. Guinevere had sent a clerk over to help him address the envelopes. After that, he was committed. Panic had set in almost at once. Now he was beyond panic. He had placed himself in Guinevere's hands, and Lord only knew what the result would be. One thing was certain: He was going to be a lot poorer when it was all over.

But that was the thing about Guinevere Jones. Life hadn't been the same for Zac since he had met her. And when all was said and done, he knew he wouldn't ever want to go back to the way things had been before she had entered his world. Zac tended to take a realistic, pragmatic view of life and of himself. He knew himself well enough, for example, to know he'd do anything to keep Guinevere safe. It was a measure of the differences between them that she would undoubtedly be shocked if she knew that. As far as Zac was concerned, it was just a fact of life.

CHAPTER 2

The headquarters of Gage and Watson occupied two floors in a Second Avenue high-rise that was only three blocks from Guinevere's own office. She checked in at Camelot Services to make certain Trina was on top of the early morning rush, and then she walked up the hill to Second Avenue.

It had been a while since Guinevere had gone out on one of her company's assignments. In the beginning she had done it frequently, rather than have to turn down a job from an important client. But Camelot Services was getting bigger, and her employees more diversified and efficient. It was rare these days that she found herself having to fill in on a moment's notice.

But this situation was different, Guinevere reminded herself as she walked through the revolving doors and into the two-story lobby of the building. This time she was undertaking her own investigation. This was her first, very own big case. She couldn't wait until she could put the results in front of Zac. He was going to have to admit that she had definite talent in the investigative business. Besides, she thought, as she rode the elevators up to the nineteenth floor, where she was to report in for work, this whole thing was going to be rather exciting. She would be on her own this time around. Damned if she would ask Zac Justis for any more advice. Zac could be a wet blanket at times—usually when she was really getting excited or involved in something of which he did not approve. Zac didn't seem to realize just how many things there were in this world of which he didn't approve.

On the nineteenth floor, Guinevere stepped out of the elevator into the lobby of Gage and Watson. There was the usual confusion at the reception desk while the receptionist sorted out the situation. After three phone calls the woman looked up with a cheerfully relieved smile.

"You're to report in to Miss Malcolm at the end of the hall. She's in charge of the typists and word processors."

"Thank you," Guinevere said politely, and turned in the direction indicated. She ducked into a ladies' room halfway down the hall and double-checked her appearance in the mirror. The royal blue blazer fit like a glove, nipping in slightly at her slender waist and causing her small bust to appear a bit fuller than nature had ordained. Guinevere had had her own blazer especially tailored and hadn't regretted the expense. With the blazer, she wore a narrow tan skirt that fit smoothly over her hips. She considered this portion of her anatomy a bit too well-rounded, although Zac certainly didn't seem to mind. Zac, however, tended toward an earthy view, and his taste couldn't be relied on when it came to matters of fashion and style.

Guinevere frowned slightly at her image, turning her head a little to make sure the neat coffee-brown hair was still firmly knotted at the nape of her neck. Smiling at the small Camelot Services crest on her pocket, she turned and walked out of the ladies' room—and promptly collided with the man in the corridor outside. So much for professional decorum.

"Excuse me," Guinevere mumbled hastily, disengaging herself and stooping quickly to pick up the file folder she had just dropped. "Very clumsy of me. They ought to put mirrors up across the hall, so that when you open the door, you know what's coming!"

"If I'd known who was coming out of the restroom," the man said as he bent down to help her with the folder, "I'd have made certain I was standing exactly where I was. As it is, I guess I was just lucky. Hello, Guinevere Jones. It's been a long time."

Guinevere's fingers tightened convulsively around the folder as shock went through her. She raised her head and slowly got to her feet. There were several skills one learned when one ran a service-oriented business. One of them was how to smile even though you were recovering from stunned amazement. She called upon that skill now. "Hello, Rick. What a surprise. I had no idea you worked for Gage and Watson."

"For almost a year now," Rick Overstreet answered easily. His golden-brown eyes moved over Guinevere with interested appraisal. "What are you doing here? A couple of years ago I had the impression you were planning to go into business for yourself."

Guinevere had forgotten just how intimate Rick's glances could be. He had the unsettling ability to make a woman feel pinned like a butterfly beneath his gaze. Overstreet was forty by now, she figured, and he had definitely aged well. His body was still austerely lean and obviously in good shape. He wore his expensive business suit well. The thick, tawny-brown hair was laced with a hint of gray at the temples, giving him a sophisticated, male-in-his-prime look that complemented the straight nose, firm mouth, and strong jaw. His features were regular and well fashioned, strong and masculine, but it had always been his eyes that had attracted women. Rick Overstreet had the eyes of a big, tawny cat. He also had the morals of one, as far as Guinevere was concerned.

"My business is doing fine," she told him calmly. "But we're a little busy at the moment, so I'm taking one of the field assignments. If you'll excuse me, I should be moving along. Professional temps are never supposed to be late, you know. Nice to see you again, Rick."

He smiled lazily. "How about coffee later this morning?"

"Thanks, but I'm probably going to have to work straight through," she lied. "I understand the Gage and Watson typing pool is swamped this week. I'm here to help with the overload. How's your wife?" Guinevere asked with cool bluntness.

Rick's smile disappeared, and he fished out a pack of cigarettes, the expensive French brand he had favored two years ago. "Elena died almost two years ago. Shortly after you and I stopped seeing each other, in fact." He lit the cigarette with a small gold lighter.

The news of Elena's death jolted Guinevere. "I'm sorry, Rick. I didn't know."

"It's been two years. I don't think about it too much anymore. She died in a car accident on her way to Portland to see her family."

Guinevere nodded, not knowing what to say. She had never met Elena Overstreet, hadn't known of the woman's existence until it was almost too late. "Well, good-bye, Rick. I really must be going." She turned away and moved hurriedly down the hall, aware of Rick Overstreet's golden eyes following her into a large room at the end of the corridor. The moment she was out of his sight she realized she was breathing too quickly, as if she had been running. Guinevere forced herself to take a deep, calming breath, as a businesslike, auburn-haired woman in her thirties came forward with a smile.

"You must be Miss Jones, from the agency. Very glad to see you. I understand your typing is excellent. We were worried when we learned that Sally was ill, but Camelot Services assured us someone would be along to replace her. You wouldn't happen to know anything about word processors, too, would you?"

Guinevere smiled at the familiar question. "I'm reasonably familiar with the standard office models." She glanced around and saw
what brand was in use at Gage and Watson. "I think I can manage."

"Thank goodness. We could have used you as a typist, but frankly,
you'll be far more useful on the word processor. Come over here and
meet Francine Bates. She'll show you the ropes."

Francine Bates was everyone's idea of a mother figure. Warm,
slightly plump, her gray hair worn in a soft halo around her smiling
features, she might have just stepped out of the kitchen with a tray
of cookies and milk. Guinevere remembered vaguely that Sally Evenson had mentioned her.

"Sit down, and I'll show you what we're doing," Francine invited
cheerfully. "Don't worry, Lisa," she added to the typing pool super-
visor. "I'll have her up and running in no time. Do you want her to
start on the Copperfield report?"

"That would be great," Lisa Malcolm said. "It's due on Friday."
She smiled and went off to organize the early morning chaos at the
other end of the room.

"I appreciate the help," Guinevere said, tucking her shoulder bag
into her desk drawer as she sat down in front of the word processor.

"No problem. You're from the same agency little Sally Evenson
was from, aren't you? I recognize the jacket."

"That's right. Sally had to take the rest of the week off. I'm filling
in for her."

Francine nodded. "Sally's a sweet thing, a sensitive young woman.
I've enjoyed working with her for the past few weeks. I hope she's
all right?"

"Oh, yes. Just a slight cold."

Francine clucked sympathetically as she arranged papers on
Guinevere's desk. "Such a frail little thing. Probably doesn't take
much to make her ill. I told her she wasn't eating properly. Lord knows

what she does eat. Probably just fast food. I've thought about taking her over to my sister's place on the coast for a few days. My sister's a great cook. She could put a little meat on Sally's bones. Well, back to business, here's what the big rush is all about," she went on, pointing to the papers she had placed on the desk. "This report is due on Friday. Of course, management didn't get it to us until the last minute, and there have been changes almost every day. I don't know how they expect us to do a final version by Friday, when they're probably still going to be making revisions on Thursday night. But I guess that's management for you."

"Yes," Guinevere agreed feelingly, "that's management."

The work occupied Guinevere throughout the morning. During that time she met the other people who worked in the office, all of whom were women. She was invited to accompany Francine Bates and a few of the others on coffee break in the building cafeteria and accepted the invitation with alacrity. She wanted to become part of the group as quickly as possible, not only because it was company policy for a Camelot Services employee to be friendly, but because it would be the fastest way to make contact with Madame Zoltana.

The conversation at coffee break covered everything from troublesome teenagers to the new fall styles showing up in the local department stores. Guinevere listened and participated while she sipped her coffee, but she was disappointed when no one mentioned Madame Zoltana. That was the thing about undercover investigations, she decided. You had to have patience. Hadn't Zac always told her that? Unfortunately, patience was not one of her virtues.

Guinevere glanced at her watch as she thought of Zac. She was due to meet him for lunch. She had vowed she wouldn't ask him for any more advice, but she decided to change her mind. Perhaps he could suggest some method of bringing up the subject of Madame Zoltana without arousing suspicion. She'd probably have to listen to another lecture on not getting involved, but it would be worth it if she got some useful pointers.

Zac left his office a few minutes before noon and strolled down to Second Avenue to pick up Guinevere for lunch. He was pleased with the way plans were going for his big move up. The movers had promised to arrive on the specified day, and the new furniture was already in a warehouse, waiting to be delivered. As far as Zac could see, there were no real glitches on the horizon in the moving department, but he knew that some were bound to develop. It was a law of nature.

The real problem was getting Guinevere to send him some secretarial candidates. He was beginning to think he'd made a mistake, asking her to handle the initial interviews. At the time it had seemed reasonable enough. After all, she was the expert at hiring secretaries, and she had a whole stable of them to draw on. But so far he hadn't been presented with a single live choice, and it was beginning to worry Zac. What was the holdup? He wanted the secretary to move into the new office suite on the same day that the furniture was installed. Zac liked things neat and tidy.

The August sun was heating the city to a mellow seventy-eight degrees. As he neared the high-rise where Guinevere was working, he removed his jacket and slung it over his shoulder. Perhaps it would be a good day to eat at one of the restaurants in the Pike Place Market. Zac considered the matter closely as he approached the revolving doors of the building. He was hungry. Through narrowed eyes he spotted a blue blazer among a crowd of people stepping out of an elevator, as he walked into the cool lobby.

Guinevere didn't notice him immediately. She was talking to a man who had exited the elevator beside her. Zac watched the two of them cross the wide slate lobby floor, and something tightened inside him.

Guinevere was smiling, but there was something unnatural about her normally warm, charming smile. Zac frowned at the way the man's tawny head was bent toward her. He got the impression Guinevere's companion was trying to talk her into something. Probably lunch.

Impelled by a distinctly primitive need to stake his claim in front of the other man, Zac went forward purposefully. "Hi, Gwen. Ready for lunch?" His voice was a low-pitched, gravelly sound that was meant to catch the attention of both parties. It did.

Guinevere's reaction startled Zac. She turned her head at once, something akin to relief in her eyes. Then she was hurrying toward him, her high heels clicking on the slate floor. "Oh, there you are, Zac. I'm ready." The smile was as full of relief as her eyes, and she did something she almost never did in public. She came to a halt in front of him, stood on her toes, and kissed him.

Zac recovered almost instantly from the shock and took her arm with possessive force. He was intensely aware of the tawny-haired man watching them. Zac glanced back casually as he guided Guinevere toward the door, and his gaze collided with that of the watching man. Zac decided he didn't like him at all. Coolly he turned his back on him and ushered Guinevere through the revolving doors.

"Who was that?" he asked without preamble as they reached the sidewalk.

"Nobody important. Just someone who works for Gage and Watson," Guinevere said quickly. "Where are we going?"

"How about down to the market?" Was she brushing off his question because she had no interest in the man who had stepped out of the elevator with her, or because she didn't want to discuss him?

"That sounds fine. I feel like pasta today."

"You always feel like pasta," he reminded her indulgently.

So they ate pasta in a trendy little café, and afterward they wandered back through the vegetable stalls that lined the cobbled street of the Pike Place Market. Guinevere bought two plump peaches for dessert and sliced them with a plastic knife. It was tricky eating the juicy fruit on the sidewalk, but there was something pleasantly romantic about the business, too, Zac decided. Lately he had been more and more aware of the feeling of being one half of a couple. It was the first time in his life he had felt like this. Guinevere Jones was occasionally infuriating, frequently charming, often recklessly impulsive, but above all, she was his. She belonged to him now, Zac reminded himself complacently. She was in love with him. And he was in love with her.

This business of being in love was still new to both of them, Zac realized. They were both learning the parameters of the commitment, discovering its depths, being careful not to rush through the fascinating discoveries they were making. Maybe this was the reward for waiting and falling in love in your thirties instead of at eighteen. You were more aware of the subtler aspects of the whole process. On the other hand, Zac decided, subtlety wasn't always such a great thing. It left small questions unanswered.

But there were certain straightforward questions that could still be asked. Zac finished his peach and wiped his hands on a paper napkin. "What time are you serving dinner tonight?"

Guinevere made a face. "Oh, Zac, you're so romantic."

He grinned. "You're going to owe me a lot of dinners for the next few weeks. I intend to get something in exchange for all the Free Enterprise Security cash you're spending on the party."

Trina Hood was still in the office when Guinevere returned to Camelot Services after work that day. Trina looked up with a glimmer of mischief in her eyes as her boss came through the door. "I think I've found her, Gwen."

"Found who?" Guinevere went to her desk to sort through the messages.

"The new secretary for your friend Zac."

Guinevere's head came up quickly. "You did?"

"Uh-huh. And she's perfect, Gwen. You aren't going to be able to find fault with her, the way you have with all the others. If Zac knew how many secretarial candidates you've turned down on his behalf, he'd explode."

Guinevere frowned thoughtfully, sitting down. "Now, Trina, you know I'm only trying to be careful. Zac will probably be a difficult employer. He can be short-tempered, dictatorial, and difficult. No one knows that better than I. It will take a very calm, mature person to work in his office."

Trina was trying to stifle a broad grin. "By calm, you mean placid, and by mature, you mean someone over fifty, right? You can't kid me, Guinevere Jones. You've turned down every potential candidate for a week, because each one has been cute and under thirty."

"Zac doesn't need an ex-cheerleader in his office," Guinevere informed her loftily.

"He needs someone who can type and answer phones. Ninety percent of the people you've interviewed could probably have handled the job, Gwen." Trina held up a hand. "But don't worry, I understand, even if Zac wouldn't. This time you don't have to fret. Evelyn Pemberton is exactly what you want for Zac. She's fifty-three, well-groomed, intelligent, well-mannered, and poised. She's also happily married, with grandchildren."

"How's her typing?"

Trina pretended to look surprised. "I didn't know that was as important as the fact that she's not likely to seduce Zac."

Guinevere laughed ruefully. "Have I been so obvious?"

"Just a tad, but I won't tell. Evelyn Pemberton types seventy-five words a minute. Flawlessly. I tested her on your machine."

"Okay, Trina. Set up an appointment with her for me." Guinevere leaned forward to study her calendar. "How about on my lunch hour tomorrow?"

"I already have," Trina informed her blandly. "I made one for her with Zac for the day after tomorrow."

"You're that sure?"

"I'm positive this is the one you've been looking for, Gwen. Take my word for it. But you know, you've been worrying needlessly about putting temptation in Zac's office. I've seen the way that man looks at you. He's got a one-track mind, and that applies to his love life, as well as everything else. You're the only woman on the track."

Guinevere sighed. "I just want to make sure it stays that way."

That night after dinner Guinevere told Zac she thought his opening for a secretary was about to be filled. It gave her a marvelously self-righteous feeling to be able to say that Trina Hood had found the likely candidate. This way Zac couldn't accuse her of being too picky. Curled up beside him on the black leather couch in her brightly colored apartment, Guinevere sipped a small glass of brandy and told him about Evelyn Pemberton.

"Trina said she sounds perfect. Types seventy-five words a minute and is very poised. I'm going to meet her tomorrow. If everything clicks, I'll send her over for you to interview the next day. How's that?"

Zac cradled her against his shoulder, his fingertips resting lightly over the small curve of her breast. "It's about time. What took you so long? You've got dozens of secretaries, who probably all want to go to work full time for a great employer like me."

"I wanted someone very special for you, Zac," she told him sweetly.

"I'll bet. A nice, robust, grandmotherly type, right? Has it taken you this long to find someone gray-haired and over fifty?"

Guinevere blinked. "Now, Zac . . ."

He grinned and pulled her closer. "It's all right. I understand completely. Besides, I've always had a thing for older women."

"Zachariah Justis!"

He tightened his grip as she indignantly tried to pull away. "Calm down. You didn't have to worry, you know. It wears me out just keeping up with you. I wouldn't have the energy to make it with my secretary even if she looked like a *Playboy* centerfold."

"Hah. That's what they all say."

To Guinevere's surprise, Zac took the remark seriously. "Who all says that? The guy who got off the elevator with you, maybe? I could see him having an affair with his secretary, while his wife waits at home. He looks the type."

In spite of Zac's enveloping warmth, a tiny shiver went through Guinevere. She suppressed it almost at once, but she was afraid Zac might have sensed it. "I was making a generalization," she said with a deliberate smile.

"Who is he?"

"The man on the elevator with me? His name is Rick Overstreet. I told you, he works at Gage and Watson. Want some more brandy?"

"No."

Zac hesitated, and Guinevere held her breath, afraid he was going to ask more questions. But his strong, blunt fingers slipped inside the collar of her blouse instead.

"No," Zac repeated, his voice darkening, as he began to unbutton the blouse. "What I really want at the moment is you."

Guinevere shivered again, but not from the tension connected with Rick Overstreet's name. This time it was strictly a result of the excitement that flared when Zac touched her.

"Zac," she whispered, eyes luminous, as he slipped the blouse off her shoulders.

"Come here," he murmured. "Give me something to think about besides my new secretary."

Guinevere sighed softly and went into his arms with the hot, exciting sense of abandon that always swept over her when Zac made love to her. Locked safely in his massive embrace, she gave herself wholeheartedly, rejoicing in the love that was growing steadily between them. She would let nothing interfere with this new love, Guinevere vowed silently. She would protect it and nurture it and care for it as if it were a delicate plant. She would let nothing come between herself and Zac.

The subject of Madame Zoltana came up spontaneously the next day during coffee break, when two of the women sharing the table with Guinevere and Francine Bates mentioned the psychic as they sat sipping their morning coffee. Guinevere was elated, because Zac had been singularly unhelpful in suggesting ways of steering the conversation in a specific direction. This was a stroke of luck, and it was the first break she'd had in her investigation. She tried to seize it without being too obvious.

"It's absolutely incredible, even if it is just clever guessing," confided Mary Hutchins. "I didn't believe anyone could really know that kind of stuff about a person's past, until Ruth introduced me to Madame Zoltana. It was amazing. She knew about my husband's gallbladder operation. She told me Harold had just gotten a promotion and could expect another one next year. She even knew that my mother-in-law was coming for a visit in the near future. Gives you the willies, when you think about it."

"Are you going back for another appointment?" Guinevere asked.

Mary hesitated. "I'm not sure. She told me last time she had to cut the session short because she was growing tired, but she promised me she could give me some helpful hints about decisions I'm going to have to make in the future if I returned. The thing is, I don't really believe in this psychic nonsense, but this Madame Zoltana is—well, different than I expected. She really knows things. I'm not sure if I want to go back or not."

"What can it hurt, Mary?" Francine Bates asked logically. "You might learn something useful, something that could help you."

Ruth, the other woman at the table, bit her lip but said nothing. Guinevere wondered just exactly what Ruth had been told and how often she was going to have to return to Madame Zoltana in order to keep her own personal secret from haunting her. Ruth reminded Guinevere a lot of Sally Evenson. There was that same fragile, uncertain air about both, as if they had been kicked in the teeth by life and were having a hard time recovering. Madame Zoltana was definitely not helping Sally, and Guinevere had a hunch she wasn't doing poor Ruth much good, either.

"I don't know," Mary Hutchins was saying. "I'm not sure I like this psychic business. Going once for a lark was fine, but I don't think I'll go back. It was a little spooky, if you want to know the truth." She looked at Guinevere. "What about you? Are you into the psychic bit?"

"I don't know," Guinevere said slowly, trying to sound convincingly uncertain. "I've never been to a psychic. It sounds fascinating, though." She turned to Ruth. "What do you think about this Madame Zoltana, Ruth?"

Ruth gnawed on her lower lip and studied the dregs of her coffee. "It's true," she said in a low voice. "She does see things, things she couldn't possibly know any other way except through her powers. And . . . and she tries to help."

"Help?" Guinevere prompted.

Ruth nodded slowly. "Sometimes she can use her power to . . . to change things just a little. Enough to keep them from hurting you." Ruth seemed to run out of words at that point. She lifted her head to look at Guinevere. "I don't know what to think, to tell you the truth. Would you like to meet her?"

Guinevere glanced at Francine Bates. "What do you think, Francine?"

"I went to her a couple of times. Nothing much came of it, but it was kind of fun. Like going to a gypsy fortune-teller at a fair or something. I didn't take it seriously."

"How much does it cost?" Guinevere asked.

"Just twenty dollars for one visit," Mary answered. "I guess it's worth it just for the experience. As I said, I'm not sure I'll go back, though."

"I think," Guinevere said carefully, "that I'd like to try it at least once. How do I set up an appointment?"

"That's easy," Mary assured her. "One of us who's already been to her can call and set it up. She only takes referrals, you know."

"That's interesting," said Guinevere. "The psychic business must be pretty good if she can depend on making a living just on a referral basis."

"She doesn't want to be pestered by a bunch of skeptics trying to make fun of her power," Ruth explained in a small voice. "She doesn't mind people who are seriously interested, or even just curious, but she sees no need to waste her time with casual walkins. She says she's not a carnival sideshow and she doesn't want to be treated as one."

"I see," said Guinevere. "All right. I can't claim to be a believer, but I am genuinely curious. Go ahead and set up an appointment for me."

CHAPTER 3

The next day at Gage and Watson Guinevere deposited her shoulder bag in her desk drawer and went to work immediately. She had assigned herself this job in order to investigate Madame Zoltana, but that didn't mean she could stiff Gage and Watson. She had her professional ethics, and she would make certain the company got its money's worth from a Camelot Services employee. She was well into the document she was entering into the word processor, when Francine Bates arrived.

"Hey, it's all set, Gwen," the older woman announced lightly as she went to her desk. "I just saw Ruth and Mary in the hall. One of them made an appointment for you with Madame Zoltana. It's for this afternoon, right after work. I wrote down the address. It's a small house up on First Hill."

"I didn't know there were any houses left on First Hill," Guinevere said dryly. "I thought the hospitals had taken over most of the neighborhood." Several of Seattle's fine medical establishments had located in the district known as First Hill, an older area that looked out over the heart of the city toward Elliott Bay.

Francine laughed. "Not quite. There are a lot of apartments, and a few houses, still left."

"You said you'd only been to visit this Madame Zoltana once or twice, Francine?" Guinevere opened her drawer and stuffed the slip of paper with the address on it into her purse.

"That's all. I'm afraid I'm not a true believer. Or maybe I just don't want to believe, if you know what I mean." Francine paused thoughtfully as she started her word processor. Her voice grew more serious. "She really can tell you some incredible things. It can be . . . well, unsettling. But I think she helps some people."

"Helps them?"

Francine nodded. "Poor little Sally Evenson, who used to sit at the desk you're using, has really come to rely on her lately. Madame Zoltana has been a counselor and a sort of therapist for her."

Some therapist, Guinevere thought grimly. One who left the patient in a far worse condition than the one in which she'd found her. Whatever Zoltana's game with Sally had been, as far as Guinevere was concerned it was the next best thing to blackmail. "Well, I'll withhold judgment until I've met the woman," she told Francine, just as Miss Malcolm arrived.

Two hours later, at eleven o'clock, Guinevere got up from the word processor with a small sigh of relief. She forgot sometimes just how hard this kind of work could be. Coffee break was hailed joyously by one and all when it arrived.

"I'll see you down in the cafeteria," Guinevere said to Francine as they left the office and started down the hall. "I want to stop by the ladies' room first."

Francine nodded. "Okay. We'll be waiting."

Inside the restroom, Guinevere checked her hair, washed her

hands, and straightened her royal blue blazer. A Camelot Services employee was supposed to look professional at all times. Satisfied, she went back out to the corridor, deciding to give Zac a ring. He was supposed to be meeting with the interior designer of his new office today for a final rundown on plans and preparations. Zac had not gotten along well with the interior designer during the past few weeks. There had been numerous arguments over what constituted essential furnishings and what nonessential furnishings. There had also been several knock-down-drag-out discussions over the cost of everything from the floor covering to the desk calendars. On most of those occasions only Guinevere's presence had forestalled all-out warfare. Unfortunately, she couldn't attend today's conference.

She was halfway down the hall en route to the pay phone at the other end when Rich Overstreet glided out of his office and into her path. His movements were catlike, like his eyes. Guinevere, who had been doing her best to avoid any such accidental meetings, managed a polite smile.

"Good morning, Rick." She accompanied the greeting with a small nod and attempted to step past him.

"Join me for a cup of coffee, Gwen." Rick did not move out of her way. The golden cat's eyes were intent and serious. "It's been a long time."

"I'm afraid I can't just now. I have to make a phone call, and then I've got to meet some friends down in the cafeteria."

His mouth crooked sardonically. "Don't I qualify as a friend?"

Guinevere gave up any pretense of superficial politeness. Two years had not changed Rick Overstreet; you still had to be blunt to get through to him. "Not exactly, no."

He put out a hand and caught her arm, his fingers resting on the fabric of her blazer. "Gwen, you know that's not true. It's been two long years and everything's changed now."

She lifted her chin, her eyes scathing. "Because your wife is dead? That doesn't change a thing, Rick. Please let me go."

"Did I hurt you so badly two years ago?" he asked gently.

"No."

"I think you're lying, Gwen."

"I was never the one who lied, Rick. You were the one who had that bad habit."

He shrugged slightly. "Can you blame me? I wanted you very badly, Gwen. I knew you wouldn't come to me if you found out about Elena."

"You were right." She had found out about Elena, just before she had been about to leave on that first weekend trip with Rick. Guinevere had been horrified, hurt, and infuriated. But she had been grateful she'd discovered the truth before she had gone to bed with Rick Overstreet. The thought of being the other woman made her sick.

His eyes warmed with masculine promise. "Elena's gone now."

"So is whatever we once had," Guinevere said heartily. "Please let go of my arm, Rick."

"How long have you been seeing that guy who met you for lunch yesterday? He looked as if he owned you."

Guinevere's eyes narrowed. "No one owns me, Rick. You of all people should know that."

Rick ignored the crack. "He didn't look like your type at all, Gwen."

"You're hardly an authority."

"More of an authority than you want to admit, and you know it," he said softly, his fingers still gripping her sleeve. "We could have been good together, Gwen, if you hadn't lost your nerve."

"It was hardly a question of losing my nerve. What I lost was my faith in you. You were a lying, cheating bastard then, Rick, and I doubt you've changed one bit. Excuse me." She jerked free of his grip and strode briskly down the hall, not looking back. What rotten luck to run into him here at Gage and Watson after all this time. One of the perils of being an undercover investigator, Guinevere told herself with an inner sigh.

Zac answered the phone on the third ring. Guinevere knew at once that things were not going well on the other end.

"I hope you're not yelling at her again, Zac. If you're not careful, she's going to abandon the whole job before you move in, and then where will you be?"

"Not much worse off, if you ask me. Do you know what she wants to do now, Gwen? She wants to put grass on one entire wall. *Grass*, of all things. She's gone crazy."

"I expect she's talking about grass cloth, Zac. It makes a very handsome wall covering."

"There's already a nice coat of paint on all the walls."

"Yes, but having one wall papered will soften the overall effect. Trust her, Zac. You hired her for her advice, so take it. Listen, I called to tell you I've got my big break in the Zoltana case," she went on excitedly.

"I'm not sure if I can stand the suspense."

"Now, Zac, don't be condescending. This is important. I'm going to have my first appointment with Madame Zoltana tonight after work."

"Ask her to look into her crystal ball and tell you whether this interior designer of mine is going to survive until the end of the week or if I'll be charged with justifiable homicide."

"You aren't taking this seriously, are you?"

"Damn right, I'm taking it seriously. Between you and the interior designer, the assets of Free Enterprise Security are going to be wiped out before I ever get into my new office."

"I mean my case. You're not taking my case seriously."

"You want me to get on your case?" he threatened mildly.

"Not particularly," she retorted. "All right, Zac, go back to sniping at your interior designer. I've got more important things to do. I just thought I'd let you know where I'll be after work, since you said something about having dinner together this evening."

"I'll be at your place when you get home. Don't be late, or I'll eat without you." Zak broke off to yell at the hapless designer. "For God's sake," Guinevere heard him shout, "put away that damn baby blue. I am not having baby blue in my new office."

"I'll see you for dinner," Guinevere said into the phone. "You can cook." She hung up the phone before Zac could respond, wondering what he would end up bringing home for dinner. He was spending a great deal of time at her apartment these days, moving in slowly but surely, as if he hoped she wouldn't notice. A couple of his shirts were now hanging unobtrusively in her closet, and he kept a toothbrush in the bathroom. His socks and underwear were starting to show up in a dresser drawer, all carefully folded. At least he was neat.

Guinevere smiled to herself at the thought of Zac trying to be subtle. She left the pay phone and started toward the elevators. It was as she pressed the call button that she glanced back and saw Rick Overstreet leaning casually in the doorway of his office, lighting one of his fancy cigarettes. His eyes never left her as she got into the elevator. Guinevere shuddered as the elevator doors slid shut. He was beginning to make her feel like prey, she realized. And she hated the sensation.

At lunchtime she hurried back to Camelot Services to conduct the interview with Evelyn Pemberton. Trina smiled knowingly as the secretarial candidate walked through the door, and Guinevere had to smile back. Mrs. Pemberton appeared at first glance to be exactly what she had been waiting for. In her early fifties, the handsome, gray-haired woman wore her years and experience with a womanly authority that Guinevere responded to at once. She'd like to have that same confident authority when she reached Mrs. Pemberton's age. Guinevere rose to greet her, giving the woman her most charming smile.

"How do you do, Mrs. Pemberton. Please sit down. I'm so glad you could come. Miss Hood has explained the job to you?"

"She gave me an overview when I talked to her." Evelyn Pemberton nodded cordially at Trina, who was getting ready to leave for lunch. "Mr. Justis sounds as if he can be a bit of a handful at times, but I've been married for twenty-five years and raised two sons. I'm quite familiar with the male of the species. They have their occasional ego problems, and they can be temperamental, but I've learned to manage over the years."

Guinevere nodded in enthusiastic agreement. "Mr. Justis needs someone who can maintain a calm office environment. His clients are often nervous and worried, as you can imagine. It's the nature of his business, of course. During the past year, his client list has been growing quite steadily, and he's reached the point where he needs full-time secretarial assistance. The job routines will be quite varied, and confidentiality is an absolute must." Guinevere glanced shrewdly at Evelyn Pemberton. "You do understand that? Mr. Justis would let you go in an instant if he thought you had been indiscreet about one of his cases." But first, Guinevere added silently, he'd probably chew you to pieces.

"And he'd probably chew me up into little bits before he fired me, right?" Evelyn Pemberton asked easily.

Guinevere grinned. "I think, Mrs. Pemberton, that you have a good grasp of the job requirements. I'll send you over to talk to Mr. Justis first thing in the morning."

"That will be fine."

Guinevere found the little house on First Hill without too much trouble. It was located in the shade of an old brick apartment building that filled up most of the rest of the block. Madame Zoltana apparently did not believe in advertising. There was no sign out front announcing the sort of service being offered inside. The house was a basic, old-fashioned frame structure with a well-tended garden stretching around to the back. The curtains in the windows were dark and heavy and pulled shut, which was surprising on such a pleasant, sunny day.

There was nothing to announce that this was the abode of a rip-off psychic. Guinevere checked the address one more time before going up the front porch steps. As she lifted her hand to knock on the screen door, it occurred to her that she was nervous. She had a fleeting wish that Zac had accompanied her, and instantly gave herself a mental kick for being so chicken. This was her case, not his.

The door was opened on the second knock, and Guinevere found herself facing a bosomy woman in her late fifties. Her face was serenely austere, almost aristocratic. Piercing blue eyes regarded Guinevere with cool inquiry. The woman was dressed in a black caftan trimmed at hem and sleeve with a white, embroidered design. Her hair was silvered and worn very long. It fell down her back in soft waves. Several silver bracelets and necklaces jangled lightly when she moved. A cigarette dangled carelessly from her right hand. The room behind her was quite dark, due to the drawn curtains, and smelled of stale cigarette smoke, and Guinevere could see very little in the darkness.

"Madame Zoltana?"

The woman inclined her head regally. "I am she. What can I do for you?"

"I'm Guinevere Jones. I have an appointment with you." Guinevere was still fighting a strange sense of nervousness. Planning the big exposé of Madame Zoltana's shady business practices was one thing; carrying out those plans was clearly going to be another. For some reason, Madame Zoltana wasn't quite what she had expected. There was too much shrewd intelligence in those blue eyes and an unnerving degree of quiet arrogance in Madame Zoltana's posture.

It occurred to Guinevere that she might have bitten off more than she could chew. Instantly she pushed aside the notion and summoned up one of her famous, charming smiles—the kind of smile Zac claimed made people want to instantly confide their most secret thoughts. Madame Zoltana did not respond to the smile.

"Come in," the woman said coolly, standing aside.

Guinevere took a few steps into the darkened room, and as her eyes grew accustomed to the shadows, she glanced around at the simple, old-fashioned overstuffed furniture, which appeared to date from the forties, as did the house itself. Several overflowing ashtrays were scattered around. On one side of the room an arched opening revealed a small dining alcove, and on the other side a doorway opened onto a dark hall that apparently led to the bedrooms.

"My contemplation room is through here," Madame Zoltana said quietly, moving past Guinevere soundlessly.

Guinevere followed her into the dim hall and through a doorway that opened onto a small carpeted and heavily draped chamber. The only furniture here was a round table and two chairs. The walls were painted a dark gray, giving the whole room a cloudy appearance. In the center of the table was a thick crystal dish in the shape of a large salad bowl. Not the traditional crystal ball, Guinevere thought disparagingly.

"Please sit down." Madame Zoltana lowered herself into one of the chairs and waited until Guinevere was seated. She looked at her client over the top of the crystal bowl. "You are not a believer."

"No," Guinevere said, opting for honesty. "But I am interested and curious. I'm also open-minded. I've never met a psychic. My friends at work tell me you're quite genuine. I wanted to see for myself."

Madame Zoltana continued to stare, her blue eyes riveting in their intensity. "I accept that your interest is genuine. You must understand that I do not normally like to waste my time trying to convince skeptics. I have too many other important things to do. I can only see a limited number of clients. The sessions are very tiring for me, and it takes several hours to renew my energies after a client has left."

"I understand."

"My fees have been explained to you?"

That's right, Guinevere thought grimly, get the money settled first. "Of course." She reached into her purse and removed a twenty-dollar bill from her wallet. "Will this cover the session?"

"Yes." Madame Zoltana took the money. It vanished into a caftan pocket. She leaned forward, cradling the heavy crystal bowl between her hands. There was a long silence, and then Zoltana said, "You are here only to explore the matter of psychic powers. Therefore, I will not attempt to read the future for you. It requires much effort, and in this case it does not seem to be worth it. You probably wouldn't believe what I had to tell you anyway. But perhaps I can satisfy your intellectual interest with some observations about you and your past."

"Why do you use a bowl?"

"Instead of a crystal ball, you mean?" Madame Zoltana smiled thinly. "It doesn't matter what shape the crystal takes, so long as it is of the best quality. Crystal has curious properties. It enables one to focus more easily. It is possible to work without the aid of crystal, but much more difficult. What really makes the difference is having the Gift. Without it, it wouldn't matter how much crystal one used. Seeing through the veils of the past and the future would be impossible."

"And you have the Gift?" Guinevere was careful to keep the question sincere.

Madame Zoltana inclined her head. "It is both a blessing and a curse." She stubbed out her cigarette in a nearby ashtray.

Just like running any small business, Guinevere thought wryly. A blessing and a curse. She wondered how Zoltana listed her occupation with the IRS.

Guinevere waited as Madame Zoltana composed herself and stared into the crystal bowl. There was another long period of silence, during which Guinevere felt her palms grow moist again. Zac would laugh at her if he knew how anxious she felt at the moment. Surreptitiously she dried her palms on her skirt and waited.

At first Guinevere thought the room was growing marginally darker, then she realized that the bowl in the center of the table seemed to be glowing very faintly. Probably her imagination, she told herself. Either that or some lighting trick. No telling what gadgets were concealed under or in the table.

Finally Madame Zoltana began to speak. The words came out faintly, with what sounded like a great deal of effort. Guinevere leaned forward to hear clearly.

"I see many things," Madame Zoltana whispered. "Some are insignificant. You are not married. You live alone, although there is a man who shares more and more of your life these days. You have a younger sister, a very beautiful sister, who has at times been a trial to you. You work in an office, using a typing machine of some sort, but you aren't a secretary or clerk." Madame Zoltana frowned. "I don't understand. . . . Ah, yes, it becomes clear. You own your own business, one that involves secretaries and clerks and various other kinds of office personnel. At times, you, too, do such work."

Guinevere was startled, by the references both to Carla and to the fact that she herself wasn't just an employee of Camelot Services. This woman had definitely done some research. Guinevere kept her mouth shut, waiting for Madame Zoltana to continue.

"You are thirty years old. This man with whom you are presently involved is somewhat older, perhaps in his mid-thirties." Zoltana's brow wrinkled slightly. "But even though he is only a few years older than you, in some ways he is much older. He has perhaps seen too much of some things in life. Perhaps this is why he needs you.

He is very strong in many ways." Zoltana hesitated and her brow relaxed. "Ah, yes, he is a good lover."

Guinevere flushed in spite of herself. She would have to remember to mention that last observation to Zac.

Madame Zoltana fell silent for a few minutes, and Guinevere began to wonder if the session was already over. But the psychic did not look up from the faintly glowing bowl. She appeared to be contemplating something she saw in the crystal depths. "There is something more that has to do with this man, but it is not clear. I told you that I would not put myself to the effort of reading the future for you, but I am getting hints of it. I cannot ignore them. Do you wish me to look forward?" Madame Zoltana did not raise her head.

"How much?" Guinevere asked dryly.

"Another twenty dollars."

She would consider it as expenses having to do with the investigation, Guinevere decided. Zac always kept a precise expense account when he was working. She reached into her wallet and withdrew another twenty. "All right. Tell me what you see."

"It has to do with this man in your life. There are indications of danger." Zoltana hesitated again. "I cannot tell if the danger is aimed at him or emanates from him. Perhaps both." Another tense pause. "I see fear in you. Fear of this man you love. There is a threat, and you do not know how to deal with it. You, too, are in danger. You must be very, very careful, because when the moment of truth arrives, you will not be certain you can trust this man."

Guinevere realized she was holding her breath. The nervousness she had been experiencing was now tinged with dread. She forced herself to take a calming breath, reminding herself that creating this kind of vague fear was Madame Zoltana's stock in trade. Guinevere had to admit the woman was surprisingly good at it. Angry at her own unexpected gullibility, Guinevere tried to shake off the uneasy sensation that was enveloping her. She waited tensely for Madame Zoltana to continue. The psychic continued to stare into the crystal bowl, her forehead lined again with concentration, but eventually she sighed and sat back, breaking the spell. Her blue eyes were fixed on Guinevere's face.

"I can tell you no more today. I am at the limit of my abilities. If you wish to know more, you must return at another time. Please go now. I must rest."

Madame Zoltana got to her feet, steadying herself with a hand on the back of her chair. Reaching for a cigarette, she waited for Guinevere to precede her out of the room.

With a last glance at the crystal bowl, Guinevere obeyed the woman's instructions to leave. At the doorway, she looked back once more, trying to decide if the bowl had really glowed for a few moments. She still couldn't be certain.

As soon as she stepped outside into the warm summer day, Guinevere managed to forget much of the odd sensation that had gripped her during those tense moments inside the house. The power of suggestion really was quite amazing, she marveled as she hurried toward her compact, parked at the curb. She couldn't wait to tell Zac.

Zac was aware of a comfortable, homey feeling as he heard Guinevere's key in the lock. He put down the knife he was using to slice tomatoes, picked up his glass of tequila and the glass of wine he had poured for Guinevere, and went to meet her. She came through the door looking mildly disheveled and more concerned than he had expected. He bent his head to give her a short, forceful kiss and handed her the wine.

"Hey, what happened? Madame Zoltana get to you after all? The woman must be a real pro."

Guinevere took a grateful swallow of wine and held up the glass. "Thanks, I needed that. Madame Zoltana was a strange experience, Zac. Not quite what I was expecting." She sniffed appreciatively. "What's cooking?"

"I'm glad to see the experience didn't manage to spoil your appetite. I'm making tacos." He turned back toward the kitchen, and Guinevere followed, tossing her purse into a hall closet en route. He set his tequila back down on the counter and picked up the knife. "So tell me all about it. How's the big-time psychic investigation going?"

Guinevere sat on a kitchen stool, one leg swinging idly over the other as she sipped her wine and watched Zac prepare the taco fillings. "Well, for openers, she told me right away I didn't just work as a temporary secretary. She knew I owned Camelot Services, Zac."

"Is that so?" He was amused, but he kept a serious expression on his face as he grated cheese. "Anything else?"

"She knew about Carla. Knew she was beautiful and that she's occasionally been a pain in the ass."

"Uh-huh. What else?"

He thought Guinevere hesitated a long time before she continued. It was obvious she had been slightly disconcerted by her experience. "She mentioned a man in my life," Guinevere said slowly. "I'm sure it was you. She seemed to know something about you."

"What, exactly?" Zac asked sardonically as he picked up his glass of tequila.

"She mentioned danger around you, for one thing."

"Must have guessed I was going to be slicing tomatoes tonight. I've been known to cut myself with a sharp knife while slicing tomatoes. Anything else?"

Again Guinevere paused. "No, not really."

"How much did this little investigation set you back?"

"Forty bucks," Guinevere said, grimacing.

"And, of course, if you want to know the good stuff, you'll have to go back."

"Precisely. Madame Zoltana exhausts herself easily."

Zac leaned back against the counter, taking pity on her, she seemed so serious. "What's the problem, Gwen? You knew she was a con artist."

"Well, yes. But she did seem to know things, Zac. I was very careful about what I said around Gage and Watson. I don't see how some of that information could have gotten back to her."

"Sounds to me as if she just had someone take a look inside your purse."

Guinevere's eyes opened wide. "My purse!"

Zac's mouth curved faintly. "Follow me." He sauntered back into the hall, opened the closet, and removed Guinevere's shoulder bag. He unzipped it and turned it upside down, emptying the contents onto a small table. Tossing aside the leather purse, he pushed his fingers idly through the motley collection.

"Here we go, a business card with *Camelot Services* stamped on it in nice big letters, and you listed as president. Your driver's license, identifying you as Guinevere Jones, the same name as the president of Camelot Services. It also tells us several other things about you, including the fact that you are thirty years old." He flicked through a few other items. "A note to call Carla. A photo of Carla standing outside her new art gallery, and an announcement of the opening of the gallery. Carla's last name is the same as your last name. It wouldn't take much guesswork to figure out she's your sister, and everyone knows younger sisters are occasionally pains in the ass, especially when they're good-looking. It's all here, Gwen. Everything Madame Zoltana revealed to you was revealed to her first by someone who went through your purse."

"You're absolutely right," Guinevere breathed. "That explains everything. It also fits with my theory of her having an inside person at Gage and Watson. I left my purse in my desk drawer several times yesterday and again today. It would have been very easy for someone to have a look through it."

"Yeah."

"But what about you, Zac? She knew about you, too."

He grinned. "What did she know about me? Use your head, Gwen. Whoever works for her at G and W probably saw you meet me for lunch yesterday. It wouldn't have taken any great psychic power to figure out that you and I are seeing each other for some nonplatonic reasons." *Especially not after the way you kissed me in front of that turkey who was trying to make a pass at you as you got off the elevator,* Zac added to himself.

"What about the danger she hinted at?"

"That was the hook, the bait to make you return for a few more visits. Vague references to danger are probably standard operating procedure for her. By the next time she would have learned even more about you."

Guinevere's mood lightened several degrees as she assimilated his logic. "Yes, it all makes sense. What a racket. The thing is, Zac, she's really very good. She creates this odd atmosphere that is very convincing."

"Good con artists are all very convincing. They have to be in order to make a living. Ready to eat?"

"Mmm-hmm." Guinevere followed him back through the kitchen door, wondering why she hadn't told him everything Madame Zoltana had said. For some reason she didn't want to examine too closely, Guinevere didn't want to bring up the fact that Zoltana had warned her she would soon feel fear around Zac. And Guinevere didn't want to think about the other warning, the one that implied she might not be able to trust Zac when the chips were down. The problem was, she had let Zoltana get to her, allowed the woman to prey on her imagination. Gullible Guinevere.

"You know, Zac," she said as she set the table, "you look cute in an apron."

CHAPTER 4

It was touching, Zac decided the next day as he interviewed Evelyn Pemberton, really touching. When he thought of how hard Guinevere must have worked to avoid sending him a bright-eyed, sexy little ex-cheerleader, he got a nice, warm feeling deep inside. Somewhere in the vicinity below his belt to be precise. The notion of Guinevere going out of her way to make certain he wouldn't be put in any danger of being seduced by a sweet young thing amused him no end. After all her hard work, he almost hated to have to tell her that Evelyn Pemberton was exactly what he'd had in mind from the beginning.

Already he was beginning to relax around Mrs. Pemberton. No doubt about it, the woman inspired confidence. He could envision her already seated at the desk in the outer office of the new suite upstairs, organizing the daily business and calming clients. The fact that she could type was simply an added bonus, as far as Zac was concerned. He couldn't wait to put everything in her hands.

"Mrs. Pemberton, I think this is going to work out beautifully," he announced with satisfaction after only fifteen minutes of interviewing. "Free Enterprise Security will be moving upstairs to its new offices on the twentieth. I'd like you to start on that date. Now, Gwen tells me there are some tax forms we have to fill out." He scrabbled around in a desk drawer trying to find them as he spoke. "And I think we have to file something with Social Security, too. I'm not exactly sure what, but Gwen will know." He looked up hopefully. "Or perhaps you know the routine?"

She smiled benignly at his blatant relief and enthusiasm. "I know the routine, Mr. Justis," she said gently, "but I don't think we're quite ready for it yet."

He stared at her blankly. "Not ready?"

"Mr. Justis, I assure you the opening you have sounds very interesting, and I will give it my closest consideration, but I really must have a few days to think about it. And I'm sure you'll want to interview other people."

"Uh, no, I don't," he said flatly, stunned by this turn of events. "I'm offering you the job."

"Well, I certainly appreciate it. I'll let you know my decision next week."

"Next week?" he repeated. "Next *week*?"

"Yes. At that time, if I decide to accept your offer, we can discuss the pension plan you're offering." She rose to leave, a graceful woman who moved with confidence. "Good-bye, Mr. Justis. I'll call you as soon as I've made my decision."

Zac stared after her, stricken. The closing of the door jolted him out of his trance. He grabbed the phone and dialed the number of Camelot Services. When Trina answered, he didn't even give her time to finish the greeting.

"Put Gwen on the phone," Zac ordered. "Now."

"I'm sorry, Zac, I can't do that. She's at Gage and Watson."

"Oh, hell, that's right." He glanced irritably at his watch. "Then call Gage and Watson, and tell her I want to talk to her immediately."

"What's the matter, Zac? Didn't Evelyn Pemberton work out?"

"Just get hold of Gwen. Tell her she's got a very unhappy client on her hands. Namely, me." He dropped the receiver into the cradle and waited for Gwen to call, drumming his fingers on the desk. It took ten long minutes. When the instrument did ring, he snatched it up.

"Zac? What's wrong? Trina said you sounded upset."

"You told me Evelyn Pemberton was mine if I wanted her."

"She is."

"Well, I want her, and she doesn't seem to want me. What the hell went wrong? I thought you knew what you were doing when it came to this sort of thing. Lord knows, I waited long enough to get even one potential candidate out of you. Now the candidate tells me she'll think about the offer and get back to me next week sometime. Furthermore, if she does decide to take the job, she made it clear she wants to know about my pension plan. Gwen, I haven't *got* a pension plan."

"Is that all? Zac, she's a pro. She's going to make you cool your heels a bit so you'll appreciate her all the more when she agrees to take the job. Don't worry, she'll say yes when she calls."

"Christ, you'd think I was asking her to marry me!"

"She's not being coy; she's being businesslike. Trust me, Zac."

"You keep saying that," he complained. "What about my nonexistent pension plan?"

"I know what I'm doing. And I'll put you in touch with the people who can help you set up a small pension plan. Now stop worrying. Listen, I was going to call you anyway. Meet me for lunch, okay? I want to consult."

"Consult about what?" Then it clicked. "Oh, yeah, your big case."

"Why is it I keep getting the impression you're not taking my big case seriously?"

"I am taking it seriously. I think it's a complete and utter waste of your time and money, but I'm taking it seriously."

"Sure." She didn't sound mollified. "All right, pick me up for lunch at noon. I'll meet you in the lobby of the building."

"Okay. Listen, Gwen, are you sure about Evelyn Pemberton?"

"Trust me, Zac."

Zac hung up with a groan and sat glaring for a few minutes at the two Mason Adair paintings he had hanging on the walls of his tiny office. For a moment he simply stared at them. Then he thought about Gwen and her big case, and a reluctant smile curved the edges of his mouth. He was beginning to enjoy her Nancy Drew enthusiasm. There were a lot of things he enjoyed about Guinevere Jones.

Guinevere was all business as she sat down to lunch with Zac in a small deli between First and Western Avenues. "I've been thinking all morning about what you said last night," she began, watching him bite into a huge sandwich.

"Nice to know you're hanging on my every word."

"About my purse," she reminded him. "Zac, please pay attention. I'm trying to consult with you."

"My usual consulting fee is two hundred dollars an hour."

"How about I pay for lunch?"

"It's a deal." He glanced at his watch. "You've got fifty minutes left."

Guinevere considered giving him a swift kick under the table but decided against it. She realized Zac was finding her current efforts amusing, but that didn't mean she couldn't pick his brain—if she could just keep his attention from wandering. She leaned forward intently.

"I think you're right about someone having gone through my

purse, reporting certain details to Madame Zoltana before my appointment last night."

"I know I'm right." He took another satisfying bite of his sandwich.

"I've done some observation this morning, and the way I figure it, there aren't too many people who would have had access to my purse. The most likely suspect is Francine Bates, and she's the one who originally turned Sally on to Madame Zoltana. Francine has this nice, motherly sort of personality. I can just see Sally confiding in her about the baby and everything."

"Have you got any evidence against Francine?"

"Nope. So I've decided to set a trap."

Zac chewed thoughtfully for a moment before repeating cautiously, "A trap?"

"That's right. I want to see what you think of my idea." Guinevere sat back and smiled brilliantly.

He sighed. "Go ahead. It's your hour."

"Here's what I'm going to do. I'm going to give Francine some exciting little tidbit and make sure that no one besides her knows about it. Then I'll see if Madame Zoltana mentions it at the next session."

"Hmm. When's the next session?"

"I'm going to call Zoltana this afternoon and set it up as soon as possible."

Zac finished the first half of his sandwich. "What's the tidbit you're going to give Francine?"

"Oh, I thought I'd tell her I'm worrying about my brother going back to jail," Guinevere said airily.

"You don't have a brother."

"That's the whole point, Zac. When that false bit of information crops up during a session, I'll know for sure that Francine was the one who planted it. Then I'll have proof that she and Zoltana are working together."

Zac shook his head and reached for the other half of his sandwich. "The only one you'll prove anything to is yourself. Zoltana's clients probably won't believe you."

"Well, I can certainly make a scene at Gage and Watson, and most of the doubters will believe me."

"Does it occur to you that Madame Zoltana and her cohort aren't going to be thrilled when you start accusing them of conspiracy?"

"What can they do about it?"

"Sue you for slander," Zac suggested mildly.

Guinevere frowned. "Nonsense. I'll be telling the truth."

"It's going to be your word against theirs," he pointed out.

"Well, at the very least, I'm going to make sure Sally Evenson knows the truth. Besides, someone like Zoltana is not about to sue. She'd have to prove her powers are for real, and she couldn't do that."

"Just keep telling yourself that when you find yourself hiring a lawyer."

"Don't try to alarm me, Zac."

"Okay. Is the consultation over?"

"I guess so," Guinevere said reluctantly. "Although you haven't exactly been a big help."

"Consultants get paid whether they're a big help or not. It's one of the joys of consulting work. Now, if you're finished, you can tell me how the hell I'm supposed to set up a pension plan for a single employee."

Guinevere grinned. "That kind of consulting will cost you lunch tomorrow."

"You're a hard woman, Guinevere Jones."

"It's the company I've been keeping lately," she explained.

Guinevere planted her false tidbit with great care right after lunch. She walked back into the office with her head bent over a letter she held in her hand, making sure her expression was troubled, and when she sat down beside Francine Bates, she didn't give her the usual friendly greeting.

Francine watched for a while as Guinevere made a show of concentrating intently on her work. Finally the older woman spoke.

"Everything okay, Gwen? You look worried."

Guinevere sniffed slightly and reached for a tissue. "I'm fine," she said through a bleak smile as she dabbed delicately at her nose. She'd never done any acting. Warning herself not to overplay the part, she added wearily, "Family problems. You know how it is."

"That's for sure," Francine said consolingly. "Sometimes it helps to talk about it, though."

"I wouldn't want to burden you with my personal problems," Guinevere said bravely, stuffing the tissue back into her purse.

"I don't mind, Gwen. What are friends for?"

After that it was easy. During the afternoon coffee break, Guinevere allowed Francine to coax the whole sordid story out of her.

"We all thought he was doing so well," she concluded dismally. "My parents had such hopes, and now he goes and gets himself arrested again. Oh, he claims he's innocent, of course, but who's going to believe him with his record? If only he hadn't gone to Los Angeles."

"Just another young kid drawn by the bright lights of Southern California," Francine said sadly. "Happens all the time. How is the rest of the family coping?"

"About as you'd expect. My mother is heartbroken. Dad is disgusted. I'm not sure he's going to be willing to hire a lawyer this time."

"What an awful situation."

"If only I knew what to do and what was going to happen next." Guinevere summoned a shaky smile. "I'm half thinking about going back to Madame Zoltana's. I'm not sure I believe in her powers, but I honestly don't know where else to turn."

"Why not?" Francine agreed gently. "She might be able to give you a little hope, and we all need that from time to time."

"I think I'll give her a call before we go back to work," Guinevere said with sudden conviction.

But there was no answer when Guinevere dialed Madame Zoltana's number. She waited impatiently another hour and then slipped out of the office to try calling again.

"Any luck?" Francine asked when Guinevere returned from the second attempt.

"No. I guess she's out for the day."

"Maybe you'll be able to reach her this evening."

"Maybe."

But Guinevere couldn't get hold of Madame Zoltana that evening, either. It was very frustrating, and she told Zac as much when he showed up at her door after work.

"My big plan is going down the tubes, Zac. Why isn't she answering her phone? I was all set to see her again today after I left Gage and Watson."

"Who knows? Maybe she's taken a temporary vacation on another astral plane." Zac wandered into the kitchen to see what Guinevere had going for dinner.

"I do wish you'd stop making jokes about this case, Zac," she muttered as she followed him into the bright yellow kitchen.

"You never want me to have any fun," he observed as he reached for the tequila bottle in her cupboard.

Guinevere mumbled something under her breath. "Did you mention earlier that you were inviting yourself for dinner this evening?" she asked meaningfully.

"I don't believe I did. When I left the office my feet just sort of naturally turned in this direction." He poured the tequila and recapped the bottle. "Did you make enough for two?"

Guinevere grinned. "Luckily for you I just sort of naturally bought enough shrimp for two."

"I think I begin to see a pattern developing in our lives," Zac said with a certain satisfaction.

Guinevere had no more luck getting hold of the elusive Zoltana the following morning. She was becoming increasingly frustrated, but she forgot some of her irritation when Francine Bates showed up late for work. For the first time since she had met Francine, the older woman was not cheerful or friendly. She seemed withdrawn and preoccupied. Guinevere began to wonder if perhaps Francine and Madame Zoltana had put two and two together and decided they were being set up by one Guinevere Jones.

"I think my cover may be blown," Guinevere confided to Zac at lunchtime. "Francine hasn't said two words to me all day, and I can't get hold of Madame Zoltana. Do you think they might have become suspicious when they discovered I was really the owner of Camelot Services, and not just another employee?"

"I don't see why. As far as they know, you were just filling in for one of your employees and didn't want to have everyone know you owned the firm," Zac reassured her.

"Well, what do I do now?"

Zac shrugged. "You could see if anyone else has had any better luck getting an appointment with Zoltana. If someone else has, you can assume Zoltana's probably avoiding you."

Guinevere brightened. "That's an excellent idea, Zac. Sometimes you're positively brilliant."

"I know," he said modestly.

She went back to Gage and Watson determined to track down Mary and Ruth. Mary hadn't tried to get hold of Madame Zoltana, but Ruth had made an effort three times the previous day and had failed. She seemed very depressed about the situation.

"I don't know what to do," she confided to Guinevere. "I've got to talk to her. I'm going crazy with worry. She always seems to know what's happening, and she's been keeping things under control for me. I know you might not believe it, but it's true. Now I can't reach her, and I'm frantic."

On a hunch, Guinevere tried Sally Evenson next. Sally seemed happy enough in her new temporary assignment, but when Guinevere asked her about Madame Zoltana, she didn't sound quite so cheerful.

"I have an appointment with her after work this afternoon, Miss Jones. I know you think I shouldn't go, but I *have* to go."

"I understand, Sally. Look, do me a favor, and call me after you've seen her, all right? I want to talk to you about the session."

"Well, all right."

But when Sally phoned Guinevere at home that evening, her voice sounded odd, as if she was half relieved, half terrified. "There was no one home, Miss Jones. I went to her house just like I always do, and she wasn't there. What do you think it means? Maybe she isn't going to help me anymore."

"Sally, listen to me. Madame Zoltana wasn't helping you to begin with. She has no more psychic power than I do. You've just saved twenty bucks."

"Thirty," Sally said almost inaudibly.

"Thirty!"

"That's what I've been paying lately, ever since she said she could keep things under control for me. Oh, Miss Jones, I don't know what to do!"

Guinevere glanced through the kitchen door at Zac, who had

his feet up on her coffee table while he read the evening paper. He seemed to be ignoring the conversation. "Sally, you're an adult woman with a good job. You have your own life under control. You don't need anyone else to control it for you. Now, tell me how you like your new assignment."

They talked for a few more minutes, and Guinevere tried to find lots of encouraging things to say. When they hung up, she went thoughtfully out into the living room, plunking herself down beside Zac on the sofa.

"You know what I think?" she demanded.

"What?" He looked up from the newspaper.

"I think Madame Zoltana is lying low."

"You could be right. But I'm not quite sure why she would bother. To be honest, Gwen, you aren't much of a threat."

"Hah! I'll bet Madame Zoltana thinks I am," Guinevere said with some satisfaction. "Let me have the comics." She reached for a section of the paper. "I think I'll drive by Madame Zoltana's tomorrow and see if she's at home."

"Waste of time," Zac promised.

Zac was right, Guinevere had to admit the next day after work when she parked in front of Madame Zoltana's little house. There was no sign of Madame Zoltana. All the drapes were still pulled, so she couldn't peer through the windows, but after she'd knocked loudly several times, Guinevere was sure no one was home.

She walked back down the front path to the sidewalk and glanced around at the neighborhood. The only real neighbors lived in the big brick apartment house that filled up the block. They weren't likely to have noted the actions of the local psychic who lived in the little house on the corner. Guinevere decided she could hardly just start knocking on apartment doors and asking questions. People would think she was nuts.

The following day, Francine Bates failed to show up for work. Guinevere was on the phone to Zac by noon.

"She's not here, Zac. Miss Malcolm says she hasn't phoned in sick or made any excuses. She simply didn't show up. That's very unusual behavior for Francine, according to everyone else in the office. I tried calling her at home, and there's no answer. And no one has been able to get hold of Madame Zoltana, either. Zac, this is getting very mysterious."

"Not nearly as mysterious as these forms I'm supposed to fill out for an employee pension plan. What have you gotten me into, Gwen?"

"Zac, your attention is wandering. We are discussing my case."

"My professional opinion is that at the moment, you don't have a case. Just as well. You weren't getting paid for solving it, anyway. Now, about these forms . . ."

Guinevere sighed and gave up. Zac was right. It was beginning to look as though she didn't have a case. She got off the phone after telling Zac to call his accountant about the pension plan forms, and she went back down the hall, ignoring Rick Overstreet as she passed him lounging in an office doorway.

"You think that's going to work forever?" Rick asked softly as she swept by. "You can't pretend I don't exist, Gwen, and you know it."

Damned if she would give him the benefit of an answer or let him know how much she resented his predatory gaze. With a woman's intuition, she sensed that she was rapidly becoming a challenge for him. If they had never run into each other again, Guinevere was certain Rick Overstreet wouldn't have thought twice about her. But now fate had thrown her back into his path, and all of his egotistical machismo was aroused. Once he'd been able to charm her with ease. Apparently it annoyed him that he'd lost his touch.

All things considered, it seemed time to throw in the towel on this assignment. It was getting hard to avoid Rick Overstreet, and her big case seemed to have disintegrated. Guinevere decided she would send Sally Evenson back to Gage and Watson in the morning.

"A wise decision," Zac said that afternoon when she told him. "I've been saying all along that you were wasting your time."

"I know," Guinevere admitted, "but it's all very disappointing. My big case has disappeared."

"Don't worry, I'll make it up to you," Zac promised with a wicked grin. "By tomorrow morning you'll have forgotten the whole thing."

"Promises, promises."

"Trust me," said Zac.

Guinevere went back to business as usual at Camelot Services for the remainder of the week, but she kept tabs on Sally Evenson. By Friday Sally seemed much happier.

"At first I was worried about what I would do without Madame Zoltana's guidance," she confided to Guinevere. "But now I feel much better. It's a relief not to have to go for those appointments. I'm not worrying the way I did when she was always telling me things that made me nervous. I talked to my friend Ruth today, and she says she's feeling better, too."

"Keep that in mind if Zoltana ever turns up again," Guinevere advised her. "You're much happier without her guidance. Did Francine Bates ever come back to work?"

"No, and it's very strange, really. No one can figure out what's happened to her. Miss Malcolm says she had personnel make some inquiries, and they can't find her, either."

Guinevere thought about that. She was grateful for the fact that Sally, at least, seemed to be much more cheerful.

Sally Evenson's cheerfulness vanished on the following Monday. She showed up at Camelot Services during her lunch hour, looking stricken. After one startled glance Guinevere and Trina rushed to her and urged her into a chair.

"Sally, what is it?" Guinevere demanded. "What's happened?"

Sally burst into tears and handed Guinevere a sheet of crumpled paper.

"Well, hell," Guinevere said as she read the message. "Looks like Zoltana is back in action."

The message was simple and to the point:

THE PRICE FOR KEEPING YOUR PAST FROM HAUNTING YOU HAS JUST GONE UP. IF YOU WANT MY CONTINUED PROTECTION, YOU MUST LEAVE ONE THOUSAND DOLLARS IN CASH AT A PLACE THAT WILL BE MADE KNOWN TO YOU IN THE NEAR FUTURE. DO NOT HESITATE WHEN YOU GET MY NEXT MESSAGE. ALREADY I HEAR THE CHILD CRYING.

Guinevere's mouth tightened at the sheer cruelty of the words. With unsteady hands she refolded the piece of paper. "Did Ruth get one of these, too?"

"I don't know." Sally sniffed. "I haven't talked to her. I haven't talked to anyone but you."

Guinevere sat down beside her and took her hand. "Sally, you know what this is, don't you? It's blackmail."

"But, Miss Jones, she was going to protect me."

"She has no power to protect you from the past. Only you can do that, by handling that past in a mature, adult fashion. Zoltana can't do anything except take your money."

"Oh, Miss Jones, I don't have a thousand dollars. I'll have to get a loan, and who would loan me money to pay Madame Zoltana?"

"Even if you did come up with the cash, you couldn't give it to a blackmailer. You know that, don't you, Sally? You must understand that it wouldn't stop with the first thousand. It would just keep going on forever."

Sally drew a deep breath. "I knew when I got that note that I had to do something, Miss Jones. At first I was just paying for her psychic services. But it's gone beyond that now. I'm frightened."

"That's the only hold she has on you, Sally. As long as she thinks she can frighten you, she'll assume she can manipulate you. I'll bet she's not sending these notes to people like Mary and me, people who don't believe in her powers."

"It's different for you, Miss Jones," Sally said sounding defeated. "You're strong."

"So are you, Sally. Not many young women could have pulled themselves together the way you have after all you went through. You're one of the strong ones, too. All you have to do is believe in yourself."

Sally looked up at her with a faint glimmer of hope. "Do you really think so, Miss Jones?"

"I really think so, Sally."

There was a short pause while Sally turned that over in her mind. "But what do I do now?"

"You will ignore this message, for one thing. For another, you and I are going to get some professional assistance in this matter. Madame Zoltana has gone too far this time. We amateur sleuths are going to call in the big guns."

"Guns?" Sally looked alarmed.

"A figure of speech," Guinevere assured her. She looked up at Trina. "Get Zac on the phone for me."

Sally looked startled. "Oh, please, I don't want anyone else to know about this!"

"Don't worry, Sally," Trina said gently. "Mr. Justis is very discreet. It's his business to be discreet. He's a confidential security consultant. He helps people who are being taken advantage of the way you are."

Sally didn't look convinced, but she waited in tense silence while Trina dialed Zac's number. Guinevere took the phone as soon as Zac came on the line. Quickly she spelled out what had happened to Sally.

"Tell her to call the Better Business Bureau and the cops," Zac said bluntly.

Guinevere smiled at Sally. "He says he'll help."

"Gwen!" Zac's protest came through the line with enough force to hurt her ear. "I did *not* say that. Don't you dare drag me into this. I've got enough on my hands as it is."

Confident that Sally couldn't overhear, Guinevere kept her smile firmly in place as she talked to Zac in soothing tones. "That's wonderful, Zac. Now, I figure the first thing we have to do is take a look around the premises."

"What premises?"

"Madame Zoltana's."

"Are you nuts?"

"I'll be glad to go by myself if you'd rather not accompany me," she said aloofly.

"Guinevere Jones," he began menacingly, "one of these days I swear, I'm going to . . ."

"Going to what?"

"We will discuss this after work," he informed her and hung up in her ear.

Guinevere replaced the receiver and kept smiling confidently at Sally Evenson. "Don't worry," she announced. "Zac's going to help us. He'll handle everything."

CHAPTER 5

"I can't believe I let myself get talked into this." Zac glanced over his shoulder once again to make sure the night-dark backyard of Madame Zoltana's house was still empty. "I must be getting soft in the head. This is what comes of indulging women. They get uppity, demanding, and headstrong."

"I don't understand why you're complaining so much," Guinevere muttered as Zac used a thin strip of metal to work the back door lock. "You do this sort of thing all the time in your line of work."

"Rarely do I do this kind of thing in my line of work," he retorted. "I find that lately I'm doing it chiefly when I'm mixed up in one of your grand schemes."

The lock surrendered in his hands, and the back door swung open with a faint squeak. Zac stood on the threshold, listening.

"What do you think?" Guinevere asked softly.

"I think no one's home."

"Well, we already know that. We knocked on the front door first, remember? And tried the phone. What can you see?" She prodded him forward until they both stood in the silent kitchen. Zac closed the door behind them.

"Did she have any pets?" he asked.

Guinevere shook her head. "None that I saw. Sally hasn't mentioned any, either." She wrinkled her nose. "But she does smoke, as you may have noticed." The stale smoke smell hung in the air, probably absorbed in the drapes and imbedded in the furniture. "I think this place has been closed for several days."

"I think you're right. But then, you already knew that, didn't you?" Zac moved slowly through the kitchen. "Remember what I told you. Don't touch anything."

"I heard you." Guinevere peered around his shoulder into the dark living room, an undeniable sense of excitement running through her veins. She ought to be ashamed of the emotion, but she couldn't pretend it didn't exist. "I can't see a thing. She left all the drapes pulled."

Zac removed a small pencil-size flashlight from the inside of his jacket. "Luckily one of us came prepared."

"I expected no less from you," she retorted with mocking admiration. "Now, where do we start?"

"Beats me. I'm a stranger here myself."

The withering look she shot him was lost in the shadows. "I wish you would take this more seriously. Come on, let's go down the hall to her contemplation room. That's where she holds her psychic sessions."

Zac shrugged and followed obediently. The contemplation room looked very much as Guinevere had last seen it. The crystal bowl was still sitting in the middle of the table.

"When she did her psychic bit in the dark room, I was almost sure the bowl glowed just a little. It was weird." Guinevere looked down into the crystal object. "I wonder how she did it."

"It's an old trick," Zac said. "There's a small drawer hidden under the table. Probably got a lightbulb in it. The crystal bowl sits over a cutout on the table surface. The light shines up through it and into the bowl. Small-time stuff. Fell for it, huh?"

Guinevere sensed his grin. "I did not fall for it," she announced loftily. "I knew it was a trick. I merely wondered how it was done." She turned away from the table and walked around the room. "I wonder if she keeps any files on her clients?"

"I wouldn't be surprised. From what you've told me, she sounds like a real businesswoman." Zac played the light around the room. "But I don't see anything in here."

"Let's check the rest of the place."

They walked through the remainder of the small house. All the drapes were pulled, and there was an ashtray in every room, the ashes and butts several days old. Zoltana's interesting collection of caftans was hung neatly in the bedroom closet. The dresser was full of clothing. There was no evidence of any filing cabinet, and the desk they discovered in the bedroom contained nothing helpful. A manual typewriter sat on top of it.

"There must be something, Zac," Guinevere said at the end of the short search.

"You mean, you hate to admit you just broke into someone else's house for no reason." He was using the flashlight to examine the inside of a closet.

Guinevere ignored that. "You said yourself she's a businesswoman. She must keep some kind of records. What about a safe?" She led the way back to the living room.

"A safe?"

"In the wall, or something. You know, behind a picture." Impatiently Guinevere went to shift the large, ornately framed painting that hung on the wall behind the sofa. She jumped as Zac snapped at her.

"I told you not to touch anything."

"Okay, okay." She pulled her fingers away before they touched the frame. "Sheesh, what a grouch. But let's look, Zac. There could be something behind that picture."

He came forward, gingerly using a handkerchief to slide the painting out of the way, and shone the flashlight against the wall. There was no sign of a hidden safe. Thoughtfully, Zac let the painting slip back into place. "Maybe the floor," he said musingly.

"What about the floor?"

"A lot of people have small home safes installed in the floor. It would be easy enough to do in an old house like this, with wooden floors. Let's have a look."

Guinevere smiled to herself. "I'm glad to see you're finally taking a real interest in this project. Where do we start?"

"By lifting the rugs." He went down on one knee and eased up the corner of the large, flower-printed area rug on the floor in front of the sofa.

Guinevere got down beside him, and together they rolled up the heavy rug. When they were finished Zac shone the flashlight over every square foot of the wooden surface, looking for a suspicious break in the lines of the boards. Nothing.

"How about the kitchen?" Guinevere suggested.

"I don't think so. The kitchen floor's covered with linoleum. You don't go rolling linoleum up every time you want to put something into your household safe." Zac got to his feet and started toward the hall. "Let's try in here."

There were two small rugs in the hallway. When they were rolled aside nothing was revealed except a discarded cigarette butt that had apparently fallen from one of the ashtrays. Guinevere let the last rug slide back onto the floor and sighed.

"This is depressing," she complained.

"Your problem is that you have a short attention span. Let's give the contemplation room a try." Zac led the way into the small room. "We'll have to move the table and chairs. Now, for Pete's sake be careful, and use that handkerchief I gave you."

"Sometimes you're extremely bossy, Zac."

"Women love masterful men."

She arched her eyebrows as she and Zac lifted the surprisingly heavy table aside. "Where did you hear that?"

"I forget. Ready? Let's have a look."

At first Guinevere saw nothing unusual when the carpet was heaved aside, but Zac went down on one knee almost at once, eyeing the line between two boards. "Here we go," he said softly.

Guinevere's sense of excitement grew at the soft note of triumph in his words. Zac's voice often got that way when he was on to something. "What is it?" She crouched down beside him.

"If someone were going to install a floorboard safe, this is the way it would look."

"I don't see anything."

"Watch." Zac pressed heavily on one of the boards. It gave almost at once with only a faint squeak of protest. Then something snapped as hidden hinges responded. A two foot square of floor popped up, revealing a dark hole. Zac aimed the flashlight inside. Metal gleamed. A numbered dial was visible.

"Zac! It's here. A real safe!" Guinevere was awed by the wonder of it all. "If she kept any useful records, I'll bet this is where they'd be. Makes sense she'd keep them here in her contemplation room."

"Mmm." Zac flashed the light around the interior of the opening. There was another discarded cigarette butt sitting near the safe, but other than that, nothing. Zac reached down and picked up the cigarette end, rotating it between his fingers.

"Put that down, Zac. It's dirty."

He gave her an odd look and obediently dropped the butt back into the dark space under the floor. "You know, you can be awfully bossy yourself at times."

"Men love masterful women. Okay, Zac," Guinevere announced cheerfully, "this is where you get to really impress me. I can't wait to watch you crack a safe."

He shot her a long-suffering glance. "I hate to disillusion you, but I am not much of a safecracker. Picking a few standard door locks is not in the same league as opening a safe, even a small one like this."

Her eyes widened in horror. "You mean you don't know how to open this thing?" In the dim reflection of the flashlight, she thought she saw his mouth curve faintly. "Zac?"

"Fortunately for my image, I don't have to try."

"What are you talking about?"

Zac leaned down and reached into the hole in the floorboards. He caught hold of the metal door of the safe and flipped it open. "Somebody else has already done the hard part for me."

Shocked, Guinevere stared down into the open safe. "Zac, it's empty!"

"Well, what did you expect? That she'd hightail it without first cleaning out any incriminating records?" Zac got to his feet again and let the hinged section of floor drop back into place. "Come on, there's one more thing I want to check. Did you bring that note Sally received?"

"You told me to bring it, remember?" Guinevere pointed out self-righteously as she dug the note out of her purse.

"And an extra sheet of typing paper?"

"Got it." She followed him down the hall again to the desk in Zoltana's bedroom. When Zac held out his hand, she gave him the blank piece of paper and watched with interest as he inserted it into the typewriter. "Do you think we'll actually be able to tell if Sally's note was done on this typewriter?"

"Maybe. Maybe not. Sometimes these old portables are eccentric enough that it's easy to tell if a letter was typed on a particular machine. Here, you type. I'm not that good at it."

"I think I detect a little sex discrimination here." Guinevere stood in front of the machine and quickly duplicated Sally's note on the fresh sheet of paper.

"Good. Now wipe the keys and the knob. We'll take a look at the two notes when we get back to your place." Zac moved around the room as Guinevere carefully wiped away any fingerprints she might have left.

Aware of a new level of tension in him she finished the task and asked, "What's wrong, Zac?"

"It's time we got out of here. Come on, let's get going."

Guinevere didn't argue. She trusted Zac's instincts. If he was getting restless, it was time to go, even if he couldn't give her a specific reason. Without a word she followed him down the hall and out the kitchen door. A few minutes later they were climbing into his three-year-old Buick, which was parked in the next block.

Guinevere stared thoughtfully out the window as Zac started the engine and drove back down First Hill toward Pioneer Square. It was shortly after midnight. "I wish I knew what Madame Zoltana used to keep in that safe."

"Well, one thing is for certain; it doesn't look as if she's planning to be away a long time. Clothing still in the closet, food in the refrigerator. Wherever she went, she intends to come back soon. We're probably lucky she didn't walk in on us," Zac noted gloomily.

"The really interesting thing is that Francine Bates has also disappeared," Guinevere remarked. "I wonder if they took off together."

"You said Francine was still at Gage and Watson the day after you saw Zoltana?"

"Yes. And she was still there that afternoon when I couldn't get hold of Zoltana. But she seemed nervous, Zac. She definitely was not her usual self. Damn. I wish I'd had a chance to set my little trap, so I'd know for certain if she was the one working with Zoltana." Guinevere brightened. "But it must have been her, Zac. She's definitely the most likely candidate."

"No one knows much about Zoltana," Zac said slowly, "but people know a few things about Francine Bates. It might be possible to find her."

"Ah-ha! And if we find her, we might be able to find out where Zoltana is. Good idea, Zac. Let's do that." Guinevere turned in the seat to gaze at him expectantly.

"You have a wonderful way of making everything sound simple, Gwen," Zac told her with a deep sigh.

"Zac, finding people is supposed to be one of your specialties."

"I suppose we might start with the sister," Zac said without much enthusiasm.

"The sister? Oh, that's right. Francine mentioned something about having a sister over on the coast." She frowned. "But Gage and Watson's personnel department isn't likely to help me find her, Zac. Personnel departments have policies about giving out that kind of information."

"I'll try it from my end. You see if any of the people she worked with knows anything about her sister."

Twenty minutes later in her apartment they put the two typewritten notes side by side on a table and examined them.

"Piece of cake," Guinevere gloated. "Look at the smudges on the

E and *T*, and the way the lines aren't quite even. It doesn't take an expert to figure out these are both from the same machine."

"It also doesn't help us very much. It just means that she returned to her house at some point to type the note she sent to Sally."

"Don't be so gloomy, Zac. You have to look on the positive side. We're getting all sorts of information tonight. With this amount of data, I expect you to solve the case in no time."

"This is your case, remember? You're supposed to solve it."

Guinevere smiled sweetly. "I'm a businesswoman. I'm smart enough to hire a professional consultant when I need one."

His own smile was wicked as he dropped the notes onto the table and pulled her into his arms. "This high-powered consultant of yours is getting anxious about his fee. He wants a little on account."

"On account of what?" she teased, twining her arms around his neck.

"On account of it's after midnight, he's tired, and he needs a little loving kindness." Zac bent his head to move his mouth lingeringly over hers. "Let's go to bed, Gwen."

She hesitated. "Maybe we should discuss the case some more, Zac. Shouldn't we make notes about everything we saw tonight at Madame Zoltana's, while it's all still fresh in our minds?"

"We've already spent half the night doing what you wanted to do. Now we're going to do what I want to do. Bed, Gwen."

"It's true, isn't it? You do have a one-track mind."

"Bed, Gwen." One arm draped around her shoulder, Zac guided her firmly down the short hall to the bedroom.

Guinevere cast one quick glance over her shoulder before they turned the corner. The two notes rested side by side on the living room table. When Zac flicked the light switch, they were hidden in darkness. They were clues, Guinevere thought, a little worried. Maybe she ought to lock them up before going to bed. But before she could voice her concern, Zac was unbuttoning her shirt and sliding his hands inside the wasteband of her jeans. She sighed contentedly and leaned against him, delighting as usual in his solid strength.

A few minutes later when that strength enveloped her completely, she forgot all about the two notes lying side by side on the table.

Guinevere phoned Sally Evenson first thing the next morning. Sally had bravely gone in to work although, Guinevere knew, the note from Madame Zoltana must be preying on her mind. Aware of the younger woman's fragile hold on her self-control, Guinevere decided on a firm, upbeat, everything's-under-control approach.

"Sally? This is Guinevere Jones. I just wanted to tell you, Mr. Justis has made terrific progress in your case. He tells me he's very near to settling matters for you."

"Miss Jones, is that for real? What's he going to do?"

"He's going to make quite certain Madame Zoltana gets out of the blackmail business once and for all. You're not to worry about a thing. You could help him get things under control even more quickly, however, if you could remember anything Francine Bates might have told you about her sister on the coast."

"Francine!" Sally was shocked. "What's she got to do with this?"

"We don't know, Sally, but there is a possibility she might be able to tell us something useful. Mr. Justis wants to talk to her. No one knows where Francine is, but he thinks there's a chance she might have gone to stay with her sister. She's never mentioned any other relative, has she?"

"Not to me. I don't know, Miss Jones," Sally said worriedly. "I don't remember much about Francine's sister. She only mentioned her a couple of times. I think she said she spent Christmas with her last year." There was a long pause while Sally tried to remember what she could about the sister. When she spoke again her voice was hesitant. "It seems to me her sister's name was Dorothy or Donna or something like that. I just can't remember."

"Do you think anyone else at work might? You could ask Ruth or Mary or one of the others. Perhaps Miss Malcolm would know."

"I'll try, Miss Jones. I'll call you back as soon as I talk to them."

"Thanks, Sally. I'll be waiting." Guinevere hung up the phone and tried to occupy herself with the usual morning chaos. But Trina was handling the flurry of panicked calls from employers who had just had essential personnel phone in sick. Guinevere spent most of the time making notes of everything she had seen in Madame Zoltana's house the previous evening. Zac was right about one thing. The unfortunate fact of the matter was that they hadn't learned all that much.

Sally finally phoned back half an hour later. "Hi, Miss Jones. I talked to everyone I could think of, and finally Ruth said she was sure Francine's sister's name was Denise. Denise Bates. She thinks she lives somewhere near Pacific Beach. That's all I could find out. I'm sorry."

"Sally, that's wonderful. You've been a tremendous help. I'll call you as soon as Free Enterprise Security finds out anything useful. And don't worry, Sally. Mr. Justis really does have it all under control."

"That's very reassuring, Miss Jones," Sally said with humble gratitude. "Thanks."

Three minutes later Guinevere was on the phone to Zac, who yawned in her ear when she gave him the news.

"Excuse me," he said politely. "I'm still working on my second cup of coffee. I think I'm getting too old for the late nights and wild life you lead, Gwen. You're going to have to slow down for me."

Guinevere said something short and rude. "We would have gotten to bed quite a bit earlier if you hadn't decided to take advantage of me. Now, quit complaining, and tell me what you're going to do next."

"Have a third cup of coffee."

"Zac!"

"Okay, okay. A name and an approximate location should be sufficient. A little time on the telephone should give me an address for Denise Bates. I'll let you know when I've got it. Oh, by the way, I'm going to be a little late getting home tonight. I've got to see a new client around four thirty. Chances are I'll be tied up until six or so. Your turn to cook dinner."

The phone clicked in Guinevere's ear, and she sat looking at the humming instrument. *I'll be home a little late tonight.* It was getting to be so casual, so understood, so very routine. Zac was practically living with her these days. Guinevere tried to decide just how she felt about that, but before she could come to any earthshaking decisions, Trina was interrupting to tell her about the latest crisis. Guinevere sighed and gave up the task of analyzing her relationship with Zac. There didn't seem to be much point analyzing it, anyway. It was just happening.

At five thirty that evening the doorbell chimed demandingly. Guinevere put down the knife she had been using to chop mushrooms and wiped her hands on a towel. It couldn't be Zac, unless he had lost his key. She went into the entry hall and peered through the peephole. A shaft of nervous unease went through her when she saw who stood on her threshold.

Frowning, Guinevere held the door open a few inches but did not stand aside invitingly. "Rick! What on earth are you doing here?"

He lounged in the doorway, golden eyes moving over her with a familiarity that did nothing to stem the anxiety Guinevere was feeling. She refused to let him see how he was affecting her.

"I came to see you."

"I'm busy."

He looked amused. "So I see. Cooking dinner for that big, plodding hulk you're dating these days? What a waste of time. You can do better than him, Gwen."

"I doubt it. Now, would you kindly leave? I've got a lot to do." Guinevere tried to shove the door closed but found it stopped by Rick Overstreet's shoe. She glanced down, annoyed, and the next instant he had pushed his way inside and was closing the door behind him. Guinevere glared at him, refusing to give in to the small, niggling panic that had sprung up out of nowhere. "I'm asking you to leave, Rick." She kept her voice steady and very, very cool.

"I'm not ready to leave." He prowled through her living room as though he found it fascinating. "I'm curious about you, Gwen. I want to see just how much you've changed. You were living up on Capitol Hill when I knew you. This is all new."

"How did you get my address?" she demanded icily.

"It took some work, but I managed." He scanned the books in her huge yellow bookcase, his hands shoved casually into the pockets of his slacks.

"Rick, I—"

He swung around abruptly, facing her. "I've been thinking about us, Gwen."

"I wish you wouldn't," she said bluntly, not liking the glitter in those golden eyes.

"I've decided there's unfinished business between us."

"No, Rick. You finished it before it even began. You must have known I'd never play the role of the other woman. Not for any man."

"I knew. That's why I never told you about Elena. But I wanted you, Gwen. After you lost your nerve and broke off what was between us, I told myself I'd give you some time to calm down. Then . . . things happened. I got the new position with Gage and Watson, and shortly after that Elena died. By the time everything had settled down I'd lost track of you."

"Not only lost track, but lost interest, too, I suspect. I'm sure you went on to bigger and better things—and more cooperative women. Don't try to pretend that what you felt was a timeless passion, Rick. You know as well as I do that you were only looking for a convenient affair. I realized that as soon as I found out you'd lied to me."

He shrugged. "It doesn't matter now. We've run into each other again. There was always something about you, Gwen. . . ." He let the sentence trail off, his eyes intent. "I've discovered I want you again."

Guinevere smiled wryly. "Only because you can't have me. I'm a challenge for you now because I didn't fall right back into your hands the moment you encountered me again. Forget it."

There was a flare from the gold lighter as Rick lit one of his elegant cigarettes. He exhaled deeply, fixing her with a lambent gaze through the smoke. "No," he said finally. "I don't think I will forget it. It's fate, Gwen."

"The hell it is." She held the door open for him. "Please leave," she said very steadily. "Now."

"Before the hulk gets here, you mean?"

"Before I lose my temper and call the police to throw you out!" Guinevere heard the edge in her voice and frantically tried to bring herself back under control. She must not let him affect her this way. She refused to let him frighten her. "Listen to me, Rick. I will try to spell this out as simply as possible. I am not interested in you anymore. I want nothing to do with you. Find some other woman to hypnotize, because I'm immune to your brand of charm. It's shallow and it's meaningless. *Now get out!*"

He approached her with indolent grace, eyes narrowed and gleaming. "You say I'm only attracted by the challenge? Better watch out, Gwen. You're making yourself more of a challenge each minute.

Two years ago you got away with walking out on me, only because I had other things to handle at the time. But now it's different. Now I can do what I should have done then. Are you sleeping with the hulk or keeping him dangling, the way you kept me dangling?"

"That's none of your damn business."

He nodded as if she had answered his question. "You're sleeping with him, I'm sure of it. There's something about the way he looks at you, the way he touches you. He tried to warn me off the other day when he saw me with you, did you know that? In a way, that added to the challenge, too. It would be interesting to take you away from him, just to see how he would react. All things considered, I'm afraid you're becoming damn-near irresistible, Guinevere Jones. I want you, and this time I'm going to have you." He smiled grimly around the cigarette. "But first I think I'll let *you* dangle a bit. It will serve you right. It's time you learned a lesson."

"Rick, if you don't leave, I swear, I'll have you thrown out." Guinevere's teeth were locked together with tension. She watched him take the cigarette from his mouth and casually grind it out in a small pottery bowl that stood on the hall table. It was the bowl where Guinevere kept her car keys. She wanted to scream at him that he had no business using the lovely bowl for an ashtray, but common sense told her to hold her tongue. She wanted to do nothing that would give him an excuse for staying any longer, and losing her temper would accomplish only that. He would delight in making her lose control.

"Good-bye, Gwen." He nodded with a mocking courtesy and walked out the door.

Guinevere shut the door behind him and locked it, leaning against it with her eyes closed in relief. Holding her breath, she waited for the sound of his footsteps to die on the stairs. Only after she heard the faint noise of the outer door closing did she release her breath.

Her heart was pounding with a fear that seemed wholly out of proportion to the incident.

The first thing that caught her attention was the smell of cigarette smoke. Guinevere wrinkled her nose in disgust. It wasn't just that it was smoke; it was Rick Overstreet's smoke. She hurried around the room, opening the windows as wide as possible. She didn't want the smell in the apartment when Zac arrived. She didn't want to have to try to explain Rick Overstreet to Zac. Her own foolishness two years ago was a source of embarrassment, and Zac would simply not understand why the man felt he could show up at her apartment uninvited. Lately Guinevere had begun to sense the streak of possessiveness that ran through Zac. She didn't approve of it, but she had no wish to bring it to the surface. Far better to let sleeping dogs lie.

When she'd finished with the windows, she grabbed the bowl from the hall table and took it into the kitchen. There she held the butt under running water until she was certain it was extinguished and tossed it into the trash can under the sink. She rinsed out the bowl and replaced it just as she heard Zac's key in the lock. Taking a deep breath, she managed what she hoped was a bright smile as he came through the door.

"You're late," she announced, going forward to kiss him with more passion than she'd intended.

"I've got an excuse. I think I've located Francine Bates's sister," he said.

CHAPTER 6

"She's over on the coast, all right," Zac explained as he lounged at the kitchen table while Guinevere finished preparing dinner. He rested one foot on the chair opposite the one he occupied and wrapped his large fist around the small glass of tequila. His tie had been discarded and his collar loosened. He was the picture of domesticity—relaxing after a hard day's work while watching the little woman bustle around the kitchen. Zac intended to take advantage of the domestic scene as long as Guinevere would allow him to do so. "I got an address and a phone number. I tried phoning, but there was no answer, so I'll try again tomorrow."

"What if we can't reach her?" Guinevere dumped the pile of mushrooms into a frying pan and let them sizzle in butter.

"I guess if we can't get hold of her in a couple of days, we can drive over to the coast and see if we can find her," Zac said reluctantly.

"Good idea! I'm impressed that you found her so quickly." Guinevere picked up her wineglass and took a rather large swallow. "You really are awfully good at your work, aren't you, Zac?"

Zac blinked lazily, watching her movements with a shuttered curiosity. The tension in her this evening was new. He'd seen it the moment he'd come through the door. Because of it, he'd refrained from asking her who had been smoking a cigarette in the apartment before he'd arrived. He'd caught the lingering scent of burning tobacco as soon as he'd entered the hall. But before he could casually ask who'd been visiting, Guinevere had thrown herself into his arms. Instinct had warned Zac to wait and see. "In my own slow, humble way I try to do my job," he said with grave modesty. To his surprise she reacted strongly to the joke.

"You are not slow or humble or plodding or anything like it," Guinevere said fiercely. "You are downright brilliant at times."

"Gosh, lady, I didn't know I'd made such a great impression."

She turned back to the stove brusquely. "Well, you have. Are you ready? The salmon is done and so are the mushrooms."

Zac cocked one thick brow. "Salmon? Now I'm the one impressed. What did I do to deserve salmon tonight?" He swung his foot down off the chair and got up to pour another glass of tequila.

"Nothing special. I stopped by the market on the way home from work and spotted a great buy on salmon, so I got some for us. Ready?"

"I'm ready."

She continued to chatter throughout dinner. Zac let her, content to eat the beautifully poached salmon and listen to Guinevere's conversation. The truth was, most of the time he liked listening to her talk. She had a talent for soothing him or teasing him or nagging him or arguing with him that was very satisfying. Zac had a feeling he could listen to her for the rest of his life, merely taking steps to close her mouth when he was ready to take her to bed. Maybe not even then. He liked the small, passionate sounds she made in bed. But there was no getting around the fact that her conversation tonight contained a thread of tension. Zac waited. He was a patient man, and he'd always been good at waiting when it was necessary.

After dinner Guinevere sat back in her chair and drained the last of her wine. "That," she announced, "was terrific salmon, even if I do say so myself."

"It was," Zac agreed, smiling at her. "And this kitchen will smell of fish tomorrow if I don't empty your garbage for you tonight. I'll take care of it while you start the dishes."

"Why do I always get to start the dishes while you empty the trash? There's a male-chauvinist pattern developing in this household, Zac Justis." But she got to her feet and began rinsing dishes under the faucet.

"Some things are biologically preordained," Zac explained as he hauled the garbage out from under the sink. "Women have evolved with a certain innate ability to do dishes, and men seem to have gotten stuck with a talent for emptying garbage. I suppose it's all fair enough, when you consider the great cosmic scheme of things. Be back in a minute."

He opened a drawer and found a twist tie for the garbage sack and headed for the front door. The building's garbage chute was located near the stairs in the outside hall. Standing before the metal panel that opened onto the chute, Zac caught the stale cigarette smell as he started to twist the tie around the plastic bag.

He stood still for a moment, thinking. Then he calmly opened the bag and glanced inside. He found the damp cigarette butt under the paper that had been used to wrap the salmon. Zac stared at it for a moment and then twisted the bag closed and dumped it down the chute. He would be patient.

The damning photos arrived in Guinevere's mail the following day.

She had decided to go back to the apartment before returning to the office after lunch, and her mail had already arrived. The lack of a return address in the upper left-hand corner made her curious about the plain manila envelope. She tore it open with an inexplicable sense of urgency. The message was as straightforward as the one Sally Evenson had received. It also appeared to have been typed on the same typewriter. Madame Zoltana had been busy.

Guinevere stood in the hall of her apartment building, reading and rereading the message.

IF YOU WOULD PREFER THAT MR. JUSTIS DID NOT SEE THESE PHOTOS, YOU WILL STOP MAKING INQUIRIES ABOUT ME. I DO NOT APPRECIATE THE INTERFERENCE IN MY BUSINESS.

After having read the message through at least four times, Guinevere unwrapped the black-and-white photos with a sense of dread. She was not surprised when she saw the crude shots of herself lying naked in Rick Overstreet's arms. No, she was not surprised, but she was suddenly physically sick.

Stuffing the photos and the message back into the envelope, Guinevere ran up the two flights of stairs and stabbed her key into her lock. It took several tries before she could control her shaking hand long enough to get the door open. Her breath was coming in tight gasps and her stomach threatened to rebel. She was damp with perspiration. Blindly she groped her way down the hall to the bathroom and sat down on the edge of the tub, waiting to see if she was going to lose her lunch.

Crouched on the cold porcelain edge of the tub, she clutched the terrible envelope in both hands and thought, This was what it was like for poor Sally. I didn't understand. How could I have known how awful it really is. *Blackmail.*

The photos were fakes, of course. Someone had cleverly taken head shots of her and Rick and applied them to two anonymous nude bodies. But they looked perfectly real. Modern photography techniques could mask almost any kind of fakery.

She had never been to bed with Rick Overstreet, not two years ago, not this past week, not *ever*. But, oh God, the photos looked so real. What's more, they were definitely recent shots. She had not worn her hair that way two years ago. It was the way she wore it now. Zoltana had made certain these pictures appeared very current. Zac would have understood Guinevere's involvement in an affair with another man two years ago. He wouldn't appreciate having it thrown in his face—no man would—but he'd have understood.

But he would never tolerate being a cuckold. Zoltana had wanted her victim to see these shots, to know that if Zac saw them, he must certainly assume Guinevere was currently having an affair with Rick Overstreet. Any man who looked at these photos would believe the worst.

Guinevere sat waiting for the nausea to pass and tried desperately to think. For a few perilous moments it all seemed too much. She wanted to run and hide from Zac and the world. The only way she could steady herself was by thinking of Sally Evenson. That poor, poor woman. How easy it had been to give her bracing advice and tell her not to worry. How easy it had been to hand out the usual trite words about never paying off a blackmailer. Only now, finding herself in the same position, did she know the sense of awful doom and the utter helplessness. Guinevere opened her eyes and stared across the room. At this moment she understood completely how any blackmail victim might commit murder. But she didn't even have that option. Madame Zoltana had disappeared.

The phone rang in the kitchen. For a moment Guinevere blocked the intrusion out of her mind. She couldn't handle anything as normal as the phone right now. Besides, she wasn't even supposed to be home at this hour of the day. But it rang again and again, and at last Guinevere responded out of the habit of a lifetime. Ringing phones had to be answered. Like a zombie she walked into the kitchen.

"Hello?"

"Gwen? What the hell are you doing home at this time of day?"

When she heard Zac's voice, Guinevere thought her throat would close up completely. "I had lunch nearby. Just thought I'd stop and grab my mail."

"I see. When I couldn't get hold of you at the office, I decided to take a chance and try the apartment. Trina said you should have been back from lunch by now."

"What did you want, Zac?"

"I was just doing my consultant's duty and reporting in. I still can't get hold of Denise Bates. I think we're going to have to drive over to the coast. What about tomorrow morning?"

She nodded, realized belatedly he couldn't see her response, and finally found her voice. "Yes. Tomorrow would be fine, Zac. I'll tell Trina she'll be in charge all day."

"Okay, then I'll make arrangements here. Maybe it's all for the best. I was supposed to meet with that crazy interior designer in the morning. This will give me a perfect excuse for canceling the meeting. Oh, by the way, the caterer called to discuss adding a basil dip, for the vegetables, and a bunch of miniature eggplants. I told him to forget both, but he insisted on talking to you first."

"I'll give him a call, Zac."

"I don't care what you do about the basil dip, but I do not want to waste a dime on eggplant, miniature or otherwise. I hate eggplant. Is that clear?"

"Yes, Zac."

"I mean it, Gwen. No eggplant," he said, suspicious of her quick, obedient response.

"I heard you. No eggplant. I'll call him this afternoon. Is that all, Zac?"

There was a short pause. "Are you going back to the office now?"

"Yes."

"I'll pick you up after work. We can walk back to your place together this evening."

Guinevere cleared her throat in a wave of panic. "Uh, Zac, you've been over here for dinner every night this week. And you've stayed the night every night this week. Don't you need to take care of some things around your own apartment? What about your laundry?"

"My laundry's under control, Gwen," he said laconically. "Don't worry, if you don't feel like cooking, I'll handle it. We can have tacos again."

She wanted to cry, and instead she had to sound calm and firm. "Zac, I think we need a little time apart, don't you? After all, we've been almost living together lately. I think . . . I think we're rushing things. We need to maintain our separate identities. We haven't really discussed this, I know, but I thought we understood each other. Please, Zac." She held her breath, knowing her inner agitation was showing and unable to control it.

There was another brief pause from Zac's end of the line, and then he said quietly, "I thought we understood each other, too. I'll pick you up tomorrow for the drive to the coast. Have a good evening, Gwen."

When he gently hung up on her, Guinevere let go of the hold she had been maintaining while on the phone. The tears fell freely until there were no more left inside. Then she picked up the phone again, called the office, and calmly told Trina that she would not be in for the rest of the afternoon or tomorrow.

"Is anything wrong, Gwen?" Trina added, concern in her voice.

"No, Trina. Nothing's wrong." She replaced the receiver and went into the living room. There she spread out the awful photos on the coffee table and tried to imagine exactly how Zac would respond if he ever saw them. When her mind refused to form a picture of his reaction, she decided it was because she couldn't bear to think about it.

Feeling weary and drained, Guinevere leaned back against the couch cushions and wondered vaguely how Madame Zoltana had learned about her and Zac. She wondered how Zoltana knew enough to select Rick Overstreet to use in the photos. And she wondered how Zoltana had found out that Guinevere was making inquiries.

When she got nowhere with that line of questioning, she remembered something Zoltana had said about Zac. *You will not be able to trust him.*

"Oh, Zac," Guinevere whispered wretchedly, "it's not a question of trust." But it was, wasn't it? Yet how could any woman expect a man to look at such pictures and not believe the lie they portrayed? If only Rick Overstreet had not shown up in her life a second time.

Which led back to the interesting question of how Zoltana could have known about Overstreet. Someone at Gage and Watson might have seen them together, Guinevere speculated listlessly. Or perhaps Rick had commented on their past relationship. Gossip could have filtered back to Zoltana's informant.

Guinevere tried pursuing that line of thought for a while, but it led nowhere. Nothing led anywhere. All her thoughts were running in useless little circles. An hour later she was still sitting on the couch, staring helplessly at the photos.

Zac found his own apartment very dull and very confining. It was not a place of relaxation and refuge, and it hadn't been for some time, he realized. Guinevere's apartment was home now. And he hadn't been invited home this evening.

He sat with his feet propped on his coffee table and stared out of his high-rise window, watching night settle on Elliott Bay. He was on his second tequila and was seriously thinking of forgoing dinner altogether in favor of getting disgustingly drunk. He rarely got disgustingly drunk. He couldn't even remember the last time. Probably back in college shortly before he'd dropped out in his junior year. Maybe not even then.

He liked his tequila, but the truth was, he wasn't the type of man who did anything that would take him beyond his own self-control. Except make love to Guinevere Jones. Zac had to admit that when she came alive under his hands, he forgot everything else in the world but their combined excitement and satisfaction.

He wondered what she was doing at this particular moment. Eating, probably. He glanced at his watch. No, by now she would have finished eating. It was almost seven thirty.

Why hadn't she wanted him there tonight? He had to face the fact that he might have worn out his welcome. Zac took another sip of tequila, and when he was tired of confronting that fact, he went on to the next fact, which was that Guinevere Jones had said she loved him. She belonged to him.

Maybe she just wanted some time to herself. Everyone needed time alone. She was right, he had practically moved in with her lately, and she wasn't accustomed to having a man in the house. Of course, the reverse was true, too. He wasn't accustomed to living with a woman. They both had adjustments to make. They both needed time to make those adjustments. Perhaps he had been rushing things lately, but it had all seemed so right.

But tonight everything seemed very, very wrong. He didn't like the feeling. There was the same sense of wrongness he felt when a case was going sour. But this hardly constituted a Free Enterprise Security case. This was Guinevere Jones.

Zac's mind jumped to the matter of the cigarette butt in Guinevere's garbage. That led to the memory of her tension last night. She had even been tense in bed for a while. He hadn't tried to make love to her. Instead he had pulled her close, his arm wrapped around her bare waist, and just held her. Eventually she had fallen into a heavy sleep. When he knew for certain she was no longer awake, he, too, had been able to sleep.

The vague tension he had sensed in her last night was nothing compared to the tension that had gripped her this afternoon when he had phoned her at home. Hell, if it were any other woman, he would have thought he'd interrupted an afternoon tryst with a lover.

The tequila in his glass slopped onto the coffee table as that last thought flashed through his mind. No. Not Guinevere. She wouldn't do that to him.

The memory of cigarette smoke drifted through his mind again, nagging at him, refusing to let go.

She wouldn't betray him with another man. She would be totally honest. She would tell him if she had fallen in love with someone else.

Unless she sensed how hard he would fight to keep her from walking out of his life.

She would still be honest. It was her nature.

This was getting him nowhere. He was a patient man, Zac told himself. A slow, patient, plodding man. Hell, the people he'd once worked with had called him the Glacier. But he had his limits. Zac set down the tequila glass and got to his feet. Taking his windbreaker out of the hall closet, he opened the door, went out into the hall, and took the elevator down to the lobby.

Out on First Avenue he caught a bus that took him to Pioneer Square. He got off near Guinevere's apartment house and stood on the sidewalk looking up at her window. The arched panes of glass were dark. If she wasn't home, he'd go out of his mind.

He used the key she had given him to let himself inside the apartment house door, and then he steadily climbed the two flights to Guinevere's door. When he stood outside her apartment, he hesitated a moment, listening. Slowly he inserted his key into the lock.

Guinevere was stricken with a curious sense of inevitability when she heard the key turn in the lock. She didn't move, but she turned her head to look at him as he opened the door. She hadn't bothered to turn on the lights, and in the shadows he seemed to fill the doorway. Carefully she set down her half empty wineglass. She couldn't find any words, so she stared mutely. It was Zac who spoke first, not moving from the threshold.

"You want to tell me what this is all about?" he asked, far too softly.

"I can't."

"Why not?"

"Because I love you," she whispered hoarsely.

"Then you have to tell me," he said simply. He still didn't move. "I'll go crazy if you don't."

"You'll despise me if I do."

Unexpectedly he smiled at that. "You know that's not true."

She shook her head helplessly. "Please go away, Zac."

"Don't you trust me?"

She caught her breath. *You won't be able to trust him.* "She said I wouldn't, you know. That afternoon when I had the psychic session with Madame Zoltana, she said I would be afraid to trust you when the chips were down."

"And are you?" he asked heavily.

She considered the question for the thousandth time. "It isn't exactly a question of trust."

"Isn't it?"

Guinevere looked down at the envelope on the coffee table. "Yes," she said quietly, "I guess it is." She stood up, the sense of inevitability stronger than ever. There really was no alternative. Zac had to know, and she had to face his reaction, whatever it might be. She picked up the envelope and held it out to him. "I love you, Zac."

He closed the door and came forward to take the envelope from her hand. "I know," he said. Then he calmly reached out and switched on a lamp. He turned the envelope upside down, spilled the photos and the typed message out onto the table, and stood quietly looking down at them.

Guinevere looked down at the damning evidence, too, her emotions as chaotic as if she were seeing the photos for the first time. Her voice stark, she said, "They're fakes, Zac. I have never been to bed with Rick Overstreet. I swear I would never betray you with him."

"Don't you think I know that?" Zac asked with a curious half smile.

She looked at him, the emotional trauma of the past few hours plain in her eyes. "Oh, Zac!" Then he was holding out his arms, and she was throwing herself against the safety of his chest, burying her face against his shoulder. She felt his arms tighten around her protectively, felt the strength in him, and then she was crying again. But this time the tears were the healing kind.

Zac held her for a long while, his hands moving on her back with strong, soothing movements that seemed to comfort him as much as they did Guinevere. He cradled her close until the tremors stopped shaking her body. Finally Guinevere lifted her head and looked up at him, her eyes still damp.

"I'm sorry, Zac. When I got home this afternoon and found those pictures, it was just more than I could handle. I couldn't think straight—couldn't think how to explain them to you. I was sure you would take one look at them and that would be the end of everything."

"That, sweetheart, is why blackmail often works. The victim is sure that if the secret is revealed, it will be the end of everything."

"But, Zac, there's no secret. It's all a fake. Photographic tricks."

"I know."

"But how can you be sure?" Guinevere wailed, irrationally upset by his calm acceptance of the horror that had nearly driven her out of her mind that afternoon. "You barely glanced at them. And even if you study them you can't tell where the photos of the heads were joined to the bodies. I know—I've been studying them for hours."

"Gwen, my love, you wouldn't do that to me. If you had fallen for someone else, you'd make a clean break with me first. You wouldn't betray me."

"I know, but . . ."

His mouth crooked faintly at the corners, and he reached down and scooped up one of the photos. "And even if I weren't such a trusting soul, I do have eyes and a very vivid memory. I know every square inch of your sweet body, Guinevere Jones, and this ain't it. Whoever posed for the nude portion of this shot is a little too big on top and much too small on the bottom."

"What?" Guinevere tore her gaze from his face to look at the picture. In the photo, the man's hand was cupping the woman's breast, and there was no doubt that there was a fair amount of bosom left over. When Zac's hand covered Guinevere's breast, he cupped the whole of it in his fingers. Guinevere was not built like a centerfold model. She smiled mistily as she met Zac's eyes again. "Are you saying I'm flat-chested and plump in the rear?"

"I'm saying you're perfect the way you are," Zac said diplomatically, shoving the photos back into the envelope. "Do you mind if we put these away for now, and talk about them later? I've had a very difficult afternoon."

"Because of me?"

He nodded solemnly. "Because of you. Don't ever do that to me again, honey. I couldn't take it."

"Zac, I'm so sorry," she whispered. "I've been so scared."

"You should have told me immediately what had happened." He cradled her face between his palms, his eyes intent and serious. "You know that, don't you?"

"Yes. Now I do. But I was in shock most of the afternoon. I couldn't seem to think straight."

"And you're still used to handling your problems on your own, aren't you?"

"I suppose so. Not that I was doing much of a job handling this one. My God, Zac, now I know what poor Sally Evenson must have felt like when she got her note from Madame Zoltana. It's the most incredibly helpless sensation. You just want to reach out and kill the blackmailer."

Zac paused. "An interesting thought."

Guinevere tilted her head, not understanding. "What do you mean?"

"Just what I said. It's an interesting thought. But we will pursue it later, along with a few other outstanding questions."

"What questions?"

"Never mind. They can wait. Right now I can't. I am going to take you to bed, Guinevere Jones, and together we are going to reassure each other."

"Are we?" She smiled tremulously as his big hands slid over her shoulders and down to her waist.

"Can you think of anything else you'd rather do?"

"No." She wrapped her arms around him. "Love me, Zac. I've never felt as alone as I did this afternoon."

"Neither have I."

He picked her up and carried her into the bedroom, not bothering with the light. "Undress me, Gwen," he muttered as he began removing her clothing. "Undress me and tell me how much you want me."

"More than anything else in the world," she answered tightly as the melting heat flooded her body. She felt her shirt fall from her shoulders, and then he was cupping her small breasts, his fingers enclosing her completely. His palms moved tantalizingly on the nipples, coaxing them into tingling firmness.

Guinevere sighed and leaned against his chest as she pushed off his shirt. She threaded her fingers through the curling hair that tapered down to his flat, strong stomach. She could feel the hardness of him through the fabric of his slacks. His hands went around her, urging her close until the waiting heaviness of him was pressed against her soft thighs.

"I want you, Gwen."

"I know," she whispered as he tugged her jeans and panties down over her hips. Then he was lowering himself slowly to his knees, his mouth moving over her breasts and soft belly until her senses were reeling.

"Ah, *Zac*." She inhaled sharply when he dipped his fingers between her legs and found the warm, silky moisture that betrayed her readiness. She steadied herself, her fingertips digging into his broad shoulders, as she felt his mouth in a stunningly intimate kiss. "Oh, my darling!"

"Come to bed, sweetheart. It's been a long day." He rose slowly, stepping out of his slacks. Gently he tumbled her down into the sheets and came down beside her, one thigh anchoring her firmly beneath him. "Wrap yourself around me and tell me I'm home."

"You're home, Zac. So am I."

Her fingers flicked along his hot skin, seeking the thrusting contours of his back and hips. When he pushed her thighs apart with one hand and settled himself between her legs, she urged him closer with eager hands. She loved the heavy weight of him along her body, loved the full, waiting male power in him. Most of all, Guinevere realized, she loved Zac Justis.

He came to her with a sure, surging strength that filled her completely, unleashing the exciting, twisting rhythms of her own body. She moved beneath him, glorying in the almost savage force of his possession. Her nails bit into his back with feminine hunger. Guinevere gave herself completely when she gave herself to Zac, and he responded just as totally. Neither of them held back anything during these wild, sweet moments of physical union.

When the culmination overtook them, it did so almost simultaneously. Guinevere was unaware of how Zac made himself wait so that he could watch the passion in her face as she cried out his name, but she heard his echoing response a moment later and felt the shudders of his hard, solid body.

When it was all over, Guinevere turned and nestled against Zac's warm body, content at last and ready for sleep.

"Not just yet, Gwen," Zac said quietly. "You can sleep later. Right now we're going to talk."

CHAPTER 7

"Who is Rick Overstreet?" Zac asked. "I'd like the whole story this time."

Guinevere stirred in the cradle of his arm. "Do we have to talk about him now?"

"Mmm. I think so, yes."

She sighed, knowing there was no way of postponing the discussion. When Zac asked a direct question in that tone of voice, he didn't let go until he had the answer. Guinevere knew better than to argue. "Rick Overstreet was a mistake."

"An old lover?" His voice was almost perfectly neutral.

"No. I told you, I've never been to bed with him. Not recently and not two years ago when I met him. But I dated him for a while. I met him while working at the company he was with at the time. I was with a temp firm. It was shortly before I opened Camelot Services. Rick can be very . . ." She broke off, looking for the right word. "Very charming. He has a way of casting out lures to women. Two years ago, I suppose I had hopes that something more might develop between us."

"What happened?"

"I found out that he was married. He hadn't bothered to inform me of that fact. When I realized he'd lied to me and saw him for what he was, I told him I had no intention of being the other woman."

Zac considered that for a long moment. "Didn't he tell you he was on the verge of divorcing his wife? That's the usual line in a situation like that."

"It wouldn't have made any difference, because I'd never marry a man who divorced his wife because of me. But now that you mention it, no, he never did try that line. Maybe he realized it wouldn't have worked. I was very angry at the time, and I made it very clear I never wanted to see him again."

"He let you go without a fight?" Zac sounded skeptical.

Guinevere smiled, her lips moving slightly against his chest. "Not everyone is as tenacious as you are."

"I wouldn't have let you walk out that easily."

She lifted her head and looked down at him. "You wouldn't have lied to me about a wife in the first place."

"No," he agreed, watching her face. He was quiet for another long moment. "You ran into Overstreet again at Gage and Watson, didn't you?"

Guinevere nodded. "I suppose it was bound to happen sooner or later. Seattle isn't that big, and I have contacts with many of the companies with offices downtown. As long as he and I were both working in downtown Seattle, the possibility of running into him existed. Frankly, I hadn't worried about it, because I hadn't given him much thought in the past two years. He hadn't thought about me very often, either, as far as that goes. He admitted it. A lot of things happened to him shortly after I stopped seeing him. He got distracted, I suppose. And then, knowing him, there would have been other women closer at hand than I was."

"What kind of things distracted him?"

"Well, his wife died, for one thing. And he got a new job. The position at Gage and Watson, I guess. I don't know what else might have happened. I haven't talked to him that much. Just a few times in the hall at Gage and Watson."

"So he wrote you off until he ran into you again at Gage and Watson. Did he tell you right away that his wife had died?"

"Well, yes," Guinevere admitted.

"And then he decided to see if he could pick up where he left off two years ago."

"I told him I wasn't interested," Guinevere said earnestly, alarmed by the emotionless tone of Zac's voice. "It was the truth."

He looked at her through lazily lowered lids, which concealed the expression in the ghost-gray eyes. "But he's still trying?"

Guinevere took a deep breath. "I think he sees me as a challenge now. Unfinished business. He came over here last night, before you got here."

"I know."

Guinevere's eyes widened. Then she nodded slightly. "Yes, you do, don't you? I should have known."

"Why didn't you tell me?"

"Because I wasn't sure what you would do. I was afraid things might get violent if you knew he was pestering me. I didn't want you involved in a brawl on my behalf. I also felt that Rick Overstreet was my problem, something I had to handle. I'm a big girl, Zac. I'm supposed to be able to handle my own problems. And I *am* dealing with him."

"The hell you are. He's hunting you. I saw his face the other day when you got off the elevator with him. And now he's come to your apartment."

"I threw him out!"

"Next time I'll throw him out," Zac told her evenly. "That should settle the matter."

"Zac, you make me sound like a stupid, silly little female who can't handle a man who's making a pass." Guinevere realized she was beginning to sound shrewish. "I'm thirty years old, and I am not weak or stupid or silly. Furthermore, I do not want any violence. Do you understand?"

"Let's forget that subject and go on to the next."

"Which is?" she asked, suspiciously, not ready to let go of the first topic of discussion.

"Those pictures in the envelope."

The fight went out of Guinevere. She collapsed against him. "My God, Zac, I thought I was going to be sick when I saw them. I never knew how bad blackmail really is. It hits you right in the stomach. When I think of all the little lectures I gave Sally, I get thoroughly disgusted with myself. I didn't really understand what she was going through."

"Don't knock your little lectures to Sally. From what you've told me, they helped her a great deal. She was actively helping us find Francine Bates's sister, wasn't she? She has the feeling that something is being done. She's fighting back. That's the important thing, Gwen."

"You're right. It's the feeling of being totally helpless that gets you. Like I said, I just wanted to commit murder."

"Yes. The thought has crossed my mind more than once this evening. Gwen, if it's crossed our minds, I'm sure the solution has occurred to a few other people, too."

"What do you mean?"

Zac crooked an arm behind his head, his brows meshing into a thick line above his narrowed eyes. "Maybe Madame Zoltana is lying low because she's nervous about one of her 'clients' doing something drastic."

"You read that note she sent. She wants me to stop making inquiries."

"Which means," said Zac, "that she knows you've been making them. She also knows something about you and Rick Overstreet. At least, she knew enough to use him in her threat. She must have realized that photos of you with that particular man would really upset you, because you had a link to him in the past. You must be right about her having an insider at Gage and Watson."

"I suppose anyone could have seen me talking to Rick in the hall at work and then seen me with you. Whoever saw me could have put two and two together. It's even possible Rick made some comment. I wouldn't put it past him to . . . to imply things to other men. You know what I mean." Guinevere paused a moment. "I get a little nervous around Rick," she went on in a low voice. "I don't like him. Someone might have noticed that I wasn't comfortable with him and decided to use the information somehow. I still think the most likely candidate is Francine Bates."

"We'll see what we can find out in the morning." Zac's voice changed abruptly, returning to normal. Gently he lifted her aside and pushed back the sheet. "Hungry?" He slapped her lightly on her lush rear.

Guinevere blinked. "I hadn't thought about it."

"Well, I am. I didn't have dinner tonight. Too busy sitting alone in my apartment stewing over you. I'm going to fix myself a bite to eat. Taking you to bed always gives me an appetite."

Guinevere smiled, watching him as he walked across the room to retrieve his Jockey shorts. Then he disappeared into the bathroom. She liked the solid, hard planes of his body. There was something very substantial about Zac, both physically and mentally. She got to her feet and reached for a robe.

A few minutes later she found him in the kitchen, slicing cheese and arranging crackers on a plate. He was eating a saltine as he worked. She watched him from the doorway for a moment.

"Thank you, Zac," she said softly.

He looked up, still munching. His ghost-gray eyes were full of the rare warmth he reserved for her alone. "For what?" he asked around the cracker.

"Believing me."

He swallowed the cracker. "Next time something like this happens, keep in mind that you could tell me the IRS is a benevolent association devoted to the preservation of hamsters, and I'd believe you." He popped another cracker into his mouth.

Guinevere came up behind him and wrapped her arms around his waist. "I love you, Zac."

He turned around, smiling, and shoved a cracker into her mouth. "I love you, too. Let's eat."

After a fairly lengthy drive, Zac and Guinevere reached the coast around nine o'clock the next morning, and sometime later they finally found the Bates cottage. It took three stops to ask directions and several wrong turns, but at last Zac was parking the Buick on the side of the road in front of the weathered gray structure. He sat for a moment with his hands on the wheel, studying the house.

The cottage was quite isolated. It sat alone on a bluff overlooking the ocean. There was a thick group of trees to the rear that marched up a hill and disappeared on the other side. A car was parked out front.

"I think the best way to handle this is the straightforward

approach," he finally said. "I could pretend to be an insurance sales-man or something, but I think that would be a waste of time."

"Do you think anyone's at home?" Guinevere peered at the cot-tage windows.

"I think so. Let's go." He got out of the car and walked around to the passenger side to open Guinevere's door.

The brisk breeze off the sea caught her neatly bound hair as she stepped out of the Buick, sending wispy little tendrils fluttering around her face. Guinevere automatically put up one hand to keep the hair out of her eyes as she followed Zac to the front door.

It took three knocks before anyone answered. The woman who reluctantly opened the door appeared to be in her late fifties or early sixties and resembled Francine Bates. She wore her blond-tinted hair in a short, curling bob, and looked at Zac with suspicious eyes.

"Yes? What do you want?" she asked bluntly.

"We're here to see Francine Bates. Please tell her it's important and that we won't be leaving until we've talked to her."

"She's not here." The woman tried to close the door but found its progress impeded by the presence of Zac's foot. "Now, look here, mister—"

"Justis is the name. Zachariah Justis. My friend here is Guine-vere Jones. Francine knows her."

"I don't see what that has to do with anything. I've told you my sister isn't home!" The woman looked desperately at Guinevere, as if hoping she would find the woman less implacable than the man. "Please, I'm telling you she isn't here. I haven't seen her in ages. She lives in Seattle."

Guinevere sensed the near hysteria in her voice and moved closer, smiling gently. "It's all right, Miss Bates. I only want to talk to your sister. It's very, very important. We've been trying to find her for several days. Please help us."

"What's going on here?" the woman demanded shrilly. "I tell you, I've had it with all this nonsense. I can't take any more. Now, get out of here and don't come back, do you hear me?"

Guinevere sensed Zac was about to move forward aggressively. She put her hand on his arm and spoke again soothingly to the woman. "Please, Miss Bates. We must talk to her. A great deal depends on what she can tell us about Madame Zoltana."

The older woman opened her mouth to protest once more, but her words were cut off by another voice. Francine Bates appeared behind her sister, her face drawn and tense. She looked at Guinevere, ignoring Zac.

"It's all right, Denise. I knew that sooner or later someone would find me," she said wearily. "Let them in. I'll talk to them."

There was a moment of silent tension as the four people regarded one another, and then Denise opened the door to admit Zac and Guinevere. She stood stiffly aside as they entered.

"Sit down," Francine said quietly. "Denise, would you fix us all some tea?"

Denise hesitated, her eyes on her sister. Then she turned and marched into the kitchen.

Guinevere glanced around at the comfortable old cottage, with its old-fashioned, slightly shabby furniture and the amateurish seascapes on the walls. She sank into the depths of the sofa, and Zac sat down beside her. Francine sat across from them, still looking only at Guinevere.

"You've found me," Francine said finally. "What do you want?"

It was Zac who responded, hard, his voice dark. "Some answers."

Francine nodded to herself. "Yes, I guess you do. I wish I had all of them."

Guinevere leaned forward. "Francine, tell me. Were you Madame Zoltana's inside woman at Gage and Watson? Was it you who told her who I was and gave her the kind of information she needed to impress her clients?"

Francine's mouth tightened. Her hands clenched in her lap. "It seemed harmless at first," she finally whispered. "Just a game. Everyone got a kick out of it."

"And Madame Zoltana split the twenty dollar fees with you?" Zac asked, hazarding a guess.

Francine flashed him a quick glance and nodded. "I realized it was getting to be more than a clever little game, but somehow I couldn't stop it. Zoltana seemed to have certain people hooked. She kept making them return, and the fees she charged got higher. But people like Sally and Ruth seemed to want to go back to her."

"How did you meet her?" Guinevere asked kindly.

Francine sighed. "By accident. I went to her myself one day for a psychic reading. I was just curious, you understand. I don't really believe in that stuff. But she was good. Very clever. I was intrigued. When it was over, she suggested I tell some of my friends at work. She said she would give me a finder's fee for every new client I sent to her. I didn't see anything wrong with that, so I agreed. I got a fee even if someone else made the appointment for a new client, the way Ruth did with you."

Zac shifted slightly on the old sofa. "But things got more complicated, right? The next thing you knew, she was asking you for information about the clients before she gave them their sessions."

Francine looked at him helplessly. "She just wanted to know a few details here and there. Said it would make the sessions more entertaining for the people." Francine bit her lip. "She also said she would give me a larger percentage of the fee. I shouldn't have done it. I know I shouldn't have done it. But somehow it was all so easy, and I needed the money, and I didn't think I was really hurting anyone, and . . ." Her voice trailed off as she looked down at her twisting hands.

"Where is Madame Zoltana, Francine?" Zac asked.

"I don't know." The response was barely audible. She didn't look up.

"Yes, you do," Zac insisted.

"No! I swear I don't know." Francine's head lifted. Her eyes held a look of desperation.

"But you're afraid," Zac went on ruthlessly. "You disappeared a day or two after Zoltana did. Why?"

"Because I don't know what happened to her! Don't you understand? I'm afraid that whatever happened to her might happen to me. If anyone guessed that I worked with her . . ."

"What makes you think anything did happen to her?" Zac demanded.

Francine shook her head again. "I don't know. It's just a feeling. I went to her place that evening after Guinevere had her appointment, just like I always do, to collect my share of the week's fees. But she wasn't there. I tried her again later that night, and she still wasn't there. I began to get worried. Zoltana never went out at night, you see. She was home most of the time, in fact. Every time I saw her, she was cooped up in that dark house with all the drapes pulled and the smoke so thick you could cut it with a knife. She told me once she couldn't stand being out at night because it made her nervous. I teased her about being afraid of ghosts or something, and she just looked at me and said it was the truth. I believed her. You see, I—I got to know her a little during the months I was sending clients to her. Once in a while, she talked to me when I went to get my cut. I think I'm probably the only one she ever did talk to about anything personal. She was a very odd woman in a lot of ways. Sometimes I got the impression she really did think she had a few of those psychic powers she pretended to have."

The woman's fear was a tangible thing. Guinevere could feel it emanating from her in waves. "Francine, what is it? Do you think one of Zoltana's clients got angry enough to do something drastic? Who would do such a thing? I've seen the ones she really victimized. They were people such as Sally Evenson and Ruth what's-her-name at Gage and Watson. Zoltana knew what she was doing. She picked on the fragile people, the ones who wouldn't fight back. From what I can tell, Zoltana was a shrewd operator. She wouldn't have tried to run her scam on someone who might have retaliated."

Francine sucked in her breath and reached for a hanky just as Denise returned with the tea tray. Francine stared at the teapot, gathering her self-control.

"I think she had something else going on besides the psychic sessions," Francine said after a long moment.

Zac pounced. "What makes you think that?"

"Something she said a couple of times. I once asked her if she was really making much of a living off the psychic sessions, and she told me it was enough to get by on but that she had a . . . a pension plan for her old age."

"A pension plan?" Guinevere stared at Francine's troubled face.

"She used to say that every time she looked into her bowl, she saw a comfortable future for herself. I couldn't figure out what she was talking about, so one night I asked her. She just said she had something big going on the side. Something that was making a lot more money for her than the piddling little psychic sessions, and that in another couple of years she was going to have enough to retire and move to Arizona."

"All right, Francine," Zac said flatly, "what do you think she had going on the side?"

Denise spoke up before her sister could respond. "Franny, no, don't say anything. I think you should keep quiet about this."

Francine gave her a bleak glance. "Why, Denise? If they found me, someone else could, too. What good does keeping silent do? We can't stay locked up in this house forever."

Denise closed her eyes and sat back in her chair.

"Well?" Zac prompted with a ruthlessness that made Guinevere wince. The man had no subtlety, but he got answers.

"I think," Francine said slowly, "that Zoltana was blackmailing someone."

Guinevere frowned. "All her little scams could be called blackmail."

"No, not those little twenty- and thirty-dollar psychic sessions she conned people into. I mean real blackmail. Thousands of dollars. I think she had someone important on the hook and that person finally figured out who was doing it."

"And you think that same someone killed her? You think she's dead?" Zac concluded.

Francine nodded miserably. "I'm afraid that if he or she ever finds out I was working with Zoltana, I'll be next. Whoever it is will assume I know whatever it is that Zoltana knew."

"But you don't," Guinevere said.

"No. If I did, I'd know whom I had to fear, wouldn't I? As it is, I'm living in terror of almost everyone. It's very hard to live that way, Gwen. The truth is, I was almost glad to see you standing out there on the porch a few minutes ago. I knew you must have come about Zoltana, and I didn't think you could be the one she was blackmailing."

"Why not?"

Francine shrugged. "I don't know. I just didn't think the killer would look like you." She swung her weary gaze to Zac. "Him, maybe, but not you."

"Zac is investigating Madame Zoltana's disappearance," Guinevere said firmly. "He's not interested in killing her."

"Yet—at any rate," Zac added laconically. "Francine, what would you say if I told you we have some reason to think Zoltana is still alive?"

Francine looked startled. "You do?"

"Since she disappeared, two different people have received blackmail threats. Not penny-ante stuff, but real threats."

"I don't understand," Francine said in confusion. "I've been so convinced that she must have been killed, I can hardly believe she's alive."

"We don't know if she is or not. There's another possibility," Zac went on, ignoring Guinevere's questioning glance. "You might be right. Whomever she was blackmailing might have killed her and then decided to use her files to continue fleecing her victims. He or she might not have been able to resist the easy pickings. One thing's for certain, the price of Zoltana's silence has risen considerably. One threat said the payoff would be a thousand dollars."

"Good lord," Francine whispered. "I don't understand this. I just don't understand."

"Neither do we," Zac informed her, "but we're going to find some answers. That's why we're here." He pulled a notepad out of his jacket pocket. "Let's run through everything again, Francine, step by step. I want you to try to remember every conversation you had with Zoltana concerning her 'pension plan.'"

Denise shuddered and looked at her sister. "What's going to happen?"

"Whoever has decided to go into blackmail in a big way is going to find that it doesn't always pay," Zac said softly. "He or she has already made one serious mistake."

"What's that?" Francine asked urgently.

"Whoever it is tried to blackmail Gwen," Zac explained calmly. "That's the end of the line." His ballpoint pen clicked. "Now, tell me again about Zoltana looking into her own future."

Guinevere sat back and watched Zac lead Francine Bates through a detailed history of her association with Madame Zoltana. It took almost an hour, and Zac had the blunt techniques of an inquisitor. At the end of the hour poor Francine Bates was exhausted. When Zac finally closed his little book with a snap, the older woman looked at him anxiously.

"What should I do now?"

"Stay out of sight while I see what I can do back in Seattle. We know the envelopes containing the new blackmail threats were mailed in the city, so chances are whoever's behind them, whether it's Zoltana or someone else, is still in town. I'll be in touch as soon as I know anything."

"But, Mr. Justis, I'm frightened," Francine said as Zac got to his feet.

"Maybe you should have thought about that before you started helping Zoltana con people like Sally Evenson," he remarked, taking Guinevere's arm and heading toward the door. He didn't wait for a response. He pushed open the door, got Guinevere outside, and let the screen slam shut behind them.

"You were rather hard on her, Zac," Guinevere said quietly as they walked to the car.

"No, I wasn't. You've seen me when I come down hard on people, Gwen. I treated Francine Bates with kid gloves, and you know it."

Everything was relative, Guinevere decided as she slipped into the front seat of the Buick. She had seen Zac pin a man against a wall by the throat while he asked his questions. Compared to that, she supposed it could be said that Zac hadn't been hard on Francine Bates.

"Do you think she's safe here?"

"I don't know," Zac admitted as he put the car in gear. "But I can't protect her and she's not willing to go to the police, so there's not much anyone can do except try to find out what happened to Zoltana. That's the only way to put a stop to this mess."

"What do we do next?"

"Eat. It's almost noon."

"Be serious, Zac."

"I am serious. I've got a taste for razor clams, and this is supposed to be a good place to find them. Let's go find a restaurant."

There was something about his voice that alerted her. "You're on the edge of Deep Think," she accused.

"Deep Think?"

"You know, when you turn off the outside world and go someplace inside your head and think. You always do it when you're getting near the turning point in a case. Before you do, tell me what you think happened to Zoltana. Do you believe she might have been killed?"

"It's a possibility. If Francine's right about there being a major blackmail victim somewhere in the picture, someone who was shelling out thousands of dollars for Zoltana's silence, then, yes, it's a possibility."

"And that same someone might have discovered her client files and decided to try to get what he or she could out of them." Guinevere thought about it. "Whoever it was had to know I was starting to ask questions."

"True. Which suggests that if someone else is involved, he or she is probably associated with Gage and Watson."

"Or knows Sally Evenson. Sally might have said more than she should have, if someone pumped her carefully enough. She's very sweet, but not the most sophisticated thinker in the world."

"She was afraid of Madame Zoltana. Do you think she might have killed her, Gwen?"

"No."

"Are you sure? Anyone can kill, given the right set of circumstances," Zac said.

"You have a very low view of human nature."

"I have a realistic view of it."

Guinevere turned the matter over in her mind. "I suppose Sally might have been capable of murder if she was sufficiently frightened. But I don't see her figuring out how to get rid of the body or how to open the safe. Furthermore, I don't think she'd try to blackmail Zoltana's clients. It just isn't in her to be that organized and ruthless, Zac. Murder in the heat of fear and anger, possibly. But not cold-blooded blackmail later."

"Okay, who does that leave?"

Guinevere ran through the list of people who had gone to Madame Zoltana. "There's Ruth. But she's a lot like Sally. Then there's Mary, who's much tougher. One or two others. But Zac, why assume Zoltana's dead? Those last blackmail threats came from her typewriter, don't forget."

"I haven't forgotten. But if someone killed her, it would make sense for the killer to make it look as if Zoltana was still behind the blackmail attempts. It would be simple enough to slip back into Zoltana's house and use the typewriter."

The razor clams were perfectly fried and accompanied by huge, chunky fries. Guinevere and Zac ate their fill in a rustic little café down by the water's edge, and afterward they drove back to Seattle.

Zac moved in and out of what Guinevere termed Deep Think during most of the long drive home. He would surface long enough to ask her a question or two and then grow silent again, driving without a word for long stretches of time. By the time they reached Seattle he had almost ceased communicating altogether. Guinevere waited patiently for the results, but none were forthcoming.

As soon as they reached Guinevere's apartment, Zac checked in with his answering service. He hung up the phone with an expression of satisfaction on his face.

"Well, one good thing came out of today, at any rate. Gertie says Evelyn Pemberton tried to get in touch to tell me she's going to accept the job. She says we can discuss the pension plan next week. What a relief."

"I was sure of her all along," Guinevere informed him confidently.

"I'm glad somebody was. Now, as long as I don't find any eggplant being served at the party, I will count myself a reasonably lucky man."

Zac awoke early the next morning, fully alert and hating the uncomfortable sensation of being too *aware*. It meant matters were getting serious. He rose on one elbow and looked down at Guinevere, who slept peacefully curled against him. Whoever had tried to terrorize her would pay a heavy price. Attacking Guinevere was not within the rules of the game. Since Zac had made this particular rule himself, he intended to enforce it.

CHAPTER 8

At eight o'clock on the morning after the interview with Francine Bates, Zac sat at his desk and gazed moodily out of his cubicle window. The view across the hall was as uninviting as ever. The salesman who usually occupied the cubicle on the other side of the corridor was out of town and had left his drapes pulled. Zac was staring at a wall of beige drapery, which did nothing to stimulate his mental acuity. He was looking forward to having a real view when he moved upstairs the following week.

Zac was steadily working his way through his second cup of coffee while he considered everything he had on the Madame Zoltana mess. The more he thought about it, the more he decided to spend the morning tying up a couple of loose ends. They might or might not relate directly to the matter, but in any event, his own curiosity would be satisfied. Zac finished the coffee and decided to walk down Fourth to the Seattle Public Library as soon as it opened.

Two hours later he was seated in front of a microfilm reader scanning the obituary sections of two-year-old editions of the *Seat-*

tle Times and the *Post-Intelligencer.* It took a while, but with the help of a librarian and an index he found what he wanted. Overstreet was not a very common name. The obituary on Elena Overstreet was brief and to the point. In a copy of one of the other papers he found a short article on Mrs. Overstreet's death. Zac dug out his notebook and made a few entries. Then he thanked the librarian and went back to his office to see how good his newly formed contacts with the police were. Shortly before lunch Zac called Guinevere.

"I'll pick you up in a few minutes. We have a few things to talk about."

Guinevere hung up the phone feeling uneasy. Zac's voice had taken on that cold, detached manner it always had when he was closing in for the kill.

The kill. It was only a casual phrase used to describe the finale of a case, but somehow the words seemed underlined in her mind. Guinevere shook off the feeling and turned to Trina.

"Mind if I take lunch first? Zac's on his way over. He wants to talk to me about the Zoltana case."

"No problem. I'm supposed to be dieting this week, anyway. Take your time, but think of me while you're wolfing down french fries and spinach pasta."

"French fries and spinach pasta?"

"That's what I'm craving at the moment."

When Zac arrived a few minutes later, it was clear that food was not uppermost in his mind. The night before Zac had been sliding in and out of his Deep Think state. Today she knew instinctively he was on the edge of that other state of being she had seen him in when a case was closing. He was turning into a hunter. It was on these occasions that Guinevere was painfully conscious of the essential core of hardness in the man.

"I'm supposed to order french fries and spinach pasta," she said lightly as they walked the two blocks to the waterfront.

"We'll eat at a fish and chips stand. I don't want to waste time at a full-service restaurant," Zac said flatly.

"Well, at least I'll get the french fries," Guinevere muttered to herself. This was not the time to argue. Zac had his mind on something else.

They gave their orders at the counter of a sidewalk fish bar and waited until the trays were ready. Then they carried the food to the patio eating area and sat down across from each other.

"Okay, what gives?" Guinevere couldn't stand the suspense any longer.

"I did a little checking this morning."

"On what? Or should I say, on whom?"

"On Rick Overstreet." Zac reached for the vinegar bottle.

Guinevere halted the french fry that was halfway to her mouth. "Why?" she asked simply.

"Curiosity. Plus the fact that he's at least peripherally involved in this case. Don't forget that whoever was trying to put pressure on you knew there was some reason you would panic at the sight of photos of you and Overstreet. That means someone knew the two of you were more than passing acquaintances."

"Not necessarily," Guinevere said slowly.

"Blackmail works on an emotional level. That means there has to be something emotional on which the blackmailer can base the threat. Somebody knew he or she could scare you to death with a threat involving Rick Overstreet. The next question we have to ask ourselves is whether Zoltana would know that much about you and Overstreet."

"If Rick had talked about us at work," Guinevere began uncer-

tainly, not wanting to speculate on what he might have said, "someone could have heard and reported to Zoltana."

"The only one reporting to Zoltana was Francine Bates. She
admitted yesterday she'd seen you and Rick in the hall, but I didn't
get the impression it had struck her as a major event. The only man
she mentioned to Zoltana was me, and only because she'd seen us
leave for lunch together and assumed we were involved. It was a
logical assumption. It would not have been logical to assume you
and Overstreet had a secret past just because she saw you with him
in the corridor at Gage and Watson."

"We do not have a secret past!"

Zac ignored the protest, using his plastic fork to break up a chunk
of fried fish. "As far as I can tell, Overstreet is the only one who
knew about your past relationship with him."

"But, Zac, why would he use that information to blackmail me
into staying out of the Zoltana case? Unless—" She broke off,
shocked. "Surely you don't think he's involved—or do you?"

Zac lifted his head, munching fish. "I went to the library and
checked the obit on Elena Overstreet's death. Did you know she died
in a car accident? Went off the edge of the highway somewhere
along the Oregon coast."

Guinevere swallowed her french fry. "No. I didn't know. Rick
told me she died a couple of years ago, shortly after I stopped seeing
him, but he didn't say how."

"There's more. I made a few phone calls this morning after I'd
checked the old newspapers. Elena Overstreet was a very wealthy
woman. Family money. Rick was the chief beneficiary in her will.
When she died, he became a comfortably wealthy man."

Guinevere thought of those gleaming golden eyes and shivered.
Her mouth went dry. "Do you think he killed her, Zac?"

"I don't know. I talked to the cops about the accident. According to the report, there was no sign of foul play. There was a lot of fog that night, and Elena Overstreet had been drinking. Given the circumstances, her going over a cliff wasn't all that surprising."

"What was she doing driving the coastal highway? Why wasn't she on the interstate? She was a Northwest native. She wouldn't have been terribly concerned with taking the scenic route, especially at night," Guinevere noted thoughtfully.

"Mmm. The question occurred to me, too. How long has Overstreet smoked those French cigarettes?"

Guinevere stared at him. "How did you know about his choice in cigarettes?"

"I carried out the trash for you the night he visited your apartment, remember? I found the butt in the garbage."

"Oh, yes. Quite the master detective, aren't you?" She didn't know whether to be annoyed or resigned. Zac hadn't said a word to her about the smell of smoke that night. He'd simply waited until disaster had struck to inform her he already knew about her visitor. There were times when Zac frightened her a little. He had a lethal sense of timing. "He was smoking them two years ago when I first met him. He still is. I don't know how long he's preferred them. Why do you ask?"

"Remember the cigarette butt we found next to Zoltana's floor safe?"

Guinevere's stomach went tight. "I remember." She waited for the punch line, knowing already what it would be.

"It was the same French brand that Overstreet smokes. I didn't check the contents of her ashtrays that night. They might have all contained that brand. Who knows? It could be a coincidence. She might just happen to prefer the same brand as Overstreet. But I don't think it's very likely."

Guinevere absorbed that information for a long moment. "But, Zac, what can it possibly mean?"

"It means I think we should take another look around Madame Zoltana's this evening. If nothing else, we can verify what type of cigarette she smokes. I should have done that last time. There are other things I want to check, too."

"We've already been through her house."

"I think we missed something," he said calmly, forking up the last of his fish.

"What makes you think that?"

He shrugged. "I don't know. A hunch."

She nodded, knowing better than to argue with him about one of his hunches. She had learned to respect them. "All right. What time shall we go? Midnight again?"

"That should be about right."

Guinevere sat watching him polish off his french fries and wondered if Zac's hunches were becoming contagious. She suddenly had the same need to take another look around Zoltana's house.

At five minutes to twelve Zac again picked the lock on the back door of Zoltana's small cottage. The door opened, and Zac and Guinevere stepped over the threshold.

There was no sign that anything had been touched since their last midnight visit. Cautiously they walked through the house, using Zac's slender flashlight.

"We know someone must have used the typewriter since we were last in here," Guinevere said as they moved into the bedroom.

"True, but if he was careful, there wouldn't be any evidence. I doubt he'd be stupid enough to leave prints." Zac played the light over the desk and started opening drawers.

"Zac, what exactly are we looking for? Surely the important stuff was in Zoltana's safe, and if she was killed, the killer has whatever she was hiding."

"I think the client files were in that safe, but I don't think the heavy-duty stuff was," Zac said, scanning through some notepads he'd found. "If Zoltana was into big-time blackmail, I doubt she kept her evidence in that safe."

"Why not?"

"It's too obvious, for one thing. Look how easily we found it. Floor safes are fairly common. Besides, it would make sense to keep her client files separate from the really incriminating stuff."

Guinevere opened a closet door, using her handkerchief. "Maybe she put the juicy stuff in a safe-deposit box at the bank."

"Maybe, but I doubt it. I don't think she was the type. Besides, blackmailers usually keep the evidence close at hand."

"Why?"

"Beats me. I told you, blackmail is an emotional business—on both sides. The blackmailer knows his or her life is probably only as safe as the evidence being used against the victim. There's an emotional need to keep that evidence under tight wraps, where it can be checked frequently. Blackmail is also very illegal, remember? The blackmailer prefers not to involve the establishment or the authorities in any way, so it makes sense to stay clear of banks. Too much chance of being observed. On top of everything else, Francine told us Madame Zoltana was a very private, almost housebound person. My guess is, she hid her evidence here in the house, and I don't think the blackmailer found it after he killed her. If he had found it and destroyed it, he probably wouldn't have sent you the faked pictures and the note telling you to stay out of the mess."

"I don't know, Zac, it just doesn't make a lot of sense. If Rick did kill his wife, how on earth would Madame Zoltana know about it?

And what evidence could she possibly have had? For Pete's sake, we don't even know that she's dead or that Rick was responsible, if she is."

"Right now it's all guesswork. If we can find the blackmail evidence, we'll have something to go on."

Guinevere closed the closet door with sudden decision. "The most important room in this house is Madame Zoltana's contemplation room."

Zac was crouched beside the desk, checking the back of a drawer. He looked up and met Guinevere's eyes. "A good point."

"But we already found her secret safe in there," Guinevere felt obliged to note. "How much could be hidden in that room?"

"Why don't we find out?"

He got to his feet and led the way back down the hall, coming to a halt in the doorway to the contemplation room. He shone the light around the gloomy interior.

"What about the walls?" Guinevere asked, running her fingertips along the surface of one wall.

"I don't think so. Not easily accessible. She would have had to tear up the wall every time she wanted to check her evidence. And she would have checked the evidence frequently, just to make sure it was safe."

"Another floor safe?"

"Possible, but not likely."

Guinevere glanced around the room. Her eyes fell on the crystal bowl in the center of the table. A thought occurred to her, and she went forward slowly, staring down into the bowl. "Francine said something," she murmured. "Remember? Something about Zoltana saying she looked into her own future every time she gazed into the crystal bowl?"

Zac froze, his eyes on Guinevere's profile as she stood looking at the bowl. "Lady, there are times when I think you might have missed your calling." He strode forward and used a cloth to lift the crystal bowl aside. There was a small panel of not quite opaque plastic in the table on which the bowl had sat. Zac pressed it gingerly, but nothing happened. Then he went down on one knee, shining the flashlight up under the table.

Guinevere crouched beside him as he reached up to trace a faint line in the wooden undersurface. She recalled the small, hidden drawer he had noted on their last visit. For a few minutes nothing happened, but then Zac let out a soft, satisfied exclamation as something gave. An instant later Guinevere was gazing up into a small hidden compartment. There was a tiny battery-powered lightbulb inside. There was also a small package wrapped in a plastic sandwich bag.

"So that's how she made the bowl glow," Guinevere observed as Zac removed the package. "A lightbulb, just as you guessed."

"Uh-huh." Zac sat cross-legged on the carpet and focused the flashlight on the plastic bag. "Too bad I didn't have enough sense to keep making guesses when I was hot. I should have checked the table the last time I was here."

Guinevere leaned forward on her knees and read the gold embossed letters on the leather book in the bag. "It's a diary."

Zac peeled open the bag and pulled out the small book. He flipped it open to the first page. "Elena Overstreet," he read.

Guinevere got to her feet. "Let's get out of here. I don't want to read that diary in this house."

He didn't argue, merely looked at her curiously for a few seconds and nodded. "We'll take it back to your apartment."

Back at her apartment Guinevere practically ran up the stairs, carrying the diary in both hands. As soon as Zac had opened the door she headed straight for the kitchen and opened the little book on the table.

"What do you think it's all about, Zac?"

"Calm down and we'll find out." He pulled the book toward him as he sat down. Guinevere leaned forward, craning her neck to read the fine, feminine hand.

The diary dated from three years previously. The last date was August fourteenth, two years earlier.

"She died August seventeenth, according to the newspapers," Zac said as he scanned the last entry first.

Guinevere stared as a familiar name leapt off one of the pages. "Look! There's a reference to Madame Zoltana. Damn, I wish Elena's handwriting was easier to read. Go back a few pages, Zac. I want to see where Madame Zoltana first appears."

Zac obediently flipped through the pages. Zoltana's name first occurred some six months before Elena's death.

It is clear the woman has a genuine talent. At our first session she demonstrated her abilities beyond a shadow of a doubt. She knew how unhappy I am and how fearful I have become lately. Unlike Dr. Stevens, she doesn't try to tell me it's all in my head and then write out a prescription for more pills. Madame Zoltana is a great comfort to me. I fully intend to make another appointment. I am not going to tell Rick about her. He would only ridicule me, and I can't take any more of his mockery.

Guinevere sucked in her breath. "So Madame Zoltana was Elena's psychic counselor during those months before her death."

"Looks like it." Zac turned a few more pages, reading quickly. "Elena Overstreet was one scared woman, Gwen. Listen to this."

I can't shake the feeling of foreboding. I talked to Madame
Zoltana about it again yesterday, and she told me that she sees a
great darkness on my horizon. I told her about my panic attacks
in the middle of the night, and she said they were meant as
warnings. She is hoping that if she sees me on a frequent basis
she will be able to determine the nature of the warnings. I am
going back to her again tomorrow. Rick is not home tonight. No
doubt he is out with another of his whores.

Guinevere winced as she read the last line. "It wasn't me," she
told Zac defensively. "I didn't even meet him until a month after
that."

"And you were never one of his whores, so relax," Zac said
grimly.

"I think I'm going to feel guilty when this is all over," Guinevere
said sadly.

"Why? When you were seeing Rick, you didn't even know Elena
existed."

"That's true."

"And when you found out about her, you told Overstreet to take
a flying leap."

Guinevere nodded again, mutely seeking reassurance.

"So stop making guilty noises and help me figure out what's
going on in this diary."

His utter lack of patience with her attack of guilt made Guinevere
smile in spite of herself. "That's what I like about you, Zac. You're
so straightforward about life's little problems."

"I do make an effort not to let them bend my brain into spaghetti,
unlike some people I could mention," he retorted dryly. "Ah, here
we go, another entry mentioning Rick."

If I tell anyone about what happened last night, I know I will be
told I'm mentally ill. Perhaps they will send me back to the
hospital. I couldn't stand that. No one but Zoltana believes me. I
know Rick tried to kill me last night. All those pills he insisted I
take, and then the alcohol he encouraged me to drink. I know he
wanted me to overdose. Thank God I had the sense not to swallow
the pills. He must have been amazed when I appeared at breakfast
this morning.

"She thought he was trying to kill her, Zac!"

"It gets worse."

Together they pored over the diary, following Elena's heart-
wrenching story. The woman had been terrified of reporting her
fears to anyone but Zoltana, apparently because Elena had had a
history of psychological problems. Eventually Zoltana became her
confidant, and it was obvious Zoltana had made the most out of the
situation. Toward the end of the diary Elena was visiting Zoltana
three or four times a week, while Rick was at work. She never told
her husband of the psychic counseling sessions.

There were two more incidents in the diary that Elena reported
as attempts on her life. Both would have looked like accidents or
suicide if they had succeeded. By the next to the last entry it was
obvious that Elena was nearly hysterical with fear.

I don't think I will live out the week. Rick is a total stranger to
me now. Perhaps he always was. I have never been so terrified in
my life. I think he bought a gun yesterday. Perhaps he has given
up trying to make my death appear to be a suicide. I must get out
of this house. I have made up my mind. There is no one who will
believe me or shelter me except Zoltana. I cannot ask her to take

the risk of offering shelter. If Rick discovered I was hiding with her, he would surely kill her, too. No, I must go off by myself and hide. I have taken money out of the bank, and I have the keys to the car. Rick had hidden them, but I found them anyway. I will leave this diary with Zoltana, along with my written request that any accident I appear to suffer be investigated as a possible case of homicide. I will instruct her that if anything should happen to me, she is to turn the diary and my request over to the police. Heaven help me, I should have left long ago. But perhaps there never was a time when I would have been safe. From the moment Rick married me, I have been his victim. He has watched me as a cat watches a mouse, waiting to pounce.

There was a handwritten note folded up in the back of the diary. A neat, formal little request from Elena Overstreet to the authorities. Guinevere's eyes burned when she read it. "That poor woman," she breathed.

Zac closed the diary. "Well, it's obvious she didn't make the best possible choice of confidants when she picked Madame Zoltana. Zoltana took her for a ride as long as she was alive, and after Elena died, she decided to go big time and blackmail Rick Overstreet. I think we can guess what finally happened to Madame Zoltana."

"I wonder how Rick found out she was the blackmailer."

"Any number of ways. Given enough time, Zoltana probably would have made a few slips and exposed herself. Once Overstreet knew who she was and what she had on him, she didn't stand a chance." Zac tapped the small book against the tabletop, his eyes unreadable. "The problem is that Overstreet can't relax completely, even if he has gotten rid of Zoltana."

"Because he didn't find the diary," Guinevere concluded.

"Exactly. He must have emptied out the safe that night and assumed he'd found what he needed. But all he got were the client files."

"This diary is not going to be enough to convict him of murder, Zac. There's no proof here, only his poor wife's fears and suspicions."

"True, but there's enough to put him in a very untenable position and probably enough to reopen the investigation of Elena's accident. No telling where that might lead. Furthermore, we've got a missing person on our hands and more than enough evidence to send the police to Overstreet asking pointed questions."

"You know what really worries me?" Guinevere asked quietly.

"What?"

"Francine Bates. Zac, if Rick didn't find this diary the night he ransacked the safe, he's bound to wonder where it went. And if he ever figures out that Francine was Zoltana's inside person at Gage and Watson, he'll assume she has the diary."

"I know," Zac said simply. He reached for the phone and dug his notebook out of his pocket.

"What are you going to do?"

"Tell Francine and her sister to take a short vacation until I can convince the authorities to look into this. That's going to take some doing, and I'd just as soon the Bates sisters were staying anonymously in a hotel. If we found them, Overstreet could find them."

"He'd have to figure out first that Francine was involved with Zoltana."

"That's not so difficult to figure out, Gwen."

"You're right. Even I did it." She waited anxiously while Zac dialed the Bates cottage on the coast. After a few minutes it was obvious there wasn't going to be an answer. Zac hung up with a grim expression.

"Maybe they're not home."

"I think it's more likely they still aren't answering the phone. They're scared, remember."

A new level of alarm flared in Guinevere. "Zac, we've got to warn them."

He eyed her. "The only way to do that is to drive over to the coast."

"I know."

"We're talking a two-and-a-half-hour drive, and it's already twelve thirty."

"I know," Guinevere said again.

There was silence in the kitchen while Zac and Guinevere sat looking at each other. Then Zac got to his feet.

"Right," he said decisively. "Let's get going."

The drive to the coast seemed endless, although in truth Zac made excellent time on the empty highway. Fifty miles out of Seattle it became obvious there was a storm brewing. By the time they neared the ocean it had arrived in full force.

"Thank heavens we didn't have this rain to drive through until the last few miles," Guinevere remarked as Zac turned on the windshield wipers. "It would have slowed us down."

"Let's just hope the whole damn trip hasn't been wasted."

She gave him an alarmed glance. "What do you mean? You don't think anything has happened to Francine and Denise, do you?"

He exhaled patiently. "I only meant I hope they really are in that cottage and not out for the evening visiting friends or something. Be just our luck to make this drive when a phone call in the morning might have been all that was needed."

"I would have been a nervous wreck by morning," Guinevere told him.

"Theoretically, they aren't in any more danger now than they have been for the past few days."

"Except that Rick might be closing in on Francine." Guinevere chewed her lower lip. "I just hope he doesn't figure out her connection to Madame Zoltana too quickly."

Zac slowed for the turnoff to the Bates cottage. It was nearly three o'clock in the morning, and the lights were off in the house.

"They're probably in bed," Guinevere said reasonably.

"Probably."

"So why am I so jumpy all of a sudden?"

Zac gave her a faint smile as he parked the car. "Damned if I know. I was hoping you could tell me why I'm so jumpy."

"You're never jumpy," she accused him, holding her purse up to shield herself from the rain as she got out of the car. "You're always cool, calm, and collected. I don't know how you do it."

"Vitamins. Ready?"

"Wish you kept an umbrella in the trunk," Guinevere muttered as she hastened after him.

"Seattlelites don't carry umbrellas."

"A myth." She ducked under the shelter of the porch and brushed rain from her leather purse as Zac rang the doorbell. When there was no response, he tried pounding heavily. Guinevere frowned. "They might be afraid of anyone coming to the door at this time of night. Perhaps they're playing possum."

"Miss Bates!" Zac shouted through the door. "It's Zac and Gwen. We have to talk to you."

"Open the door, Zac." Guinevere was compelled by a fierce sense of urgency. Apparently Zac was feeling the same force.

"It's open," he said, shoving at the door.

"Don't waste your time," Rick Overstreet said from the far end of the porch. "They're not home."

Guinevere whirled around to see him step out of the shadows, an ugly, snub-nosed gun in his hand.

"Zac!"

Zac didn't bother to answer. His hand closed around her wrist, and he yanked her forward into the house, slamming the door behind them. A shot cracked viciously as the door shut, the bullet slicing through the air where Guinevere had been standing a second earlier.

CHAPTER 9

Guinevere got only a brief view of the dark living room and kitchen of the cottage as Zac raced her through both rooms, but they appeared empty. There was no sign of either Bates sister.

"Zac, what are we going to do?"

"The woods out back," he bit off, yanking her through the kitchen. "With any luck, Overstreet will think we're hiding in the house, at least for a few minutes. That might give us some time. Why is that goddamn Beretta of mine always stuck under the sink in my apartment when I need it most?"

Guinevere didn't argue, as he paused for a second to open the back door and glance outside. The rain was coming down in thick, heavy torrents now. The endless dull pounding of it was a blessing, as far as Guinevere was concerned. The sound masked their movements through the house. The oppressive darkness visible through the back door offered a haven. Guinevere plunged into it without any hesitation. She had no desire to huddle under a bed inside the house waiting for Rick Overstreet to hunt down his quarry. She'd had one horrifying glimpse into his face out there on the porch, and she knew without a shadow of a doubt that Rick had murder in mind.

"It won't take him long to figure out we're not hiding in the house," Zac said as they plunged into the heavily wooded area.

"The car . . .?" Guinevere's breath was coming quickly already. The wet undergrowth slapped and clawed at her jeaned legs. She didn't know how far she could run, although being pursued by a man with a gun was probably going to be an excellent incentive.

In the wet darkness Zac shook his head. "The area around it is too open. No cover. We'd never make it if he spotted us. Our best bet is to draw him as far as we can into these trees."

"And then what?" Guinevere gasped.

"Then we do something real clever."

"Like what?"

"I'll let you know as soon as I think of it. Come on, behind those bushes."

"I think those are blackberry bushes, Zac. Be careful. Full of thorns."

Zac dodged around the edge of the looming clump of bushes, and Guinevere followed. Her wrist was getting sore from the relentless pressure Zac was exerting on it. She didn't complain.

"You think he'll come after us?" she asked, glancing back over her shoulder. She could see little in the darkness. The dark bulk of the house was a featureless blot barely visible between the trees.

"He'll come after us." Zac sounded grimly certain. "He has to come after us. He's got too much at stake. We know who he is and what he's done. He can't afford to let us get away."

"Somehow," Guinevere muttered dismally, "I didn't expect my big case to end quite this way."

"Neither did I. Life with you is full of surprises, Gwen." The observation was clearly not meant as a compliment.

A harsh, cracking sound echoed through the rain. Guinevere gulped air. "Zac!"

"He's shooting blindly. He can't possibly see us."

"Zac, I saw a light," Guinevere whispered after another quick glance over her shoulder. "He's got a big flashlight."

"Well, at least we'll always know right where he is, won't we? That flashlight will act as a beacon."

"I love the way you always look on the bright side."

"Come on, I think this is about as far as we can go. The trees are starting to thin out again, and we need their protection. We have to stay among them." Zac slowed to a halt and tugged Guinevere to the right.

She struggled after him, her chest tight with the effort of drawing in oxygen. "If we get out of this, I think I'd better sign up for an aerobics class. No stamina."

"You're doing fine. I'm the one who'd better sign up for the class." He pushed her down behind a massive, chest-high cluster of twisted berry bushes. "Listen to me, Gwen. I want you to stay here, understand?"

Guinevere ignored the stinging in her palm as she unthinkingly closed her hand around a thorny branch. She looked up, trying to see his face in the darkness and rain. In the wet shadows she got only an impression of harsh planes and angles. His eyes seemed colorless, but the glittering intensity in them was frightening. It was the image of a face belonging to a creature that hunted and killed to survive. It crossed her mind that it was because of her that Zac had once again been transformed into this grim, relentless, very dangerous being.

"I'm sorry, Zac," she heard herself whisper, her voice a mere thread of sound.

He didn't pay any attention to the useless apology. "Don't move, Gwen."

"Yes, Zac."

He urged her down until she was crouched in the mud, and then he was gone, his passage soundless in the night. Guinevere hugged herself, recovering her breath as she strained to listen. She became aware of a weight on her right shoulder and realized in vague surprise that she still had her leather bag. Amazing how strong a woman's instinct was when it came to hanging on to her purse.

Minutes passed. Guinevere could hear nothing but the endlessly thudding rain. She knew Zac was out there somewhere, hunting the man who was hunting them. Her mind conjured up a bizarre scene of two dangerous wild animals prowling through the night, seeking each other's throats. She thought of Rick Overstreet's golden cat's eyes, and of Zac's strong, quiet strength.

Another shot cracked through the trees. Instinctively, Guinevere ducked, although she knew Rick couldn't possibly see her. The strain of waiting behind the berry bushes was quickly eating at her nerves, though. She needed to know where Overstreet was.

She crawled through the mud on her hands and knees, peering around the edge of the berry thicket. For a moment she could see nothing, and then Rick's flashlight cut a vicious swath through the night. She froze, trying to spot Zac and wondering how long it would take Rick to find Zac's hiding place or her own.

When the light shifted in another direction Guinevere caught an impression of movement to her left and realized it was probably Zac. She narrowed her eyes, struggling to see through the pouring rain, and decided he was working his way around an invisible circle that would ultimately bring him to a point directly across from her.

It made sense from his viewpoint, she realized. He would be able to keep an eye on her location and make sure Overstreet didn't find her first. He would also be able to track Rick's progress through the woods. But as far as Guinevere could tell, the only action Zac would be able to take would be to leap out and try to take Rick by surprise. She shuddered. Rick had a gun and a flashlight. It was going to be damn risky.

Minutes slipped past. Guinevere was soaked, and she was getting chilled, but still she crouched where Zac had left her. The slanting flashlight beam kept cutting through the night in a pattern that indicated Rick was methodically searching every inch of the wooded terrain. He must have realized that Zac was unarmed.

Guinevere flinched as the flashlight began moving closer. Zac was right. In one respect the light made it easy to keep tabs on Rick. But there was a certain horrifying inevitability about its movement. Given enough time, Rick was sure to find one or both of them. Guinevere huddled more tightly into herself, watching the flashlight through the twisted berry vines. She was soaking wet.

"You should never have gotten involved, Gwen."

Rick's voice shocked her. For some reason, she hadn't expected him to start talking. He must be feeling very confident. Or perhaps he thought he could rattle her and Zac.

"What made you do it? How did you figure out that Zoltana bitch was blackmailing me? It was a mistake to drag your lover into this. I'm going to have to kill you both now. You know that, don't you? And when I'm done with you two, I'll take care of that goddamn Francine Bates. Zoltana gave that stupid diary to her, didn't she? It's the only explanation. It took me a while to put it all together. I didn't realize the Bates woman was connected with Zoltana until today, when I had a talk with one of your silly little temps at work. She let it slip, and then I realized what must have happened to Elena's diary. But I can't figure you out, Gwen, or that bastard with you. How the hell did you get involved?"

Rick was edging closer, the flashlight still moving in sweeping arcs. Overstreet was only a dark, lethal shadow behind the glare of the light. Guinevere wished she could make herself smaller. The temptation to break and run was almost overwhelming, but instinct warned her that that would be stupid. Rick was too close now. He would detect the movement. Her fingers closed around a rock lying in the mud beside her. It was a poor excuse for a weapon, but she didn't have anything else. Guinevere held her breath, aware her fingers were shaking around the cold, hard rock.

She was tensing herself for a wild, desperate throw, when she realized Rick had changed direction. He was no longer coming toward her berry-bush cover. The flashlight was moving toward a point diametrically across from her. It was the direction in which Zac had disappeared.

Guinevere moved her head slightly, trying to follow the beam of light. It glanced off several trees and then skimmed over a small, tumbled pile of rocks. It froze on the rocks, and Guinevere knew for certain Rick had found Zac's hiding place. What's more, she knew Rick had realized the same thing. The light didn't shift from the rocks.

"Come on out and I'll make it quick and clean," Rick promised with a hungry anticipation that went well with his catlike eyes. "I want to get this over with. Come on," he urged, moving slowly toward the jumble of granite. *"Come on!"*

Zac didn't stand a chance. His hiding place was exposed in the full glare of the flashlight. The most he could hope to do was make a break for it, and Guinevere knew he'd never make it. Rick would cut him down in a split second. Fury overwhelmed her. She was on her feet before she had time to think, heaving the shoulder bag uselessly in Rick's direction. It fell short, but it brought Rick around with jolting swiftness, the flashlight blinding her.

"You bastard!" she yelled and then dove for the mud as Rick lifted the gun. A shot slammed through the berry bushes above her head, and the flashlight swung wildly, as though Rick had staggered. She flattened herself, waiting for the next shot, but it never came. Instead there was a shout of rage from Rick Overstreet and the unmistakable sound of bodies hitting the ground.

Guinevere jerked to her feet, knowing Zac must have jumped the other man. The flashlight lay on the soggy ground, its steady beam revealing a twisting flurry of arms and legs. Guinevere raced forward, but she knew even before she reached the light that Zac had everything under control. She was in time to see the final savage blows as he straddled Overstreet and slammed his fist against Rick's jaw. Overstreet went abruptly still.

"Zac! Are you all right?" Guinevere scrambled for the flashlight, aiming it at his face. Blood glinted on his mouth. In that instant he was the hunter who had made his kill. In the brilliant glare of the flashlight his eyes were pools of slowly retreating menace.

"I'm fine. Would you kindly stop trying to blind me with that goddamn flashlight?"

"Oh, sorry." Hastily she swerved the light out of his eyes and aimed it at Overstreet. There was considerably more blood on Rick's handsome features than there was on Zac's face. "I was scared to death."

"Not half as scared as I was when you stood up and threw that stupid purse at him," Zac muttered, reaching for the gun, which had fallen into the mud. He climbed to his feet. "What the hell did you think you were doing? I thought I told you to stay behind those bushes."

"He had you pinned behind those rocks. He was going to kill you!"

"I wasn't behind the rocks," Zac said mildly, watching her. "I was over there behind those trees. That pile of rocks was a little too obvious."

Guinevere stared at him. "You weren't behind the rocks? But I was sure I'd seen you disappear in this direction."

"We can discuss this at some other time. Not now. Help me get this bastard back to the house."

Guinevere bit her lip at the disgusted anger in his voice. It was obvious Zac was not in a cheerful mood. She could hardly blame him. Silently she bent to grab one of Rick's limp arms.

It was six o'clock in the morning before Guinevere and Zac finally checked in to a small beachfront motel. The desk clerk had taken one look at Zac's bruised face and cold eyes, and hadn't argued about the fact that his new guests had neither luggage nor a semblance of respectability. He pointedly pretended to ignore Guinevere's disreputable appearance. Her hair was hanging in damp tendrils around her shoulders, and she was wearing an oversize shirt that had been loaned to her by a sheriff's deputy.

Zac accepted the key without a word and led the way along the second floor to the room they had been assigned.

"First, a shower." He slammed the door shut and locked it.

Guinevere didn't want to argue with him any more than the desk clerk had. Obediently she headed toward the bathroom, stripping off the borrowed shirt and the rest of her clothing as she went. Zac followed, leaving a trail of muddy clothes behind him. When she had the hot water on full blast, he stepped in beside her.

Guinevere waited until she could stand it no longer. Zac had been dangerously silent too long. The only real talking he had done had been to the sheriff's men, whom he had called from the Bates cottage. Clutching the bar of soap, she looked up at him through the steaming water.

"Why don't you just chew me out and get it over with? I can't stand the suspense."

He opened his eyes beneath the water and glared at her. For a moment he was silent, but there was emotion moving now in his eyes. That had to be some sort of improvement, Guinevere figured. She hated it when Zac's eyes went cold.

"You little fool. You almost got yourself killed." He didn't touch her, but Guinevere got the impression that was because he didn't quite trust himself to touch her.

"Zac, I've already apologized for that scene back in the woods. I told you, I thought Rick had found your hiding place. How was I to know you weren't behind those rocks? It was a logical place to hide." Her eyes widened slightly. "Which was exactly what you wanted Rick to think, didn't you? You were going to jump him from behind when he tried to flush you out from the cover of the rocks."

"That was the general idea," Zac said through gritted teeth. "How was I to know you were going to pop up and start yelling and throwing purses?"

"But Zac, you've got to admit it provided a useful distraction for you," Guinevere said logically. "Who knows? You might not have gotten a good chance at Rick otherwise."

"That is not the point, Gwen." He put his big hands on her bare shoulders and brought her close. "The point is that you risked your neck out there, after I had given you strict orders to stay down and keep out of sight."

"Yes, well, I felt I had to improvise. And it worked, Zac. You got a clear shot at him. Admit it. Admit my causing that distraction was very useful for you."

"I'll admit nothing of the kind. I ought to turn you over my knee."

She grinned, relaxing slightly as she sensed some of the tension draining from him at last. She put her arms around his neck and let the tips of her breasts brush his chest. "How long have you had this kinky streak in you?"

Zac groaned and pulled her closer. "If I weren't so damn tired,

I'd do it, you know. But somehow, after that little game of hide-and-seek in the woods, plus two hours of talking myself hoarse trying to explain this mess to the authorities, I find my reserves of energy are totally depleted. Turn off the water and let's go to bed, Gwen. We both need some sleep before we drive back to Seattle. I'll finish yelling at you later."

"Whatever you say, Zac." She turned off the taps and reached for a towel.

Twenty minutes later they collapsed side by side beneath the covers, the drapes firmly pulled against the early morning light. A waiting silence hung over the bed for a few minutes, and then Zac tucked Guinevere against him, his leg settling with possessive intimacy over hers.

"Gwen?"

"Hmm?"

"You probably saved our lives back there in the woods."

Guinevere's lashes lifted. "What?"

He sighed and settled her closer. "You were right. The distraction you caused bought me the time I needed."

"Oh, Zac . . ."

"I don't want to think about how many years it took off my life, however," he concluded.

"I wouldn't worry about it," she smiled. "You're in great shape."

There was another stretch of silence, and then Zac spoke again, into Guinevere's ear.

"Gwen?"

"Hmm?"

"It turns out I'm not sleepy. Too much adrenaline, I guess."

"That's too bad, seeing as how you've already charged this room to your corporate account," she reminded him regretfully. "You're going to have to pay for it whether we use it or not."

"We can always put the bed to another use." His palm closed possessively over her breast as he nuzzled the sensitive place behind her ear.

Guinevere sighed contentedly. "Yes, I suppose we could. Waste not, want not."

Zac pushed her back against the mattress. Then he came down on top of her with a sudden urgency that whipped the banked fires of her own sensuality into a glowing blaze. They made love until the jagged edges of the night's danger and terror were dulled, and then finally they slept.

Three days later Guinevere stood in the center of Zac's new office suite talking to Sally Evenson and Evelyn Pemberton. She was entertaining them with the details of the Zoltana case, while Zac worked himself into a frenzy of anxiety and party-giver's panic. Periodically he moved through the room, double-checking the position of the caterer's platters. Then he disappeared into the second office to count champagne glasses. The reception was due to start in fifteen minutes, and Zac had convinced himself that no one would appear.

"Zoltana had been running her little con game for years," Guinevere explained to Sally, who listened with avid attention. Sally was wearing her royal blue blazer tonight and was thrilled to have been invited as one of Zac's clients, even though she didn't pay one penny of Zac's usually hefty fees for his services. Sally was unique in that she had gotten his help for free. Still, ultimately she had been a client, and as such she deserved an invitation to the evening's festivities.

Evelyn Pemberton nodded, one eye on Zac, who was adjusting a canapé tray for the tenth time. "I can understand how it would work. She gave her clients the impression she really could read their past and guide them in making decisions about the future. Then the susceptible ones kept coming back for more. A nice, steady income."

Sally sighed. "She could be very persuasive."

"I don't doubt it," Guinevere agreed. "She certainly had Elena Overstreet on a string. The poor woman latched onto Madame Zoltana and clung to her. Zoltana fed her fears, the way she normally did, probably assuming they were false. It undoubtedly came as a shock when Elena died. There sat Zoltana with the incriminating diary and enough knowledge to guess what might have happened. She hesitated for several months, but then she contacted Rick Overstreet anonymously and let him know her silence could be bought for a price. For a while she got away with it."

"How did he find out she was the blackmailer?" Evelyn Pemberton asked. She swung around suddenly. "Mr. Justis, please don't worry about that canapé tray. It's perfect the way it is."

"I was just straightening it," he muttered, stalking into the other office.

"According to the cops, Rick finally tracked Zoltana down by keeping an eye on the drop point she chose for the payoffs. It wasn't easy, because she changed the points constantly, and Rick couldn't take long hours off from work to watch bus depot lockers and private post office boxes all day long. But one day a couple of months ago he got lucky."

"Then he set about planning to kill her." Sally shuddered.

"He took his time about planning her death. He still hasn't admitted he did it. But the police said a Jane Doe that fit the description of Madame Zoltana turned up in Lake Washington last week. They think they can tie Rick to it. If nothing else, they've got him for attempted murder," Guinevere said.

"Attempted murder of you and Zac," Evelyn Pemberton said, shaking her head. "What about Francine Bates and her sister?" Before Guinevere could answer, Evelyn called through the doorway into the next office, "Mr. Justis, don't touch the glasses. You'll get fingerprints on them. Just let the caterer's staff handle things. That's what they're here for."

Guinevere hid a grin as Zac reluctantly refrained from picking up one of the glasses that sat on his desk in the second office. He paced restlessly back out into the main room, straightening his already straight tie. He answered Evelyn's question. "Before he killed Zoltana, Rick forced her to reveal the safe. She kept quiet about the other hiding place, hoping to use it to bargain for her life. He grabbed the contents of the safe without looking at them, assumed he had what he needed, and shot Zoltana before she could convince him there was a second hiding place. Then he dumped her body in the lake, knowing it was going to take a long time before anyone reported her missing. It was only later that he realized he didn't have the evidence against himself that he'd gone after. But he was a greedy man. He couldn't resist trying to squeeze some easy money out of Zoltana's victims, so he sent a note to Sally and some of the others. In the meantime, he kept wondering what had happened to the diary."

Zac reached the far end of the room and spun around, pacing back past Guinevere and the other two women. "He also decided to make a pass at Gwen. He went over to her apartment one evening and saw the note he'd sent to Sally, the one he'd signed with Zoltana's name. It was lying right out there in the open on a table. He also saw the note Gwen and I typed on Zoltana's typewriter. At that point he knew he had real trouble. Gwen was obviously asking questions about Madame Zoltana, and that was dangerous for him."

"I see," Evelyn Pemberton said slowly. "But he assumed you didn't know anything about the diary."

"True, and at that point we didn't," Guinevere agreed, knowing neither she nor Zac intended to talk about Rick's blackmail attempt.

Overstreet had originally prepared the photos intending to use them to coerce Guinevere into going to bed with him. But after he'd seen the notes, he'd used the doctored pictures in an attempt to scare her off the case instead. "He was, however, holding all the client data he'd taken from the safe. He also had a list of payoffs to Zoltana's inside person at Gage and Watson, although she hadn't put down Francine Bates's name, thank heaven. It gave poor Francine some time. But eventually Rick figured out what the record of payments was, and then he decided to get rid of Francine on the assumption that she knew too much. She might also have the diary. It was logical that Zoltana might have told her about it."

Sally's eyes widened. "But then you found the diary, and decided to warn poor Francine she might be in great danger."

Zac whipped around from the other side of the room, glancing at his watch. "But Francine had gotten nervous enough to move out of the cottage and take her sister with her. When Gwen and I found her, she realized the murderer could, too. So she and Denise headed for Oregon. The cops located them yesterday and told them they had Overstreet in custody. Where the hell is everyone?"

"It's only five forty-five, Zac," Mrs. Pemberton said firmly. "Relax."

He ran a finger around his collar and glared at Guinevere. "If no one shows up, I'm holding you personally responsible. This was all your idea. You said it would be good public relations."

"Calm down, Zac. Everything's going to be fine," Guinevere soothed gently, aware that her eyes were undoubtedly mirroring her amusement.

Sally Evenson finished the tale. "I guess it was my fault Mr. Overstreet got the final bit of information he needed to know Francine was involved. He stopped me in the hall and asked me all sorts of questions."

"He knew you were one of Zoltana's victims," Zac pointed out. "And he was blackmailing you himself. It was logical you might be able to tell him who the inside person was, even if you didn't realize you knew. He was fishing for information."

"I didn't understand what he was asking," Sally explained unhappily. "He just started talking about Francine and a few of the other women in the office. I answered his questions, and I guess I told him something that pinpointed Francine. Thank heaven she wasn't at the cottage when Rick arrived."

"Yes," responded Zac dryly. "Unfortunately, not all of us were quite that lucky." He shot a baleful glance at Guinevere.

Before Guinevere could respond, a voice hailed them from the open doorway.

"Hey, is this the office where the free food is supposed to be?" Mason Adair, the artist, sauntered into the room, Guinevere's sister Carla on his arm. Both were smiling broadly. "Nice spread, Zac. I suppose we have to wait until the big-time clients arrive before we tear it apart?"

Zac was visibly relieved that someone had shown up after all. "Help yourself. How are you, Mason?"

"Doing great, thanks. Carla here has my career well in hand." He glanced at the canvases on the walls. "Glad you like the pictures."

"They look terrific in here," Carla observed. "But then, they would, of course. A Mason Adair picture is an asset to any important room."

Zac was nodding his head in willing agreement when another couple appeared in the doorway.

"Good evening, Zac. Are we on time?"

Zac grinned. "Come on in. Evelyn, this is Edward Vandyke and his wife. Mr. Vandyke is a former client of mine. Mr. and Mrs. Vandyke, this is my new executive secretary, Evelyn Pemberton."

"How do you do, Mrs. Pemberton?" Mrs. Vandyke said with a warm smile. "I'm sure you'll find working with Zac very interesting." She turned to Guinevere. "Good to see you again. How is the temporary-service business doing?"

Guinevere responded to the easy inquiry as someone else walked into the room. Out of the corner of her eye she watched the trickle turn into a rush, and within half an hour the small suite was crowded with people. Zac was the perfect host, relaxing finally, as it became obvious the reception was not going to be a social disaster. Guinevere found him alone for a moment in the inner office, where he had gone to bring out more champagne. She cornered him at the desk and held out her glass for a refill.

"Congratulations, Mr. Justis. You're a success."

His gray eyes gleamed as he looked down at her. "Thanks to you. I couldn't have done it without you, Gwen. I'll admit it."

"My tab is paid for your services on the Zoltana case, then?"

"We can discuss what you still owe tonight after we get home," he returned smoothly.

Her mouth curved. "Home," she repeated. "I like the sound of that."

"So do I. It strikes me that maintaining two apartments has become an unnecessary expense. What do you think?" There was a sudden, curious tension in him, although his voice was casual.

"I think so, too," she agreed softly.

He bent his head and kissed her briefly, his mouth warm with promise.

"Did I ever tell you what Madame Zoltana said about you the day I went to see her?" Guinevere asked musingly as Zac raised his head.

"I don't believe you went into great detail."

"She said you were a good lover."

"Ah," said Zac complacently. "I always knew the woman had a certain amount of true psychic ability."

"Yes," said Guinevere, remembering the events of the past few days. "I think she did."

Keep reading for a special excerpt from Jayne Castle's

DESPERATE
AND DECEPTIVE

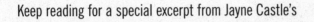

THE GUINEVERE JONES COLLECTION, VOLUME 1

Available now from Berkley Books

He was the ugliest man in the bar, and he had his eye on her.

It figured, Guinevere Jones decided as she swept up an empty bottle of imported British ale. Give her one entire evening in the trendiest yuppie bar in Seattle, and she would end up attracting the attention of the only nontrendy, nonyuppie in the room. Deliberately she avoided looking at the corner table where he sat brooding under a huge fern.

Deftly she replaced the empty bottle with a full one, made change with a charming smile, and thanked the attractive young urban professional male who had just ordered the ale. It took an effort to project her voice over the monotonous din of music currently considered hot. By the time the bar closed for the night she would be hoarse.

She was also going to have very sore feet. The black pumps that were a part of the cocktail waitress uniform had become uncomfortable five minutes after she'd stepped into them. The pencil-slim black skirt and the mauve blouse weren't as unpleasant as the shoes, but Guinevere felt conspicuous. Skirts cut as narrowly as the one she wore were designed for what the fashion industry termed the junior figure. She knew her derriere had not fallen within the junior parameters since she was twelve years old. Unfortunately the blouse seemed to have been styled for a Hollywood starlet, and her bustline had maintained its petite dimensions even though she was now thirty.

Ah, well. Such was the price one paid for the joys of being one's own boss. She'd spent worse evenings. The client was happy, and the image of being totally dependable had been maintained. One always had to consider the image.

Guinevere made her way to the next tableful of fashionably casual up-and-comers and dutifully took their orders for California wines and an imported light beer. Sooner or later she was going to have to go back to the table in the corner. The nonyuppie had almost finished his small glass of tequila. It was after she'd taken his order the first time that she'd become aware of his intent scrutiny. Might as well get it over and done. Resolutely Guinevere headed for the fern-shrouded table.

"Another tequila?" She kept her voice bright and her smile brilliantly professional.

He nodded once and swallowed the last sip in the small glass. Guinevere stifled a shudder.

"When do you get off work?"

The low, dark shade of his voice surprised her for some reason, perhaps because it didn't sound in the least affected by the tequila.

"I don't. I work twenty-four hours a day. No time off for good behavior. Or bad either." She made her response polite but firmly discouraging.

"Just one long hustle, hmmm?"

"A woman's work is never done." She scooped up the little glass, her tone dropping several degrees in temperature. "I'll be right back."

"I put in a lot of twenty-four-hour days myself. Or at least it seems that way sometimes."

"Fascinating. Excuse me." Without another word she took the glass and hurried back to the long, ornate bar at the far end of the room. In all fairness the man wasn't really ugly. It was just that in this terribly chic environment he tended to stand out. Like a sore thumb.

For one thing, he was definitely older than almost everyone else in the room, probably near forty. The typical young, upwardly mobile urban professional tended to be around thirty—a good age for making it big or at least living well so that everyone was convinced you were making it big. Same difference.

The man crouching like a malevolent frog under the fern was dressed much more conservatively than those around him. His white shirt and bland tie were definitely nondesigner, and his short, no-nonsense haircut was not the product of a blow dryer. She hadn't peeked under the table, but Guinevere was willing to bet the shoes would be wing tips.

In the dimly lit room it was difficult to get a good look at his face, but she'd seen enough to know the frog drinking tequila among princes had not been cloned from the same designer genes as the rest of the crowd in the bar.

And the heavy-handed pass he was attempting to make could have used some social polish, to say the least.

"Order in," Guinevere called to the busy bartender. Jerry nodded once to show he'd heard and went on blending the frothy pink strawberry daiquiri someone had ordered. His expression was polite, but she had a hunch what he was thinking. Bartenders, Guinevere had learned, were very disdainful of people who ordered fluffy drinks. She waited patiently until he was done.

"Two more chardonnays, three draft bitters, and another tequila straight."

"Who's the guy drinking the tequila?" Jerry smoothly poured the white wines.

"A frog that never metamorphosed into a prince."

"Huh?"

"Never mind. Don't they ever turn that music down, Jerry?"

"Nope. It's after midnight. The meat-market action is going to be getting very intense soon. The music helps."

"Helps what?"

Jerry shrugged with the wisdom of bartenders the world over. "Helps make it all right, I guess. How are you holding up?"

"My feet are killing me, but I'll last."

"You get used to it after a while." Jerry grinned abruptly. "But I guess that bit of information doesn't matter much to you. You're here only for the night."

"Thank heaven. I think I'm getting too old for this sort of thing. Be back in a few minutes."

Guinevere picked up the drink-laden tray and moved back into the crowd. Jerry was right. The action was getting intense. There was an air of urgency hanging over some of the participants. It was Friday evening, and a lot of the people in the room were going to be facing a lonely weekend if they didn't connect with someone soon.

She would have found the whole scene sociologically interesting if she hadn't been so tired, Guinevere realized. And if her feet weren't hurting so much. She saved the tequila order for last.

"You didn't answer my question," the man under the fern said just as if their earlier conversation hadn't been terminated.

Guinevere set down the tequila. "Seven, please."

"What time do you get off work?" He pushed eight dollar bills toward her. They were left over from the change she had made on his first drink.

"I told you, never. They lock me up in a little cage in the back room from two A.M. until six. Then I start all over again." Guinevere found fifty cents in change and set it in front of him. "Thank you." She turned to leave.

"I'm thinking of locking you up in a cage myself." He gave her a contemplative glance, ghost gray eyes moving over her with grave consideration.

Guinevere knew she was close to losing her temper. Only the necessity of maintaining a good image in front of the client kept her from dropping the tray on the Frog's head. Smiling very sweetly, she leaned a little closer.

"Allow me to point out that you have wandered into the wrong pond tonight, sir. This is trendy, young, go-getter territory. Not really suited for frogs. Try your luck in one of the big hotel bars downtown or out on the airport strip. I think that would be more your style. Better hurry. It's getting late."

"Whatever luck I'm going to have will be here." He picked up the tequila. "You see, I'm not looking for just any woman tonight. I'm looking for you, Guinevere Jones. And I've found you."

She drew in her breath slowly, hiding the jolt he had given her. The fact that the Frog knew her name introduced a vaguely alarming element into the atmosphere. She wished he looked more like a drunken businessman attempting a clumsy pass. She didn't care for the steady regard of those dark eyes.

"Just what," she said calmly, "did you intend to do with me after you found me?"

"I told you. Put you in a cage."

There was always the possibility, of course, that he was simply crazy. But Guinevere couldn't find any sign of obvious insanity in the unrelenting face of the man under the fern. It was the fact that he knew her name that really disturbed her.

"Would you care to explain yourself so that I can make a decision?" she inquired politely.

"Make a decision about what?"

"About whether to call the cops or the mental health folks."

A faint smile flickered briefly at the edge of his grim mouth. "I don't think you want to call either crowd, Miss Jones. The police would be an embarrassment to you, and the mental health people have more important things to do."

Guinevere went still, the tray balanced precariously on one hand as she eyed the Frog. "Why," she asked distinctly, "would the cops prove embarrassing?"

Looking thoughtful, he tasted the tequila and then reached up to push aside a trailing piece of fern that seemed to be trying for a sample of his drink. "Because then I would have to go into long and rather detailed explanations about who I am and why I'm spending an evening fighting off a fern and making threats to a particular cocktail waitress, all of which would be awkward for a supposedly upright, tax-paying small businessperson such as yourself."

The tray wavered a bit on her hand. Guinevere steadied it. "Okay, I'll ask the obvious. Who are you?"

"Zachariah Justis. You can call me Zac."

"Why would I want to call you Zac?"

"Because you'll soon be working for me and I'd like to try for a certain degree of informality on the job. I've heard it, uh, lubricates the channels of communication. Smooths the ripples in the chain of command. Makes for an atmosphere of teamwork. That sort of thing."

Guinevere was aware of a growing sensation of light-headedness.

Frantically she kept a hold on the tray and her nerves. Her throat felt a little dry. "Where did you hear that, Mr. Justis?"

He opened one large, square hand in a negligent gesture. "I think I read it in a recent issue of some business management magazine."

"You read a lot of those?"

"Not as many as I should, I'm afraid." There was no real note of apology in the words. "I find them irritating."

"I'll just bet you do." He looked like a man who would in general find irritating excessive demands for polite, socially acceptable behavior, let alone the courtesies of modern management.

"How soon can you leave?" he asked, ignoring her comment.

"You have a one-track mind. I'm not going anywhere with you, Mr. Justis."

"This is where I get to say the magic word."

"Which is?"

"StarrTech."

Guinevere let out the breath she hadn't realized she'd been holding. A small, nasty sensation of prickly awareness went down her spine. "For a frog you know some interesting magic words."

"I thought you'd appreciate that particular one. Can you leave now?"

She shook her head instantly. "No."

"When?"

"Not until two."

He glanced at the clock over the bar. "That's another hour."

"Don't let me keep you. If you're bored with waiting, feel free to leave." She swung around and started for the next table.

"I'll wait," he said behind her.

Guinevere didn't doubt it.

Zac watched her as she moved off into the crowded room. She'd handled it well. When he'd mentioned StarrTech, there had been no furious denials, no loud exclamations of angered innocence, no contrived demands for an explanation. She had assessed the single word and figured out for herself all the ramifications. She'd be going home with him at two.

He appreciated that kind of direct acceptance of reality. He hadn't expected to find it in Guinevere Jones. But, then, she was a small businessperson, just as he was, and people struggling to keep small businesses afloat learned in a hurry to deal with reality.

It was an interesting concept, Zac decided, this notion of having something in common with Miss Guinevere Jones. He wondered how she'd react to the idea. Probably wouldn't be thrilled. What was it she had called him? A frog. That was it. Absently he shoved the fern frond off his shoulder. The damn thing seemed to be alive, the way it was attempting to climb into his drink. Suddenly he realized how he must look sitting in this dark corner under the overly healthy plant. Rather like a frog.

Miss Jones, on the other hand, didn't look at all like a frog. She also didn't look like the stereotype of the young, urban professional either, although she was about the right age. Zac was willing to bet his IRS deductions for an entire year's office expenses that Guinevere Jones had never been a cheerleader in high school or homecoming queen. That pleased him in a vague sort of way. He had never been captain of the football team or homecoming king. Something else in common.

Her hair was longer than that of most of the other women in the room. Every other female seemed to be wearing a sleek, expensively styled cut that probably cost a fortune and looked as if it had come out of *Vogue* magazine. Guinevere's below-shoulder-length hair was braided and coiled at the nape of her neck in an old-fashioned style that was timeless in its simplicity. Zac liked its coffee brown color.

It annoyed him that he was trying so hard to analyze her, but he couldn't deny his own curiosity. He'd spent a lot of time deciding whether to move in on her and even more time figuring out how to do it. It was his nature to take his time reaching conclusions. During the hours he'd spent making his decisions, Zac had also had plenty of opportunity to wonder about the woman he was planning to cage.

The first thing he'd noticed when he'd finally identified her in the shadowy bar was that she seemed to be wearing a skirt that was a size too small and a blouse that was at least a size too big. It was probably the tequila that made him want to reach out and explore firsthand both ends of the spectrum.

It was amazing how professionally she handled the cocktail waitress role. Apparently she'd filled the job at StarrTech just as easily. Zac was impressed. He'd have to ask her where she'd learned the knack of blending into such varied situations. It was a talent he could use.

She didn't return to his table for the rest of the remaining hour. But Zac knew Guinevere was aware of his watching her. There was a hint of tension in the way she held her shoulders and in the scrupulous way she avoided his eyes. But he was certain she wouldn't run. Guinevere Jones was the kind who held her ground and went down fighting. Zac knew he lacked finesse when it came to handling people, but his instincts about them were usually sound. He winced as another round of prerecorded music hit the speakers. It seemed to him that someone was deliberately turning up the volume.

At closing time Guinevere considered her options and realized she really didn't have any. If the Frog had put her name together with StarrTech, Inc. so long after she'd quit working there, he definitely knew too much. There was no safety in running. Hiding her head in the sand wasn't going to make this particular frog disappear. She could tell that by the way he sat under the fern with such lethal patience. By the time she had collected her oversize red canvas tote and made her way out onto the sidewalk, she was prepared for the fact that Zachariah Justis would be waiting.

"Do you want some help with that?" He stepped out of the shadows and indicated the tote.

"No, thanks. I can carry my own purse," she told him tartly.

"Purse? I thought it was a piece of luggage." His hand dropped quickly. He shoved it and his other fist into the front pockets of the tweed jacket he wore. "What the hell have you got in there?"

"A very large assault rifle."

He nodded, walking toward a cab that waited at the curb. "I understand that a woman living alone has to protect herself."

Guinevere gritted her teeth and got into the cab without protest. "You seem to know a great deal about me, Mr. Justis."

"I try to learn as much as possible before attempting to blackmail someone, Miss Jones. May I call you Gwen?"

"No." Blackmail? That wasn't quite what she had been expecting. Guinevere's palm was damp against the soft red leather of the tote. For a moment she wished devoutly for the assault rifle she'd told him was inside her bag.

"Every report I have on you implies that you can be a very warm and charming woman, someone who wouldn't hesitate to let another person call her by a short form of her name," Zac said as the cab swung away from the curb.

Guinevere noticed that the driver already seemed to have the address. The cab was speeding along Western Avenue toward the Pioneer Square area. In other words, she was being taken home. That information brought an element of relief but not much. Out on the darkness of Elliott Bay a huge cargo ship was making its way cautiously into the port of Seattle. She caught glimpses of its lights between buildings as she looked out through the cab's windows.

"I limit my warmth and charm to people who aren't prone to kidnapping and blackmail," Guinevere said finally. The backseat of the cab felt crowded. Zac Justis was a little less than six feet in height, and she hadn't noticed any fat on him, but he somehow seemed to fill up all the available space. She felt he was pushing her in more ways than one.

"Aren't you worried about limiting your circle of acquaintances?"

"I have a feeling that I've got more friends than you have, Mr. Justis." She kept her eyes on the night-darkened scene visible through the cab's windows.

"You're probably right," he admitted dryly. Then he leaned forward to tap the driver's shoulder. "That's the building there on the left."

Guinevere resisted the urge to comment scathingly on his knowledge of her address. He was probably trying to impress her with just how much information he had. She wouldn't give him the satisfaction of demanding further explanations.

Without a word she stepped out of the cab and waited stoically while her unwanted escort paid the driver. She noticed out of the corner of her eye that he tipped carefully but not at all lavishly. A man who watched his money. She could identify, however unwillingly, with that. Sighing, she fished her key out of a zippered pocket on the tote.

"I suppose you intend to come upstairs?" she muttered as Zac walked toward her.

"How can I turn down such a generous invitation?"

Closing her teeth very firmly against the retort that hovered in her throat, Guinevere led the way through the well-lit entrance of the brick building and up one flight of stairs. The façade of her apartment building was a stately design of arching windows and ornamental detail that dated back to the turn of the century. The inside had been gutted and completely renovated with the goal of capturing the attention of the new urban pioneer: the single person who wanted to live downtown and demanded something more interesting than a bare box.

"All right, Mr. Justis," Guinevere said as she opened the door of her apartment, "let's hear what you have to say about blackmail and StarrTech. And then you can leave."

His mouth curved slightly at one corner and there was a reluctantly appreciative expression in his eyes as he followed her through the door. He came to a halt on the threshold and absorbed the brilliant impact of color that greeted him.

"Somehow it looks like you. Unexpected."

He walked toward the floor-to-ceiling bookcase, which was painted with yolk-colored enamel. En route he noticed slate gray carpets bordered in red. There was more red throughout the apartment: a red window seat, a red-painted desk with red bookcases behind it, and a red shelf in the entrance hall. The yellow reappeared elsewhere in the shape of a tea cart and a trash can beside the desk. The room seemed to be anchored by the few pieces of furniture, all of which were in black. The night was locked out with miniblinds custom-designed to fit the high, arched windows.

"I'm surprised you find anything about me unexpected. You seem to have done a fairly thorough job of snooping." Guinevere tossed her tote bag onto the tea cart and stepped out of the pumps with an exclamation of relief. Barefooted, she lost a couple of inches of height, but a few centimeters weren't enough to make her feel any more in charge of the situation anyway, so why suffer? She walked to the black leather love seat and threw herself down into a corner. "My God, I'm exhausted. Say what you have to say and then leave, Mr. Justis."

"You've had a long day," he observed mildly. He took the black-wire diamond-shaped chair across from her and eyed her feet. "You were in the offices of Camelot Services at seven o'clock this morning, ate a sandwich at your desk for lunch, grabbed a bite of supper on your way to the bar, and then put in a full shift as a cocktail waitress."

"The woman who was assigned to take the waitress job phoned

in sick at the last minute." Guinevere decided trying to keep him from using the short form of her name would be pointless. Another small battle lost. Sooner or later she was going to have to find a defensible position.

"Do you always sub for your people when they can't go out on one of the temporary assignments?"

"Someone has to do it. As you must know from your prying, Camelot Services is still a very small operation. I didn't have anyone else I could call in at the last minute."

"And you didn't want to offend the client by being unable to meet the request for a temporary cocktail waitress," he said softly.

"When you're in the temporary help business, you can't come up with too many excuses or you'll lose clients."

"Yes. I know how important it is to please clients. Which brings me to the reason I'm here."

"I'm glad something is going to get you to explain yourself. Do me a favor and lay it all out in short, pithy sentences. I'm too tired to fence with you."

"I want to please one of my clients, Gwen. I think you can help."

She eyed him narrowly. "What client?"

"StarrTech."

"I see." She thought about that for several long seconds. Then she thought about the future of Camelot Services. It was the same as thinking about her own future. At the moment both were beginning to look shaky. "What, exactly, are you doing for StarrTech?"

"It's hired my firm to take a private, very quiet look at a problem it's been having with lost equipment shipments. The people there think the problem is originating within their computer department."

"Your firm?"

"Free Enterprise Security, Incorporated." There was a hint of satisfaction underlining the words.

Guinevere blinked. "You're an investigating agency? A private detective service?"

He shook his head. Then he frowned down at his hands. He'd clasped them loosely between his knees, his elbows resting on his thighs. "My firm offers consultations to businesses."

"What sort of consultations?" It was like pulling teeth, Guinevere decided. But she was going to get some answers if it killed her. Perhaps a little more liquor would make him chattier. And heaven knew she could use a drink. She got to her feet, wincing a little. "Would you like some brandy?"

"Thank you." He watched her as she walked into the kitchen, but he didn't follow. When she reappeared, holding two small snifters of brandy, he accepted the offer with a polite inclination of his head.

"You didn't answer my question." Guinevere prompted him, resuming her seat. "Just what sort of consultations do you provide?"

"Security consultations."

"Ah." She swallowed some of the brandy. It might not make her guest any more comprehensible, but it certainly made it easier to sit here and deal with his presence in her apartment. She took another sip. "Ah," she said again, and wondered if it sounded any wiser this time.

"My firm provides very discreet services, Gwen. We're called in when management does not want to create a stir or make accusations. Generally corporate managements hate to create stirs or make accusations. Bad for the image and stockholders take a dim view of that sort of trouble. If we learn that there's something worth creating a stir about or decide that accusations should be made, we go ahead and make the recommendation. It's up to the client to pursue it into court."

"You keep saying 'we.' Just how big is Free Enterprise Security?"

He hesitated, then shrugged. The small movement emphasized the width of his shoulders. "You will have the distinction of being my first employee. I just got started a few months ago, and until now I've been a one-man operation. A small business, just like your own."

Guinevere stared at him and then seized on the most puzzling element in his explanation. "Your employee?"

"Ummm."

"I don't understand."

"Of course not. That's where the blackmail comes in." He lifted the snifter to his mouth and took a healthy swallow.

Guinevere placed her glass down very carefully on the table beside the small sofa. "Let me get this straight. You're not planning on impressing your client by dragging me in chains into StarrTech headquarters?"

"The image is intriguing, but frankly I've got bigger fish to fry. Your bit of finagling with StarrTech's computerized benefits program is not what I'm investigating."

Guinevere closed her eyes briefly. Hearing it put into words made it suddenly very, very real. This man knew what she had done during her short stint as a clerk in the computer department of StarrTech. "How did you find out?" she asked bleakly.

"Russ Elfstrom is a friend of mine." Zac was calm, almost placid. A man in control. "He came across your little maneuvers a couple of weeks ago. Just about the same time that management began to worry about bigger problems it had discovered."

Russ Elfstrom, Guinevere remembered, had been in charge of all computer systems at StarrTech. She hadn't liked the man. No one in the department did. The programmers had called him the Elf behind his back. He wasn't particularly short, but there was a kind of high-strung quality about the man. He smoked incessantly, and occasionally, while she was at StarrTech, Guinevere had seen him furtively pop a couple of small pills. Wiry and balding, with restless, pale eyes, the Elf had ruled the department with little regard for the delicate egos of programmers and even less for the hopeful computer operators who had dreams of using the machines as a way out of the clerical pool.

On the other hand, Russ Elfstrom was a good company man. He got things done. Management liked him, and as long as he was content to run a department that had a high turnover in personnel, management was content to leave him alone. Management didn't really understand computers, anyway, let alone computer personnel. Results were all that mattered.

"So the Elf tossed me into your clutches," Guinevere murmured. "Why?"

"He was simply going through every detail he could think of that might be helpful to me in my examination of the missing shipments. In the process he uncovered your manipulation of the benefits plan. He was on the verge of mentioning you to management. I persuaded him to let me have you instead. I think you might prove useful, Gwen."

"I sound like an odd little tool you've discovered and aren't quite certain how to use," she snapped bitterly.

"Oh, I think I know how to use you. I'm offering to keep your name clear at StarrTech if you'll give me a hand on this other problem." Something a little fierce flared in his eyes for an instant. "Keeping your name clean should be important to you, Gwen. After all, independent businesspeople have to maintain spotless reputations, don't they? It wouldn't do at all to have potential clients thinking that you use your services as a cover for theft and other assorted activities, would it?"

In spite of her resolve to stay absolutely cool, that stung. Guinevere sat upright, her hazel eyes narrowed, her mouth tight. "Camelot Services is utterly reliable, Mr. Justis. There has never been a complaint or a doubt about the ethics of my company!"

"Until your venture into StarrTech?" He leaned back in the black steel-mesh chair, apparently satisfied with the results of his accusation.

Guinevere fought a short, violent battle for control and surprised herself by winning. "My *venture* into StarrTech was a different matter. A private matter." She picked up the brandy, her grip so savage that it was a wonder the glass didn't shatter. She forced herself to drink.

"There was something different about your contract with Starr-Tech?" Zac inquired benignly. "Something that set it apart from other short-term temporary assignments?"

"If you're going to make an accusation, I'll get a lawyer. If you're not, then I don't need one, do I? Either way, I don't intend to say anything further on the subject of my business at StarrTech."

Zac waited for a long moment, watching her. "I won't be making any accusations to StarrTech management, Guinevere Jones, because I think you're going to cooperate. Isn't that right?"

She made herself inhale slowly, seeking a way to calm herself. "Blackmail."

"Just as I promised."

"Do you always make good on your promises?"

"Keeping my promises is one of the few things in which I still believe, Gwen."

She focused on the massive yellow bookcase across the room. "What is it you want me to do in exchange for your silence?"

"I want you to go back into the computer services department at StarrTech, doing pretty much the same sort of clerical work you did the first time. But this time around you're going to be my eyes and ears in the department. I need some answers, and you're going to get them for me."

She moved her head in a vague denial. "What about the Elf? How do I know he'll keep quiet?"

"As I said, Russ is a friend of mine. He'll do whatever I ask him to do in this matter."

"Somehow I find it hard to imagine," Guinevere said.

"What? That you're being blackmailed?"

"No, that you and Russ Elfstrom are such close friends. You're not a friendly type, Mr. Justis."

"Russ and I go back a long way together."

"How unfortunate for you. That's just about the most depressing thing I've heard since the last time I talked to my sister's shrink."

Justis blinked owlishly, assimilating that information and trying to make sense of it. "What's this got to do with your sister?"

"Never mind. Tell me what you want, Mr. Justis. And then go back to your pond."